The Collected Stories of
Robert Silverberg

VOLUME ONE

To Be Continued

The Collected Stories of
Robert Silverberg

VOLUME ONE

To Be Continued

ROBERT SILVERBERG

SUBTERRANEAN PRESS 2012

Trade Paperback

ISBN: 978-1-59606-507-9

Subterranean Press
PO Box 190106
Burton, MI 48519

www.subterraneanpress.com

ACKNOWLEDGMENTS

"The Road to Nightfall," "Absolutely Inflexible," "The Macauley Circuit," "Counterpart," "The Artifact Business," and "The Outbreeders" first appeared in *Fantastic Universe*.

"Gorgon Planet" first appeared in *Nebula Science Fiction*.

"The Silent Colony" and "A Man of Talent" first appeared in *Future Science Fiction*.

"To Be Continued" first appeared in *Astounding Science Fiction*.

"Alaree" first appeared in *Saturn Science Fiction and Fantasy*.

"Collecting Team" and "World of a Thousand Colors" first appeared in *Super-Science Fiction*.

"One-Way Journey," "There Was An Old Woman," and "Ozymandias" first appeared in *Infinity Science Fiction*.

"Warm Man" and "The Man Who Never Forgot" first appeared in *Fantasy and Science Fiction*.

"Blaze of Glory" and "The Iron Chancellor" first appeared in *Galaxy Science Fiction*.

"Sunrise on Mercury," "Delivery Guaranteed," "The Songs of Summer," and "Why?" first appeared in *Science Fiction Stories*.

TABLE OF CONTENTS

INTRODUCTION

The present volume represents the beginning of my third try at putting together my Collected Short Stories. I hope to get it right this time.

I've been assembling my stories in collections almost since the beginning of my career. The first, a paperback called *Next Stop the Stars*, was published in 1962 and contained five very early stories, three of which ("Blaze of Glory," "Warm Man," and "The Songs of Summer") have been carried forth into this very book. Then came *Godling, Go Home* in 1964—eleven more stories, of which another trio ("Why?", "A Man of Talent," and "The Silent Colony" are to be found here), and then *To Worlds Beyond*, a nine-story book of 1965, and so on and on and on through an inordinate number of collections over the years, that because of their various overlappings are the bane of bibliographers (especially the one called *Needle in a Timestack*, published in two different editions with largely different tables of contents, neither volume containing the short story of that name).

Finally, in 1991, I felt it was appropriate to bring some order out of all this chaos by doing a systematic series of books collecting all the stories of mine that I thought were worth preserving in such a set. And so, the following year, Bantam Books published *The Collected Stories of Robert Silverberg, Volume One: Secret Sharers*. Alas, Volume One of this ambitious series did not begin with my earliest stories. For commercial reasons the publisher thought it best to start the project off with my more recent work, material that was, unsurprisingly, rather more skillful than the stories I had written in my twenties and therefore might be deemed a more auspicious way to launch the project. And so Volume One, a fine, fat book of 546 pages, included two dozen stories and novellas that had been written between 1982 and 1988, a cluster of award-winners among them.

And then there was no Volume Two. Lou Aronica, the editor who had championed my short-story series at that publishing house, resigned; his successor was not interested in continuing it; and that was that. Meanwhile, though, I had found another champion overseas: my longtime British publisher and friend, Malcolm Edwards, who agreed to bring out a six-volume set. Since *Secret Sharers* was already assembled, Malcolm started with that, splitting it into two volumes under the titles *Pluto in the Morning Light* and *The Secret Sharer*, and following them in due course with a third volume covering 1969 to 1974; a fourth that (at last!) offered my earliest stories, those of 1953 to 1958 that you will find here; a fifth spanning 1962 to 1970; and a sixth and last in this zigzag progression, embracing the work of 1989 to 1995.

These six books left out a good many short stories of mine that Malcolm had previously published in other collections, and some of my best novellas, too, had to be omitted for reasons of space. And, of course, the jumbled chronological sequence, with a big group of my most recent stories again coming first in the British set, my earliest ones to be found in Volume Four, and so forth, made things perplexing for readers trying to follow the course of my development in some rational way.

So, after a lapse of some years, I'm trying again. This time it is my hope the stories will appear, volume by volume, in strict chronological order, by which I mean in the order in which they were written, not in order of first publication. (They differ in this from the British books, in which, for some reason that I no longer remember, the order of stories is not quite chronological.) So here we have the stories of the dawn of my career, written between 1953 and 1958. 1958 makes a natural ending place for this volume, because that year marked the termination of my period of high-velocity science-fiction story output; I wrote practically no short s-f in the next three years, and when we resume with Volume Two, it will be with stories from 1962.

I don't know how many short stories I've written. There may be a thousand of them.

Since 1954 I've kept a ledger listing every work of fiction and non-fiction that I've sold, in chronological order—its original title, the publisher that bought it, the number of words, the payment I received, and the date and place of first publication. The ledger also includes a cumulative count of my published words—the total is just past 25 million now, which puts me up there with Simenon and John Creasey and a few other very prolific writers. And I used to number each individual item in order of its sale.

Somewhere along the way I stopped tallying that last statistic. The most recent catalog number I can find—1093—accompanies an entry for April, 1973. The succeeding decades were not as productive for me as the ones from 1954 to 1973 (there was a period of nearly five years—1974-1978—when I didn't write anything at all!) but it's a fair guess that I added several hundred more items to the record during the 1980s and 1990s. So the tally might be in the vicinity of 1500 or so items by now, maybe even a little more. That number would include books and magazine articles as well as short stories; but stories very likely make up two thirds of my total output, which is why I suspect I've written about a thousand of them over the past fifty-some years, a stupefying number: just about one every two weeks, on the average, for more than a generation. The ledger in which I list them, each entry taking up a single line, occupies one volume close to an inch thick and in 1998 overflowed to a second volume.

A lot of those stories, of course, were mere rent-payers, spun out at furious speed when I was very young to meet the voracious needs of low-grade magazines. A writer had to be prolific in order to survive, back then—very prolific indeed.

A career in science fiction in the 1950s almost invariably meant a career writing a multitude of short pieces. Unless your name was Heinlein or Asimov or Bradbury, you didn't think much about getting books published at that time. If you wrote for a living, without holding any sort of outside job, what you wrote was short stories and novelettes for the magazines, and you wrote them just as quickly as you could.

The magazines would pay you anywhere from one to three cents a word: a 5000-word story therefore would bring you $50 to $150, before such things as your agent's commission and the exactions of the Internal Revenue Service were figured in. It wasn't much, but at least the magazine market was big—fifteen or twenty different titles, many of them published every month. If you worked fast enough, using an assortment of pseudonyms so that the readers didn't weary of your name, you might hope to earn $15,000 a year or so, not a bad livelihood back then, when rent on a fine apartment in New York City was $150 a month and dinner for two at a deluxe restaurant cost less than $25, including a good bottle of wine. To do that, though, you had to write and sell a short story to some magazine or other a couple of times a week, every week of the year—a constant, unending stream of publishable material. No wonder we called ourselves "full-time writers." I allowed myself weekends off right from the start, but otherwise I worked at my fiction-making tasks day in and day out, mornings and afternoons, no time off for headaches or hangovers or a daytime visit to the movies. Those of us who considered ourselves full-time science-fiction writers needed not only to be capable of generating salable story concepts at will but to be cognizant at all times of each magazine's buying status—which one was in desperate need of copy, which one was currently overstocked, which one was overstocked on *your* stuff and didn't want to look at any more just now. It was an insane way to live and an almost impossible thing to succeed at; but those of us who chose to live that way and who did actually succeed at it (there were only about a dozen of us) usually didn't stop to think that it couldn't be done, and so we just went ahead and did it.

So you wrote what you could sell, and you wrote it fast. Looking through my battered old ledger now, I see a myriad such potboilers popping out at me: "Gambler's Planet," August 1955, "Swords Against the Outworlders," May 1956, "The Mystery of Deneb IV," July 1956, "Peril of the Earthlings," November 1956, and so on and on and on, at least five or six of them a month all through 1957 and 1958 and 1959, onward to "Kill That Babe," April 1959, "See You In Hell," August 1959, "Bridegrooms Scare Easy," December 1959, et cetera etcetera, several yards of entries all told. I have no more idea of what most of those stories were about, now, than you do. I probably forgot about them as soon as I cashed the checks. A lot of them were mystery stories, westerns, even some sports fiction, mixed in with a vast mass of slam-bang science-fiction stuff full of monsters, space battles, swordfights, and hideous slime. Whenever the science-fiction market took a dip—and it took a huge one in the summer of 1958, when most of the magazines in the field went out of business—I would swiftly switch gears and write fiction of some other kind.

Few of those stories have been reprinted since their first published appearances. I will probably allow the mystery stories and the sports fiction to languish forever in oblivion, but I do feel some affection for my early pulp-magazine science fiction, and for a detailed view of this phase of my career I refer you to my Subterranean Press book *In the Beginning,* published in February, 2006, which contains sixteen of these pulp stories plus detailed accounts of how and why they came to be written, and serves as a kind of overture to the present series.

But along with that incredible outpouring of swiftly concocted action tales in my youth—for which I make no apologies; quickly writing a lot of simple, unambitious stories in order to pay the rent seems no more shameful to me than working as a bookstore clerk or shoe salesman for the same purpose—came plenty of stories into which I poured my heart and soul and all the skill I had at my command. If I could have earned my living back then by writing only stories that expressed my deepest feelings about the universe, I would surely have done it. How I admired people like Ray Bradbury and Theodore Sturgeon and Fritz Leiber, whose fiction was almost always a reflection of inner passion and creative need, and who rarely if ever descended to mere hackery!

But I was younger than they were, just starting out in the world, with only a few dollars in the bank, and I felt the need to establish my economic security first and look to the artistic side of things afterward. In those days of cent-a-word magazines, where a thoughtful and polished 5000-word story that might take a week or more to write could earn a payment of $50 (minus ten percent for the agent's commission, and income tax due besides) I couldn't see any way to find that economic security by limiting my writing output entirely to pure and holy work. (Bradbury wrote for slick magazines that paid ten or twenty times as much as the ones I dealt with; Leiber had an editorial job and wrote his fiction on the side; Sturgeon, I would later learn, lived a difficult hand-to-mouth existence as the price of his integrity.) Still, I had some measure of self-respect to guard; and so, whenever I felt I could afford the luxury of doing some serious work, I would, throughout those dreary years of spinning out the hackwork, attempt from time to time to write the sort of science fiction that meant something to me, the kind of thing I valued as a reader.

It is those personally rewarding stories, out of all the millions of words of my early years as a writer, that I have chosen to preserve in this first volume of my collected stories. The selection of stories we have here represents my best work from the stories written between 1953 and 1958, the first five years of my career. I don't mean to imply that the stories in this book are immortal classics of science fiction. I was, yes, an unusually precocious writer, who began selling stories at the age of 18 and was doing it with numbing regularity before he was 21. But, however skillful those stories were (and I think some of them were quite skillful indeed) they were nevertheless the work of a very young man who had seen relatively little of the world and who had not yet had a chance to pass through the emotional trials of adulthood out of which the best fiction is compounded. I was in my second year in college when the first of my published stories, "Gorgon Planet," appeared. I include it in this volume to show you that even in 1953 I knew how to write a publishable story; but I wouldn't want you to think that because I was able to get it published I look upon it as the equal of what such writers of the time as Philip K. Dick, Robert Sheckley, Algis Budrys, or C.M. Kornbluth were doing then. I didn't then, and I don't now.

All the same, I was pretty good right at the outset. I may have been glib and opportunistic, but I could handle dialog and exposition effectively, I knew almost intuitively how to alternate them to provide an agreeable narrative texture, and my notions of plotting, though marked by an occasional tendency to reach for easy solutions, show a solid grounding in classical technique. Many of these early stories of mine have frequently been reprinted in anthologies and most of them, I suspect, would find publishers even in today's market, which is a far more limited one than the one I grew up in. (In 1953, when I first became serious about launching a career as a professional writer, there were *dozens* of science fiction magazines in the United States, and new ones popped up sporadically over the next few years. Today there are four or five, I think, aside from the assortment of ephemeral on-line publications.) And so—by way of demonstrating my contention that I knew what I was doing pretty much from the start of my career—here is a selection, a rather selective selection, from the scores and scores of stories and millions and millions of published words I produced in the first five years of my career. It begins with the just-about-okay material of the teenage apprentice that I was in the early 1950s, shows the rapid development into the cool-eyed professional I soon became, and concludes with the smooth, competent work of a writer in his mid-twenties about to enter into the fullness of his mature powers as a writer. A kind of autobiography in fiction, actually. I hope you'll agree that these stories are worth investigating for more than pure historical interest. For me it has been a remarkable experience to carry out this enterprise in literary archaeology into my own past and rediscover the writer I was, more than fifty years ago.

Robert Silverberg

GORGON PLANET

All through my adolescence there was very little I wanted as badly as to see a story bearing my name appear in one of the science-fiction magazines. I was a passionate s-f fan, and in those days the magazines were the center of the s-f world; any member of the small cult-group that called itself "fandom" who sold a story to one of the professional magazines attained an increment of instant fame and prestige that can barely be comprehended today. (Among the writers who emerged from fandom in the 1940s via those gaudy-looking magazines were such people as Ray Bradbury, Isaac Asimov, Frederik Pohl, and Arthur C. Clarke.) If I could sell a story, I told myself, it would in a single stroke free me from every aspect of teenage insecurity and admit me to the adult world of achievement and community respect.

In some ways, that's very much what happened, since my debut as a professional writer coincided with my transition from awkward, uncertain adolescent to poised and confident adult. But it didn't happen overnight and there were a few ironic complications along the way. For one thing, my first sale (barring a couple of semiprofessional things) was a novel that was to be published in hard covers, which to me meant that it would be far less visible and impressive to my friends in fandom than, say, a short story printed in the awesomely prestigious magazine Astounding Science Fiction, *which everybody read. So that book sale, significant though it was to my career, failed to transform my self-image in the way I had hoped. And then I did sell a story to one of the professional science-fiction magazines—in January, 1954, while I was still finishing a very ambitious novelette that I called "Road to Nightfall." The story had the title of "Gorgon Planet," and*

I had written it in September, 1953 for the first s-f editor I had come to know personally: Harry Harrison, who had just taken over the editorship of three magazines. That summer Harrison had asked me to write a short article explaining s-f fandom for one of his magazines—my first real professional sale, though because it was nonfiction it didn't really count in my eyes. A few weeks later I brought him "Gorgon Planet," which he said wasn't quite good enough for his top-of-the-line magazine, Science Fiction Adventures, but which he was willing to publish in one of its lesser companions, Rocket Stories or Space Science Fiction. So I had sold a story at last! (But I hadn't exactly sold it yet, merely had had it accepted, because Rocket and Space paid only on publication).

Since Harry would buy only North American rights, I was free to submit my story overseas—and immediately did, to Nebula Science Fiction, a pleasant, somewhat old-fashioned magazine that had begun operations in Scotland the year before. Reasoning correctly that Nebula's youthful editor, Peter Hamilton, might be having difficulties getting stories from the better-known writers, I had begun sending him mine as soon as I learned of his magazine's existence. He replied with rejection letters containing friendly encouragement: "If you like to go on trying," he told me in July of 1953, "I'll be only too happy to continue to advise you. If you become a big name through Nebula it will be as big a thing for me (nearly) as it will be for you." And on January 11, 1954, he wrote to me to say, "You will be pleased to hear that I have accepted 'Gorgon Planet,' and it will appear in the 7th issue of Nebula (due out early February)." Through Hamilton's American agent I duly received my payment—$12.60—and, a few weeks later, a copy of the published story itself.

So, this time, I really had sold a story to one of the magazines! But where was my instant fame, where was my sudden prestige? Nowhere, as a matter of fact, because Nebula was virtually unknown in the United States and gained me no awe whatever from my friends in fandom. I would have to wait until the story appeared in Rocket Stories or Space Science Fiction for that.

But Rocket and Space went out of business almost at once, neither publishing my story nor paying me for it. To Peter Hamilton of Nebula went the glory, such as it was, of bringing Robert Silverberg's first professionally-published science fiction story into print. And here it is—mainly for the historical record, I suppose. (I finally did sell it to an American magazine, by the way—in 1958, to a short-lived item called Super-Science Fiction. The editor retitled it "The Fight With the Gorgon," which didn't strike me as an improvement, but I kept my mouth shut and cashed my check.) The story's not terrible, actually. It's something less than a masterpiece, I suppose; but, glancing through it now, I can see that even at the age of eighteen I had mastered the fundamentals of storytelling as it was practiced in the science-fiction magazines of the day. Despondent as I often was in those days as story after story came back rejected, I was obviously on the brink of a writing career. All that was missing was an editor willing to say yes, and finally I had found one. Peter Hamilton published seven more stories of mine in the remaining five years of his magazine's life, and he always seemed as delighted to have discovered me as I had been to be discovered by him.

Our troubles started the moment the stiffened corpse of Flaherty was found, standing frozen in a field half a kilometer from the ship. We had all hated the big Irishman's guts, but finding his body, completely unharmed, stock-still and standing alone, was quite a jolt. There was no apparent sign of death—in fact, at first we thought he was sleeping on his feet. Horses do it, and Flaherty wasn't far removed from a horse.

But he wasn't. He was dead, dead as hell. And when the entire human population of a planet consists of eight, and one of those eight dies suddenly of unknown causes, the framework of your existence tends to sag a bit. We were scared.

"We" being the first Earth Exploratory Party (Type A-7) to Bellatrix IV in Orion. Eight men, altogether, bringing back a full report on the whole planet. Eight, of whom one, ox-like Flaherty, was stiff as a board before us.

"What did it, Joel?" asked Tavy Ramirez, our geologist.

"How the blazes do I know?" I snapped. I regretted losing my temper instantly. "Sorry, Tavy. But I know as much as you do about the whole thing. Flaherty is dead, and there's something out there that killed him."

"But there's *nothing* out there," protested Kai Framer, the biologist. "For three days we've hunted up and down and haven't found a sign of animal life."

Jonathan Morro, biologist, unwound his six-feet-eight and stretched. "Maybe an intelligent plant did him in, eh, Kaftan?"

I shook my head. "Doubt it, Jon. No sign of violence, no plants in the vicinity. We found him standing in the middle of a field, on his two big feet, frozen dead. Doesn't figure."

Over in the corner of the cabin, Steeger—medical officer—was puttering around the corpse. Steeger was an older man than most of us, one who had literally rotted in the service. He had contracted frogpox on Fomalhaut 11, and now wore two chrome-jacketed titanium legs. I looked over at him.

"Any report, Doc?"

Steeger turned watery eyes towards me. "No sign of any physical harm, Joel. But his muscles are all tensed, as if—as if—well, I can't phrase it. He seems to have been frozen in his tracks by some strange force. I'm stuck, Joel."

Phil Janus, our chronicler, looked up from the chess game he'd been playing with pilot Curt Holden and laughed. "Maybe he had an overdose of his own joy-juice and it hardened all his arteries."

That was a reference to the crude still Flaherty had rigged the day we landed on Bellatrix IV. His duties as navigator had kept the big fellow pretty busy all trip, but first day down-planet and he spent his first idle hour building the still. He didn't say a word about it to anyone, but had shown up at mess that night pretty high. He never told us where the still was, though we searched all over. The second day Janus had located a liter flask of whisky, home-brewed, and his sampling had cost him a black eye.

"No," said Framer. "Let's be serious a moment. One of our group is dead, and we don't know what killed him. There's something out there that Flaherty crossed. I move we organize a searching party to find out what."

"Seconded," murmured Morro.

I looked at the corpse for a moment, then at the six men around me. Framer was my solid man, I knew, the leader of the group. Morro was strong, too, but usually too bored to bother with the welfare of the group. Young Holden, the pilot, was a follower; he didn't have any thoughts of his own, or at least he didn't express any. Tavy Ramirez I knew: quiet, smiling, unassuming—not very strong a person. Doc Steeger was small, frightened, not at all the sort of man who'd go gallivanting around space as part of an exploratory crew. Janus was like Morro in many ways: he just didn't care. Flaherty, thank the Lord, was dead. The big ox had threatened nasty incidents many times, and had been a constant source of dissension on-ship.

As for me—Joel Kaftan, Lieut. (Spatial)—I was scared. Plenty scared. Visible monsters on a planet are bad enough; invisible ones were hell. I looked out at the port and saw the vast, empty, tree-studded plain that was our chunk of Bellatrix IV, and looked back at the men.

"All in favor of a searching party, say aye."

Aye it was, and we divided up. There were seven of us, now, and that made things awkward. Steeger was indispensable, as our doctor, and he was of no use outdoors anyway. Holden was theoretically dispensable—in a pinch I could probably have piloted the ship—but I would have hated to try, and so I confined him to quarters too. That left just five men for the search.

It was logical to split into two groups, one of three men and one of two. But I didn't think too clearly for a moment, and announced we'd have *three* groups. I didn't figure that one poor chap would have to go out alone.

I teamed up with Ramirez, and Framer with Morro. That left Janus as a searching party of one.

Janus didn't mind. Phil rarely minded anything. "Looks like I'm lone wolf," he said. "Okay, gentlemen. If you hear a loud silence from my neck of the woods, run like hell."

The airlock was open anyway (Bellatrix IV has an atmosphere roughly that of Earth's, which was a boon) and the five of us left.

I started out with Tavy and we headed towards the site of Flaherty's finish, very much scared. When your life span is 150 or so years, and you've got a hundred of them left, you're not too anxious to die young, even as a hero on an alien planet. Framer and Morro wandered up towards the big ridge behind the spaceship, and Janus headed for the clump of twisted red-leaved trees about two hundred meters away.

Tavy and I moved slowly, casting our eyes in all directions. As usual, there was no sign of any animal life. Bellatrix IV had an abundance of plants (not chlorophyll-based plants, but ones with some sort of iron-compound base), a temperate climate, flowing streams of real H_2O water. But no visible animals. Of course, we hadn't covered very much territory yet, maybe two or three square kilometers.

No one dared to make a sound. Then suddenly, in about two seconds flat, we got our first taste of Bellatrician life. Poor Janus came flying out of his copse, and lumbering behind him out of nowhere came a bizarre thing about ten feet high, with non-functional wings, gleaming golden scales, and a headful of writhing, pencil-like tentacles.

We stood transfixed for a moment. I drew my rifle and put a shot into the scales, without any seeming effect. And then Janus turned and stared up at the beast for a fraction of a second as he ran.

The beast stared too, and the frantic pursuit came to an end. They glared at each other for just a moment, and then the monster wheeled and ran off in the other direction. It disappeared over the hill.

But Janus remained where he was, frozen dead.

We planted our second corpse and sat morosely in the cabin. We missed Flaherty just a bit, but not too much. But Janus, though, genial, clever, enormously capable—it was hard to believe he was dead, killed by a gorgon.

For the beast of the forest was unquestionably a gorgon, right out of the old mythology. Doc Steeger gave us the first inkling when he pointed out that death had been caused by a sudden neural blast.

Framer looked up at this. "We didn't see any physical contact between Phil and the monster, though."

"No," broke in Ramirez. "Janus just looked at the thing, and then he froze stiff—"

The thought came to Morro and myself almost instantaneously.

"A gorgon," I said.

"Gorgon," he echoed. He stood up—preposterous lanky fellow— and stared outside at the wide plain with its deadly clump of trees at one corner. "A gorgon."

"Pardon me, sir." It was Holden. "Just exactly what *is* a gorgon, sir? They said nothing about them in the Academy."

Framer muttered something under his breath. Kal, I knew, was a man of wide learning, and he had nothing but scorn for modern educational methods, which are highly specialized. Morro spoke.

"A gorgon, Curt, is a mythological beast. It killed by a glance; if you looked at its eyes, you were turned to stone. The thing outside is almost a living version of a gorgon, complete to those tentacles on its head. The original gorgon was supposed to have living snakes instead of hair."

Holders said nothing, but his eyes widened.

Ramirez scratched his long nose with a thick finger. "Joel, how are we going to fight our friend outside?"

"The same way Perseus did," I said.

And so Operation Medusa got under way. It took some preliminary discussion. For one thing, Holden, who held most of our technological information behind his freckled forehead, had not the slightest knowledge of the Perseus myth, and we had to bring him up to date.

Morro patiently did most of the explaining.

"A Greek hero named Perseus boasted he could kill Medusa, the gorgon," the giant said, smothering a yawn. "With the help of the gods he got a pair of magic sandals which enabled him to fly, and a cap of invisibility. Then he polished his shield to mirror brightness and swooped down on the gorgon, watching her in his mirror-shield, and without ever looking her in the face he cut off her head."

"I see," Curt said. "We have to hunt down this gorgon too, and we can't look at it either, or—" He nodded outside at the two brown mounds of earth.

"Right," Framer said. "But we don't have a mirror. And we can't build one. What now?"

We racked our brains. Morro wondered if we could somehow polish the ship to the proper brightness, but we saw the scheme was impractical.

"Try radar," Tavy offered.

"That's it!" I whooped. "Hunt down the gorgon with radar and blast it without ever looking at the damned thing!"

From there on Medusa's number was up. But she didn't go down without a fight.

Holden had the radar screen dismantled and set up for gorgon-hunting in no time at all. The boy's horizons were limited, perhaps, but in the fields for which he had been educated he was tops. On a warm, summery day, we set out on our gorgon-hunt.

We always had difficulty adjusting to the red leaves on the trees and especially the carpet of red grass on the ground. Bellatrix IV, as far as we could see, was a huge plain, covered with what seemed to be a bloody carpet. Every time I looked down I felt a twinge, and thought of the two graves near the ship, and of the two explorers who would never get back for another lecture tour on Earth.

Steeger remained behind on ship, peering intently into the radar screen. The five of us fanned out slowly, armed to the teeth and scared stiff. I could see myself that evening being borne back to the ship, frozen, and sharing that impromptu graveyard with Janus and Flaherty.

Steeger had more to worry about than any of us. Hunched over the radar screen, his job was to relay instructions to us. We knew the gorgon was somewhere in the copse, because Framer had seen the great thing go thundering into the clump of trees the day before, and no one had seen or heard it since. But only a fool would go in there after a beast that killed by a glance.

Slowly, painfully, the five of us formed a wide circle around the copse, standing no closer than a hundred meters from the edge. Not one of us dared to look up, of course; our eyes remained fixed on the blood-red grass and Steeger directed us to our positions, step by painful step. It took half an hour to form the circle, as Doc would tell first one, then another of us, to move a couple of steps to right or left. Finally the circle was complete—five Perseuses, frightened green.

Then came the rough part, as we waited for the attack. When the call came over the phones from Steeger, I was going to hurl a Johnson flare into the copse, and, if all went right, the gorgon would come lumbering out. Without looking, we would fire.

As I look back, I see it was a pretty harebrained scheme. So many things could have gone wrong that it's a wonder we ever went ahead with it.

Doc gave the signal, and I drew back my arm and flung the flare, automatically looking up as I did. For one horror-stricken second I feared the gorgon might approach just as I looked up, but there was no sign of it.

Then all hell broke loose in the copse.

A Johnson flare goes off like a lithium bomb—at least it creates enough light to simulate one. That copse lit up bright yellow, and I caught the odd contrast between the red of the leaves and the yellow of the light. And I saw something huge thrashing around in the heart of the copse before I jerked my head down. I stared at my feet.

Try blindfolding yourself some time and walking down a city street, an empty street, at dawn. The terror is something unimaginable, the unreasoning terror of the blind. That's the way I felt, knowing that at

24

any moment a monster might pop out of the clump of trees and leap at me while I stood studying my boots. An awful ten seconds passed, and seemed like days, and I grew progressively more numb with fear, until I passed the point of fright and seemed almost calm. Nothing happened, though the flare continued to kick up a powerful light. I heard rustling noises in the copse.

And then all at once I heard Steeger's tinny yell in my phones.

"Joel!"

In the same instant I drew with my right hand and flung my left hand behind my neck, forcing my head down. I aimed the blaster up at a 45-degree angle and began sizzling away for all I was worth. Over to my left I could hear Morro doing the same.

There was the sound of thunder, as of a great beast lumbering around near me. I could hear Steeger screaming something in my phones, but I was unable to stop yelling myself. And I didn't dare look up.

For all I knew the gorgon was standing right over me and bending to bite me in two. But I had passed the point of any coherent reasoning. I was still screaming and squeezing the trigger of the burned-out blaster five minutes later, when Morro and Framer came over to me and led me back to the ship.

We had killed it, then. And I, Lieut. (Spatial) Joel Kaftan, commander of EExP A-7 to Bellatrix IV, was Perseus.

"We thought we'd never get you up," said Morro.

Steeger said, "I saw that gorgon come out, and I yelled to you. You started waving the blaster around, and Morro came over too. But by the time he reached you, you had blasted Medusa in the neck and pretty near cut that head right off."

Ramirez took up the story. "You were still blasting away without looking, even though the gorgon had fallen on its face. Holden came up and cut its head off, but it's still thrashing its wings out there."

"You ruined about three trees with your blaster," Morro added. "Damned careless of you, Joel."

I looked up. The accumulated tension had built up to such a pitch while I was waiting for the thing to come out of its lair that I felt I had been through a wringer and had been squeezed flat. I looked around at the men ranging the couch on which I lay.

I saw great Morro standing at my feet, and old Steeger looking even older after his remote-control chess-game with the gorgon. And there was Holden, and Ramirez. Four. And I made five. Two dead made seven. It took me another second to realize we were not all together.

"Where's Framer?"

"Out there," Ramirez said. "The biologist in him got the upper hand, and he's out there examining our defunct friend."

"But you said the wings were still thrashing," I yelled, leaping from the couch. "That means—"

But the others realized what it meant, too, and we raced through the airlock door in no time at all.

We were too late, of course. We found the biologist bent over the decapitated gorgon, examining the head with interest. And frozen stiff.

Averting our eyes, we carried Kal back to the ship and buried him next to Flaherty and Janus. More than any of us, Kal had been a scientist, and he couldn't resist trying to solve the puzzle of the gorgon. Whether he had or not we would never know—but apparently the gorgon's neural network had been of a low order, low enough to remain functioning for a while after the organism's death. And there had been enough of a charge left in those deadly eyes to give Framer a freezing blast.

I directed operations from the door of the ship, trying hard not to stare at the upturned gorgon-head. Upton and Morro crept up blindfolded and slipped the gorgon's head into a thick plasticanvas bag, and zipped up the top. We stuck a "danger—do not open" sign on it.

Medusa had cost us three men, but we had beaten her. We loaded her headless corpse into the deep freeze for Earth's scientists to puzzle over. It took all five of us to lift the huge thing and stow it away, and we were glad to see the end of it. No more monsters, we thought; the expedition would be restful from here on.

Until the next day, when Ramirez found that Sphinx crouching near the ship—

THE ROAD TO NIGHTFALL

I was in my late teens, an undergraduate at Columbia University, when I began sketching this story out in the fall of 1953. I had, I remember, been reading a story by the French writer Marcel Ayme called "Crossing Paris," in the July-August 1950 issue of Partisan Review—a literary magazine that I followed avidly in those days. This was how it opened:

"The victim, already dismembered, lay in a corner of the cellar under wrappings of stained canvas. Jamblier, a little man with graying hair, a sharp profile, and feverish eyes, his belly girded with a kitchen apron which came down to his feet, was shuffling across the concrete floor. At times he stopped short in his tracks to gaze with faintly flushed cheeks and uneasy eyes at the latch of the door. To relieve the tension of waiting, he took a mop which was soaking in an enamelled bucket, and for the third time he washed the damp surface of the concrete to efface from it any last traces of blood which his butchery might have left there...."

It sounds like the beginning of a murder mystery, or a horror story. But in fact "Crossing Paris" dealt with the complicated problem of transporting black-market pork by suitcase through the Nazi-occupied city. The grim, bleak wartime atmosphere and the situational-ethics anguish of the characters affected me profoundly; almost at once I found myself translating the story's mood into science-fictional terms. What if, I asked myself, I were to take Ayme's trick opening paragraph literally? Assume that the "victim" is not a pig but a man, as I had thought until the second page of the story, and the city is suffering privations far more intense even than those of the war, so that cannibalism is being practiced and the

27

illicit meat being smuggled by night through the streets is the most illicit meat of all.

I wrote it in odd moments stolen from class work over the next couple of months, intending to submit it to a contest one of the science-fiction magazines was running that year, and finished it during my Christmas break from college. A thousand-dollar prize (the equivalent of at least ten thousand in today's money) was being offered for the best story of life in twenty-first-century America written by a college undergraduate. For some reason I never entered the contest—missed the deadline, perhaps—but in the spring of 1954 I started sending my manuscript around to the science-fiction magazines. I was nobody at all, then, an unpublished writer (though to my own amazement I had just had my first novel, Revolt on Alpha C, accepted for hardcover publication in 1955). Back the story came with great speed, just as all the fifteen or twenty other stories I had sent out over the previous five years had done. (I had been thirteen or fourteen when I first began sending my stories to the magazines.) When it had been to all seven or eight of the magazines that existed then, and every editor had told me how depressing, morbid, negative, and impossible to publish it was, I put it aside and wrote it off as a mistake.

A couple of years went by. By then I was selling my stories at a rapid clip and had become, before I was twenty-one, a well-known science-fiction writer. I was earning a nice living from my writing while still an undergraduate at Columbia. (You will find an account of how all that happened in my collection of pulp-adventure stories, In the Beginning.)

Meanwhile a kid from Cleveland had come to New York, moved in next door to me, and set up shop as a writer as well. His name was Harlan Ellison. One day in 1956 I told him that I had been able to sell all my stories except one, which no editor would touch, and he demanded to see it. He read it on the spot. "Brilliant!" he said. "Magnificent!" Or words to that effect. Harlan was indignant that such a dark masterpiece would have met with universal rejection, and he vowed to find a publisher for it. Just about then, the kindly and unworldly Hans Stefan Santesson took over the editorship of a struggling magazine called Fantastic Universe, and Harlan told him I had written a story too daring for any of his rivals to print—virtually defying him not to buy it. Hans asked for the manuscript, commented in his mild way that the story was pretty strong stuff, and, after hesitating over it for nearly two years, ran it in the July, 1958 issue of his magazine.

After more than half a century I find it hard to see what was so hot to handle about "Road to Nightfall." Its theme—that the stress of life in a post-atomic society could lead even to cannibalism—seemed to upset many of the editors who turned it down, but there was no taboo per se against that theme. (Cf. Damon Knight's 1950 classic, "To Serve Man," just to name one.) Most likely the protagonist's moral collapse at the end was the problem, for most s-f editors of the time preferred stories in which the central figure transcends all challenges and arrives at a triumphant conclusion to his travail. That I had never published anything at the time was a further drawback. Theodore Sturgeon or Fritz Leiber, say, might have persuaded an editor to buy a story about cannibalism, or one with a downbeat ending—but a downbeat cannibal story by an unknown author simply had too much going against it, and even after my name had become established it still needed the full force of the Harlan Ellison juggernaut to win it a home. To me it still seems like a pretty good job, especially for a writer who was still a considerable distance short of his twentieth birthday. It moves along, it creates character and action and something of a plot, it gets its point across effectively. If I had been an editor looking at this manuscript back then, I would certainly have thought its writer showed some promise.

The dog snarled, and ran on. Katterson watched the two lean, fiery-eyed men speeding in pursuit, while a mounting horror grew in him and rooted him to the spot. The dog suddenly bounded over a heap of rubble and was gone; its pursuers sank limply down, leaning on their clubs, and tried to catch their breath.

"It's going to get much worse than this," said a small, grubby-looking man who appeared from nowhere next to Katterson. "I've heard the official announcement's coming today, but the rumor's been around for a long time."

"So they say," answered Katterson slowly. The chase he had just witnessed still held him paralyzed. "We're all pretty hungry."

The two men who had chased the dog got up, still winded, and wandered off. Katterson and the little man watched their slow retreat.

"That's the first time I've ever seen people doing that," said Katterson. "Out in the open like that—"

"It won't be the last time," said the grubby man. "Better get used to it, now that the food's gone."

Katterson's stomach twinged. It was empty, and would stay that way till the evening's food dole. Without the doles, he would have no idea of where his next bite of food would come from. He and the small man walked on through the quiet street, stepping over the rubble, walking aimlessly with no particular goal in mind.

"My name's Paul Katterson," he said finally. "I live on 47th Street. I was discharged from the Army last year."

"Oh, one of those," said the little man. They turned down 15th Street. It was a street of complete desolation; not one pre-war house was standing, and a few shabby tents were pitched at the far end of the street. "Have you had any work since your discharge?"

Katterson laughed. "Good joke. Try another."

"I know. Things are tough. My name is Malory; I'm a merchandizer."

"What do you merchandize?"

"Oh...useful products."

Katterson nodded. Obviously Malory didn't want him to pursue the topic, and he dropped it. They walked on silently, the big man and the little one, and Katterson could think of nothing but the emptiness in his stomach. Then his thoughts drifted to the scene of a few minutes before, the two hungry men chasing a dog. Had it come to that so soon? Katterson asked himself. What was going to happen, he wondered, as food became scarcer and scarcer and finally there was none at all?

But the little man was pointing ahead. "Look," he said. "Meeting at Union Square."

Katterson squinted and saw a crowd starting to form around the platform reserved for public announcements. He quickened his pace, forcing Malory to struggle to keep up with him.

A young man in military uniform had mounted the platform and was impassively facing the crowd. Katterson looked at the jeep nearby, automatically noting it was the 2036 model, the most recent one, eighteen years old. After a minute or so the soldier raised his hand for silence, and spoke in a quiet, restrained voice.

"Fellow New Yorkers, I have an official announcement from the Government. Word has just been received from Trenton Oasis—"

The crowd began to murmur. They seemed to know what was coming.

"Word has just been received from Trenton Oasis that, due to recent emergency conditions there, all food supplies for New York City and environs will be temporarily cut off. Repeat: due to recent emergency in the Trenton Oasis, all food supplies for New York and environs will temporarily be cut off."

The murmuring in the crowd grew to an angry, biting whisper as each man discussed this latest turn of events with the man next to him. This was hardly unexpected news; Trenton had long protested the burden of feeding helpless, bombed-out New York, and the recent flood there had given them ample opportunity to squirm out of their responsibility. Katterson stood silent, towering over the people around him, finding himself unable to believe what he was hearing. He seemed aloof, almost detached, objectively criticizing the posture of the soldier on the platform, counting his insignia, thinking of everything but the implications of the announcement, and trying to fight back the growing hunger.

The uniformed man was speaking again. "I also have this message from the Governor of New York, General Holloway: he says that attempts at restoring New York's food supply are being made, and that messengers have been dispatched to the Baltimore Oasis to request food supplies. In the meantime the Government food doles are to be discontinued effective tonight, until further notice. That is all."

The soldier gingerly dismounted from the platform and made his way through the crowd to his jeep. He climbed quickly in and drove off. Obviously he was an important man, Katterson decided, because jeeps and fuel were scarce items, not used lightly by anyone and everyone.

Katterson remained where he was and turned his head slowly, looking at the people round him—thin, half-starved little skeletons, most of them, who secretly begrudged him his giant frame. An emaciated man with burning eyes and a beak of a nose had gathered a small group around himself and was shouting some sort of harangue. Katterson knew of him—his name was Emerich, and he was the leader of the colony living in the abandoned subway at 14th Street. Katterson instinctively moved closer to hear him, and Malory followed.

"It's all a plot!" the emaciated man was shouting. "They talk of an emergency in Trenton. What emergency? I ask you, what emergency? That flood didn't hurt them. They just want to get us off their necks by starving us out, that's all! And what can we do about it? Nothing. Trenton knows we'll never be able to rebuild New York, and they want to get rid of us, so they cut off our food."

By now the crowd had gathered round him. Emerich was popular; people were shouting their agreement, punctuating his speech with applause.

31

"But will we starve to death? We will not!"

"That's right, Emerich!" yelled a burly man with a beard.

"No," Emerich continued, "we'll show them what we can do. We'll scrape up every bit of food we can find, every blade of grass, every wild animal, every bit of shoe-leather. And we'll survive, just the way we survived the blockade and the famine of '47 and everything else. And one of these days we'll go out to Trenton and—and—roast them alive!"

Roars of approval filled the air. Katterson turned and shouldered his way through the crowd, thinking of the two men and the dog, and walked away without looking back. He headed down Fourth Avenue, until he could no longer hear the sounds of the meeting at Union Square, and sat down wearily on a pile of crushed girders that had once been the Carden Monument.

He put his head in his hands and sat there. The afternoon's events had numbed him. Food had been scarce as far back as he could remember—the twenty-four years of war with the Spherists had just about used up every resource of the country. The war had dragged on and on. After the first rash of preliminary bombings, it had become a war of attrition, slowly grinding the opposing spheres to rubble.

Somehow Katterson had grown big and powerful on hardly any food, and he stood out wherever he went. The generation of Americans to which he belonged was not one of size or strength—the children were born under-nourished old men, weak and wrinkled. But he had been big, and he had been one of the lucky ones chosen for the Army. At least there he had been fed regularly.

Katterson kicked away a twisted bit of slag, and saw little Malory coming down Fourth Avenue in his direction. Katterson laughed to himself, remembering his Army days. His whole adult life had been spent in uniform, with soldier's privileges. But it had been too good to last; two years before, in 2052, the war had finally dragged to a complete standstill, with the competing hemispheres both worn to shreds, and almost the entire Army had suddenly been mustered out into the cold civilian world. He had been dumped into New York, lost and alone.

"Let's go for a dog-hunt," Malory said, smiling as he drew near.

"Watch your tongue, little man. I might just eat you if I get hungry enough."

"Eh? I thought you were so shocked by two men trying to catch a dog."

Katterson looked up. "I was," he said. "Sit down, or get moving, but don't play games," he growled. Malory flung himself down on the wreckage near Katterson.

"Looks pretty bad," Malory said.

"Check," said Katterson. "I haven't eaten anything all day."

"Why not? There was a regular dole last night, and there'll be one tonight."

"You hope," said Katterson. The day was drawing to a close, he saw, and evening shadows were falling fast. Ruined New York looked weird in twilight; the gnarled girders and fallen buildings seemed ghosts of long-dead giants.

"You'll be even hungrier tomorrow," Malory said. "There isn't going to be any dole, any more."

"Don't remind me, little man."

"I'm in the food-supplying business, myself," said Malory, as a weak smile rippled over his lips.

Katterson picked up his head in a hurry.

"Playing games again?"

"No," Malory said hastily. He scribbled his address on a piece of paper and handed it to Katterson. "Here. Drop in on me any time you get really hungry. And—say, you're a pretty strong fellow, aren't you? I might even have some work for you, since you say you're unattached."

The shadow of an idea began to strike Katterson. He turned so he faced the little man, and stared at him.

"What kind of work?"

Malory paled. "Oh, I need some strong men to obtain food for me. *You* know," he whispered.

Katterson reached over and grasped the small man's thin shoulders. Malory winced. "Yes, I know," Katterson repeated slowly. "Tell me, Malory," he said carefully. "What sort of food do you sell?"

Malory squirmed. "Why—why—now look, I just wanted to help you, and—"

"Don't give me any of that." Slowly Katterson stood up, not releasing his grip on the small man. Malory found himself being dragged willy-nilly to his feet. "You're in the meat business, aren't you, Malory? *What kind of meat do you sell?*"

Malory tried to break away. Katterson shoved him with a contemptuous half-open fist and sent him sprawling back into the rubble-heap. Malory twisted away, his eyes wild with fear, and dashed off down 13th

Street into the gloom. Katterson stood for a long time watching him retreat, breathing hard and not daring to think. Then he folded the paper with Malory's address on it and put it in his pocket, and walked numbly away.

Barbara was waiting for him when he pressed his thumb against the doorplate of his apartment on 47th Street an hour later.

"I suppose you've heard the news," she said as he entered. "Some spic-and-span lieutenant came by and announced it down below. I've already picked up our dole for tonight, and that's the last one. Hey—anything the matter?" She looked at him anxiously as he sank wordlessly into a chair.

"Nothing, kid. I'm just hungry—and a little sick to my stomach."

"Where'd you go today? The Square again?"

"Yeah. My usual Thursday afternoon stroll, and a pleasant picnic that turned out to be. First I saw two men hunting a dog—they couldn't have been much hungrier than I am, but they were chasing this poor scrawny thing. Then your lieutenant made his announcement about the food. And then a filthy meat pedlar tried to sell me some 'merchandize' and give me a job."

The girl caught her breath. "A job? Meat? What happened? Oh, Paul—"

"Stow it," Katterson told her. "I knocked him sprawling and he ran away with his tail between his legs. You know what he was selling? You know what kind of meat he wanted me to eat?"

She lowered her eyes. "Yes, Paul."

"And the job he had for me—he saw I'm strong, so he would have made me his supplier. I would have gone out hunting in the evenings. Looking for stragglers to be knocked off and turned into tomorrow's steaks."

"But we're so hungry, Paul—when you're hungry that's the most important thing."

"*What?*" His voice was the bellow of an outraged bull. "What? You don't know what you're saying, woman. Eat before you go out of your mind completely. I'll find some other way of getting food, but I'm not going to turn into a bloody cannibal. No longpork for Paul Katterson."

She said nothing. The single light-glow in the ceiling flickered twice.

34

"Getting near shut-off time. Get the candles out, unless you're sleepy," he said. He had no chronometer, but the flickering was the signal that eight-thirty was approaching. At eight-thirty every night electricity was cut off in all residence apartments except those with permission to exceed normal quota.

Barbara lit a candle.

"Paul, Father Kennon was back here again today."

"I've told him not to show up here again," Katterson said from the darkness of his corner of the room.

"He thinks we ought to get married, Paul."

"I know. I don't."

"Paul, why are you—"

"Let's not go over that again. I've told you often enough that I don't want the responsibility of two mouths to feed, when I can't even manage keeping my own belly full. This is the best—each of us on our own."

"But children, Paul—"

"Are you crazy tonight?" he retorted. "Would you dare to bring a child into this world? Especially now that we've even lost the food from Trenton Oasis? Would you enjoy watching him slowly starve to death in all this filth and rubble, or maybe growing up into a hollow-cheeked little skeleton? Maybe you would. I don't think I'd care to."

He was silent. She sat watching him, sobbing quietly.

"We're dead, you and I," she finally said. "We won't admit it, but we're dead. This whole world is dead—we've spent the last thirty years committing suicide. I don't remember as far back as you do, but I've read some of the old books, about how clean and new and shiny this city was before the war. The war! All my life, we've been at war, never knowing who we were fighting and why. Just eating the world apart for no reason at all."

"Cut it, Barbara," Katterson said. But she went on in a dead monotone. "They tell me America once went from coast to coast, instead of being cut up into little strips bordered by radioactive no-man's-lands. And there were farms, and food, and lakes and rivers, and men flew from place to place. Why did this have to happen? Why are we all dead? Where do we go now, Paul?"

"I don't know, Barbara. I don't think anyone does." Wearily, he snuffed out the candle, and the darkness flooded in and filled the room.

35

Somehow he had wandered back to Union Square again, and he stood on 14th Street, rocking gently back and forth on his feet and feeling the lightheadedness which is the first sign of starvation. There were just a few people in the streets, morosely heading for whatever destinations claimed them. The sun was high overhead, and bright.

His reverie was interrupted by the sound of yells and an unaccustomed noise of running feet. His Army training stood him in good stead as he dove into a gaping trench and hid there, wondering what was happening.

After a moment he peeked out. Four men, each as big as Katterson himself, were roaming up and down the now deserted streets. One was carrying a sack.

"There's one," Katterson heard the man with the sack yell harshly. He watched without believing as the four men located a girl cowering near a fallen building.

She was a pale, thin, ragged-looking girl, perhaps twenty at the most, who might have been pretty in some other world. But her cheeks were sunken and coarse, her eyes dull and glassy, her arms bony and angular.

As they drew near she huddled back, cursing defiantly, and prepared to defend herself. *She doesn't understand,* Katterson thought. *She thinks she's going to be attacked.*

Perspiration streamed down his body, and he forced himself to watch, kept himself from leaping out of hiding. The four marauders closed in on the girl. She spat, struck out with her clawlike hand.

They chuckled and grabbed her clutching arm. Her scream was suddenly ear-piercing as they dragged her out into the open. A knife flashed; Katterson ground his teeth together, wincing, as the blade struck home.

"In the sack with her, Charlie," a rough voice said.

Katterson's eyes steamed with rage. It was his first view of Malory's butchers—at least, he suspected it was Malory's gang. Feeling the knife at his side, in its familiar sheath, he half-rose to attack the four meat-raiders, and then, regaining his sense, he sank back into the trench.

So soon? Katterson knew that cannibalism had been spreading slowly through starving New York for many years, and that few bodies of the dead ever reached their graves intact—but this was the first time, so far as he knew, that raiders had dragged a living human being from the streets and killed her for food. He shuddered. The race for life was on, then.

The four raiders disappeared in the direction of Third Avenue, and Katterson cautiously eased himself from the trench, cast a wary eye in all directions, and edged into the open. He knew he would have to be careful; a man his size carried meat for many mouths.

Other people were coming out of the buildings now, all with much the same expression of horror on their faces. Katterson watched the marching skeletons walking dazedly, a few sobbing, most of them past the stage of tears. He clenched and unclenched his fists, angry, burning to stamp out this spreading sickness and knowing hopelessly that it could not be done.

A tall thin man with chiseled features was on the speaker's platform now. His voice was choked with anger.

"Brothers, it's out in the open now. Men have turned from the ways of God, and Satan has led them to destruction. Just now you witnessed four of His creatures destroy a fellow mortal for food—the most terrible sin of all.

"Brothers, our time on Earth is almost done. I'm an old man—I remember the days before the war, and, while some of you won't believe it, I remember the days when there was food for all, when everyone had a job, when these crumpled buildings were tall and shiny and stream-lined, and the skies teemed with jets. In my youth I traveled all across this country, clear to the Pacific. But the War has ended all that, and it's God's hand upon us. Our day is done, and soon we'll all meet our reckoning.

"Go to God without blood on your hands, brothers. Those four men you saw today will burn forever for their crime. Whoever eats the unholy meat they butchered today will join them in Hell. But listen a moment, brothers, listen! Those of you who aren't lost yet, I beg you: save your-selves! Better to go without food at all, as most of you are doing, than to soil yourselves with this kind of new food, the most precious meat of all."

Katterson stared at the people around him. He wanted to end all this; he had a vision of a crusade for food, a campaign against cannibal-ism, banners waving, drums beating, himself leading the fight. Some of the people had stopped listening to the old preacher, and some had wandered off. A few were smiling and hurtling derisive remarks at the old man, but he ignored them.

"Hear me! Hear me, before you go. We're all doomed anyway; the Lord has made that clear. But think, people—this world will shortly pass away, and there is the greater world to come. Don't sign away your chance for eternal life, brothers! Don't trade your immortal soul for a bit of tainted meat!"

The crowd was melting away, Katterson noted. It was dispersing hastily, people quickly edging away and disappearing. The preacher continued talking. Katterson stood on tip-toes and craned his neck past the crowd and stared down towards the east. His eyes searched for a moment, and then he paled. Four ominous figures were coming with deliberate tread down the deserted street.

Almost everyone had seen them now. They were walking four abreast down the center of the street, the tallest holding an empty sack. People were heading hastily in all directions, and as the four figures came to the corner of 14th Street and Fourth Avenue only Katterson and the preacher still stood at the platform.

"I see you're the only one left, young man. Have you defiled yourself, or are you still of the Kingdom of Heaven?"

Katterson ignored the question. "Old man, get down from there!" he snapped. "The raiders are coming back. Come on, let's get out of here before they come."

"No. I intend to talk to them when they come. But save yourself, young man, save yourself while you can."

"They'll kill you, you old fool," Katterson whispered harshly.

"We're all doomed anyway, son. If my day has come, I'm ready."

"You're crazy," Katterson said. The four men were within speaking distance now. Katterson looked at the old man for one last time and then dashed across the street and into a building. He glanced back and saw he was not being followed.

The four raiders were standing under the platform, listening to the old man. Katterson couldn't hear what the preacher was saying, but he was waving his arms as he spoke. They seemed to be listening intently. Katterson stared. He saw one of the raiders say something to the old man, and then the tall one with the sack climbed up on the platform. One of the others tossed him an unsheathed knife.

The shriek was loud and piercing. When Katterson dared to look out again, the tall man was stuffing the preacher's body into the sack. Katterson bowed his head. The trumpets began to fade; he realized that resistance was impossible. Unstoppable currents were flowing.

Katterson plodded uptown to his apartment. The blocks flew past as he methodically pulled one foot after another, walking the two miles through the rubble and deserted, ruined buildings. He kept one hand on his knife and darted glances from right to left, noting the furtive scurryings in the side streets, the shadowy people who were not quite visible behind the ashes and the rubble. Those four figures, one with the sack, seemed to lurk behind every lamppost, waiting hungrily.

He cut into Broadway, taking a shortcut through the stump of the Parker Building. Fifty years before, the Parker Building had been the tallest in the Western world; its truncated stump was all that remained. Katterson passed what had once been the most majestic lobby in the world, and stared in. A small boy sat on the step outside, gnawing a piece of meat. He was eight or ten; his stomach was drawn tight over his ribs, which showed through like a basket. Choking down his revulsion, Katterson wondered what sort of meat the boy was eating.

He continued on. As he passed 44th Street, a bony cat skittered past him and disappeared behind a pile of ashes. Katterson thought of the stories he had heard of the Great Plains, where giant cats were said to roam unmolested, and his mouth watered.

The sun was sinking low again, and New York was turning dull grey and black. The sun never really shone in late afternoon any more; it sneaked its way through the piles of rubble and cast a ghostly glow on the ruins of New York. Katterson crossed 47th Street and turned down towards his building.

He made the long climb to his room—the elevator's shaft was still there, and the frozen elevator, but such luxuries were beyond dream—and stood outside for just a moment, searching in the darkness for the doorplate. There was the sound of laughter from within, a strange sound for ears not accustomed to it, and a food-smell crept out through the door and hit him squarely. His throat began to work convulsively, and he remembered the dull ball of pain that was his stomach.

Katterson opened the door. The food-odor filled the little room completely. He saw Barbara look up suddenly, white-faced, as he entered. In his chair was a man he had met once or twice, a scraggly-haired, heavily bearded man named Heydahl.

"What's going on?" Katterson demanded.

Barbara's voice was strangely hushed. "Paul, you know Olaf Heydahl, don't you? Olaf, Paul?"

"What's going on?" Katterson repeated.

"Barbara and I have just been having a little meat, Mr. Katterson," Heydahl said, in a rich voice. "We thought you'd be hungry, so we saved a little for you."

The smell was overpowering and Katterson felt it was all he could do to keep from foaming at the lips. Barbara was wiping her face over and over again with the napkin; Heydahl sat contentedly in Katterson's chair.

In three quick steps Katterson crossed to the other side of the room and threw open the doors to the little enclosed kitchenette. On the stove a small piece of meat sizzled softly. Katterson looked at the meat, then at Barbara.

"Where did you get this?" he asked. "We have no money."

"I—I—"

"I bought it," Heydahl said quietly. "Barbara told me how little food you had, and since I had more than I wanted I brought over a little gift."

"I see. A gift. No strings attached?"

"Why, Mr. Katterson! Remember, I'm Barbara's guest."

"Yes, but please remember this is my apartment, not hers. Tell me, Heydahl—what kind of payment do you expect for this—this gift? And how much payment have you had already?"

Heydahl half-rose in his chair. "Please, Paul," Barbara said hurriedly. "No trouble, Paul. Olaf was just trying to be friendly."

"Barbara's right, Mr. Katterson," Heydahl said, subsiding. "Go ahead, help yourself. You'll do yourself some good, and you'll make me happy too."

Katterson stared at him for a moment. The half-light from below trickled in over Heydahl's shoulder, illuminating his nearly bald head and his flowing beard. Katterson wondered just how Heydahl's cheeks managed to be quite so plump.

"Go ahead," Heydahl repeated. "We've had our fill."

Katterson turned back to the meat. He pulled a plate from the shelf and plopped the piece of meat on it, and unsheathed his knife. He was about to start carving when he turned to look at the two others.

Barbara was leaning forward in her chair. Her eyes were staring wide, and fear was shining deep in them. Heydahl, on the other hand, sat comfortably in Katterson's chair, with a complacent look on his face that Katterson had not seen on anyone's features since leaving the Army.

A thought hit him suddenly and turned him icy-cold. "Barbara," he said, controlling his voice, "what kind of meat is this? Roast beef or lamb?"

"I don't know, Paul," she said uncertainly. "Olaf didn't say what—"

"Maybe roast dog, perhaps? Filet of alleycat? Why didn't you ask Olaf what was on the menu. *Why don't you ask him now?*"

Barbara looked at Heydahl, then back at Katterson.

"Eat it, Paul. It's good, believe me—and I know how hungry you are."

"I don't eat unlabeled goods, Barbara. Ask Mr. Heydahl what kind of meat it is, first."

She turned to Heydahl. "Olaf—"

"I don't think you should be so fussy these days, Mr. Katterson," Heydahl said. "After all, there are no more food doles, and you don't know when meat will be available again."

"I like to be fussy, Heydahl. What kind of meat is this?"

"Why are you so curious? You know what they say about looking gift-horses in the mouth, heh heh."

"I can't even be sure this is horse, Heydahl. What kind of meat is it?" Katterson's voice, usually carefully modulated, became a snarl. "A choice slice of fat little boy? Maybe a steak from some poor devil who was in the wrong neighborhood one evening?"

Heydahl turned white.

Katterson took the meat from the plate and hefted it for a moment in his hand. "You can't even spit the words out, either of you. They choke in your mouths. Here—cannibals!"

He hurled the meat hard at Barbara; it glanced off the side of her cheek and fell to the floor. His face was flaming with rage. He flung open the door, turned, and slammed it again, rushing blindly away. The last thing he saw before slamming the door was Barbara on her knees, scurrying to pick up the piece of meat.

Night was dropping fast, and Katterson knew the streets were unsafe. His apartment, he felt, was polluted; he could not go back to it. The problem was to get food. He hadn't eaten in almost two days. He thrust his hands in his pocket and felt the folded slip of paper with Malory's address on it, and, with a wry grimace, realized that this was his only source of food and money. But not yet—not so long as he could hold up his head.

Without thinking he wandered towards the river, towards the huge crater where, Katterson had been told, there once had been the United Nations buildings. The crater was almost a thousand feet deep; the United Nations had been obliterated in the first bombing, back in 2028. Katterson had been just one year old then, the year the War began. The actual fighting and bombing had continued for the next five or six years, until both hemispheres were scarred and burned from combat, and then the long war of attrition had begun. Katterson had turned eighteen in 2045—nine long years ago, he reflected—and his giant frame made him a natural choice for a soft Army post. In the course of his Army career he had been all over the section of the world he considered his country—the patch of land bounded by the Appalachian radioactive belt on one side, by the Atlantic on the other. The enemy had carefully constructed walls of fire partitioning America into a dozen strips, each completely isolated from the next. An airplane could cross from one to another, if there were any left. But science, industry, and technology were dead, Katterson thought wearily, as he stared without seeing at the river. He sat down on the edge of the crater and dangled his feet.

What had happened to the brave new world that had entered the twenty-first century with such proud hopes? Here he was, Paul Katterson, probably one of the strongest and tallest men in the country, swinging his legs over a great devastated area, with a gnawing pain in the pit of his stomach. The world was dead, the shiny streamlined world of chrome plating and jet planes. Someday, perhaps, there would be new life. Someday.

Katterson stared at the waters beyond the crater. Somewhere across the seas there were other countries, broken like the rest. And somewhere in the other direction were rolling plains, grass, wheat, wild animals, fenced off by hundreds of miles of radioactive mountains. The War had eaten up the fields and pastures and livestock, had ground all mankind under.

He got up and started to walk back through the lonely street. It was dark now, and the few gaslights cast a ghostly light, like little eclipsed moons. The fields were dead, and what was left of mankind huddled in the blasted cities, except for the lucky ones in the few Oases scattered by chance through the country. New York was a city of skeletons, each one scrabbling for food, cutting corners and hoping for tomorrow's bread.

A small man bumped into Katterson as he wandered unseeing. Katterson looked down at him and caught him by the arm. A family man, he guessed, hurrying home to his hungry children.

"Excuse me, sir," the little man said, nervously, straining to break Katterson's grip. The fear was obvious on his face; Katterson wondered if the worried little man thought this giant was going to roast him on the spot.

"I won't hurt you," Katterson said. "I'm just looking for food, Citizen."

"I have none."

"But I'm starving," Katterson said. "You look like you have a job, some money. Give me some food and I'll be your bodyguard, your slave, anything you want."

"Look, fellow, I have no food to spare. Ouch! Let go of my arm!"

Katterson let go, and watched the little man go dashing away down the street. People always ran away from other people these days, he thought. Malory had made a similar escape.

The streets were dark and empty. Katterson wondered if he would be someone's steak by morning, and he didn't really care. His chest itched suddenly, and he thrust a grimy hand inside his shirt to scratch. The flesh over his pectoral muscles had almost completely been absorbed, and his chest was bony to the touch. He felt his stubbly cheeks, noting how tight they were over his jaws.

He turned and headed uptown, skirting around the craters, climbing over the piles of rubble. At 50th Street a Government jeep came coasting by and drew to a stop. Two soldiers with guns got out.

"Pretty late for you to be strolling, Citizen," one soldier said.

"Looking for some fresh air."

"That all?"

"What's it to you?" Katterson said.

"Not hunting some game too, maybe?"

Katterson lunged at the soldier. "Why, you little punk—"

"Easy, big boy," the other soldier said, pulling him back. "We were just joking."

"Fine joke," Katterson said. "You can afford to joke—all you have to do to get food is wear a monkey suit. I know how it is with you Army guys."

"Not any more," the second soldier said.

"Who are you kidding?" Katterson said. "I was a Regular Army man for seven years until they broke up our outfit in '52. I know what's happening."

"Hey—what regiment?"

"306th Exploratory, soldier."

"You're not Katterson, Paul Katterson?"

"Maybe I am," Katterson said slowly. He moved closer to the two soldiers. "What of it?"

"You know Mark Leswick?"

"Damned well I do," Katterson said. "But how do you know him?"

"My brother. Used to talk of you all the time—Katterson's the biggest man alive, he'd say. Appetite like an ox."

Katterson smiled. "What's he doing now?"

The other coughed. "Nothing. He and some friends built a raft and tried to float to South America. They were sunk by the Shore Patrol just outside the New York Harbor."

"Oh. Too bad. Fine man, Mark. But he was right about the appetite. I'm hungry."

"So are we, fellow," the soldier said. "They cut off the soldiers' dole yesterday."

Katterson laughed, and the echoes rang in the silent street. "Damn them anyway! Good thing they didn't pull that when I was in the service; I'd have told them off."

"You can come with us, if you'd like. We'll be off-duty when this patrol is over, and we'll be heading downtown."

"Pretty late, isn't it? What time is it? Where are you going?"

"It's quarter to three," the soldier said, looking at his chronometer. "We're looking for a fellow named Malory; there's a story he has some food for sale, and we just got paid yesterday." He patted his pocket smugly.

Katterson blinked. "You know what kind of stuff Malory's selling?"

"Yeah," the other said. "So what? When you're hungry, you're hungry, and it's better to eat than starve. I've seen some guys like you—too stubborn to go that low for a meal. But you'll give in, sooner or later, I suppose. I don't know—you look stubborn."

"Yeah," Katterson said, breathing a little harder than usual. "I guess I am stubborn. Or maybe I'm not hungry enough yet. Thanks for the lift, but I'm afraid I'm going uptown."

And he turned and trudged off into the darkness.

There was only one friendly place to go.

Hal North was a quiet, bookish man who had come in contact with Katterson fairly often, even though North lived almost four miles uptown, on 114th Street.

Katterson had a standing invitation to come to North at any time of day or night, and, having no place else to go, he headed there. North was one of the few scholars who still tried to pursue knowledge at Columbia, once a citadel of learning. They huddled together in the crumbling wreck of one of the halls, treasuring moldering books and exchanging ideas. North had a tiny apartment in an undamaged building on 114th Street, and he lived surrounded by books and a tiny circle of acquaintances.

Quarter to three, the soldier said. Katterson walked swiftly and easily, hardly noticing the blocks as they flew past. He reached North's apartment just as the sun was beginning to come up, and he knocked cautiously on the door. One knock, two, then another a little harder.

Footsteps within. "Who's there?" in a tired, high-pitched voice.

"Paul Katterson," Katterson whispered. "You awake?"

North slid the door open. "Katterson! Come on in. What brings you up here?"

"You said I could come whenever I needed to. I need to." Katterson sat down on the edge of North's bed. "I haven't eaten in two days, pretty near."

North chuckled. "You came to the right place, then. Wait—I'll fix you some bread and oleo. We still have some left."

"You sure you can spare it, Hal?"

North opened a cupboard and took out a loaf of bread, and Katterson's mouth began to water. "Of course, Paul. I don't eat much anyway, and I've been storing most of my food doles. You're welcome to whatever's here."

A sudden feeling of love swept through Katterson, a strange, consuming emotion which seemed to enfold all mankind for a moment, then withered and died away. "Thanks, Hal. Thanks."

He turned and looked at the tattered, thumb-stained book lying open on North's bed. Katterson let his eye wander down the tiny print and read softly aloud.

"The emperor of the sorrowful realm was there,
Out of the girding ice he stood breast-high
And to his arm alone the giants were
Less comparable than to a giant I."

North brought a little plate of food over to where Katterson was sitting. "I was reading that all night," he said. "Somehow I thought of browsing through it again, and I started it last night and read 'till you came."

"Dante's *Inferno*," Katterson said. "Very appropriate. Someday I'd like to look through it again too. I've read so little, you know; soldiers don't get much education."

"Whenever you want to read, Paul, the books are still here." North smiled, a pale smile on his wan face. He pointed to the bookcase where grubby, frayed books leaned at all angles. "Look, Paul: Rabelais, Joyce, Dante, Enright, Voltaire, Aeschylus, Homer, Shakespeare. They're all here, Paul, the most precious things of all. They're my old friends; those books have been my breakfasts and my lunches and my suppers many times when no food was to be had for any price."

"We may be depending on them alone, Hal. Have you been out much these days?"

"No," North said. "I haven't been outdoors in over a week. Henriks has been picking up my food doles and bringing them here, and borrowing books. He came by yesterday—no, two days ago—to get my volume of Greek tragedies. He's writing a new opera, based on a play of Aeschylus."

"Poor crazy Henriks," Katterson said. "Why does he keep on writing music when there's no orchestras, no records, no concerts? He can't even hear the stuff he writes."

North opened the window and the morning air edged in. "Oh, but he does, Paul. He hears the music in his mind, and that satisfies him. It doesn't really matter; he'll never live to hear it played."

"The doles have been cut off," Katterson said.

"I know."

"The people out there are eating each other. I saw a woman killed for food yesterday—butchered just like a cow."

North shook his head and straightened a tangled, whitened lock. "So soon? I thought it would take longer than that, once the food ran out."

"They're hungry, Hal."

"Yes, they're hungry. So are you. In a day or so my supply up here will be gone, and I'll be hungry too. But it takes more than hunger to break down the taboo against eating flesh. Those people out there have given up their last shred of humanity now; they've suffered every degradation there is, and they can't sink any lower. Sooner or later we'll come to realize that, you and I, and then we'll be out there hunting for meat too."

"Hal!"

"Don't look so shocked, Paul." North smiled patiently. "Wait a couple of days, till we've eaten the bindings of my books, till we're finished chewing our shoes. The thought turns my stomach, too, but it's inevitable. Society's doomed; the last restraints are breaking now. We're more stubborn than the rest, or maybe we're just fussier about our meals. But our day will come too."

"I don't believe it," Katterson said, rising.

"Sit down. You're tired, and you're just a skeleton yourself now. What happened to my big, muscular friend Katterson? Where are his muscles now?" North reached up and squeezed the big man's biceps. "Skin, bones, what else? You're burning down, Paul, and when the spark is finally out you'll give in too."

"Maybe you're right, Hal. As soon as I stop thinking of myself as human, as soon as I get hungry enough and dead enough, I'll be out there hunting like the rest. But I'll hold out as long as I can."

He sank back on the bed and slowly turned the yellowing pages of Dante.

Henriks came back the next day, wild-eyed and haggard, to return the book of Greek plays, saying the times were not ripe for Aeschylus. He borrowed a slim volume of poems by Ezra Pound. North forced some food on Henriks, who took it gratefully and without any show of diffidence. Then he left, staring oddly at Katterson.

Others came during the day—Komar, Goldman, de Metz—all men who, like Henriks and North, remembered the old days before the long war. They were pitiful skeletons, but the flame of knowledge burned brightly in each of them. North introduced Katterson to them, and they looked wonderingly at his still-powerful frame before pouncing avidly on the books.

But soon they stopped coming. Katterson would stand at the window and watch below for hours, and the empty streets remained empty. It was now four days since the last food had arrived from Trenton Oasis. Time was running out.

A light snowfall began the next day, and continued throughout the long afternoon. At the evening meal North pulled his chair over to the cupboard, balanced precariously on its arm, and searched around in the cupboard for a few moments. Then he turned to Katterson.

"I'm even worse off than Mother Hubbard," he said. "At least she had a dog."

"Huh?"

"I was referring to an incident in a children's book," North said. "What I meant was we have no more food."

"None?" Katterson asked dully.

"Nothing at all." North smiled faintly. Katterson felt the emptiness stirring in his stomach, and leaned back, closing his eyes.

Neither of them ate at all the next day. The snow continued to filter lightly down. Katterson spent most of the time staring out the little window, and he saw a light, clean blanket of snow covering everything in sight. The snow was unbroken.

The next morning Katterson arose and found North busily tearing the binding from his copy of the Greek plays. With a sort of amazement Katterson watched North put the soiled red binding into a pot of boiling water.

"Oh, you're up? I'm just preparing breakfast."

The binding was hardly palatable, but they chewed it to a soft pulp anyway, and swallowed the pulp just to give their tortured stomachs something to work on. Katterson retched as he swallowed his final mouthful.

One day of eating bookbindings.

"The city is dead," Katterson said from the window without turning around. "I haven't seen anyone come down this street yet. The snow is everywhere."

North said nothing.

"This is crazy, Hal," Katterson said suddenly. "I'm going out to get some food."

"Where?"

"I'll walk down Broadway and see what I can find. Maybe there'll be a stray dog. I'll look. We can't hold out forever up here."

"Don't go, Paul."

Katterson turned savagely. "Why? Is it better to starve up here without trying than to go down and hunt? You're a little man; you don't need food as much as I do. I'll go down to Broadway; maybe there'll be something. At least we can't be any worse off than now."

North smiled. "Go ahead, then."

"I'm going."

He buckled on his knife, put on all the warm clothes he could find, and made his way down the stairs. He seemed to float down, so light-headed was he from hunger. His stomach was a tight hard knot.

48

The streets were deserted. A light blanket of snow lay everywhere, mantling the twisted ruins of the city. Katterson headed for Broadway, leaving tracks in the unbroken snow, and began to walk downtown.

At 96th Street and Broadway he saw his first sign of life, some people at the following corner. With mounting excitement he headed for 95th Street, but pulled up short.

There was a body sprawled over the snow, newly dead. And two boys of about twelve were having a duel to the death for its possession, while a third circled warily around them. Katterson watched them for a moment, and then crossed the street and walked on.

He no longer minded the snow and the solitude of the empty city. He maintained a steady, even pace, almost the tread of a machine. The world was crumbling fast around him, and his recourse lay in his solitary trek.

He turned back for a moment and looked behind him. There were his footsteps, the long trail stretching back and out of sight, the only marks breaking the even whiteness. He ticked off the empty blocks.

90th. 87th. 85th. At 84th he saw a blotch of color on the next block, and quickened his pace. When he got to close range, he saw it was a man lying on the snow. Katterson trotted lightly to him and stood over him.

He was lying face-down. Katterson bent and carefully rolled him over. His cheeks were still red; evidently he had rounded the corner and died just a few minutes before. Katterson stood up and looked around. In the window of the house nearest him, two pale faces were pressed against the pane, watching greedily.

He whirled suddenly to face a small, swarthy man standing on the other side of the corpse. They stared for a moment, the little man and the giant. Katterson noted dimly the other's burning eyes and set expression. Two more people appeared, a ragged woman and a boy of eight or nine. Katterson moved closer to the corpse and made a show of examining it for identification, keeping a wary eye on the little tableau facing him.

Another man joined the group, and another. Now there were five, all standing silently in a semi-circle. The first man beckoned, and from the nearest house came two women and still another man. Katterson frowned; something unpleasant was going to happen.

A trickle of snow fluttered down. The hunger bit into Katterson like a red-hot knife as he stood there uneasily waiting for something to happen. The body lay fence-like between them.

The tableau dissolved into action in an instant. The small swarthy man made a gesture and reached for the corpse; Katterson quickly bent

49

and scooped the dead man up. Then they were all around him, screaming and pulling at the body.

The swarthy man grabbed the corpse's arm and started to tug, and a woman reached up for Katterson's hair. Katterson drew up his arm and swung as hard as he could, and the small man left the ground and flew a few feet, collapsing into a huddled heap in the snow.

All of them were around him now, snatching at the corpse and at Katterson. He fought them off with his one free hand, with his feet, with his shoulders. Weak as he was and outnumbered, his size remained as a powerful factor. His fist connected with someone's jaw and there was a rewarding crack; at the same time he lashed back with his foot and felt contact with breaking ribs.

"Get away!" he shouted. "Get away! This is mine! Away!" the first woman leaped at him, and he kicked at her and sent her reeling into the snowdrifts. "Mine! This is mine!"

They were even more weakened by hunger than he was. In a few moments all of them were scattered in the snow except the little boy, who came at Katterson determinedly, made a sudden dash, and leaped on Katterson's back.

He hung there, unable to do anything more than cling. Katterson ignored him and took a few steps, carrying both the corpse and the boy, while the heat of battle slowly cooled inside him. He would take the corpse back uptown to North; they could cut it in pieces without much trouble. They would live on it for days, he thought. They would—

He realized what had happened. He dropped the corpse and staggered a few steps away, and sank down into the snow, bowing his head. The boy slipped off his back, and the little knot of people timidly converged on the corpse and bore it off triumphantly, leaving Katterson alone.

"Forgive me," he muttered hoarsely. He licked his lips nervously, shaking his head. He remained there kneeling for a long time, unable to get up.

"No, no forgiveness. I can't fool myself; I'm one of them now," he said. He arose and stared at his hands, and then began to walk. Slowly, methodically, he trudged along, fumbling with the folded piece of paper in his pocket, knowing now that he had lost everything.

The snow had frozen in his hair, and he knew his head was white from snow—the head of an old man. His face was white too. He followed Broadway for a while, then cut to Central Park West. The snow was unbroken before him. It lay covering everything, a sign of the long winter setting in.

"North was right," he said quietly to the ocean of white that was Central Park. He looked at the heaps of rubble seeking cover beneath the snow. "I can't hold out any longer." He looked at the address— Malory, 218 West 42nd Street—and continued onward, almost numb with the cold.

His eyes were narrowed to slits, and lashes and head were frosted and white. Katterson's throat throbbed in his mouth, and his lips were clamped together by hunger. 70th Street, 65th. He zigzagged and wandered, following Columbus Avenue, Amsterdam Avenue for a while. Columbus, Amsterdam—the names were echoes from a past that had never been.

What must have been an hour passed, and another. The streets were empty. Those who were left stayed safe and starving inside, and watched from their windows the strange giant stalking alone through the snow. The sun had almost dropped from the sky as he reached 50th Street. His hunger had all but abated now; he felt nothing, knew just that his goal lay ahead. He faced forward, unable to go anywhere but ahead.

Finally 42nd Street, and he turned down towards where he knew Malory was to be found. He came to the building. Up the stairs, now, as the darkness of night came to flood the streets. Up the stairs, up another flight, another. Each step was a mountain, but he pulled himself higher and higher.

At the fifth floor Katterson reeled and sat down on the edge of the steps, gasping. A liveried footman passed, his nose in the air, his green coat shimmering in the half-light. He was carrying a roasted pig with an apple in its mouth on a silver tray. Katterson lurched forward to seize the pig. His groping hands passed through it, and pig and footman exploded like bubbles and drifted off through the silent halls.

Just one more flight. Sizzling meat on a stove, hot, juicy, tender meat filling the hole where his stomach had once been. He picked up his legs carefully and set them down, and came to the top at last. He balanced for a moment at the top of the stairs, nearly toppled backwards but seized the banister at the last second, and then pressed forward.

There was the door. He saw it, heard loud noises coming from behind it. A feast was going on, a banquet, and he ached to join in. Down the hall, turn left, pound on the door.

Noise growing louder.

"Malory! Malory! It's me, Katterson, big Katterson! I've come to you! Open up, Malory!"

The handle began to turn.

"Malory! Malory!"

Katterson sank to his knees in the hall and fell forward on his face when the door opened at last.

THE SILENT COLONY

It's not unusual or particularly disgraceful for a young writer to imitate the work of the writers he admires. That's one way to discover, from the inside, how those writers achieve the effects that the young writer finds so admirable. I'm not talking now of the various reworkings of the themes of Joseph Conrad that I've done over a period of years, or my deliberate pastiche of C.L. Moore, In Another Country. *Those were the stunts of a mature writer having a little fun. I mean a novice's flat-out imitation of his betters purely for the sake of mastering their stylistic or structural techniques.*

When I was beginning my career in the early 1950's there was a group of about a dozen science-fiction writers whose work held special meaning for me—Henry Kuttner, Cyril Kornbluth, James Blish, Alfred Bester, etc. (In 1987 I brought my favorite stories by those writers together in the autobiographical anthology, Robert Silverberg's Worlds of Wonder, *more recently issued under the title,* Science Fiction 101, *which I recommend to any beginning writer who is as hungry to see print as I was fifty-plus years ago.) There was a particular cluster within my group of favorites whose work I paid special attention to: Robert Sheckley, Philip K. Dick, Jack Vance. Their stories seemed to me the epitome of what I wanted my science fiction to be like; and from time to time during the first five or six years of my career I would—consciously and unabashedly—do something in the mode of one of those three, so that I could see, word by word, how they went about constructing such splendid stories.*

"The Silent Colony" is one of my Sheckley imitations: an attempt at mimicking his cool, lucid style and his ingenious plotting. I wrote it late in

the busy autumn of 1953; Sheckley, who was then about 25 years old, had begun selling only a year or two earlier, but already his fiction was appearing in leading slick magazines like Colliers and Esquire as well as in every s-f publication from the top-ranked Astounding and Galaxy to the wildest and wooliest of pulps. He had even had a collection of his stories published in book form by a major publisher. It was a dazzling beginning to a career: I, seven years younger, envied him frantically. If I couldn't be Robert Sheckley, I could at least learn to write like him. "The Silent Colony," it seems to me now, is a creditable try at a Sheckley story, given the difference in our ages and technical skills. It didn't sell to Esquire, or even Galaxy, but it did sell. On the strength of my contract for my novel Revolt on Alpha C I had acquired an agent by then—Scott Meredith, who represented such top figures in the field as Vance, Dick, Arthur C. Clarke, and Poul Anderson—and in June of 1954, after nine tries, he sold it (for $15) to Robert W. Lowndes, editor of Future Science Fiction. Lowndes needed a very short story to fill his next issue, the Future dated October, 1954, to be published in August; and so, most unusually, "The Silent Colony" was in print just a couple of months after it was accepted.

I spent the summer of 1954 editing a mimeographed newspaper in a children's camp a hundred miles north of New York City; and great was my pride when the October Future arrived up there and I displayed my story to my fellow campers—three pages tucked away at the end of the issue, with stories by Philip K. Dick, Algis Budrys, and Marion Zimmer Bradley much more prominently displayed. I didn't mind its inconspicuousness. One didn't expect a little snippet of a story like that to be featured prominently. And Dick, Budrys, and Bradley all were older than I was and each of them had been writing professionally for two or three years already, so I didn't begrudge them their names on the cover. What mattered was that I was in the issue too—my first short story to be published in a widely distributed American magazine. Only three pages now: but bigger and better things were to come. I was sure of that.

Skrid, Emerak, and Ullowa drifted through the dark night of space, searching the worlds that passed below them for some sign of their own kind. The urge to wander had come over them, as it does inevitably to all inhabitants of the Ninth World. They had been drifting through space for eons; but time is no barrier to immortals, and they were patient searchers.

"I think I feel something," said Emerak; "the Third World is giving off signs of life."

They had visited the thriving cities of the Eighth World, and the struggling colonies of the Seventh, and the experienced Skrid had led them to the little-known settlements on the moons of the giant Fifth World. But now they were far from home.

"You're mistaken, youngster," said Skrid. "There can't be any life on a planet so close to the sun as the Third World—think of how warm it is!"

Emerak turned bright white with rage. "Can't you *feel* the life down there? It's not much, but it's there. Maybe you're too old, Skrid."

Skrid ignored the insult. "I think we should turn back; we're putting ourselves in danger by going so close to the sun. We've seen enough."

"No, Skrid, I detect life below." Emerak blazed angrily. "And just because you're leader of this triad doesn't mean that you know everything. It's just that your form is more complex than ours, and it'll only be a matter of time until—"

"Quiet, Emerak." It was the calm voice of Ullowa. "Skrid, I think the hothead's right. I'm picking up weak impressions from the Third World myself; there may be some primitive life-forms evolving there. We'll never forgive ourselves if we turn back now."

"But the sun, Ullowa, the sun! If we go too close—" Skrid was silent, and the three drifted on through the void. After a while he said, "All right, let's investigate."

The three accordingly changed their direction and began to head for the Third World. They spiraled slowly down through space until the planet hung before them, a mottled bowl spinning endlessly.

Invisibly they slipped down and into its atmosphere, gently drifting towards the planet below. They strained to pick up signs of life, and as they approached the life-impulses grew stronger. Emerak cried out vindictively that Skrid should listen to him more often. They knew now, without doubt, that their kind of life inhabited the planet.

"Hear that, Skrid? Listen to it, old one."

"All right, Emerak," the elder being said, "you've proved your point. I never claimed to be infallible."

"These are pretty strange thought-impressions coming up, Skrid. Listen to them, they have no minds down there," said Ullowa. "They don't think."

"Fine," exulted Skrid. "We can teach them the ways of civilization and raise them to our level. It shouldn't be hard, when time is ours."

"Yes," Ullowa agreed, "they're so mindless that they'll be putty in our hands. Skrid's Colony, we'll call the planet. I can just see the way the Council will go for this. A new colony, discovered by the noted adventurer Skrid and two fearless companions—"

"Skrid's Colony, I like the sound of that," said Skrid. "Look, there's a drifting colony of them now, falling to earth. Let's join them and make contact; here's our chance to begin."

They entered the colony and drifted slowly to the ground among them. Skrid selected a place where a heap of them lay massed together, and made a skilled landing, touching all six of his delicately constructed limbs to the ground and sinking almost thankfully into a position of repose. Ullowa and Emerak followed and landed nearby.

"I can't detect any minds among them," complained Emerak, frantically searching through the beings near him. "They look just like us— that is, as close a resemblance as is possible for one of us to have to another. But they don't think."

Skrid sent a prying beam of thought into the heap on which he was lying. He entered first one, then another, of the inhabitants.

"Very strange," he reported. "I think they've just been born; many of them have vague memories of the liquid state, and some can recall as far back as the vapor state. I think we've stumbled over something important, thanks to Emerak."

"This is wonderful!" Ullowa said. "Here's our opportunity to study newborn entities firsthand."

"It's a relief to find some people younger than yourself," Emerak said sardonically. "I'm so used to being the baby of the group that it feels peculiar to have all these infants around."

"It's quite glorious," Ullowa said, as he propelled himself over the ground to where Skrid was examining one of the beings. "It hasn't been for a million ten-years that a newborn has appeared on our world, and here we are with billions of them all around."

"Two million ten-years, Ullowa," Skrid corrected. "Emerak here is of the last generation. And no need for any more, either, not while the mature entities live forever, barring accidents. But this is a big chance for us—we can make a careful study of these newborn ones, and perhaps set up a rudimentary culture here, and report to the Council once these babies have learned to govern themselves. We can start completely from scratch on the Third Planet. This discovery will rank with Kodranik's vapor theory!"

"I'm glad you allowed me to come," said Emerak. "It isn't often that a youngster like me gets a chance to—" Emerak's voice tailed off in a cry of amazement and pain.

"Emerak?" questioned Skrid. There was no reply.

"Where did the youngster go? What happened?" Ullowa said.

"Some fool stunt, I suppose. That little speech of his was too good to be true, Ullowa."

"No, I can't seem to locate him anywhere. Can you? Uh, Skrid! Help me! I'm—I'm—Skrid, it's killing me!"

The sense of pain that burst from Ullowa was very real, and it left Skrid trembling. "Ullowa! Ullowa!"

Skrid felt fear for the first time in more eons than he could remember, and the unfamiliar fright-sensation disturbed his sensitively balanced mind. "Emerak! Ullowa! Why don't you answer?"

Is this the end, Skrid thought, the end of everything? Are we going to perish here after so many years of life? To die alone and unattended, on a dismal planet billions of miles from home? Death was a concept too alien for him to accept.

He called again, his impulses stronger this time. "Emerak! Ullowa! Where are you?"

In panic, he shot beams of thought all around, but the only radiations he picked up were the mindless ones of the newly born.

"Ullowa!"

There was no answer, and Skrid began to feel his fragile body disintegrating. The limbs he had been so proud of—so complex and finely traced—began to blur and twist. He sent out one more frantic cry, feeling the weight of his great age, and sensing the dying thoughts of the newly born around him. Then he melted and trickled away over the heap, while the newborn snowflakes of the Third World watched uncomprehending, even as their own doom was upon them. The sun was beginning to climb over the horizon, and its deadly warmth beat down.

ABSOLUTELY INFLEXIBLE

Despite the rigors of college work, I wrote short stories steadily throughout 1954—one in April, two in May, three in June, two in October after the summer break. And I eventually sold them all, too. But progress was slow and often discouraging, and it wasn't until the summer of 1955 that there was any pattern of consistent sales.

I had finished my third year of college by then, and—though I intended to return for the final year and collect my degree—I was already beginning to believe that I might actually be able to earn a modest living of some sort as a professional science-fiction writer. The evidence in favor of that, so far, was pretty slim: "Gorgon Planet," "The Silent Colony," the book Revolt on Alpha C, and then a couple of stories, "The Martian" and "Yokel with Portfolio," that were bought by a minor magazine called Imagination in February and May of 1955. My total income from all of that was $352.60 spread over a year and a half, not a great deal even in those days. But I was finding it easier and easier to construct short stories that—to me—seemed at least as good as most of those that the innumerable s-f magazines of the day were publishing, and I was getting encouraging response from my agent about the new pieces I sent him once or twice a month. What I didn't know was that most of the boom-era magazines that had begun publication in 1953 were on their last legs by the early months of 1955, and that my agent's enthusiasm didn't mean much, because it was his usual practice to send a cheery note (ghostwritten by one of his employees) about any story that stood half a chance of being published by someone, somewhere, eventually. So I stepped up my pace of production *as the college year came to its close, and by June of 1955 I was writing a story a week.*

"Absolutely Inflexible" was among them—one of my first successful tries at the time-paradox theme. I suppose it's more than a little indebted to Robert A. Heinlein's classic "By His Bootstraps," but what time-paradox story isn't? And it has some strength of its own, enough to have seen it through an assortment of anthology appearances over the years, and even, for a while, to be a best-seller for one of the pioneering on-line publishers of the 1990s. It was bought, after making the rounds for about six months, by the veteran editor-publisher Leo Margulies, who ran it in the July 1956 issue of the underrated magazine he had founded and edited, Fantastic Universe.

The detector over in one corner of Mahler's little office gleamed a soft red. He indicated it with a weary gesture of his hand to the sad-eyed time jumper who sat slouched glumly across the desk from him, looking cramped and uncomfortable in the bulky spacesuit he was compelled to wear.

"You see," Mahler said, tapping his desk. "They've just found another one. We're constantly bombarded with you people. When you get to the Moon, you'll find a whole Dome full of them. I've sent over four thousand there myself since I took over the bureau. And that was eight years ago—in 2776. An average of five hundred a year. Hardly a day goes by without someone dropping in on us."

"And not one has been set free," the time jumper said. "Every time-traveler who's come here has been packed off to the Moon immediately. Every one."

"Every one," Mahler said. He peered through the thick shielding, trying to see what sort of man was hidden inside the spacesuit. Mahler often wondered about the men he condemned so easily to the Moon. This one was small of stature, with wispy locks of white hair pasted to his high forehead by perspiration. Evidently he had been a scientist, a respected man of his time, perhaps a happy father (although very few of the time jumpers were family men). Perhaps he possessed some bit of scientific knowledge that would be invaluable to the twenty-eighth century; perhaps not. It did not matter. Like all the rest, he would have to be sent to the Moon, to live out his remaining days under the grueling, primitive conditions of the Dome.

"Don't you think that's a little cruel?" the other asked. "I came here with no malice, no intent to harm whatsoever. I'm simply a scientific observer from the past. Driven by curiosity, I took the Jump. I never expected that I'd be walking into life imprisonment."

"I'm sorry," Mahler said, getting up. He decided to end the interview; he had to get rid of this jumper because there was another coming right up. Some days they came thick and fast, and this looked like one of them. But the efficient mechanical tracers never missed one.

"But can't I live on Earth and stay in this spacesuit?" the time-jumper asked, panicky now that he saw his interview with Mahler was coming to an end. "That way I'd be sealed off from contact at all times."

"Please don't make this any harder for me," Mahler said. "I've explained to you why we must be absolutely inflexible about this. There cannot—must not—be any exceptions. It's two centuries since last there was any occurrence of disease on Earth. In all this time we've lost most of the resistance acquired over the previous countless generations of disease. I'm risking my life coming so close to you, even with the spacesuit sealing you off."

Mahler signaled to the tall, powerful guards waiting in the corridor, grim in the casings that protected them from infection. This was always the worst moment.

"Look," Mahler said, frowning with impatience. "You're a walking death-trap. You probably carry enough disease germs to kill half the world. Even a cold, a common cold, would wipe out millions now. Resistance to disease has simply vanished over the past two centuries; it isn't needed, with all diseases conquered. But you time-travelers show up loaded with potentialities for all the diseases the world used to have. And we can't risk having you stay here with them."

"But I'd—"

"I know. You'd swear by all that's holy to you or to me that you'd never leave the confines of the spacesuit. Sorry. The word of the most honorable man doesn't carry any weight against the safety of the lives of Earth's billions. We can't take the slightest risk by letting you stay on Earth. It's unfair, it's cruel, it's everything else. You had no idea you would walk into something like this. Well, it's too bad for you. But you knew you were going on a one-way trip to the future, and you're subject to whatever that future wants to do with you, since there's no way of getting back."

Mahler began to tidy up the papers on his desk in a way that signaled finality. "I'm terribly sorry, but you'll just have to see our way of thinking about it. We're frightened to death at your very presence here. We can't allow you to roam Earth, even in a spacesuit. No; there's nothing for you but the Moon. I have to be absolutely inflexible. Take him away," he said, gesturing to the guards. They advanced on the little man and began gently to ease him out of Mahler's office.

Mahler sank gratefully into the pneumochair and sprayed his throat with laryngogel. These long speeches always left him feeling exhausted, his throat feeling raw and scraped. Someday I'll get throat cancer from all this talking, Mahler thought. And that'll mean the nuisance of an operation. But if I don't do this job, someone else will have to.

Mahler heard the protesting screams of the time jumper impassively. In the beginning he had been ready to resign when he first witnessed the inevitable frenzied reaction of jumper after jumper as the guards dragged them away, but eight years had hardened him.

They had given him the job because he was hard, in the first place. It was a job that called for a hard man. Condrin, his predecessor, had not been the same sort of man Mahler was, and for that reason Condrin was now himself on the Moon. He had weakened after heading the Bureau for a year and had let a jumper go; the jumper had promised to secrete himself at the tip of Antarctica, and Condrin, thinking that Antarctica was as safe as the Moon, had foolishly released him. That was when they called Mahler in. In eight years Mahler had sent four thousand men to the Moon. (The first was the runaway jumper, intercepted in Buenos Aires after he had left a trail of disease down the hemisphere from Appalachia to Argentine Protectorate. The second was Condrin.)

It was getting to be a tiresome job, Mahler thought. But he was proud to hold it. It took a strong man to do what he was doing. He leaned back and awaited the arrival of the next jumper.

The door slid smoothly open as the burly body of Dr Fournet, the Bureau's chief medical man, broke the photo-electronic beam. Mahler glanced up. Fournet carried a time-rig dangling from one hand.

"Took this away from our latest customer," Fournet said. "He told the medic who examined him that it was a two-way rig, and I thought I'd bring it to show you."

Mahler came to full attention quickly. A two-way rig? Unlikely, he thought. But it would mean the end of the dreary jumper prison on the Moon if it were true. Only how could a two-way rig exist?

He reached out and took it from Fournet. "It seems to be a conventional twenty-fourth century type," he said.

"But notice the extra dial here," Fournet said, pointing. Mahler peered and nodded.

"Yes. It *seems* to be a two-way rig. But how can we test it? And it's not really very probable," Mahler said. "Why should a two-way rig suddenly show up from the twenty-fourth century when no other traveler's had one? We don't even have two-way time-travel ourselves, and our scientists don't think it's possible. Still," he mused, "it's a nice thing to dream about. We'll have to study this a little more closely. But I don't seriously think it'll work. Bring him in, will you?"

As Fournet turned to signal the guards, Mahler asked him, "What's his medical report, by the way?"

"From here to here," Fournet said sombrely. "You name it, he's carrying it. Better get him shipped off to the Moon as soon as possible. I won't feel safe until he's off this planet." The big medic waved to the guards.

Mahler smiled. Fournet's overcautiousness was proverbial in the Bureau. Even if a jumper were to show up completely free from disease, Fournet would probably insist that he was carrying everything from asthma to leprosy.

The guards brought the jumper into Mahler's office. He was fairly tall, Mahler saw, and young. It was difficult to see his face clearly through the dim plate of the protective spacesuit all jumpers were compelled to wear, but Mahler could tell that the young time-jumper's face had much of the lean, hard look of Mahler's own. It seemed that the jumper's eyes had widened in surprise as he entered the office, but Mahler was not sure.

"I never dreamed I'd find you here," the jumper said. The transmitter of the spacesuit brought his voice over deeply and resonantly. "Your name is Mahler, isn't it?"

"That's right," Mahler agreed.

"To go all these years—and find you. Talk about improbabilities!"

Mahler ignored him, declining to take up the gambit. He had found it was good practice never to let a captured jumper get the upper hand in conversation. His standard procedure was firmly to explain to the jumper the reasons why it was imperative that he be sent to the Moon, and then send him, as quickly as possible.

"You say this is a two-way time-rig?" Mahler asked, holding up the flimsy-looking piece of equipment.

"That's right," the other agreed. "Works both ways. If you pressed the button, you'd go straight back to 2360 or thereabouts."

"Did you build it?"

"Me? No, hardly," said the jumper. "I found it. It's a long story, and I don't have time to tell it. In fact, if I tried to tell it, I'd only make things ten times worse than they are, if that's possible. No. Let's get this over with, shall we? I know I don't stand much of a chance with you, and I'd just as soon make it quick."

"You know, of course, that this is a world without disease—" Mahler began sonorously.

"And that you think I'm carrying enough germs of different sorts to wipe out the whole world. And therefore you have to be absolutely inflexible with me. I won't try to argue with you. Which way is the Moon?"

Absolutely inflexible. The phrase Mahler had used so many times, the phrase that summed him up so neatly. He chuckled to himself; some of the younger technicians must have tipped the jumper off about the usual procedure, and the jumper was resigned to going peacefully, without bothering to plead. It was just as well.

Absolutely inflexible.

Yes, Mahler thought, the words fit him well. He was becoming a stereotype in the Bureau. Perhaps he was the only Bureau chief who had never relented and let a jumper go. Probably all the others, bowed under the weight of the hordes of curious men flooding in from the past, had finally cracked and taken the risk. But not Mahler; not Absolutely Inflexible Mahler. He knew the deep responsibility that rode on his shoulders, and he had no intention of failing what amounted to a sacred trust. His job was to find the jumpers and get them off Earth as quickly and as efficiently as possible. Every one. It was a task that required unsoftening inflexibility.

"This makes my job much easier," Mahler said. "I'm glad I won't have to convince you of the necessity of my duty."

"Not at all," the other agreed. "I understand. I won't even waste my breath. You have good reasons for what you're doing, and nothing I say can alter them." He turned to the guards. "I'm ready. Take me away."

Mahler gestured to them, and they led the jumper away. Amazed, Mahler watched the retreating figure, studying him until he could no longer be seen.

If they were all like that, Mahler thought.

I could have got to like that one. That was a sensible man—one of the few. He knew he was beaten, and he didn't try to argue in the face of absolute necessity. It's too bad he had to go; he's the kind of man I'd like to find more often these days.

But I mustn't feel sympathy, Mahler told himself.

He had performed his job so well so long because he had managed to suppress any sympathy for the unfortunates he had to condemn. Had there been someplace else to send them—back to their own time, preferably—he would have been the first to urge abolition of the Moon prison. But, with no place else to send them, he performed this job efficiently and automatically.

He picked up the jumper's time-rig and examined it. A two-way rig would be the solution, of course. As soon as the jumper arrives, turn him around and send him back. They'd get the idea soon enough. Mahler found himself wishing it were so; he often wondered what the jumpers stranded on the Moon must think of him.

A two-way rig could change the world completely; its implications were staggering. With men able to move with ease backward and forward in time, past, present, and future would blend into one mind-numbing new entity. It was impossible to conceive of the world as it would be, with free passage in either direction.

But even as Mahler fondled the confiscated time-rig he realized something was wrong. In the six centuries since the development of time-travel, no one had yet developed a known two-way rig. And, more important, there were no documented reports of visitors from the future. Presumably, if a two-way rig existed, such visitors would be commonplace.

So the jumper had been lying, Mahler thought with regret. The two-way rig was an impossibility. He had merely been playing a game with his captors. This couldn't be a two-way rig, because the past held no record of anyone's going back.

Mahler examined the rig. There were two dials on it, one the conventional forward dial and the other indicating backward travel. Whoever had prepared this hoax had gone to considerable extent to document it. Why?

Could it be that the jumper had told the truth? Mahler wished he could somehow test the rig in his hands; there was always that one chance that it might actually work, that he would no longer have to be the rigid dispenser of justice, Absolutely Inflexible Mahler.

He looked at it. As a time machine, it was fairly crude. It made use of the standard distorter pattern, but the dial was the clumsy wide-range twenty-fourth-century one; the vernier system, Mahler reflected, had not been introduced until the twenty-fifth.

Mahler peered closer to read the instruction label. PLACE LEFT HAND HERE, it said. He studied it carefully. The ghost of a thought wandered into his mind; he pushed it aside in horror, but it recurred. It would be so simple. What if—?

No.

But—

PLACE LEFT HAND HERE.

He reached out tentatively with his left hand.

Just a bit—

No.

PLACE LEFT HAND HERE.

He touched his hand gingerly to the indicated place. There was a little crackle of electricity. He let go, quickly, and started to replace the time-rig on his desk when the desk abruptly faded out from under him.

The air was foul and grimy. Mahler wondered what had happened to the conditioner. Then he looked around.

Huge, grotesque buildings raised to the sky. Black, despairing clouds of smoke overhead. The harsh screech of an industrial society.

He was in the middle of an immense city, with streams of people rushing past him on the street at a furious pace. They were all small, stunted creatures, angry-looking, their faces harried, neurotic. It was the same black, frightened expression Mahler had seen so many times on the faces of jumpers escaping to what they hoped might be a more congenial future.

He looked at the time-rig clutched in one hand, and knew what had happened.

The two-way rig.

It meant the end of the Moon prisons. It meant a complete revolution in civilization. But he had no further business back in this age of nightmare. He reached down to activate the time-rig.

Abruptly someone jolted him from behind. The current of the crowd swept him along, as he struggled to regain his control over himself. Suddenly a hand reached out and grabbed the back of his neck.

"Got a card, Hump?"

He whirled to face an ugly, squinting-eyed man in a dull-brown uniform with a row of metallic buttons.

"Hear me? Where's your card, Hump? Talk up or you get Spotted."

Mahler twisted out of the man's grasp and started to jostle his way through the crowd, desiring nothing more than a moment to set the time-rig and get out of this disease-ridden squalid era. As he shoved people out of his way, they shouted angrily at him.

"There's a Hump!" someone called. "Spot him!"

The cry became a roar. "Spot him! Spot him!"

Wherever—whenever—he was, it was no place to stay in long. He turned left and went pounding down a side street, and now it was a full-fledged mob that dashed after him, shouting wildly.

"Send for the Crimers!" a deep voice boomed. "They'll Spot him!"

Someone caught up to him, and without looking Mahler reached behind and hit out, hard. He heard a dull grunt of pain, and continued running. The unaccustomed exercise was tiring him rapidly.

An open door beckoned. He stepped inside, finding himself inside a machine store of sorts, and slammed the door shut. They still had manual doors, a remote part of his mind observed coldly.

A salesman came towards him. "Can I help you, sir? The latest models, right here."

"Just leave me alone," Mahler panted, squinting at the time-rig. The salesman watched uncomprehendingly as Mahler fumbled with the little dial.

There was no vernier. He'd have to chance it and hope he hit the right year. The salesman suddenly screamed and came to life, for reasons Mahler would never understand. Mahler averted him and punched the stud viciously.

It was wonderful to step back into the serenity of twenty-eighth-century Appalachia. Small wonder so many time jumpers come here, Mahler reflected, as he waited for his overworked heart to calm down. Almost anything would be preferable to *then*.

He looked around the quiet street for a Convenience where he could repair the scratches and bruises he had acquired during his brief stay in the past. They would scarcely be able to recognize him at the Bureau in his present battered condition, with one eye nearly closed, a great livid welt on his cheek, and his clothing hanging in tatters.

He sighted a Convenience and started down the street, pausing at the sound of a familiar soft mechanical whining. He looked around to see one of the low-running mechanical tracers of the Bureau purring up the street towards him, closely followed by the two Bureau guards, clad in their protective casings.

Of course. He had arrived from the past, and the detectors had recorded his arrival, as they would that of any time-traveler. They never missed.

He turned and walked towards the guards. He failed to recognize either one, but this did not surprise him; the Bureau was a vast and wide-ranging organization, and he knew only a handful of the many guards who accompanied the tracers. It was a pleasant relief to see the tracer; the use of tracers had been instituted during his administration, so at least he knew he hadn't returned too early along the time-stream.

"Good to see you," he called to the approaching guards. "I had a little accident in the office."

They ignored him and methodically unpacked a spacesuit from the storage trunk of the mechanical tracer. "Never mind talking," one said. "Get into this."

He paled. "But I'm no jumper," he said. "Hold on a moment, fellows. This is all a mistake. I'm Mahler—head of the Bureau. Your boss."

"Don't play games with us, fellow," the taller guard said, while the other forced the spacesuit down over Mahler. To his horror, Mahler saw that they did not recognize him at all.

"If you'll just come peacefully and let the Chief explain everything to you, without any trouble—" the short guard said.

"But I *am* the Chief," Mahler protested. "I was examining a two-way time-rig in my office and accidentally sent myself back to the past. Take this thing off me and I'll show you my identification card; that should convince you."

"Look, fellow, we don't want to be convinced of anything. Tell it to the Chief if you want. Now, are you coming, or do we bring you?"

There was no point, Mahler decided, in trying to prove his identity to the clean-faced young medic who examined him at the Bureau office. That would only add more complications, he realized. No; he would wait until he reached the office of the Chief.

He saw now what had happened: Apparently he had landed somewhere in his own future, shortly after his own death. Someone else had taken over the Bureau, and he, Mahler, was forgotten. (Mahler suddenly realized with a shock that at this very moment his ashes were probably reposing in an urn at the Appalachia Crematorium.)

When he got to the Chief of the Bureau, he would simply and calmly explain his identity and ask for permission to go back the ten or twenty or thirty years to the time in which he belonged, and where he could turn the two-way rig over to the proper authorities and resume his life from his point of departure. And when that happened, the jumpers would no longer be sent to the Moon, and there would be no further need for Absolutely Inflexible Mahler.

But, he realized, if I've already done this then why is there still a Bureau now? An uneasy fear began to grow in him.

"Hurry up and finish that report," Mahler told the medic.

"I don't know what the rush is," the medic said. "Unless you like it on the Moon."

"Don't worry about me," Mahler said confidently. "If I told you who I am, you'd think twice about—"

"Is this thing your time-rig?" the medic asked boredly, interrupting.

"Not really. I mean—yes, yes it is," Mahler said. "And be careful with it. It's the world's only two-way rig."

"Really, now?" said the medic. "Two ways, eh?"

"Yes. And if you'll take me in to your Chief—"

"Just a minute. I'd like to show this to the Head Medic."

In a few moments the medic returned. "All right, let's go to the Chief now. I'd advise you not to bother arguing; you can't win. You should have stayed where you came from."

Two guards appeared and jostled Mahler down the familiar corridor to the brightly lit little office where he had spent eight years. Eight years on the other side of the fence.

As he approached the door of what had once been his office, he carefully planned what he would say to his successor. He would explain the accident, demonstrate his identity as Mahler, and request permission to use the two-way rig to return to his own time. The Chief would probably be belligerent at first, then curious, finally amused at the chain of events that had ensnarled Mahler. And, of course, he would let him go, after they had exchanged anecdotes about their job, the job they both held at the same time and across a gap of years. Mahler swore never again to touch a time machine, once he got back. He would let others undergo the huge job of transmitting the jumpers back to their own eras.

He moved forward and broke the photoelectronic beam. The door to the Bureau Chief's office slid open. Behind the desk sat a tall, powerful-looking man, lean, hard.

Me.

Through the dim plate of the spacesuit into which he had been stuffed, Mahler saw the man behind the desk. Himself. Absolutely Inflexible Mahler. The man who had sent four thousand men to the Moon, without exception, in the unbending pursuit of his duty.

And if he's Mahler—

Who am I?

Suddenly Mahler saw the insane circle complete. He recalled the jumper, the firm, deep-voiced, unafraid time jumper who had arrived claiming to have a two-way rig and who had marched off to the Moon without arguing. Now Mahler knew who that jumper was.

But how did the cycle start? Where did the two-way rig come from in the first place? He had gone to the past to bring it to the present to take it to the past to—

His head swam. There was no way out. He looked at the man behind the desk and began to walk towards him, feeling a wall of circumstance growing around him, while he, in frustration, tried impotently to beat his way out.

It was utterly pointless to argue. Not with Absolutely Inflexible Mahler. It would just be a waste of breath. The wheel had come full circle, and he was as good as on the Moon. He looked at the man behind the desk with a new, strange light in his eyes.

"I never dreamed I'd find you here," the jumper said. The transmitter of the spacesuit brought his voice over deeply and resonantly.

THE MACAULEY CIRCUIT

This, too, was written in June of 1955. Like most of my stories at that time it made its modest way from editor to editor, steadily descending from the top-paying markets to those farther down the pecking order, and early in 1956 was bought, for a glorious $40, by Leo Margulies, who was beginning to accept my work with some regularity. He published it in the August 1956 issue of Fantastic Universe. *Like the rest of my work of that period, it's no masterpiece: I wasn't really up to turning out a lot of masterpieces when I was twenty years old. But it stands up pretty well, I think—an intelligent consideration of some of the problems that the still virtually unborn computer age was likely to bring. (And when you read it, please bear in mind that computers, in 1955, were still considered experimental technology—generally "thinking machines" or "electronic brains"—and music synthesizers existed only in the pages of science fiction.)*

I don't deny I destroyed Macauley's diagram; I never did deny it, gentlemen. Of course I destroyed it, and for fine, substantial reasons. My big mistake was in not thinking the thing through at the beginning. When Macauley first brought me the circuit, I didn't pay much attention to it—certainly not as much as it deserved. That was a mistake, but I couldn't help myself. I was too busy coddling old Kolfmann to stop and think what the Macauley circuit really meant.

71

If Kolfmann hadn't shown up just when he did, I would have been able to make a careful study of the circuit and, once I had seen all the implications, I would have put the diagram in the incinerator and Macauley right after it. This is nothing against Macauley, you understand; he's a nice, clever boy, one of the finest minds in our whole research department. That's his trouble.

He came in one morning while I was outlining my graph for the Beethoven *Seventh* that we were going to do the following week. I was adding some ultrasonics that would have delighted old Ludwig—not that he would have heard them, of course, but he would have *felt* them—and I was very pleased about my interpretation. Unlike some synthesizer-interpreters, I don't believe in changing the score. I figure Beethoven knew what he was doing, and it's not my business to patch up his symphony. All I was doing was *strengthening* it by adding the ultrasonics. They wouldn't change the actual notes any, but there'd be that feeling in the air which is the great artistic triumph of synthesizing.

So I was working on my graph. When Macauley came in I was choosing the frequencies for the second movement, which is difficult because the movement is solemn but not *too* solemn. Just so. He had a sheaf of paper in his hand, and I knew immediately that he'd hit on something important, because no one interrupts an interpreter for something trivial.

"I've developed a new circuit, sir," he said. "It's based on the imperfect Kennedy Circuit of 2261."

I remembered Kennedy—a brilliant boy, much like Macauley here. He had worked out a circuit which almost would have made synthesizing a symphony as easy as playing a harmonica. But it hadn't quite worked—something in the process fouled up the ultrasonics and what came out was hellish to hear—and we never found out how to straighten things out. Kennedy disappeared about a year later and was never heard from again. All the young technicians used to tinker with his circuit for diversion, each one hoping he'd find the secret. And now Macauley had.

I looked at what he had drawn, and then up at him. He was standing there calmly, with a blank expression on his handsome, intelligent face, waiting for me to quiz him.

"This circuit controls the interpretative aspects of music, am I right?"

"Yes, sir. You can set the synthesizer for whatever aesthetic you have in mind, and it'll follow your instructions. You merely have to establish the aesthetic coordinates—the work of a moment—and the synthesizer will handle the rest of the interpretation for you. But that's not exactly the goal of my circuit, sir," he said gently, as if to hide from me the fact that he was telling me I had missed his point. "With minor modifications—"

He didn't get a chance to tell me, because at that moment Kolfmann came dashing into my studio. I never lock my door, because for one thing no one would dare come in without good and sufficient reason, and for another my analyst pointed out to me that working behind locked doors has a bad effect on my sensibilities, and reduces the aesthetic potentialities of my interpretations. So I always work with my door unlocked and that's how Kolfmann got in. And that's what saved Macauley's life, because if he had gone on to tell me what was on the tip of his tongue I would have regretfully incinerated him and his circuit right then and there.

Kolfmann was a famous name to those who loved music. He was perhaps eighty now, maybe ninety, if he had a good gerontologist, and he had been a great concert pianist many years ago. Those of us who knew something about presynthesizer musical history knew his name as we would that of Paganini or Horowitz or any other virtuoso of the past, and regarded him almost with awe.

Only all I saw now was a tall, terribly gaunt old man in ragged clothes who burst through my door and headed straight for the synthesizer, which covered the whole north wall with its gleaming complicated bulk. He had a club in his hand thicker than his arm, and he was about to bash it down on a million credits' worth of cybernetics when Macauley effortlessly walked over and took it away from him. I was still too flabbergasted to do much more than stand behind my desk in shock.

Macauley brought him over to me and I looked at him as if he were Judas.

"You old reactionary," I said. "What's the idea? You can get fined for wrecking a cyber—or didn't you know that?"

"My life is ended anyway," he said in a thick, deep, guttural voice: "It ended when your machines took over music."

He took off his battered cap and revealed a full head of white hair. He hadn't shaved in a couple of days, and his face was speckled with stiff-looking white stubble.

"My name is Gregor Kolfmann," he said. "I'm sure you have heard of me."

"Kolfmann, the pianist?"

He nodded, pleased despite everything. "Yes, Kolfmann, the *former* pianist. You and your machine have taken away my life."

Suddenly all the hate that had been piling up in me since he burst in—the hate any normal man feels for a cyberwrecker—melted, and I felt guilty and very humble before this old man. As he continued to speak, I realized that I—as a musical artist—had a responsibility to old Kolfmann. I still think that what I did was the right thing, whatever you say.

"Even after synthesizing became the dominant method of presenting music," he said, "I continued my concert career for years. There were always some people who would rather see a man play a piano than a technician feed a tape through a machine. But I couldn't compete forever." He sighed. "After a while anyone who went to live concerts was called a reactionary, and I stopped getting bookings. I took up teaching for my living. But no one wanted to learn to play the piano. A few have studied with me for antiquarian reasons, but they are not artists, just curiosity-seekers. They have no artistic drive. You and your machine have killed art!"

I looked at Macauley's circuit and at Kolfmann, and felt as if everything were dropping on me at once. I put away my graph for the Beethoven, partly because all the excitement would make it impossible for me to get anywhere with it today and partly because it would only make things worse if Kolfmann saw it. Macauley was still standing there, waiting to explain his circuit to me. I knew it was important, but I felt a debt to old Kolfmann, and I decided I'd take care of him before I let Macauley do any more talking.

"Come back later," I told Macauley. "I'd like to discuss the implications of your circuit, as soon as I'm through talking to Mr Kolfmann."

"Yes, sir," Macauley said, like the obedient puppet a technician turns into when confronted by a superior, and left. I gathered up the papers he had given me and put them neatly at a corner of my desk. I didn't want Kolfmann to see *them,* either, though I knew they wouldn't mean anything to him except as symbols of the machine he hated.

When Macauley had gone I gestured Kolfmann to a plush pneumochair, into which he settled with the distaste for excess comfort that is characteristic of his generation. I saw my duty plainly—to make things better for the old man.

"We'd be glad to have you come to work for us, Mr Kolfmann," I began, smiling. "A man of your great gift—"

He was up out of that chair in a second, eyes blazing. "Work for you? I'd sooner see you and your machines dead and crumbling! You, you scientists—you've killed art, and now you're trying to bribe me!"

"I was just trying to help you," I said. "Since, in a manner of speaking, we've affected your livelihood, I thought I'd make things up to you."

He said nothing, but stared at me coldly, with the anger of half a century burning in him.

"Look," I said. "Let me show you what a great musical instrument the synthesizer itself is." I rummaged in my cabinet and withdrew the tape of the Hohenstein *Viola Concerto,* which we had performed in '69—a rigorous twelve-tone work which is probably the most demanding, unplayable bit of music ever written. It was no harder for the synthesizer to counterfeit its notes than those of a Strauss waltz, of course, but a human violist would have needed three hands and prehensile nose to convey any measure of Hohenstein's musical thought. I activated the playback of the synthesizer and fed the tape in.

The music burst forth. Kolfmann watched the machine suspiciously. The pseudo-viola danced up and down the tone row while the old pianist struggled to place the work.

"Hohenstein?" he finally asked timidly. I nodded.

I saw a conflict going on within him. For more years than he could remember he had hated us because we had made his art obsolete. But here I was showing him a use for the synthesizer that gave it a valid existence—it was synthesizing a work impossible for a human to play. He was unable to reconcile all the factors in his mind, and the struggle hurt. He got up uneasily and started for the door.

"Where are you going?"

"Away from here," he said. "You are a devil."

He tottered weakly through the door, and I let him go. The old man was badly confused, but I had a trick or two up my cybernetic sleeve to settle some of his problems and perhaps salvage him for the world of music. For, whatever else you say about me, particularly after this Macauley business, you can't deny that my deepest allegiance is to music.

I stopped work on my Beethoven's Seventh, and also put away Macauley's diagram, and called in a couple of technicians. I told them what I was planning. The first line of inquiry, I decided, was to find out who Kolfmann's piano teacher had been. They had the reference books out in a flash and we found out who—Gotthard Kellerman, who had died nearly sixty years ago. Here luck was with us. Central was able to locate and supply us with an old tape of the International Music Congress held at Stockholm in 2187, at which Kellerman had spoken briefly on "The Development of the Pedal Technique": nothing very exciting, but it wasn't what he was saying that interested us. We split his speech up into phonemes, analyzed, rearranged, evaluated, and finally went to the synthesizer and began feeding in tapes.

What we got back was a new speech in Kellerman's voice, or a reasonable facsimile thereof. Certainly it would be good enough to fool Kolfmann, who hadn't heard his old teacher's voice in more than half a century. When we had everything ready I sent for Kolfmann, and a couple of hours later they brought him in, looking even older and more worn.

"Why do you bother me?" he asked. "Why do you not let me die in peace?"

I ignored his questions. "Listen to this, Mr Kolfmann." I flipped on the playback, and the voice of Kellerman came out of the speaker.

"Hello, Gregor," it said. Kolfmann was visibly startled. I took advantage of the prearranged pause in the recording to ask him if he recognized the voice. He nodded. I could see that he was frightened and suspicious, and I hoped the whole thing wouldn't backfire. "Gregor, one of the things I tried most earnestly to teach you—and you were my most attentive pupil—was that you must always be flexible. Techniques must constantly change, though art itself remains changeless. But have you listened to me? No."

Kolfmann was starting to realize what we had done, I saw. His pallor was ghastly now.

"Gregor, the piano is an outmoded instrument. But there is a newer, a greater instrument available for you, and you deny its greatness. This wonderful new synthesizer can do all that the piano could do, and much more. It is a tremendous step forward."

"All right," Kolfmann said. His eyes were gleaming strangely. "Turn that machine off."

I reached over and flipped off the playback.

"You are very clever," he told me. "I take it you used your synthesizer to prepare this little speech for me."

I nodded.

He was silent an endless moment. A muscle flickered in his cheek. I watched him, not daring to speak.

At length he said, "Well, you have been successful, in your silly, theatrical way. You've shaken me."

"I don't understand."

Again he was silent, communing with who knew what internal force. I sensed a powerful conflict raging within him. He scarcely seemed to see me at all as he stared into nothingness. I heard him mutter something in another language; I saw him pause and shake his great old head. And in the end he looked down at me and said, "Perhaps it is worth trying. Perhaps the words you put in Kellerman's mouth were true. Perhaps. You are foolish, but I have been even more foolish than you. I have stubbornly resisted, when I should have joined forces with you. Instead of denouncing you, I should have been the first to learn how to create music with this strange new instrument. Idiot! Moron!"

I think he was speaking of himself in those last two words, but I am not sure. In any case, I had seen a demonstration of the measure of his greatness—the willingness to admit error and begin all over. I had not expected his cooperation; all I had wanted was an end to his hostility. But he had yielded. He had admitted error and was ready to rechart his entire career.

"It's not too late to learn," I said. "We could teach you."

Kolfmann looked at me fiercely for a moment, and I felt a shiver go through me. But my elation knew no bounds. I had won a great battle for music, and I had won it with ridiculous ease.

He went away for a while to master the technique of the synthesizer. I gave him my best man, one whom I had been grooming to take over my place someday. In the meantime I finished my Beethoven, and the performance was a great success. And then I got back to Macauley and his circuit.

Once again things conspired to keep me from full realization of the threat represented by the Macauley circuit. I did manage to grasp that it could easily be refined to eliminate almost completely the human element in music interpretation. But it's many years since I worked in the labs, and I had fallen out of my old habit of studying any sort of diagram and mentally tinkering with it and juggling it to see what greater use could be made of it.

While I examined the Macauley circuit, reflecting idly that when it was perfected it might very well put me out of a job (since anyone would be able to create a musical interpretation, and artistry would no longer be an operative factor), Kolfmann came in with some tapes. He looked twenty years younger; his face was bright and clean, his eyes were shining, and his impressive mane of hair waved grandly.

"I will say it again," he told me as he put the tapes on my desk. "I have been a fool. I have wasted my life. Instead of tapping away at a silly little instrument, I might have created wonders with this machine. Look: I began with Chopin. Put this on."

I slipped the tape into the synthesizer and the *F Minor Fantasy* of Chopin came rolling into the room. I had heard the tired old war-horse a thousand times, but never like this.

"This machine is the noblest instrument I have ever played," he said.

I looked at the graph he had drawn up for the piece, in his painstaking crabbed handwriting. The ultrasonics were literally incredible. In just a few weeks he had mastered subtleties I had spent fifteen years learning. He had discovered that skillfully chosen ultrasonics, beyond the range of human hearing but not beyond perception, could expand the horizons of music to a point the presynthesizer composers, limited by their crude instruments and faulty knowledge of sonics, would have found inconceivable.

The Chopin almost made me cry. It wasn't so much the actual notes Chopin had written, which I had heard so often, as it was the unheard notes the synthesizer was striking, up in the ultrasonic range. The old man had chosen his ultrasonics with the skill of a craftsman—no, with the hand of a genius. I saw Kolfmann in the middle of the room, standing proudly while the piano rang out in a glorious tapestry of sound.

I felt that this was my greatest artistic triumph. My Beethoven symphonies and all my other interpretations were of no value beside this one achievement of putting the synthesizer in the hands of Kolfmann.

He handed me another tape and I put it on. It was the Bach *Toccata and Fugue in D Minor;* evidently he had worked first on the pieces most familiar to him. The sound of a super-organ roared forth from the synthesizer. We were buffeted by the violence of the music. And Kolfmann stood there while the Bach piece raged on. I looked at him and tried to relate him to the seedy old man who had tried to wreck the synthesizer not long ago, and I couldn't.

As the Bach drew to its close I thought of the Macauley circuit again, and of the whole beehive of blank-faced handsome technicians striving to perfect the synthesizer by eliminating the one imperfect element—man. And I woke up.

My first decision was to suppress the Macauley circuit until after Kolfmann's death, which couldn't be too far off. I made this decision out of sheer kindness; you have to recognize that as my motive. Kolfmann, after all these years, was having a moment of supreme triumph, and if I let him know that no matter what he was doing with the synthesizer the new circuit could do it better, it would ruin everything. He would not survive the blow.

He fed the third tape in himself. It was the Mozart *Requiem Mass*, and I was astonished by the way he had mastered the difficult technique of synthesizing voices. Still, with the Macauley circuit, the machine could handle all these details by itself.

As Mozart's sublime music swelled and rose, I took out the diagram Macauley had given me and stared at it grimly. I decided to pigeonhole it until the old man died. Then I would reveal it to the world and, having been made useless, myself (for interpreters like me would be a credit a hundred), I would sink into peaceful obscurity, with at least the assurance that Kolfmann had died happy.

That was sheer kindheartedness, gentlemen. Nothing malicious or reactionary about it. I didn't intend to stop the progress of cybernetics, at least not at that point.

No, I didn't decide to do that until I got a better look at what Macauley had done. Maybe he didn't even realize it himself, but I used to be pretty shrewd about such things. Mentally, I added a wire or two here, altered a contact there, and suddenly the whole thing hit me.

A synthesizer hooked up with a Macauley circuit not only didn't need a human being to provide an aesthetic guide to its interpretation of music, which is all Macauley claimed. Up to now, the synthesizer could imitate the pitch of any sound in or out of nature, but we had to control the volume, the timbre, all the things that made up interpretation of music. Macauley had fixed it so that the synthesizer could handle this, too. But also, I now saw that it could create its own music, from scratch, with no human help. Not only the conductor but the composer would be unnecessary. The synthesizer would be able to function independently of any human being. And art is a function of human beings.

That was when I ripped up Macauley's diagram and heaved the paperweight into the gizzard of my beloved synthesizer, cutting off the Mozart in the middle of a high C. Kolfmann turned around in horror, but I was the one who was really horrified.

I know. Macauley has redrawn his diagram and I haven't stopped the wheels of science. I feel pretty futile about it all. But before you label me reactionary and stick me away, consider this:

Art is a function of intelligent beings. Once you create a machine capable of composing original music, capable of an artistic act, you've created an intelligent being. And one that's a lot stronger and smarter than we are. We've synthesized our successor.

Gentlemen, we are all obsolete.

THE SONGS OF SUMMER

This is yet another of the stories I wrote in June of 1955; but before I discuss it, let me jump a year or so forward, to the summer of 1956. Much has happened since my first valiant sales. I have received my degree from Columbia; I have married; and, both alone and in collaboration with a roguish character named Randall Garrett, I have sold dozens and dozens of stories to all manner of magazines. (Again, I refer you to the pulp-story collection In the Beginning *for the full story of how this came about.)*

Garrett was the key figure in my sudden burst of success. A capable science-fiction writer hampered by alcoholism and incorrigible laziness, he had turned up in New York in the spring of 1955, very much at the end of his resources, and through fortuitous events had landed in the same sleazy building where Harlan Ellison and I (and a few other science-fictional types) were renting rooms. Garrett and I saw each other as complementary figures. His background was in the sciences, mine in literature. He was a clever plotter but a clumsy stylist, whereas I still was having some trouble constructing stories but told them smoothly and well. He was an ebullient extravert; I was quiet and reserved. He was a monumental procrastinator; I was a demon for work.

We took to each other immediately—attraction of opposites, I suppose— and as soon as my academic term ended early in June, we began to write stories together, Garrett typing madly until he collapsed from drink and fatigue, I taking over and working until he recovered, Garrett going on to finish the story, I giving it its final coat of polish. Everything we turned out sold. He knew all the New York editors—their foibles, their preferences—and took me

81

around to their offices to meet them. Suddenly I found myself on first-name terms with the greats of the field, John W. Campbell, Jr. of Astounding, *Horace Gold of* Galaxy, *and such lesser but distinguished figures as Robert W. Lowndes, Larry T. Shaw of the new magazine* Infinity, *and Howard Browne of* Amazing Stories. *They all saw in me a competent and ambitious story-making machine, a writer who could, working at high speed and with great reliability, turn out unspectacular but useful fiction at any length. Very quickly I made myself invaluable to them as they struggled to fill their monthly or bimonthly magazines with copy. And so I was launched.*

Now that I had so suddenly ceased to be a wistful amateur and become a busy and widely known member, at the age of 21, of the inner circle of professional science-fiction writers, I began to dig out the two or three dozen stories that I had written and failed to sell during my apprenticeship period, and submitted them one by one to the editors who were now my friends. All other things being equal, an editor will look at a manuscript by a writer he knows far more sympathetically than one that comes in from a stranger in the mail; and, one by one, all those stories that had been so extensively rejected in 1953 and 1954 and the early months of 1955 began to make their way into print in 1956.

It would take several volumes the size of this one to restore them all to print now, and I'm not sure that there's any great need to clutter people's bookshelves with fat collections of the More-or-Less-Okay-But-Not-Exactly-Great Early Stories of Robert Silverberg. A few samples like "Road to Nightfall" and "Gorgon Planet" and "The Silent Colony" should serve sufficiently to demonstrate the virtues of my prentice-work and to establish the historical record, but enough is probably enough.

But I do want to exhume one more of what I have come to think of as my "pre-professional" stories, for its own intrinsic interest and for the light it casts on later work. Once again, as with "The Silent Colony," I was imitating my betters here—this time, reaching well beyond even Robert Sheckley's league, all the way up to William Faulkner. As a Columbia undergraduate in 1954 I had read with some awe—staying up through the night and finishing it at dawn— Faulkner's As I Lay Dying. *The use not merely of multiple point of view but of multiple narrator seemed to me a startling and awesome technical device; and with the rashness of youth I tried it myself in "The Songs of Summer." Having already achieved—so it seemed to me—some mastery of the conventional single-viewpoint short story, I was now ready, at the age of twenty, to begin experimenting with more ambitious fictional forms. (And also with some themes, like that of the group mind, that I would use again and again in later years.)*

"The Songs of Summer" was another product of June, 1955. The first dozen editors to whom my agent sent it were unimpressed—or, at any rate, didn't care to print it. Whenever they felt like publishing this sort of experimentation, they had Theodore Sturgeon or James Blish to write it for them. But after it had been circulating for about a year, during which time I became well known to the New York editors and was starting to bring them the stories they had rejected the year before and have them buy them the second time around, it found a home with Robert Lowndes' magazine Science Fiction Stories *in the spring of 1956. My records indicate that I was paid 3/4 of a cent a word for it—$48.00. By then my name was becoming a familiar one on the contents pages of the s-f magazines, and I suppose Lowndes thought he could take the risk. (In fact, he ran it as the lead story in his September, 1956 issue—though it was Clifford D. Simak who got his name on the cover.) I didn't send a copy to Faulkner to see what he thought of it.*

———————

1. Kennon

I was on my way to take part in the Singing, and to claim Corilann's promise. I was crossing the great open field when suddenly the man appeared, the man named Chester Dugan. He seemed to drop out of the sky.

I watched him stagger for a moment or two. I did not know where he had come from so suddenly, or why he was here. He was short—shorter than any of us—fat in an unpleasant way, with wrinkles on his face and an unshaven growth of beard. I was anxious to get on to the Singing, and so I allowed him to fall to the ground and kept moving. But he called to me, in a barbarous and corrupt tongue which I could recognize as our language only with difficulty.

"Hey, you," he called to me. "Give me a hand, will you?"

He seemed to be in difficulties, so I walked over to him and helped him to his feet. He was panting, and appeared almost in a state of shock. Once I saw he was steady on his feet, and seemed to have no further need of me, I began to walk away from him, since I was anxious to get on to the Singing and did not wish to meddle with this man's affairs. Last year was the first time I attended the Singing at Dandrin's, and I enjoyed it very much. It was then that Corilann had promised herself. I was anxious to get on.

But he called to me. "Don't leave me here!" he shouted. "Hey, you can't just walk away like that! Help me!"

I turned and went back. He was dressed strangely, in ugly ill-arranged tight clothes, and he was walking in little circles, trying to adjust his equilibrium. "Where am I?" he asked me.

"Earth, of course," I told him.

"No," he said, harshly. "I don't mean that, idiot. Where, on Earth?"

The concept had no meaning for me. Where, on Earth, indeed? Here, was all I knew: the great plain between my home and Dandrin's, where the Singing is held. I began to feel uneasy. This man seemed badly sick, and I did not know how to handle him. I felt thankful that I was going to the Singing; had I been alone, I never would have been able to deal with him. I realized I was not as self-sufficient as I thought I was.

"I am going to the Singing," I told him. "Are you?"

"I'm not going anywhere till you tell me where I am and how I got here. What's your name?"

"My name is Kennon. You are crossing the great plain on your way to the home of Dandrin, where we are going to have the Singing, for it is summer. Come; I am anxious to get there. Walk with me, if you wish."

I started to walk away a second time, and this time he began to follow me. We walked along silently for a while.

"Answer me, Kennon," he said after a hundred paces or so. "Ten seconds ago I was in New York; now I'm here. How far am I from New York?"

"What is New York?" I asked. At this he showed great signs of anger and impatience, and I began to feel quite worried.

"Where'd you escape from?" he shouted. "You never heard of New York? You never heard of *New York*? New York," he said, "is a city of some eight million people, located on the Atlantic Ocean, on the east coast of the United States of America. Now tell me you haven't heard of that!"

"What is a city?" I asked, very much confused. At this he grew very angry. He threw his arms in the air wildly.

"Let us walk more quickly," I said. I saw now that I was obviously incapable of dealing with this man, and I was anxious to get on to the Singing—where perhaps Dandrin, or the other old ones, would be able to understand him. He continued to ask me questions as we walked, but I'm afraid I was not very helpful.

2. Chester Dugan

I don't know what happened or how; all I know is I got here. There doesn't seem to be any way back, either, but I don't care; I've got a good thing here and I'm going to show these nitwits who's boss.

Last thing I knew, I was getting into a subway. There was an explosion and a blinding flash of light, and before I could see what was happening I blanked out and somehow got here. I landed in a big open field with absolutely nothing around. It took a few minutes to get over the shock. I think I fell down; I'm not sure. It's not like me, but this was something out of the ordinary and I might have lost my balance.

Anyway, I recovered almost immediately and looked around, and saw this kid in loose flowing robes walking quickly across the field not too far away. I yelled to him when I saw he didn't intend to come over to me. He came over and gave me a hand, and then started to walk away again, calm as you please. I had to call him back. He seemed a little reluctant. The bastard.

I tried to get him to tell me where we were, but he played dumb. Didn't know where we were, didn't know where New York was, didn't even know what a city was—or so he said. I would have thought he was crazy, except that I didn't know what had happened to me; for that matter, I might have been the crazy one and not him.

I saw I wasn't making much headway with him, so I gave up. All he would tell me was that he was on his way to the Singing, and the way he said it there was no doubt about the capital S. He said there would be men there who could help me. To this day I don't know how I got here. Even after I spoke and asked around, no one could tell me how I could step into a subway train in 1956 and come out in an open field somewhere around the thirty-fifth century. The crazy bastards have even lost count.

But I'm here, that's all that matters. And whatever went before is down the drain now. Whatever deals I was working on back in 1956 are dead and buried now; this is where I'm stuck, for reasons I don't get, and here's where I'll have to make my pile. All over again—me, Dugan, starting from scratch. But I'll do it. I'm doing it.

After this kid Kennon and I had plodded across the fields for a while, I heard the sound of voices. By now it was getting towards nightfall. I forgot to mention that it was getting along towards the end of November back in 1956, but the weather here was nice and summery. There was a pleasant tang of something in the air that I had never noticed in New York's air, or the soup they called air back then.

The sound of the singing grew louder as we approached, but as soon as we got within sight they all stopped immediately.

They were sitting in a big circle, twenty or thirty of them, dressed in light, airy clothing. They all turned to look at me as we got near.

I got the feeling they were all looking into my mind.

The silence lasted a few minutes, and then they began to sing again. A tall, thin kid was leading them, and they were responding to what he sang. They ignored me. I let them continue until I formed a plan; I don't believe in rushing into things without knowing exactly what I'm doing.

I waited till the singing quieted down a bit, and then I yelled "Stop!" I stepped forward into the middle of the ring.

"My name is Dugan," I said, loud, clear, and slow. "Chester Dugan. I don't know how I got here, and I don't know where I am, but I mean to stay here a while. Who's the chief around here?"

They looked at each other in a puzzled fashion and finally an old thin-faced man stepped out of the circle. "My name is Dandrin," he said, in a thin dried little voice. "As the oldest here, I will speak for the people. Where do you come from?"

"That's just it," I said. "I came from New York City, United States of America, Planet Earth, the Universe. Don't any of those things mean anything to you?"

"They are names, of course," Dandrin said. "But I do not know what they are names of. New York City? United States of America? We have no such terms."

"Never heard of New York?" This was the same treatment I had gotten from that dumb kid Kennon, and I didn't like it. "New York is the biggest city in the world, and the United States is the richest country."

I heard hushed mumbles go around the circle. Dandrin smiled.

"I think I see now," he said. "Cities, countries." He looked at me in a strange way. "Tell me," he said. "Just *when* are you from?"

That shook me. "1956," I said. And here, I'll admit, I began to get worried.

"This is the thirty-fifth century," he said calmly. "At least, so we think. We lost count during the Bombing Years. But come, Chester Dugan; we are interrupting the Singing with our talk. Let us go aside and talk, while the others can sing."

He led me off to one side and explained things to me. Civilization had broken up during a tremendous atomic war. These people were the survivors, the dregs. There were no cities and not even small towns. People lived in groups of twos and threes here and there, and didn't come together very often. They didn't even *like* to get together, except during the summer. Then they would gather at the home of some old man—usually Dandrin; everyone would meet, and sing for a while, and then go home.

Apparently there were only a few thousand people in all of America. They lived widely scattered, and there was no business, or trade, or culture, or anything else. Just little clumps of people living by themselves, farming a little and singing, and not doing much else. As the old man talked I began to rub my hands together—mentally, of course. All sorts of plans were forming in my head.

He didn't have any idea how I had gotten here, and neither did I; I still don't. I think it just must have been a one-in-a-trillion fluke, a flaw in space or something. I just stepped through at the precise instant and wound up at that open field. But Chester Dugan can't worry about things he doesn't understand. I just accept them.

I saw a big future for myself here, with my knowledge of twentieth century business methods. The first thing, obviously was to reestablish villages. The way they had things arranged now, there really wasn't any civilization. Once I had things started, I could begin reviving other things that these decadent people had lost: money, entertainment, sports, business. Once we got machinery going, we'd be set. We'd start working on a city, and begin expanding. I thanked whoever it was had dropped me here. This was a golden opportunity for me. These people would be putty in my hands.

3. Corilann

It was with Kennon's approval that I did it. Right after the Singing ended for that evening, Dugan came over to me and I could tell from the tone of his conversation that he wanted me for the night. I had already promised myself to Kennon, but Dugan seemed so insistent that I asked Kennon to release me for this one evening, and he did. He didn't mind.

It was strange the way Dugan went about asking me. He never came right out and said anything. I didn't like anything he did that night; and he's ugly.

He kept telling me, "Stay with me, baby; we're going places together." I didn't know what he meant.

The other women were very curious about it the next day. There are so few of us, that it's a novelty to sleep with someone new. They wanted to know how it had been. I told them I enjoyed it.

It was a lie; he was disgusting. But I went back to him the next night, and the one after that, no matter what poor Kennon said. I couldn't help it, despite myself. There was just something about Dugan that drew me. I couldn't help it. But he was disgusting.

4. Dandrin

It was strange to see them standing in neat, ordered, precise rows, they who had never known any order, any rules before, and Dugan was telling them what to do. The dawn of the day before, we had been free and alone, but since then Dugan had come.

He lined everybody up, and, as I sat in the shade and watched, he began explaining his plans. We tried so hard to understand what he meant. I remembered stories I had heard of the old ones, but I had never believed them until I saw Dugan in action.

"I can't understand you people," he shouted at us. "This whole rich world is sitting here waiting for you to walk out and grab it, and you sit around singing instead. Singing! You people are decadent, that's what you are. You need a government—a good, sturdy government—and I'm here to give it to you."

Kennon and some of the others had come to me that morning to find out what was going to happen. I urged them not to do anything, to listen to Dugan and do what he says. That way, I felt, we could eventually learn to understand him and deal with him in the proper manner. I confess that I was curious to see how he would react among us.

I said nothing when he gave orders that no one was to return home after the Singing. We were to stay here, he told us, and build a city. He was going to bring us all the advantages of the twentieth century.

And we listened to him patiently, all but Kennon. It was Kennon who had brought him here, poor young Kennon who had come here for the Singing and for Corilann. And it was Corilann whom Dugan had singled out for his own private property. Kennon had given his approval, the first night, thinking she would come back to him the next day. But she hadn't; she stayed with Dugan.

In a couple of days he had his city all planned and everything apportioned. I think the thought uppermost in everyone's mind was *why:* why does he want us to do these things? Why? We would have to give him time to carry out his plans; provided he did no permanent harm, we would wait and see, and wonder why.

5. Chester Dugan

This Corilann is really stacked. Things were never like this back when! After Dandrin had told me where the unattached women were sitting, I looked them over and picked her. They were all worth a second look, but she was something special. I didn't know at the time that she was promised to Kennon, or I might not have started fooling around with her; I don't want to antagonize these people too much.

I'm afraid Kennon may be down on me a bit. I've taken his girl away, and I don't think he goes for my methods. I'll have to try some psychology on him. Maybe I'll make him my second-in-command.

The city is moving along nicely. There were 120 people at the Singing, and my figures show that fifteen were old people and the rest divided up pretty evenly; everyone is coupled off, and I've arranged the housing to fit the coupling. These people don't have children very often, but I'll fix that; I'll figure out some way of making things better for those with the most children, some sort of incentive. The quicker we build up the population, the better things will be. I understand there's a wild tribe about five hundred miles to the north of here, maybe less (I still don't have any idea where *here* is) who still have some machines and things, and once we're all established I intend to send an expedition out to conquer the wild tribe and bring back the machines.

There's an idea; maybe I'll let Kennon lead the expedition. I'll be giving him a position of responsibility, and at the same time there's a chance he might get knocked off. That kid's going to cause trouble; I wish I hadn't taken his girl.

But it's too late to go back on it. Besides, I need a son, and quickly. If Corilann's baby is a girl, I don't know what I'll do. I can't carry on my dynasty without an heir.

There's another kid here that bothers me—Jubilain. He's not like the others; he's very frail and sensitive, and seems to get special treatment. He's the one who leads the Singing. I haven't been able to get him to work on the construction yet, and I don't know if I'm going to be able to.

But otherwise everything is moving smoothly. I'm surprised that old Dandrin doesn't object to what I'm doing. It's long since past the time when the Singing should have broken up, and everyone scattered, but they're all staying right here and working as if I was paying them.

Which I am, in a way. I'm bringing them the benefits of a great lost civilization, which I represent. Chester Dugan, the man from the past. I'm taking a bunch of nomads and turning them into a powerful city. So actually, everyone's profiting—the people, because of what I'm doing for them, and me. Me especially, because here I'm absolute top dog.

I'm worried about Corilann's baby, though. If it's a girl, that means a delay of a year or more before I can have my son, and even then it'll be at least ten years before he's of any use to me. I wonder what would happen if I took a second wife—Jarinne, for example. I watched her while she was stripped down for work yesterday and she looks even better than Corilann. These people don't seem to have any particular beliefs about marriage, anyway, and so I don't know if they'd mind. Then if Corilann had a girl, I might give her back to Kennon.

And that reminds me of another thing: there's no religion here. I'm not much of a Godman myself, but I realize religion's a good thing for keeping the people in line. I'll have to start thinking about getting a priesthood going, as soon as affairs are a little more settled here.

I didn't think it was so much work, organizing a civilization. But once I get it all set up, I can sit back and cool my heels for life. It's a pleasure working with these people. I just can't wait till everything is moving by itself. I've gotten further in two months here than I did in forty years there. It just goes to show: you need a powerful man to keep civilization alive. And Chester Dugan is just the man these people needed.

6. Kennon

Corilann has told me she will have a child by Dugan. This has made me sad, since it might have been my child she would be bearing instead. But I brought Dugan here myself, and so I suppose I am responsible. If I had not come to the Singing, he might have died in the great open field. But now it is too late for such thoughts.

Dugan forbids us to go home, now that the Singing is over. My father is waiting for me at our home, and the hunting must be done before the winter comes, but Dugan forbids us to go home. Dandrin had to explain to us what "forbids" means; I still don't fully understand why or how one person can tell another person what to do. None of us really understands Dugan at all, not even Dandrin, I think. Dandrin is trying hardest to understand him, but Dugan is so completely alien to us that we do not see.

He has made us build what he calls a city—many houses close together. He says the advantage of this is that we may protect each other. But from what? We have no enemies. I have the feeling that Dugan understands us even less than we understand him. And I am anxious to go home for the autumn hunting, now that summer is almost over and the Singing is ended. I had hoped to bring Corilann back with me, but it is my own fault, and I must not be bitter.

Dugan has been very cold towards me. This is surprising, since it was I who brought him to the Singing. I think he is afraid I will try to take Corilann back; in any event, he seems to fear me and show anger towards me.

If only I understood!

7. Kennon

Dugan has certainly gone too far now. For the past week I have been trying to engage him in conversation, to find out what his motives are for doing all the things he is doing. Dandrin should be doing this, but Dandrin seems to have abdicated all responsibility in this matter, and is content to sit idly by, watching all that happens. Dugan does not make him work because he is so old.

I do not understand Dugan at all. Yesterday he told me, "We will rule the world." What does he mean? *Rule?* Does he actually want to tell everyone who lives what he can do and what he cannot do? If all of the people of Dugan's time were like this, it is small wonder they destroyed everything. What if two people told the same man to do different things? What if they told each other to do things? My head reels at the thought of Dugan's world. People living together in masses, and telling each other what to do; it seems insane. I long to be back with my father for the hunting. I had hoped to bring him a daughter as well, but it seems this is not to be.

Dugan has offered me Jarinne as my wife. Jarinne says she has been with Dugan, and that Corilann knows. Dandrin warns me not to accept Jarinne because it will anger Dugan. But if it will anger Dugan, why did he offer her to me? And—now it occurs to me—by what right does he offer me another person?

Jarinne is a fine woman. She could make me forget Corilann.

And then Dugan told me that soon there will be an expedition to the north; we will take weapons and conquer the wild men. Dugan has heard of the machines of the wild men, and he says he needs them for our city. I told him that I had to leave immediately to help my father with the hunting, that I have stayed here long enough. Others are saying the same thing: this summer the Singing has lasted too long.

Today I tried to leave. I gathered my friends and told them I was anxious to go home, and I asked Jarinne to come with me. She accepted, though she reminded me that she had been with Dugan. I told her I might be able to forget that. She said she knew it wouldn't matter to me if it had been anyone else (of course not; why should it?) but that I might object because it had been Dugan. I said good-bye to Corilann, who now is swollen with Dugan's child; she cried a little.

And then I started to leave. I did not talk to Dandrin, for I was afraid he would persuade me not to go. I opened the gate that Dugan has just put up, and started to leave.

Suddenly Dugan appeared. "Where do you think you're going?" he asked, in his hard, cold rasp of a voice. "Pulling out?"

"I have told you," I said quietly, "it is time to help my father with the hunting. I cannot stay in your city any longer." I moved past him and Jarinne followed. But he ran around in front of me.

"No one leaves here, understand?" He waved his closed hand in front of me. "We can't build a city if you take off when you want to."

"But I must go," I said. "You have detained me here long enough." I started to walk on, and suddenly he hit me with his closed hand and knocked me down.

I went sprawling over the ground, and I felt blood on my face from where he had hurt my nose. People all around were watching. I got up slowly. I am bigger and much stronger than Dugan, but it had never occurred to me that one person might hit another person. But this is one of the many things that has come to our world.

I was not so unhappy for myself; pain soon ceases. But Jubilain the Singer was watching when he hit me, and such sights should be kept from Singers. They are not like the rest of us. I am afraid Jubilain has been seriously disturbed by the sight.

After he had knocked me down, Dugan walked away. I got up and went back inside the gate. I do not want to leave now. I must talk to Dandrin. Something must be done.

8. Jubilain

Summer to autumn to every old everyone, sing winter to quiet to baby fall down. My head head hurts. My my hurts head. Bloody was Kennon.

Kennon was bloody and Dugan was angry and summer to autumn to.

Jubilain is very sad. My head hurts. Dugan hit Kennon in the face. With his hand, his hand hand hand rolled up in a ball Dugan hit Kennon. Outside the gates. Consider the gates. Consider.

They have spoiled the song. How can I sing when Dugan hits Kennon? My head hurts. Sing summer to autumn, sing every old everyone. It is good that the summer is ending, for the songs are over. How can I sing? Bloody was Kennon.

Jubilain's head hurts. It did not hurt before did not hurt. I could sing before. Summer to autumn to every old everyone. Corilann's belly is big with Dugan, and Jubilain's head hurts. Will there be more Dugans?

And more Kennons. No more Jubilains. No more songs. The songs of summer are silent and slippery. My head hurts. Hurts hurts hurts. I can sing no more. Nononononononono

9. Dandrin

This is tragic. I am an old fool.

I have been sitting in the shade, like the dried old man I am, while Dugan has destroyed us. Today he struck a man—Kennon. Kennon, whom he has mistreated from the start. Poor Kennon. Dugan has brought strife to us, now, along with his city and his gates.

But that is not the worst of it. Jubilain watched the whole thing, and we have lost our Singer. Jubilain simply was unable to assimilate the incident. A Singer's mind is not like our minds; it is a delicate, sensitive instrument. But it cannot comprehend violence. Our Singer has gone mad; there will be no more songs.

We must destroy Dugan. It is sad that we must come to his level and talk of destroying, but it is so. Now he is going to bring us warfare, and that is a gift we do not need. The fierce men of the north will prove strong adversaries for a people that has not fought for a thousand years. Why could we not have been left to ourselves? We were happy and peaceful people, and now we must talk of destroying.

I know the way to do it, too. If only my mind is strong enough, if only it has not dried in the sun during the years, I can lead the way. If I can link with Kennon, and Kennon with Jarinne, and Jarinne with Corilann, and Corilann with—

If we can link, we can do it. Dugan must go. And this is the best way; this way we can dispose of him and still remain human beings.

I am an old fool. But perhaps this dried old brain still is good for something. If I can link with Kennon—

10. Chester Dugan

All resistance has crumbled now. I'm set up for life—Chester Dugan, ruler of the world. It's not much of a world, true enough, but what the hell. It's mine.

It's amazing how all the grumbling has stopped. Even Kennon has given in—in fact, he's become my most valuable man, since that time I had to belt him. It was too bad, I guess, to ruin such a nice nose, but I couldn't have him walking off that way.

He's going to lead the expedition to the north tomorrow, and he's leaving Jarinne here. That's good. Corilann is busy with her baby, and I think I need a little variety anyway. Good-looking kid Corilann had; takes after his old man. It's amazing how everything is working out.

I hope to get electricity going soon, but I'm not too sure. The stream here is kind of weak, and maybe we'll have to throw up a dam first. In fact, I'm sure of it. I'll speak to Kennon about it before he leaves.

This business of rebuilding a civilization from scratch has its rewards. God, am I lean! I've lost all that roll of fat I was carrying around. I suppose part of the reason is that there's no beer here, yet—but I'll get to that soon enough. Everything in due time. First, I want to see what Kennon brings back from the north. I hope he doesn't ruin anything by ripping it out. Wouldn't it be nice to find a hydraulic press or a generator or stuff like that? And with my luck, we probably will.

Maybe we'll do without religion a little while longer. I spoke to Dandrin about it, but he didn't seem to go for the idea of being priest. I might just take over that job myself, once things get straightened out. I'd like to work out some sort of heating system before the winter gets here. I've figured out that we're somewhere in New Jersey or Pennsylvania, and it'll get pretty cold here unless things have changed. (Could the barbarian city to the north be New York? Sounds reasonable.)

It's funny the way everyone lies down and says yes when I tell them to do something. These people have no guts, that's their trouble. One good thing about civilization—you have to have guts to last. I'll put guts in these people, all right. I'll probably be remembered for centuries and centuries. Maybe they'll think of me as a sort of messiah in the far future when everything's blurred? Why not? I came to them out of the clouds, didn't I? From heaven.

Messiah Dugan! Lawsy-me, if they could only see me now!

I still can't get over the way everything is moving. It's almost like a dream. By next spring we'll have a respectable little city here, practically overnight. And we can hold a super-special Singing next summer and snaffle in the folk from all around.

Too bad about that kid Jubilain, by the way; he's really gone off his nut. But I always thought he was a little way there anyway. Maybe I'll teach them some of the old songs myself. It'll help to make me popular here. Although, come to think of it, I'm pretty popular now. They're all smiling at me all the time.

11.

"Kennon? Kennon? Hear me?"
"I hear you, Dandrin. I'll get Jarinne."
"Here I am. Corilann?"
"Here, Jarinne. And pulling hard. Let's try to get Onnar."
"Pull hard!"
"Onnar in." "And Jekkaman." "Hello, Dandrin."
"Hello."
"All here?"
"One hundred twenty."
"Tight now." "We're right tight."
"Let's get started then. All together."
"Hello? Hello, Dugan. Listen to us, Dugan. Listen to us. Listen to us. Hold on tight! Listen to us, Dugan."
"Open up all the way, now."
"Are you listening, Dugan?"

12. Dandrin plus Kennon plus Jarinne plus Corilann plus n

I think we'll be able to hold together indefinitely, and so it can be said that the coming of Dugan was an incredible stroke of luck for us. This new blending is infinitely better than trying to make contact over thousands of miles!

Certainly we'll have to maintain this *gestalt* (useful word; I found it in Dugan's mind when I entered) until after Dugan's death. He's peacefully dreaming now, dreaming of who knows what conquests and battles and expansions, and I don't think he'll come out of it. He may live on in his dream for years, and I'll have to hold together and sustain the illusion until he dies. I hope we're making him happy at last. He seems to have been a very unhappy man.

And just after I joined together, it occurred to me that we'd better stay this way indefinitely, just in case any more Dugans get thrown at us from the past. (Could it have been part of a Design? I wonder.) They must all have been like that back then. It's a fine thing that bomb was dropped.

We'll keep Dugan's city, of course. He did make some positive contributions to us—me. His biggest contribution was me; I never would have formed otherwise. I would have been scattered—Kennon on his farm, Dandrin here, Corilann there. I would have maintained some sort of contact among us, the way I always did even before Dugan came, but nothing like this! Nothing at all.

There's the question of what to do with Dugan's child. Kennon, Corilann, and Jarinne are all raising him. We don't need families now that we have me. I think we'll let Dugan's child in with us for a while; if he shows any signs of being like his father, we can always put him to sleep and let him share his father's dream.

I wonder what Dugan is thinking of. Now all his projects will be carried out; his city will grow and cover the world; we will fight and kill and plunder, and he will be measurelessly happy—though all these things take place only within the boundaries of his fertile brain. We will never understand him. But I am happy that all these things will happen only within Dugan's mind so long as I am together and can maintain the illusion for him.

Our next project is to reclaim Jubilain. I am sad that he cannot be with us yet, for how rare and beautiful I would be if I had a Singer in me! That would surely be the most wonderful of blendings. But that will come. Patiently I will unravel the strands of Jubilain's tangled mind, patiently I will bring the Singer back to us.

For in a few months it will be summer again, and time for the Singing. It will be different this year, for we will have been together in me all winter, and so the Singing will not be as unusual an event as it has been, when we have come to each other covered with a winter's strangeness. But this year I will be with us, and we will be I; and the songs of summer will be trebly beautiful in Dugan's city, while Dugan sleeps through the night and the day, for day and night on night and day.

TO BE CONTINUED

It was in the summer of 1955, once classes were over, that my career made its great leap forward, having been jump-started by Randall Garrett. Both in collaboration with him and on my own I started selling stories all over the place, and the big event came in August, 1955, when he and I, working under the collective pseudonym of "Robert Randall," had an 11,000-word story accepted by the editor I regarded as the greatest in the science-fiction field's history, John W. Campbell, Jr. of Astounding Science Fiction. *Campbell read the story on the spot in his office as Garrett and I watched tensely, and bought it then and there, and I went home in a daze, scarcely believing that I had actually sold a story to John W. Campbell, Jr.—and Campbell had told us also that he wanted us to write a couple of sequels to it, too.*

But my selling a collaborative story to Campbell was one thing— Garrett was already an established Campbell contributor, and I had no illusions about how it had come to pass that I was now a Campbell writer as well—and selling one that was all my own was something else again. I would appear in the magazine under a pseudonym, which was better than never appearing in it at all. But the name of Robert Silverberg on the contents page of Astounding—*I saw that as the ultimate accolade, the greatest achievement that any young science-fiction reader could aspire to.*

First, though, Garrett and I tackled one of those "Robert Randall" sequels that Campbell had requested, and sold it to him in October, 1955. Then, the following week—I was still an undergraduate at Columbia, remember, but by now I was spending as much time at my typewriter as I was in the classroom—I set out to write the story that would put me in Astounding for the first time under my own byline.

As it turned out, even this one wasn't done entirely on my own. I told Garrett what my idea was—the story of an immortal man who dreams of fatherhood, but who, for reasons inherent in the nature of immortality, has been unable to achieve it—and Garrett, whose story titles almost always embodied some sort of sly pun, said immediately, "You ought to call it 'To Be Continued.'" Which I did; and quite possibly—since our working lives were so closely intertwined at that time—he even wrote a few hundred words of the text. The first scene in the East End Bar sounds more like Garrett's work than mine. The legal drinking age in New York City then was 18, and I was a couple of years older than that, but even so I had spent very little time in bars, whereas Garrett, alas, was very familiar with them. But whether he actually wrote the scene or merely stuck in a few details of local color is something that I'm not able to recall, more than fifty years after the fact. Later in the story a character named "Corwyn" makes a brief appearance, and I know that that was a character name that Garrett frequently used in his own stories; but whether that means that Garrett wrote that scene or simply that I inserted the name as a little inside joke is, again, something I'm unable to say at this late date.

At any rate, Campbell bought the story the day I brought it to his office. The $150 he paid me for it, though quite a substantial amount of money in those pre-inflation days, was secondary for me by some distance to the thrill of knowing that I had made it into Astounding under my own name. He used the story in the May, 1956 issue. Campbell ran a readers' poll back then, with cash bonuses for the two most popular stories in each issue, and I learned a few months later that "To Be Continued" had finished in second place among the five stories of its issue, which brought me a bonus of $25. It began to seem likely now that I would become one of the regular writers for Campbell's legendary magazine, which between 1938 and 1950 or so had virtually defined modern science fiction. Clearly I was on my way.

Gaius Titus Menenius sat thoughtfully in his oddly-decorated apartment on Park Avenue, staring at the envelope that had just arrived. He contemplated it for a moment, noting with amusement that he was actually somewhat perturbed over the possible nature of its contents.

After a moment he elbowed up from the red contour-chair and crossed the room in three bounds. Still holding the envelope, he eased himself down on the long green couch near the wall, and, extending himself full-length, slit the envelope open with a neat flick of his fingernail. The medical report was within, as he had expected.

"Dear Mr. Riswell," it read. "I am herewith enclosing a copy of the laboratory report concerning your examination last week. I am pleased to report that our findings are positive—emphatically so. In view of our conversation, I am sure this finding will be extremely pleasing to you, and, of course, to your wife. Sincerely, F. D. Rowcliff, M.D."

Menenius read the letter through once again, examined the enclosed report, and allowed his face to open in a wide grin. It was almost an anticlimax, after all these centuries. He couldn't bring himself to become very excited over it—not any more.

He stood up and stretched happily. "Well, Mr. Riswell," he said to himself, "I think this calls for a drink. In fact, a night on the town."

He chose a smart dinner jacket from his wardrobe and moved toward the door. It swung open at his approach. He went out into the corridor and disappeared into the elevator, whistling gaily, his mind full of new plans and new thoughts.

It was a fine feeling. After two thousand years of waiting, he had finally achieved his maturity. He could have a son. At last!

"Good afternoon, Mr. Schuyler," said the barman. "Will it be the usual, sir?"

"Martini, of course," said W. M Schuyler IV, seating himself casually on the padded stool in front of the bar.

Behind the projected personality of W. M Schuyler IV, Gaius Titus smiled, mentally. W. M. Schuyler *always* drank martinis. And they had pretty well better be dry—very dry.

The baroque strains of a Vivaldi violin concerto sang softly in the background. Schuyler watched the swirl of colors that moved with the music.

"Good afternoon, Miss Vanderpool," he heard the barman say. "An old-fashioned?"

Schuyler took another sip of his martini and looked up. The girl had appeared suddenly and had taken the seat next to him, looking her usual cool self.

"Sharon," he said, putting just the right amount of exclamation point after it.

She turned to look at him and smiled, disclosing a brilliantly white array of perfect teeth. "Bill! I didn't notice you! How long have you been here?"

"Just arrived," Schuyler told her. "Just about a minute ago."

The barman put her drink down in front of her. She took a long sip without removing her eyes from him. Schuyler met her glance, and behind his eyes Gaius Titus was coldly appraising her in a new light.

He had met her in Kavanaugh's a month before, and he had readily enough added her to the string. Why not? She was young, pretty, intelligent, and made a pleasant companion. There had been others like her—a thousand others, two thousand, five thousand. One gets to meet quite a few in two millennia.

Only now Gaius Titus was finally mature, and had different needs. The string of girls to which Sharon belonged was going to be cut.

He wanted a wife.

"How's the lackey of Wall Street?" Sharon asked. "Still coining money faster than you know how to spend it?"

"I'll leave that for you to decide," he said. He signaled for two more drinks. "Care to take in a concert tonight? The Bach Group's giving a benefit this evening, you know, and I'm told there still are a few hundred-dollar seats left—"

There, Gaius Titus thought. The bait has been cast. She ought to respond.

She whistled, a long, low, sophisticated whistle. "I'd venture that business is fairly good, then," she said. Her eyes fell. "But I don't want to let you go to all that expense on my account, Bill."

"It's nothing," Schuyler insisted, while Gaius Titus continued to weigh her in the balance. "They're doing the Fourth Brandenburg, and Renoli's playing the Goldberg Variations. How about?"

She met his gaze evenly. "Sorry, Bill. I have something else on for the evening." Her tone left no doubt in Schuyler's mind that there was little point pressing the discussion any further. Gaius Titus felt a sharp pang of disappointment.

Schuyler lifted his hand, palm forward. "Say no more! I should have known you'd be booked up for tonight already." He paused. "What about tomorrow?" he asked, after a moment. "There's a reading of Webster's 'Duchess of Malfi' down at the Dramatist's League. It's been one of my favorite plays for a long time."

Silently smiling, he waited for her reply. The Webster was, indeed, a long-time favorite. Gaius Titus recalled having attended one of its first performances, during his short employ in the court of James I. During the next three and a half centuries, he had formed a sentimental attachment for the creaky old melodrama.

"Not tomorrow either," Sharon said. "Some other night, Bill."

"All right," he said. "Some other night."

He reached out a hand and put it over hers, and they fell silent, listening to the Vivaldi in the background. He contemplated her high, sharp cheekbones in the purple half-light, wondering if she could be the one to bear the child he had waited for so long.

She had parried all his thrusts in a fashion that surprised him. She was not at all impressed by his display of wealth and culture. Titus reflected sadly that, perhaps, his Schuyler facet had been inadequate for her.

No, he thought, rejecting the idea. The haunting slow movement of the Vivaldi faded to its end and a lively allegro took its place. No; he had had too much experience in calculating personality-facets to fit the individual to have erred. He was certain that W. M. Schuyler IV was capable of handling Sharon.

For the first few hundred years of his unexpectedly long life, Gaius Titus had been forced to adopt the practice of turning on and off different personalities as a matter of mere survival. Things had been easy for a while after the fall of Rome, but with the coming of the Middle Ages he had needed all his skill to keep from running afoul of the superstitious. He had carefully built up a series of masks, of false fronts, as a survival mechanism.

How many times had he heard someone tell him, in jest, "You ought to be on the stage?" It struck home. He *was* on the stage. He was a man of many roles. Somewhere, beneath it all, was the unalterable personality of Gaius Titus Menenius, *cives Romanus,* casting the shadows that were his many masks. But Gaius Titus was far below the surface—the surface which, at the moment, was W. M. Schuyler IV; which had been Preston Riswell the week before, when he had visited the doctor for that fateful examination; which could be Leslie MacGregor or Sam Spielman or Phil Carlson tomorrow, depending on where Gaius Titus was, in what circumstances, and talking to whom. There was only one person he did not dare to be, and that was himself.

He wasn't immortal; he knew that. But he was *relatively* immortal. His life-span was tremendously decelerated, and it had taken him two thousand years to become, physically, a fertile adult. His span was roughly a hundred times that of a normal man's. And, according to what he had learned in the last century, his longevity should be transmissible genetically. All he needed now was someone to transmit it to.

Was it dominant? That he didn't know. That was the gamble he'd be making. He wondered what it would be like to watch his children and his children's children shrivel with age. Not pleasant, he thought.

The conversation with Sharon lagged; it was obvious that something was wrong with his Schuyler facet, at least so far as she was concerned, though he was unable to see where the trouble lay. After a few more minutes of disjointed chatter, she excused herself and left the bar. He watched her go. She had eluded him neatly. Where to next?

He thought he knew.

The East End bar was far downtown and not very reputable. Gaius Titus pushed through the revolving door and headed for the counter.

"Hi, Sam. Howsa boy?" the bartended said.

"Let's have a beer, Jerry." The bartender shoved a beer out toward the short, swarthy man in the leather jacket.

"Things all right?"

"Can't complain, Jerry. How's business?" Sam Spielman asked, as he lifted the beer to his mouth.

"It's lousy."

"It figures," Sam said. "Why don't you put in automatics? They're getting all the business now."

"Sure, Sam, sure. And where do I get the dough? That's twenty." He took the coins Sam dropped on the bar and grinned. "At least you can afford beer."

"You know me, Jerry," Sam said. "My credit's good."

Jerry nodded. "Good enough." He punched the coins into the register. "Ginger was looking for you, by the way. What you got against the gal?"

"Against her? Nothin'. What do y'mean?" Sam pushed out his beer shell for a refill.

"She's got a hooker out for you—you know that, don't you?" Jerry was grinning.

Gaius Titus thought: *She's not very bright, but she might very well serve my purpose. She has other characteristics worth transmitting.*

"Hi, Sammy."

He turned to look at her. "Hi, Ginger," he said. "How's the gal?"

"Not bad, honey." But she didn't look it. She looked as though she'd been dragged through the mill. Her blonde hair was disarranged, her blouse was wrinkled, and, as usual, her teeth were discolored by the lipstick that had rubbed off on them.

"I love you, Sammy," she said softly.

"I love you, too," Sam said. He meant it.

Gaius Titus thought sourly: *But how many of her characteristics would I not want to transmit? Still, she'll do, I guess. She's a solid girl.*

"Sam," she said, interrupting the flow of his thoughts, "why don't you come around more often? I miss you."

"Look, Ginger baby," Sam said. "Remember, I've got a long haul to pull. If I marry you, you gotta understand that I don't get home often. I gotta drive a truck. You might not see me more than once or twice a week."

Titus rubbed his forehead. He wasn't quite sure, after all, that the girl was worthwhile. She had spunk, all right, but was she worthy of fostering a race of immortals?

He didn't get a chance to find out. "Married?" The blonde's voice sounded incredulous. "Who the devil wants to get married? You've got me on the wrong track, Sam. I don't want to get myself tied down."

"Sure, honey, sure," he said. "But I thought—"

Ginger stood up. "You think anything you please, Sam. Anything you please. But not marriage."

She stared at him hard for a moment, and walked off. Sam looked after her morosely.

Gaius Titus grinned behind the Sam Spielman mask. She wasn't the girl either. Two thousand years of life had taught him that women were unpredictable, and he wasn't altogether surprised at her reaction to his proposal.

But he was disturbed over this second failure of the evening nevertheless. Was his judgment that far off? Perhaps, he thought, he was losing the vital ability of personality-projection. He didn't like that idea.

For hours, Gaius Titus walked the streets of New York.

New York. Sure it was new. So was Old York, in England. Menenius had seen both of them grow from tiny villages to towns to cities to metropoli.

Metropoli. That was Greek. It had taken him twelve years to learn Greek. He hadn't rushed it.

Twelve years. And he still wasn't an adult. He could remember when the Emperor had seen the sign in the sky: *In hoc signo vinces.* And, at the age of four hundred and sixty-two, he'd still been too young to enter the service of the Empire.

Gaius Titus Menenius, Citizen of Rome. When he had been a child, he had thought Rome would last forever. But it hadn't; Rome had fallen. Egypt, which he had long thought of as an empire which would last forever, had gone even more quickly. It had died and putrefied and sloughed off into the Great River which carries all life off into death.

Over the years and the centuries, races and peoples and nations had come and gone. And their passing had had no effect at all on Gaius Titus.

He was walking north. He turned left on Market Street, away from the Manhattan Bridge. Suddenly, he was tired of walking. He hailed a passing taxi.

He gave the cabby his address on Park Avenue and leaned back against the cushions to relax.

The first few centuries had been hard. He hadn't grown up, in the first place. By the time he was twenty, he had attained his full height— five feet nine. But he still looked like a seventeen-year-old.

And he had still looked that way nineteen hundred years later. It had been a long, hard drive to make enough money to live on during that time. Kids don't get well-paying jobs.

Actually, he'd lived a miserable hands-to-mouth existence for centuries. But the gradual collapse of the Christian ban on usury had opened the way for him to make some real money. Money makes more money, in a capitalistic system, if you have patience. Titus had time on his side.

It wasn't until the free-enterprise system had evolved that he started to get anywhere. But a deposit of several hundred pounds in the proper firm back in 1735 had netted a little extra money. The British East India Company had brought his financial standing up a great deal, and judicious investments ever since left him comfortably fixed. He derived considerable amusement from the extraordinary effects compound interest exerted on a bank account a century old.

"Here you are, buddy," said the cabdriver.

Gaius Titus climbed out and gave the driver a five note without asking for change.

Zeus, he thought. *I might as well make a night of it.*

He hadn't been really drunk since the stock market collapse back in 1929.

Leslie MacGregor pushed open the door of the San Marino Bar in Greenwich Village and walked to the customary table in the back corner. Three people were already there, and the conversation was going well. Leslie waved a hand and the two men waved back. The girl grinned and beckoned.

"Come on over, Les," she yelled across the noisy room. "Mack has just sold a story!" Her deep voice was clear and firm.

Mack, the heavy-set man next to the wall, grinned self-consciously and picked up his beer.

Leslie strolled quietly over to the booth and sat down beside Corwyn, the odd man of the trio.

"Sold a story?" Leslie repeated archly.

Mack nodded. *"Chimerical Review,"* he said. "A little thing I called 'Pluck Up the Torch.' Not much, but it's a sale; you know."

"If one wants to prostitute one's art," said Corwyn.

Leslie frowned at him. "Don't be snide. After all, Mack has to pay his rent." Then he turned toward the girl. "Lorraine, could I talk to you a moment?"

She brushed the blonde hair back from the shoulders of her black turtleneck sweater and widened the grin on her face.

"Sure, Les," she said in her oddly deep, almost masculine voice. "What's all the big secret?"

No secret, thought Gaius Titus. What I want is simple enough.

For a long time, he had thought that near-immortality carried with it the curse of sterility. Now he knew it was simply a matter of time—of growing up.

As he stood up to walk to the bar with Lorraine, he caught a glimpse of himself in the dusty mirror behind the bar. He didn't look much over twenty-five. But things had been changing in the past fifty years. He had never had a heavy beard before; he had not developed his husky baritone voice until a year before the outbreak of the First World War.

It had been difficult, at first, to hide his immortality. Changing names, changing residences, changing, changing, changing. Until he had found that he didn't have to change—not deep inside.

People don't recognize faces. Faces are essentially all alike. Two eyes, two ears, a nose, a mouth. What more is there to a face? Only the personality behind it.

A personality is something that is projected—something put on display for others to see. And Gaius Titus Menenius had found that two thousand years of experience had given him enough internal psychological reality to be able to project any personality he wanted to. All he needed was a change of dress and a change of personality to be a different person. His face changed subtly to fit the person who was wearing it; no one had ever caught on.

Lorraine sat down on the bar stool. "Beer," she said to the bartender. "What's the matter, Les? What's eating you?"

He studied her firm, strong features, her deep mocking eyes. "Lorraine," he said softly, "will you marry me?"

She blinked. "Marry you? You? Marry?" She grinned again. "Who'd ever think it? A bourgeois conformist, like all the rest." Then she shook her head. "No, Les. Even if you're kidding, you ought to know better than that. What's the gag?"

"No gag," said Leslie, and Gaius Titus fought his surprise and shock at his third failure. "I see your point," Leslie said. "Forget it. Give my best to everyone." He got up without drinking his beer and walked out the door.

Leslie stepped out into the street and started heading for the subway. Then Gaius Titus, withdrawing the mask, checked himself and hailed a cab.

He got into the cab and gave the driver his home address. He didn't see any reason for further pursuing his adventures that evening.

He was mystified. How could *three* personality-facets fail so completely? He had been handling these three girls well ever since he had met them, but tonight, going from one to the next, as soon as he made any serious ventures toward any of them the whole thing folded. Why?

"It's a lousy world," he told the driver, assuming for the moment the mask of Phil Carlson, cynical newsman. "Damn lousy." His voice was a biting rasp.

"What's wrong, buddy?"

"Had a fight with all three of my girls. It's a lousy world."

"I'll buy that," the driver said. The cab swung up into Park. "But look at it this way, pal: who needs them?"

For a moment the mask blurred and fell aside, and it was Gaius Titus, not Phil Carlson, who said, "That's exactly right! Who needs them?" He gave the driver a bill and got out of the cab.

Who needs them? It was a good question. There were plenty of girls. Why should he saddle himself with Sharon, or Ginger, or Lorraine? They all had their good qualities—Sharon's social grace, Ginger's vigor and drive, Lorraine's rugged intellectualism. They were all three good-looking girls; tall, attractive, well put together. But yet each one, he realized, lacked something that the others had. None of them was really *worthy* by herself, he thought, apologizing to himself for what another man might call conceit, or sour grapes.

None of them would really do. But if somehow, some way, he could manage to combine those three leggy girls, those three personalities into one body, *there* would be a girl—

He gasped.

He whirled and caught sight of the cab he had just vacated.

"Hey, cabby!" Titus called. "Come back here! Take me back to the San Marino!"

She wasn't there. As Leslie burst in, he caught sight of Corwyn, sitting alone and grinning twistedly over a beer.

"Where'd they go? Where's Lorraine?"

The little man lifted his shoulders and eyebrows in an elaborate shrug. "They left about a minute ago. No, it was closer to ten, wasn't it? They went in separate directions. They left me here."

"Thanks," Leslie said.

Scratch Number One, Titus thought. He ran to the phone booth in the back, dialed Information, and demanded the number of the East End Bar. After some fumbling, the operator found it.

He dialed. The bartender's tired face appeared in the screen.

"Hello, Sam," the barkeep said. "What's doing?"

"Do me a favor, Jerry," Sam said. "Look around your place for Ginger."

"She ain't here, Sam," the bartender said. "Haven't seen her since you two blew out of here a while back." Jerry's eyes narrowed. "I ain't never seen you dressed up like that before, Sam, you know?"

Gaius Titus crouched down suddenly to get out of range of the screen. "I'm celebrating tonight, Jerry," he said, and broke the connection.

Ginger wasn't to be found either, eh? That left only Sharon. He couldn't call Kavanaugh's—they wouldn't give a caller any information about their patrons. Grabbing another taxi, he shot across town to Kavanaugh's.

Sharon wasn't there when Schuyler entered. She hadn't been in since the afternoon, a waiter informed him, after receiving a small gratuity. Schuyler had a drink and left. Gaius Titus returned to his apartment, tingling with an excitement he hadn't known for centuries.

He returned to Kavanaugh's the next night, and the next. Still no sign of her.

The following evening, though, when he entered the bar, she was sitting there, nursing an old-fashioned. He slid onto the seat next to her. She looked up in surprise.

"Bill! Good to see you again."

"The same here," Gaius Titus said. "It's good to see you again— Ginger. Or is it Lorraine?"

She paled and put her hand to her mouth. Then, covering, she said, "What do you mean, Bill? Have you had too many drinks tonight?"

"Possibly," Titus said. "I stopped off in the San Marino before I came up. You weren't there, Lorraine. That deep voice is quite a trick, I have to admit. I had a drink with Mack and Corwyn, Then I went over to the East End, Ginger. You weren't there; either. So," he said, "there was only one place left to find you, Sharon."

She stared at him for a long moment. Finally she said, simply, "Who are you?"

"Leslie MacGregor," Titus said. "Also Sam Spielman. And W. M. Schuyler. Plus two or three other people. The name is Gaius Titus Menenius, at your service."

"I still don't understand—"

"Yes, you do," Titus said. "You are clever—but not clever enough. Your little game had me going for almost a month, you know? And it's not easy to fool a man my age."

"When did you find out?" the girl asked weakly.

"Monday night, when I saw all three of you within a couple of hours."

"You're—"

"Yes. I'm like you," he said. "But I'll give you credit: I didn't see through it until I was on my way home. You were using my own camouflage technique against me, and I didn't spot it for what it was. What's your real name?"

"Mary Bradford," she said. "I was English, originally. Of fine Plantagenet stock. I'm really a Puritan at heart, you see." She was grinning slyly.

"Oh? Mayflower descendant?" Titus asked teasingly.

"No," Mary replied. "Not a descendant. A passenger. And I'll tell you—I was awfully happy to get out of England and over here to Plymouth Colony."

He toyed with her empty glass. "You didn't like England? Probably my fault. I was a minor functionary in King James' court in the early seventeenth century."

They giggled together over it. Titus stared at her, his pulse pounding harder and harder. She stared back. Her eyes were smiling.

"I didn't think there was another one," she said after a while. "It was so strange, never growing old. I was afraid they'd burn me as a witch. I had to keep changing, moving all the time. It wasn't a pleasant life. It's better lately—I enjoy these little poses. But I'm glad you caught on to me," she said. She reached out and took his hand. "I guess I would never have been smart enough to connect you and Leslie and Sam, the way you did Sharon and Ginger and Lorraine. You play the game too well for me."

"In two thousand years," Titus said, not caring if the waiter overheard him, "I never found another one like me. Believe me, Mary, I looked. I looked hard, and I've had plenty of time to search. And then to find you, hiding behind the faces of three girls I knew!"

He squeezed her hand. The next statement followed logically for him. "Now that we've found each other," he said softly, "we can have a child. A third immortal."

Her face showed radiant enthusiasm. "Wonderful!" she cried. "When can we get married?"

"How about tomor—" he started to say. Then a thought struck him. "Mary?"

"What...Titus?"

"How old did you say you were? When were you born?" he asked.

She thought for a moment. "1597," she said. "I'm nearly four hundred."

He nodded, dumb with growing frustration. Only four hundred? That meant—that meant she was now the equivalent of a three-year-old child!

"When can we get married?" she repeated.

"There's no hurry," Titus said dully, letting her hand drop. "We have eleven hundred years."

ALAREE

This little item displays my growing professionalism. I wrote it in March of 1956—one of eight stories that I managed to produce that month, while still carrying a full class load in college. (They all sold.) Its theme is a good indication that I was trying to address the psychological preoccupations of the brilliant, cantankerous editor Horace Gold of Galaxy, *John Campbell's most determined competitor, to whom I had not yet managed to sell a story. It's smoothly handled and I was sure that it would bring about a break-through for me there. But Gold had people like Theodore Sturgeon and Fritz Leiber to deal with matters of this sort, and evidently didn't need my attempt at it. (Though he did start buying my work a few months later.) The story went bouncing around from magazine to magazine for over a year before an equally brilliant and equally cantankerous editor, the veteran Donald A. Wollheim, purchased it for the March, 1958 issue of a short-lived and now wholly forgotten magazine called* Saturn Science Fiction *that he edited with his left hand while giving most of his attention to his highly suc-cessful and important paperback series, Ace Double Books.*

When our ship left its carefully planned trajectory and started to wobble through space in dizzy circles, I knew we shouldn't have passed up that opportunity for an overhauling on Spica IV. My men and I were anxious to get back to Earth, and a hasty check had assured us that the

Aaron Burr was in tiptop shape, so we had turned down the offer of an overhaul, which would have meant a month's delay, and set out straight for home.

As so often happens, what seemed like the most direct route home turned out to be the longest. We had spent far too much time on this survey trip already, and we were rejoicing in the prospect of an immediate return to Earth when the ship started turning cartwheels.

Willendorf, computerman first class, came to me looking sheepish, a few minutes after I'd noticed we were off course.

"What is it, Gus?" I asked.

"The feed network's oscillating, sir," he said, tugging at his unruly reddish-brown beard. "It won't stop, sir."

"Is Ketteridge working on it?"

"I've just called him," Willendorf said. His stolid face reflected acute embarrassment. Willendorf always took it personally whenever one of the cybers went haywire, as if it were his own fault. "You know what this means, don't you, sir?"

I grinned. "Take a look at this, Willendorf," I said, shoving the trajectory graphs towards him. I sketched out with my stylus the confused circles we had been traveling in all morning. "That's what your feed network's doing to us," I said, "and we'll keep on doing it until we get it fixed."

"What are you going to do, sir?"

I sensed his impatience with me. Willendorf was a good man, but his psych charts indicated a latent desire for officerhood. Deep down inside, he was sure he was at least as competent as I was to run this ship and probably a good deal more so.

"Send me Upper Navigating Technician Haley," I snapped. "We're going to have to find a planet in the neighborhood and put down for repairs."

It turned out there was an insignificant solar system in the vicinity, consisting of a small but hot white star and a single unexplored planet, Terra-size, a few hundred million miles out. After Haley and I had decided that that was the nearest port of refuge, I called a general meeting...

Quickly and positively I outlined our situation and explained what would have to be done. I sensed the immediate disappointment, but, gratifyingly, the reaction was followed by a general feeling of resigned pitching in. If we all worked, we'd get back to Earth, sooner or later. If we didn't, we'd spend the next century flip-flopping aimlessly in space.

After the meeting we set about the business of recovering control of the ship and putting it down for repairs. The feed network, luckily, gave up the ghost about ninety minutes later; it meant we had to stoke the fuel by hand, but at least it stopped that accursed oscillating.

We got the ship going, and Haley, navigating by feel in a way I never would have dreamed possible, brought us into the nearby solar system in hardly any time at all. Finally we swung into our landing orbit and made our looping way down to the surface of the little planet.

I studied my crew's faces carefully. We had spent a great deal of time together in space—much too much, really, for comfort—and an incident like this might very well snap them all if we didn't get going again soon enough. I could foresee disagreements, bickering, declaration of opinion where no opinion was called for.

I was relieved to discover that the planet's air was breathable. A rather high nitrogen concentration, to be sure—82 per cent—but that left 17 per cent for oxygen, plus some miscellaneous inerts, and it wouldn't be too rough on the lungs. I decreed a one-hour free break before beginning repairs.

Remaining aboard ship, I gloomily surveyed the scrambled feed network and tried to formulate a preliminary plan of action for getting the complex cybernetic instrument to function again, while my crew went outside to relax.

Ten minutes after I had opened the lock and let them out, I heard someone clanking around in the aft supplies cabin.

"Who's there?" I yelled.

"Me," grunted a heavy voice that could only be Willendorf's. "I'm looking for the thought-converter, sir."

I ran hastily through the corridor, flipped up the latch on the supplies cabin, and confronted him. "What do you want the converter for?" I snapped.

"Found an alien, sir," he said laconically.

My eyes widened. The survey chart said nothing about intelligent extraterrestrials in this limb of the galaxy, but then again this planet hadn't been explored yet.

I gestured towards the rear cabinet. "The converter helmets are in there," I said. "I'll be out in a little while. Make sure you follow technique in making contact."

"Of course, sir." Willendorf took the converter helmet and went out, leaving me standing there. I waited a few minutes, then climbed the catwalk to the air lock and peered out.

They were all clustered around a small alien being who looked weak and inconsequential in the midst of the circle. I smiled at the sight. The alien was roughly humanoid in shape, with the usual complement of arms and legs, and a pale-green complexion that blended well with the muted violet coloring of his world. He was wearing the thought-converter somewhat lopsidedly, and I saw a small green furry ear protruding from the left side. Willendorf was talking to him.

Then someone saw me standing at the open air lock, and I heard Haley yell to me, "Come on down, Chief!"

They were ringed around the alien in a tight circle. I shouldered my way into their midst. Willendorf turned to me.

"Meet Alaree, sir," he said. "Alaree, this is our commander."

"We are pleased to meet you," the alien said gravely. The converter automatically turned his thoughts into English, but maintained the trace of his oddly inflected accent. "You have been saying that you are from the skies."

"His grammar's pretty shaky," Willendorf interposed. "He keeps referring to any of us as 'you'—even you, who just got here."

"Odd," I said. "The converter's supposed to conform to the rules of grammar." I turned to the alien, who seemed perfectly at ease among us. "My name is Bryson," I said. "This is Willendorf, over here."

The alien wrinkled his soft-skinned forehead in momentary confusion. "We are Alaree," he said again.

"We? You and who else?"

"We and we else," Alaree said blandly. I stared at him for a moment, then gave up. The complexities of an alien mind are often too much for a mere Terran to fathom.

"You are welcome to our world," Alaree said after a few moments of silence.

"Thanks," I said. "Thanks."

I turned away, leaving the alien with my men. They had twenty-six minutes left of the break I'd given them, after which we would have to get back to the serious business of repairing the ship. Making friends with floppy-eared aliens was one thing, getting back to Earth was another.

The planet was a warm, friendly sort of place, with rolling fields and acres of pleasant-looking purple vegetation. We had landed in a clearing at the edge of a fair-sized copse. Great broad-beamed trees shot up all around us.

Alaree returned to visit us every day, until he became almost a mascot of the crew. I liked the little alien myself and spent some time with him, although I found his conversation generally incomprehensible. No doubt he had the same trouble with us. The converter had only limited efficiency, after all.

He was the only representative of his species who came. For all we knew, he was the only one of his kind on the whole planet. There was no sign of life elsewhere, and, although Willendorf led an unauthorized scouting party during some free time on the third day, he failed to find a village of any sort. Where Alaree went every night and how he had found us in the first place remained mysteries.

As for the feed network, progress was slow. Ketteridge, the technician in charge, had tracked down the foul-up and was trying to repair it without building a completely new network. Shortcuts again. He tinkered away for four days, setting up a tentative circuit, trying it out, watching it sputter and blow out, building another.

There was nothing I could do. But I sensed tension heightening among the crewmen. They were annoyed at themselves, at each other, at me, at everything.

On the fifth day, Ketteridge and Willendorf finally let their accumulated tenseness explode. They had been working together on the network, but they quarreled, and Ketteridge came storming into my cabin immediately afterward.

"Sir, I demand to be allowed to work on the network by myself. It's my speciality, and Willendorf's only snarling things up."

"Get me Willendorf," I said.

When Willendorf showed up I heard the whole story, decided quickly to let Ketteridge have his way—it was, after all, his specialty—and calmed Willendorf down. Then, reaching casually for some papers on my desk, I dismissed both of them. I knew they'd come to their senses in a day or so.

I spent most of the next day sitting placidly in the sun, while Ketteridge tinkered with the feed network some more. I watched the faces of the men. They were starting to smoulder. They wanted to get home, and they weren't getting there. Besides, this was a fairly dull planet, and even the novelty of Alaree wore off after a while. The little alien had a way of hanging around men who were busy scraping fuel deposits out of the jet tubes, or something equally unpleasant, and bothering them with all sorts of questions.

The following morning I was lying blissfully on the grass near the ship, talking to Alaree. Ketteridge came to me, and by the tightness of his lips I knew he was in trouble.

I brushed some antlike blue insects off my trousers and rose to a sitting position, leaning against the tall, tough-barked tree behind me. "What's the matter, Ketteridge? How's the feed network?"

He glanced uneasily at Alaree for a moment before speaking. "I'm stuck, sir. I'll have to admit I was wrong. I can't fix it by myself."

I stood up and put my hand on his shoulder. "That's a noble thing to say, Ketteridge. It takes a big man to admit he's been a fool. Will you work with Willendorf now?"

"If he'll work with me, sir," Ketteridge said miserably.

"I think he will," I said. Ketteridge saluted and turned away, and I felt a burst of satisfaction. I'd met the crisis in the only way possible; if I had *ordered* them to cooperate, I would have gotten no place. The psychological situation no longer allowed for unbending military discipline.

After Ketteridge had gone, Alaree, who had been silent all this time, looked up at me in puzzlement. "We do not understand," he said.

"Not *we*," I corrected. "*I*. You're only one person. *We* means many people."

"We are only one person?" Alaree said tentatively.

"No. *I* am only one person. Get it?"

He worried the thought around for a few moments; I could see his browless forehead contract in deep concentration.

"Look," I said. "I'm one person. Ketteridge is another person. Willendorf is another. Each one of them is an independent individual, an *I*."

"And together you make *we*?" Alaree asked brightly.

"Yes and no," I said. "*We* is composed of many *I*'s—but we still remain *I*."

Again he sank deep in concentration, and then he smiled, scratched the ear that protruded from one side of the thought-helmet, and said, "*We* do not understand. But *I* do. Each of you is—is an *I*."

"An individual," I said.

"An individual," he repeated. "A complete person. And together, to fly your ship, you must become a *we*."

"But only temporarily," I said. "There still can be conflict between the parts. That's necessary, for progress. I can always think of the rest of them as *they*."

"I...they," Alaree repeated slowly. *"They."* He nodded. "It is difficult for me to grasp all this. I...think differently. But I am coming to understand, and I am worried."

That was a new idea. Alaree worried? Could be, I reflected. I had no way of knowing. I knew so little about Alaree—where on the planet he came from, what his tribal life was like, what sort of civilization he had, were all blanks.

"What kind of worries, Alaree?"

"You would not understand," he said solemnly and would say no more.

Towards afternoon, as golden shadows started to slant through the closely packed trees, I returned to the ship. Willendorf and Ketteridge were aft, working over the feed network, and the whole crew had gathered around to watch and offer suggestions. Even Alaree was there, looking absurdly comical in his copper-alloy thought-converter helmet, standing on tiptoe and trying to see what was happening.

About an hour later, I spotted the alien sitting by himself beneath the long-limbed tree that towered over the ship. He was lost in thought. Evidently whatever his problem was, it was really eating him.

Towards evening, he made a decision. I had been watching him with a great deal of concern, wondering what was going on in that small but unfathomable mind. I saw him brighten, leap up suddenly, and cross the field, heading in my direction.

"Captain!"

"What is it, Alaree?"

He waddled up and stared gravely at me. "Your ship will be ready to leave soon. What was wrong is nearly right again."

He paused, obviously uncertain of how to phrase his next statement, and I waited patiently. Finally he blurted out, "May I come back to your world with you?"

Automatically, the regulations flashed through my mind. I pride myself on my knowledge of the rules. And I knew this one.

ARTICLE 101A

No intelligent extraterrestrial life is to be transported from its own world to any civilized world under any reason whatsoever, without explicit beforehand clearance. The penalty for doing so is...

And it listed a fine of more money than was ever dreamed of in my philosophy.

I shook my head. "Can't take you, Alaree. This is your world, and you belong here."

A ripple of agony ran over his face. Suddenly he ceased to be the cheerful, roly-poly creature it was so impossible to take seriously, and became a very worried entity indeed. "You cannot understand," he said. "I no longer belong here."

＊

No matter how hard he pleaded, I remained adamant. And when to no one's surprise Ketteridge and Willendorf announced, a day later, that their pooled labors had succeeded in repairing the feed network, I had to tell Alaree that we were going to leave—without him.

He nodded stiffly, accepting the fact, and without a word stalked tragically away, into the purple tangle of foliage that surrounded our clearing.

He returned a while later, or so I thought. He was not wearing the thought-converter. That surprised me. Alaree knew the helmet was a valuable item, and he had been cautioned to take good care of it.

I sent a man inside to get another helmet for him. I put it on him—this time tucking that wayward ear underneath properly—and looked at him sternly. "Where's the other helmet, Alaree?"

"We do not have it," he said.

"*We*? No more I?"

"We," Alaree said. And as he spoke, the leaves parted and another alien—Alaree's very double—stepped out into the clearing.

Then I saw the helmet on the newcomer's head, and realized that he was no double. He was Alaree, and the other alien was the stranger!

"I see you're here already," the alien I knew as Alaree said to the other. They were standing about ten feet apart, staring coldly at each other. I glanced at both of them quickly. They might have been identical twins.

"We are here," the stranger said, "We have come to get you."

I took a step backward, sensing that some incomprehensible drama was being played out here among these aliens.

"What's going on, Alaree?" I asked.

"We are having difficulties," both of them said, as one.

Both of them.

I turned to the second alien. "What's your name?"

"Alaree," he said.

"Are you all named that?" I demanded.

"We are Alaree," Alaree Two said.

"They are Alaree," Alaree One said. "And *I* am Alaree. *I*."

At that moment there was a disturbance in the shrubbery, and half a dozen more aliens stepped through and confronted Alarees One and Two.

"We are Alaree," Alaree Two repeated exasperatingly. He made a sweeping gesture that embraced all seven of the aliens to my left, but pointedly excluded Alaree One at my right.

"Are we—you coming with we—us?" Alaree Two demanded. I heard the six others say something in approximately the same tone of voice, but since they weren't wearing converters, their words were only scrambled nonsense to me.

Alaree One looked at me in pain, then back at his seven fellows. I saw an expression of sheer terror in the small creature's eyes. He turned to me.

"I must go with them," he said softly. He was quivering with fear.

Without a further word, the eight marched silently away. I stood there, shaking my head in bewilderment.

We were scheduled to leave the next day. I said nothing to my crew about the bizarre incident of the evening before, but noted in my log that the native life of the planet would require careful study at some future time.

Blast-off was slated for 1100. As the crew moved efficiently through the ship, securing things, packing, preparing for departure, I sensed a general feeling of jubilation. They were happy to be on their way again, and I didn't blame them.

About half an hour before blast-off, Willendorf came to me. "Sir, Alaree's down below," he said. "He wants to come up and see you. He looks very troubled, sir."

I frowned. Probably the alien still wanted to go back with us. Well, it was cruel to deny the request, but I wasn't going to risk that fine. I intended to make that clear to him.

"Send him up," I said.

A moment later Alaree came stumbling into my cabin. Before he could speak I said, "I told you before—I can't take you off this planet, Alaree. I'm sorry about it."

He looked up pitiably and said, "You mustn't leave me!" He was trembling uncontrollably.

"What's wrong, Alaree?" I asked.

He stared intensely at me for a long moment, mastering himself, trying to arrange what he wanted to tell me into a coherent argument. Finally he said, "They would not take me back. I am alone."

"Who wouldn't take you back, Alaree?"

"*They*. Last night, Alaree came for me, to take me back. They are a *we*—an entity, a oneness. You cannot understand. When they saw what I had become, they cast me out."

I shook my head dizzily. "What do you mean?"

"You taught me...to become an *I*," he said, moistening his lips. "Before, I was part of *we*—*they*. I learned your ways from you, and now there is no room for me here. They have cut me off. When the final break comes, I will not be able to stay on this world."

Sweat was pouring down his pale face, and he was breathing harder. "It will come any minute. They are gathering strength for it. But I am *I*," he said triumphantly. He shook violently and gasped for breath.

I understood now. They were *all* Alaree. It was one planet-wide, self-aware corporate entity, composed of any number of individual cells. He had been one of them—but he had learned independence.

Then he had returned to the group—but he carried with him the seeds of individualism, the deadly, contagious germ we Terrans spread everywhere. Individualism would be fatal to such a group mind; it was cutting him loose to save itself. Just as diseased cells must be excised for the good of the entire body, Alaree was inexorably being cut off from his fellows lest he destroy the bond that made them one.

I watched him as he sobbed weakly on my acceleration cradle. "They...are...cutting...me...loose...*now!*"

He writhed horribly for a brief moment, and then relaxed and sat up on the edge of the cradle. "It is over," he said calmly. "I am fully independent."

I saw a stark *aloneness* reflected in his eyes, and behind that a gentle indictment of me for having done this to him. This world, I realized, was no place for Earthmen. What had happened was our fault—mine more than anyone else's.

"Will you take me with you?" he asked again. "If I stay here, Alaree will kill me."

I scowled wretchedly for a moment, fighting a brief battle within myself, and then I looked up. There was only one thing to do—and I was sure, once I explained on Earth, that I would not suffer for it.

I took his hand. It was cold and limp; whatever he had just been through, it must have been hell. "Yes," I said softly. "You can come with us."

And so Alaree joined the crew of the *Aaron Burr.* I told them about it just before blast-off, and they welcomed him aboard in traditional manner.

We gave the sad-eyed little alien a cabin near the cargo hold, and he established himself quite comfortably. He had no personal possessions—"It is not *their* custom." he said—and promised that he'd keep the cabin clean.

He had brought with him a rough-edged, violet fruit that he said was his staple food. I turned it over to Kechnie for synthesizing, and we blasted off.

Alaree was right at home aboard the *Burr.* He spent much time with me—asking questions.

"Tell me about Earth," Alaree would ask. The alien wanted desperately to know what sort of a world he was going to.

He would listen gravely while I explained. I told him of cities and wars and spaceships, and he nodded sagely, trying to fit the concepts into a mind only newly liberated from the gestalt. I knew he could comprehend only a fraction of what I was saying, but I enjoyed telling him. It made me feel as if Earth were coming closer that much faster, simply to talk about it.

And he went around begging everyone, "Tell me about Earth." They enjoyed telling him, too—for a while.

Then it began to get a little tiresome. We had grown accustomed to Alaree's presence on the ship, flopping around the corridors doing whatever menial job he had been assigned to. But—although I had told the men why I had brought him with us, and though we all pitied the poor lonely creature and admired his struggle to survive as an individual entity—we were slowly coming to the realization that Alaree was something of a nuisance aboard ship.

Especially later, when he began to change.

Willendorf noticed it first, twelve days out from Alaree's planet. "Alaree's been acting pretty strange these days, sir," he told me.

"What's wrong?" I asked.

"Haven't you spotted it, sir? He's been moping around like a lost soul—very quiet and withdrawn, like."

"Is he eating well?"

Willendorf chuckled loudly. "I'll say he is! Kechnie made up some synthetics based on the piece of fruit he brought with him, and he's been stuffing himself wildly. He's gained ten pounds since he came on ship. No, it's not lack of food!"

"I guess not," I said. "Keep an eye on him, will you? I feel responsible for his being here, and I want him to come through the voyage in good health."

After that, I began to observe Alaree more closely myself, and I detected the change in his personality too. He was no longer the cheerful, childlike being who delighted in pouring out questions in endless profusion. Now he was moody, silent, always brooding, and hard to approach.

On the sixteenth day out—and by now I was worried seriously about him—a new manifestation appeared. I was in the hallway, heading from my cabin to the chartroom, when Alaree stepped out of an alcove. He reached up, grasped my uniform lapel, and, maintaining his silence, drew my head down and stared pleadingly into my eyes.

Too astonished to say anything, I returned his gaze for nearly thirty seconds. I peered into his transparent pupils, wondering what he was up to. After a good while had passed, he released me, and I saw something like a tear trickle down his cheek.

"What's the trouble, Alaree?"

He shook his head mournfully and shuffled away.

I got reports from the crewmen that day and next that he had been doing this regularly for the past eighteen hours—waylaying crewmen, staring long and deep at them as if trying to express some unspeakable sadness, and walking away. He had approached almost everyone on the ship.

I wondered now how wise it had been to allow an extraterrestrial, no matter how friendly, to enter the ship. There was no telling what this latest action meant.

I started to form a theory. I suspected what he was aiming at, and the realization chilled me. But once I reached my conclusion, there was nothing I could do but wait for confirmation.

On the nineteenth day, Alaree again met me in the corridor. This time our encounter was more brief. He plucked me by the sleeve, shook his head sadly and shrugged his shoulders, and walked away.

That night, he took to his cabin, and by morning he was dead. He had apparently died peacefully in his sleep.

"I guess we'll never understand him, poor fellow," Willendorf said, after we had committed the body to space. "You think he had too much to eat, sir?"

"No," I said. "It wasn't that. He was lonely, that's all. He didn't belong here, among us."

"But you said he had broken away from that group-mind," Willendorf objected.

I shook my head. "Not really. That group-mind arose out of some deep psychological and physiological needs of those people. You can't just declare your independence and be able to exist as an individual from then on if you're part of that group-entity. Alaree had grasped the concept intellectually, to some extent, but he wasn't suited for life away from the corporate mind, no matter how much he wanted to be."

"He couldn't stand alone?"

"Not after his people had evolved that gestalt setup. He learned independence from us," I said. "But he couldn't live with us, really. He needed to be part of a whole. He found out his mistake after he came aboard and tried to remedy things."

I saw Willendorf pale. "What do you mean, sir?"

"You know what I mean. When he came up to us and stared soulfully into our eyes. *He was trying to form a new gestalt—out of us!* Somehow he was trying to link us together, the way his people had been linked."

"He couldn't do it, though," Willendorf said fervently.

"Of course not. Human beings don't have whatever need it is that forced those people to merge. He found that out, after a while, when he failed to get anywhere with us."

"He just couldn't do it," Willendorf repeated.

"No. And then he ran out of strength," I said somberly, feeling the heavy weight of my guilt. "He was like an organ removed from a living body. It can exist for a little while by itself, but not indefinitely. He failed to find a new source of life—and he died." I stared bitterly at my fingertips.

"What do we call it in my medical report?" asked Ship Surgeon Thomas, who had been silent up till then. "How can we explain what he died from?"

"Call it—*malnutrition*," I said.

THE ARTIFACT BUSINESS

I can't remember a time when I wasn't interested in ancient civilizations and their artifacts. From childhood on I haunted the museums of New York City, at first primarily to see the dinosaurs, and then, a little later, to stare at the Sumerian and Babylonian and Egyptian relics, the Roman mosaics, the Mexican codices, the Pueblo pots. I dreamed of visiting the ruins of the lost cultures that had produced those artifacts—and, as soon as I was able to do it, off I went, year after year, to Pompeii and Chichen Itza and Rome and the Pueblo country. The distant past had the same sort of appeal for me that the distant future did; and for a considerable period of my writing career—the decade from 1961 to 1970—I was more prolific in the field of archaeological popularizations than I was as a science-fiction writer.

The story here, which reflects this early and lifelong interest in archaeology, is one that I wrote in May, 1956, during my senior year at Columbia. It wandered around unsuccessfully to several of the top-paying magazines and eventually was bought by the gentle, somewhat bumbling Hans Stefan Santesson, who had just become editor of Leo Margulies' Fantastic Universe *and who had a considerable interest in archaeology himself. Hans ran it in his April, 1957 issue.*

The Voltuscian was a small, withered humanoid whose crimson throat-appendages quivered nervously, as if the thought of doing archaeological fieldwork excited him unbearably. He gestured to me anxiously with one of his four crooked arms, urging me onward over the level silt.

"This way, friend. Over here is the Emperor's grave."

"I'm coming, Dolbak." I trudged forward, feeling the weight of the spade and the knapsack over my shoulder. I caught up with him a few moments later.

He was standing near a rounded hump in the ground, pointing downward. "This is it," he said happily. "I have saved it for you."

I fished in my pocket, pulled out a tinkling heap of arrow-shaped coins, and handed him one. The Voltuscian, nodding his thanks effusively, ran around behind me to help me unload.

Taking the spade from him, I thrust it into the ground and began to dig. The thrill of discovery started to tingle in me, as it does always when I begin a new excavation. I suppose that is the archaeologist's greatest joy, that moment of apprehension as the spade first bites into the ground. I dug rapidly and smoothly, following Dolbak's guidance.

✺

"There it is," he said reverently. "And a beauty it is, too. Oh, Jarrell-sir, how happy I am for you!"

I leaned on my spade to recover my wind before bending to look. I mopped away beads of perspiration, and thought of the great Schliemann laboring in the stifling heat of Hissarlik to uncover the ruins of Troy. Schliemann has long been one of my heroes—along with the other archaeologists who did the pioneer work in the fertile soil of Mother Earth.

Wearily, I stooped to one knee and fumbled in the fine sand of the Voltuscian plain, groping for the bright object that lay revealed. I worked it loose from its covering of silt and studied it.

"Amulet," I said after a while. "Third Period; unspecified protective charm. Studded with emerald-cut gobrovirs of the finest water." The analysis complete, I turned to Dolbak and grasped his hand warmly. "How can I thank you, Dolbak?"

He shrugged. "Not necessary." Glancing at the amulet, he said, "It will fetch a high price. Some woman of Earth will wear it proudly."

"Ah—yes," I said, a trifle bitterly. Dolbak had touched on the source of my deep frustration and sorrow.

This perversion of archaeology into a source for trinkets and bits of frippery to adorn rich men's homes and wives had always rankled me. Although I have never seen Earth, I like to believe I work in the great tradition of Schliemann and Evans, whose greatest finds were to be seen in the galleries of the British Museum and the Ashmolean, not dangling on the painted bosom of some too-rich wench who has succumbed to the current passion for antiquity.

When the Revival came, when everyone's interest suddenly turned on the ancient world and the treasures that lay in the ground, I felt deep satisfaction—my chosen profession, I thought, now was one that had value to society as well as private worth. How wrong I was! I took this job in the hope that it would provide me with the needed cash to bring me to Earth—but instead I became nothing more than the hired lackey of a dealer in women's fashions, and Earth's unreachable museums lie inch-deep in dust.

I sighed and returned my attention to the excavation. The amulet lay there, flawless in its perfection, a marvelous relic of the great race that once inhabited Voltus. Masking my sadness, I reached down with both hands and lovingly plucked the amulet from the grave in which it had rested so many thousands of years.

I felt a sudden impulse to tip Dolbak again. The withered alien accepted the coins gratefully, but with a certain reserve that made me feel that perhaps this whole business seemed as sordid to him as it did to me.

"It's been a good day's work," I told him. "Let's go back, now. We'll get this assayed and I'll give you your commission, eh, old fellow?"

"That will be very good, sir," he said mildly, and assisted me in donning my gear once again.

We crossed the plain and entered the Terran outpost in silence. As we made our way through the winding streets to the assay office, hordes of the four-armed, purple-hued Voltuscian children approached us clamorously, offering us things for sale, things they had made themselves. Some of their work was quite lovely; the Voltuscians seem to have a remarkable aptitude for handicrafting. But I brushed them all away. I have made it a rule to ignore them, no matter how delightful a spun-glass fingerbowl they may have, how airy and delicate an ivory carving. Such things, being contemporary, have no market value on Earth, and a man of my limited means must avoid luxuries of this sort.

The assay office was still open, and, as we approached, I saw two or three men standing outside, each with his Voltuscian guide.

"Hello, Jarrell," said a tall man raucously.

I winced. He was David Sturges, one of the least scrupulous of the many Company archaeologists on Voltus—a man who thought nothing of breaking into the most sacred shrines of the planet and committing irreparable damage for the sake of ripping loose a single marketable item.

"Hello, Sturges," I said shortly.

"Have a good day, old man? Find anything worth poisoning you for?"

I grinned feebly and nodded. "Nice amulet of the Third Period. I'm planning on handing it in immediately, but if you prefer I won't. I'll take it home and leave it on my table tonight. That way you won't wreck the place looking for it."

"Oh, that won't be necessary," Sturges said. "I came up with a neat cache of enameled skulls today—a dozen, of the Expansion Era, set with platinum scrollwork." He pointed to his alien guide, a dour-looking Voltuscian named Qabur. "My boy found them for me. Wonderful fellow, Qabur. He can home in on a cache as if he's got radar in his nose."

I began to frame a reply in praise of my own guide when Zweig, the assayer, stepped to the front of his office and looked out. "Well, who's next? You, Jarrell?"

"Yes, sir." I picked up my spade and followed him inside. He slouched behind his desk and looked up wearily.

"What do you have to report, Jarrell?"

I drew the amulet out of my knapsack and handed it across the desk. He examined it studiously, noticing the way the light glinted off the facets of the inset gobrovirs. "Not bad," he said.

"It's a rather fine piece, isn't it?"

"Not bad," he repeated. "Seventy-five dollars, I'd say."

"*What?* I'd figured that piece for at least five hundred! Come on, Zweig, be reasonable. Look at the quality of those gobrovirs!"

"Very nice," he admitted. "But you have to understand that the gobrovir, while attractive, is intrinsically not a very valuable gem. And I must consider the intrinsic value as well as the historical, you know."

I frowned. Now would come the long speech about supply and demand, the scarcity of gems, the cost of shipping the amulet back to Earth, marketing, on and on, on and on. I spoke before he had the chance. "I won't haggle, Zweig. Give me a hundred and fifty or I'll keep the thing myself."

He grinned slyly. "What would you do with it? Donate it to the British Museum?"

The remark stung. I looked at him sadly, and he said, "I'll give you a hundred."

"Hundred and fifty or I keep."

He reached down and scooped ten ten-dollar pieces from a drawer. He spread them out along his desk. "There's the offer," he said. "It's the best the Company can do."

I stared at him for an agonized moment, scowled, took the ten tens, and handed over the amulet. "Here. You can give me thirty pieces of silver for the next one I bring in."

"Don't make it hard for me, Jarrell. This is only my job."

I threw one of the tens to the waiting Dolbak, nodded curtly, and walked out.

I returned to my meager dwelling on the outskirts of the Terran colony in a state of deep dejection. Each time I handed an artifact over to Zweig—and, in the course of the eighteen months since I had accepted this accursed job, I had handed over quite a few—I felt, indeed, a Judas. When I thought of the long row of glass cases my discoveries might have filled, in, say, the Voltus Room of the British, I ached. The crystal shields with double handgrips; the tooth-wedges of finest obsidian; the sculptured ear-binders with their unbelievable filigree of sprockets—these were products of one of the most fertile creative civilizations of all, the Old Voltuscians—and these treasures were being scattered to the corners of the galaxy as trinkets.

The amulet today—what had I done with it? Turned it over to—to a *procurer,* virtually, to ship back to Earth for sale to the highest bidder.

I glanced around my room. Small, uncluttered, with not an artifact of my own in it. I had passed every treasure across the desk to Zweig; I had no wish to retain any for myself. I sensed that the antiquarian urge was dying in me, choked to death by the wild commercialism that entangled me from the moment I signed the contract with the Company.

I picked up a book—Evans, *The Palace of Minos*—and looked at it balefully for a moment before replacing it on the shelf. My eyes throbbed from the day's anguish; I felt dried out and very tired.

Someone knocked at the door—timidly at first, then more boldly.

"Come in," I said.

The door opened slowly and a small Voltuscian stepped in. I recognized him—he was an unemployed guide, too unreliable to be trusted. "What do you want, Kushkak?" I asked wearily.

"Sir? Jarrell-sir?"

"Yes?"

"Do you need a boy, sir? I can show you the best treasures, sir. Only the best—the kind you get good price for."

"I have a guide already," I told him. "Dolbak. I don't need another, thanks."

The alien seemed to wrinkle in on himself. He hugged his lower arms to his sides unhappily. "Then I am sorry I disturbed you, Jarrell-sir. Sorry. Very sorry."

I watched him back out despairingly. All of these Voltuscians seemed to me like withered old men, even the young ones. They were an utterly decadent race, with barely a shred of the grandeur they must have had in the days when the great artifacts were being produced. It was odd, I thought, that a race should shrivel so in the course of a few thousand years.

I sank into an uneasy repose in my big chair. About half past twenty-three, another knock sounded.

"Come in," I said, a little startled.

The gaunt figure of George Darby stepped through the door. Darby was an archaeologist who shared many of my ideals, shared my passionate desire to see Earth, shared my distaste for the bondage into which we had sold ourselves.

"What brings you here so late, George?" I asked, adding the conventional "And how was your trip today?"

"My trip? Oh, my trip!" He seemed strangely excited. "Yes, my trip. You know my boy Kushkak?"

1 nodded. "He was just here looking for a job. I didn't know he'd been working with you."

"Just for a couple of days," Darby said. "He agreed to work for five per cent, so I took him on."

I made no comment. I knew how things could pinch.

"He was here, eh?" Darby frowned. "You didn't hire him, did you?"

"Of course not!" I said.

"Well, I did. But yesterday he led me in circles for five hours before admitting he didn't really have any sites in mind, so I canned him. And that's why I'm here."

"Why? Who'd you go out with today?"

"No one," Darby said bluntly. "I went out alone." For the first time, I noticed that his fingers were quivering, and in the dreary half-light of my room his face looked pale and drawn.

"You went out alone?" I repeated. "Without a guide?"

Darby nodded, running a finger nervously through his unruly white forelock. "It was half out of necessity—I couldn't find another boy in time—and half because I wanted to strike out on my own. The guides have a way of taking you to the same area of the Burial Ground, all the time, you know. I headed in the other direction. Alone."

He fell silent for a moment. I wondered what it was that troubled him so.

After a pause he said, "Help me off with my knapsack."

I eased the straps from his shoulders and lowered the grey canvas bag to a chair. He undid the rusted clasps, reached in, and tenderly drew something out. "Here," he said. "What do you make of this, Jarrell?"

I took it from him with greet care and examined it closely. It was a bowl, scooped by hand out of some muddy-looking black clay. Fingermarks stood out raggedly, and the bowl was unevenly shaped and awkward-looking. It was an extremely uncouth job.

"What is it?" I asked. "Prehistoric, no doubt."

Darby smiled unhappily. "You think so, Jarrell?"

"It must be," I said. "Look at it—I'd say it was made by a child, if it weren't for the size of these fingerprints in the clay. It's very ancient or else the work of an idiot."

He nodded. "A logical attitude. Only—I found this in the stratum *below* the bowl." And he handed me a gilded tooth-wedge in Third Period style.

"This was below the bowl?" I asked, confused. "The bowl is more recent than the tooth-wedge, you're saying?"

"Yes," he said quietly. He knotted his hands together. "Jarrell, here's my conjecture, and you can take it for as much as you think it's worth. Let's discount the possibility that the bowl was made by an idiot; and let's not consider the chance that it might be a representative of a decadent period in Voltuscian pottery that we know nothing about.

"What I propose," he said, measuring his words carefully, "is that the bowl dates from classical antiquity—three thousand years back, or so. And that the tooth-wedge you're admiring so is perhaps a year old, maybe two at the outside."

I nearly dropped the tooth-wedge at that. "Are you saying that the. Voltuscians are hoaxing us?"

"I'm saying just that," Darby replied. "I'm saying that in those huts of theirs—those huts that are taboo for us to enter—they're busy turning out antiquities by the drove, and planting them in proper places where we can find them and dig them up."

It was an appalling concept. "What are you going to do?" I asked. "What proof do you have?"

"None, yet. But I'll get it. I'm going to unmask the whole filthy thing," Darby said vigorously. "I intend to hunt down Kushkak and throttle the truth out of him, and let the universe know that the Voltuscian artifacts are frauds, that the real Old Voltuscian artifacts are muddy, ugly things of no aesthetic value and of no interest to—anyone—but—us—archaeologists," he finished bitterly.

"Bravo, George!" I applauded. "Unmask it, by all means. Let the greasy philistines who have overpaid for these pieces find out that they're *not* ancient, that they're as modern as the radiothermal stoves in their overfurnished kitchens. That'll sicken 'em—since they won't touch anything that's been in the ground less than a few millennia, ever since this revival got under way."

"Exactly," Darby said. I sensed the note of triumph in his voice. "I'll go out and find Kushkak now. He's just desperate enough to speak up. Care to come along?"

"No—no," I said quickly. I shun violence of any sort. "I've got some letters to write. You take care of it."

He packed his two artifacts up again, rose, and left. I watched him from my window as he headed across the unpaved streets to the liquor-dispensary where Kushkak was usually to be found. He entered—and a few minutes later I heard the sound of voices shouting in the night.

The news broke the next morning, and by noon the village was in a turmoil.

Kushkak, taken unawares, had exposed all. The Voltuscians—brilliant handicrafters, as everyone knew—had attempted to sell their work to the wealthy of Earth for years, but there had been no market. "Contemporary? Pah!" What the customers wanted was *antiquity*.

Unable to market work that was labeled as their own, the Voltuscians had obligingly shifted to the manufacture of antiquities, since their ancestors had been thoughtless enough not to leave them anything more marketable than crude clay pots. Creating a self-consistent ancient history that would appeal to the imaginations of Earthmen was difficult, but they rose to the challenge and developed one to rank with those of Egypt and Babylonia and the other fabled cultures of Earth. After that, it was a simple matter of designing and executing the artifacts.

Then they were buried in the appropriate strata. This was a difficult feat, but the Voltuscians managed it with ease, restoring the disrupted strata afterwards with the same skill for detail as they employed in creating the artifacts. The pasture thus readied, they led the herd to feast.

I looked at the scrawny Voltuscians with new respect in my eyes. Obviously they must have mastered the techniques of archaeology before inaugurating their hoax, else they would never have handled the strata relationships so well. They had carried the affair off flawlessly— until the day when one of the Earthmen had unkindly disinterred a real Voltuscian artifact.

Conditions were still chaotic when I entered the square in front of the assay office later that afternoon. Earthmen and Voltuscians milled aimlessly around, not knowing what to do next or where to go.

I picked up a rumor that Zweig was dead by his own hand, but this was promptly squelched by the appearance of the assayer in person, looking rather dreadfully upset but still living. He came to the front of the office and hung up a hastily-scrawled card. It read:

NO BUSINESS TRANSACTED TODAY

I saw Dolbak go wandering by and called to him. "I'm ready to go out," I said innocently.

He looked at me, pity in his lidless eyes. "Sir, haven't you heard? There will be no more trips to the Burial Grounds."

"Oh? This thing is true, then?"

"Yes," he said sadly. "It's true."

Obviously he couldn't bear to talk further. He moved on, and I spotted Darby.

"You seem to have been right," I told him. "The whole business has fallen apart."

"Of course. Once they were confronted with Kushkak's story, they saw the game was up. They're too fundamentally honest to try to maintain the pretense in the face of our accusation."

"It's too bad, in a way," I said. "Those things they turned out *were* lovely, you know."

"And the Piltdown Man had an interesting jawbone, too," Darby retorted hotly.

"Still," I said, "it's not as if the Voltuscians were being malicious about it. Our peculiarities of taste made it impossible for them to sell their goods honestly—so it was either do it dishonestly or starve. Weren't we caught in something of the same trap when we agreed to join the Company?"

"You're right there," Darby admitted reluctantly. "But—"

"Just a second, friend," said a deep voice from behind us. We turned to see David Sturges glaring at us bitterly.

"What do you want?" Darby asked.

"I want to know why you couldn't keep your mouth shut," said Sturges. "Why'd you have to ruin this nice setup for us? What difference did it make if the artifacts were the real thing or not? As long as the people on Earth were willing to lay down real cash for them, why rock the boat?"

Darby sputtered impotently at the bigger man, but said nothing.

"You've wrecked the whole works," Sturges went on. "What do you figure to do for a living now? Can you afford to go to some other planet?"

"I did what was right," Darby said.

Sturges snorted derisively and walked away. I looked at Darby. "He's got a point, you know. We're going to have to go to another planet now. Voltus isn't worth a damn. You've succeeded in uprooting us and finishing the Voltuscian economy at the same time. Maybe you should have kept quiet."

He looked at me stonily for a moment. "Jarrell, I think I've overestimated you," he said.

A ship came for Zweig the next day, and the assay office closed down permanently. The Company wouldn't touch Voltus again. The crew of the ship went rapidly through the Terran outpost distributing leaflets that informed us that the Company still required our services and could use us on other planets—provided we paid our own fares.

That was the catch. None of us had saved enough, out of the fees we had received from the Company, to get off Voltus. It had been the dream of all of us to see Earth someday, to explore the world from which our parent stock sprang—but it had been a fool's dream. At Company rates, we could never save enough to leave.

1 began to see that perhaps Darby had done wrong in exposing the hoax. It certainly didn't help us, and it was virtually the end of the world for the natives. In one swoop, a boundless source of income was cut off and their precarious economy totally wrecked. They moved silently through the quiet streets, and any day I expected to see the vultures perch on the rooftops. Honesty had been the worst policy, it seemed.

Three days after the bubble burst, a native boy brought me a note. It was from David Sturges, and it said, briefly, "There will be a meeting at my flat tonight at 1900. Sturges."

When I arrived, I saw that the entire little colony of Company archaeologists was there—even Darby, who ordinarily would have nothing to do with Sturges.

"Good evening, Jarrell," Sturges said politely as I entered. "I think everyone's here now, and so we can begin." He cleared his throat.

"Gentlemen, some of you have accused me of being unethical," he said. "Even dishonest. You needn't deny it. I *have* been unethical. However," he said, frowning, "I find myself caught in the same disaster that has overtaken all of you, and just as unable to extricate myself. Therefore, I'd like to make a small suggestion. Accepting it will involve use of some of the—ah—moral flexibility you decry."

"What's on your mind, Sturges?" someone said impatiently.

"This morning," he said, "one of the aliens came to me with an idea. It's a good one. Briefly, he suggested that, as expert archaeologists, we teach the Voltuscians how to manufacture *Terran* artifacts. There's no more market for anything from Voltus—but why not continue to take advantage of the skills of the Voltuscians as long as the market's open for things of Earth? We could smuggle the artifacts to Earth, plant them, have them dug up again and sold there—and we'd make the entire profit, not just the miserable fee the Company allows us!"

"It's shady, Sturges," Darby said hoarsely. "I don't like the idea."

"How do you like the idea of starving?" Sturges retorted. "We'll rot on Voltus unless we use our wits."

I stood up. "Perhaps I can make things clearer to Dr. Darby," I said. "George, we're caught in a cleft stick and all we can do is try to wriggle. We can't get off Voltus, and we can't stay here. If we accept Sturges' plan, we'll build up a cash reserve in a short time. We'll be free to move on!"

Darby remained unconvinced. He shook his head. "I can't condone counterfeiting Terran artifacts. No—if you try it, I'll expose you!"

A stunned silence fell over the room at the threat. Sturges glanced appealingly at me, and I moistened my lips. "You don't seem to understand, George. Once we have this new plan working, it'll spur genuine archaeology. Look—we dig up half a dozen phoney scarabs in the Nile Valley. People buy them—and we keep on digging, with the profits we make. Earth experiences a sudden interest; there's a rebirth of archaeology. We dig up *real* scarabs."

His eyes brightened, but I could see he was still unpersuaded. I added my clincher.

"Besides, George, someone will have to go to Earth to supervise this project." I looked around the room. "We'll have to pool our cash, won't we, to get a man down there?"

I paused, caught Sturges' silent approval. "I think," I said sonorously, "that it is the unanimous decision of this assembly that we nominate our greatest expert on Terran antiquity to handle the job on Earth—Dr. George Darby."

I didn't think he would be able to resist that. I was right. Suddenly, Darby stopped objecting.

Six months later, an archaeologist working near Gizeh turned up a scarab of lovely design, finely-worked and inlaid with strange jewels.

In a paper published in an obscure journal to which most of us subscribe, he conjectured that this find represented an outcrop of a hitherto-unknown area of Egyptology. He also sold the scarab to a jewelry syndicate for a staggering sum, and used the proceeds to finance an extensive exploration of the entire Nile Valley, something that hadn't been done since the decline of archaeology more than a century earlier.

Shortly afterwards, a student working in Greece came up with a remarkable Homeric shield. Glazed pottery reached the light in Syria, and Scythian metalwork was exhumed in the wilds of the Caucasus. What had been a science as dead as alchemy suddenly blossomed into new life; the people of Earth discovered that their own world contained riches as desirable as those on Voltus and Dariak and the other planets the Company had been mining for gewgaws, and that they were somewhat less costly in the bargain.

The Voltuscian workshops are now going full blast, and the only limitation on our volume is the difficulty of smuggling the things to Earth and planting them. We're doing quite well financially, thank you. Darby, who's handling the job brilliantly on Earth, sends us a fat check every month, which we divide equally among ourselves after paying the happy Voltuscians.

Occasionally I feel regret that it was Darby and not myself who won the coveted job of going to Earth, but I reconcile myself with the awareness that there was no other way to gain Darby's sympathies. I've learned things about ends and means. Soon, we'll all be rich enough to travel to Earth, if we want to.

But I'm not so sure I *do* want to go. There was a *genuine* Voltuscian antiquity, you know, and I've become as interested in that as I am in that of Greece and Rome. I see an opportunity to do some pure archaeology in a virgin field of research.

So perhaps I'll stay here after all. I'm thinking of writing a book on Voltuscian artifacts—the *real* ones, I mean, all crude things of no commercial value whatever. And tomorrow I'm going to show Dolbak how to make Mexican pottery of the Chichimec period. It's attractive stuff. I think there ought to be a good market for it.

COLLECTING TEAM

June of 1956: the new college graduate, in his first official month as a full-time professional writer, turns out no less than eighteen stories plus two small nonfiction pieces—an average of just about one a day, considering that I always took Saturdays and Sundays off—and sells them all, to John Campbell's Astounding, *to Bob Lowndes'* Science Fiction Stories, *to William L. Hamling's* Imagination, *to Howard Browne's* Amazing Stories *and* Fantastic, *to all sorts of markets, up and down the science-fiction field and outside it as well. It is a harbinger: for years to come I will work with lunatic prolificity and not see anything at all unusual about writing two or three stories a week or even more. And, with a new apartment to furnish and rent to pay, I'll take whatever work I can get, any kind of writing assignment—and will deliver promptly and to the proper length.*

Another young writer who was living the same sort of life in New York City just then was Harlan Ellison; but he was having better luck with the mystery and crime magazines than he was at science fiction, in particular with a couple of titles called Trapped *and* Guilty. *The editor of those magazines, an amiable codger named W. W. Scott, was particularly taken not only by Harlan's writing talent but by the formidable energy with which he conducted his lively onslaught on the New York publishing world. Since Scottie, as Harlan called him—he called himself "Bill"—needed more stories for the crime magazines than even the manic Ellison could produce, Harlan brought me in as a fellow contributor: my ledger for June, 1956 shows two short crime stories sold to the Scott magazines, "Clinging Vine" and "Get Out and Stay Out," the first of dozens over the next few years.*

Then came the delicious news that Scottie was going to be editing a sci-ence-fiction magazine, too—Super-Science Fiction. (The title had already been used, for a magazine once edited by the likes of Frederik Pohl and Damon Knight, but nobody worried about that.) Scottie needed copy in a hurry for the first issue, dated December, 1956: Harlan wrote one called "Why Did Wallace Crack?" which came out as "Psycho at Mid-Point," and I turned in "Collecting Team," which Scottie retitled "Catch 'Em All Alive."

It's had quite a life, for a story turned out at white heat to meet an instant deadline. I don't have an accurate count of the number of times it's been reprinted—mainly in classroom anthologies with names like Contexts and Elements of Literature—but the number must be well up toward twenty, and hardly a year goes by without some new request to use it. I was simply trying to pay the rent when I wrote it; but this one has gone on paying for things for me for half a century. I wish I knew its secret.

From fifty thousand miles up, the situation looked promising. It was a middle-sized, brown-and-green, inviting-looking planet, with no sign of cities or any other such complications. Just a pleasant sort of place, the very sort we were looking for to redeem what had been a pretty futile expedition.

I turned to Clyde Holdreth, who was staring reflectively at the ther-mocouple.

"Well? What do you think?"

"Looks fine to me. Temperature's about seventy down there—nice and warm, and plenty of air. I think it's worth a try."

Lee Davison came strolling out from the storage hold, smelling of animals, as usual. He was holding one of the blue monkeys we picked up on Alpheraz, and the little beast was crawling up his arm. "Have we found something, gentlemen?"

"We've found a planet," I said. "How's the storage space in the hold?"

"Don't worry about that. We've got room for a whole zoo-full more, before we get filled up. It hasn't been a very fruitful trip."

"No," I agreed. "It hasn't. Well? Shall we go down and see what's to be seen?"

"Might as well," Holdreth said. "We can't go back to Earth with just a couple of blue monkeys and some anteaters, you know."

"I'm in favor of a landing too," said Davison. "You?"

I nodded. "I'll set up the charts, and you get your animals comfortable for deceleration."

Davison disappeared back into the storage hold, while Holdreth scribbled furiously in the logbook, writing down the coordinates of the planet below, its general description, and so forth. Aside from being a collecting team for the zoological department of the Bureau of Interstellar Affairs, we also double as a survey ship, and the planet down below was listed as *unexplored* on our charts.

I glanced out at the mottled brown-and-green ball spinning slowly in the viewport, and felt the warning twinge of gloom that came to me every time we made a landing on a new and strange world. Repressing it, I started to figure out a landing orbit. From behind me came the furious chatter of the blue monkeys as Davison strapped them into their acceleration cradles, and under that the deep, unmusical honking of the Rigelian anteaters noisily bleating their displeasure.

The planet was inhabited, all right. We hadn't had the ship on the ground more than a minute before the local fauna began to congregate. We stood at the viewport and looked out in wonder.

"This is one of those things you dream about," Davison said, stroking his little beard nervously. "Look at them! There must be a thousand different species out there."

"I've never seen anything like it," said Holdreth.

I computed how much storage space we had left and how many of the thronging creatures outside we would be able to bring back with us. "How are we going to decide what to take and what to leave behind?"

"Does it matter?" Holdreth said gaily. "This is what you call an embarrassment of riches, I guess. We just grab the dozen most bizarre creatures and blast-off—and save the rest for another trip. It's too bad we wasted all that time wandering around near Rigel."

"We *did* get the anteaters," Davison pointed out. They were his finds, and he was proud of them.

I smiled sourly. "Yeah. We got the anteaters there." The anteaters honked at that moment, loud and clear. "You know, that's one set of beasts I think I could do without."

"Bad attitude," Holdreth said. "Unprofessional."

"Whoever said I was a zoologist, anyway? I'm just a spaceship pilot, remember. And if I don't like the way those anteaters talk—and smell—I see no reason why I—"

"Say, look at that one," Davison said suddenly.

I glanced out the viewport and saw a new beast emerging from the thick-packed vegetation in the background. I've seen some fairly strange creatures since I was assigned to the zoological department, but this one took the grand prize.

It was about the size of a giraffe, moving on long, wobbly legs and with a tiny head up at the end of a preposterous neck. Only it had six legs and a bunch of writhing snakelike tentacles as well, and its eyes, great violet globes, stood out nakedly on the ends of two thick stalks. It must have been twenty feet high. It moved with exaggerated grace through the swarm of beasts surrounding our ship, pushed its way smoothly towards the vessel, and peered gravely in at the viewport. One purple eye stared directly at me, the other at Davison. Oddly, it seemed to me as if it were trying to tell us something.

"Big one, isn't it?" Davison said finally.

"I'll bet you'd like to bring one back, too."

"Maybe we can fit a young one aboard," Davison said. "If we can find a young one." He turned to Holdreth. "How's that air analysis coming? I'd like to get out there and start collecting. God, that's a crazy-looking beast!"

The animal outside had apparently finished its inspection of us, for it pulled its head away and, gathering its legs under itself, squatted near the ship. A small doglike creature with stiff spines running along its back began to bark at the big creature, which took no notice. The other animals, which came in all shapes and sizes, continued to mill around the ship, evidently very curious about the newcomer to their world. I could see Davison's eyes thirsty with the desire to take the whole kit and caboodle back to Earth with him. I knew what was running through his mind. He was dreaming of the umpteen thousand species of extraterrestrial wildlife roaming around out there, and to each one he was attaching a neat little tag: *Something-or-other davisoni.*

"The air's fine," Holdreth announced abruptly, looking up from his test-tubes. "Get your butterfly nets and let's see what we can catch."

There was something I didn't like about the place. It was just too good to be true, and I learned long ago that nothing ever is. There's always a catch someplace.

Only this seemed to be on the level. The planet was a bonanza for zoologists, and Davison and Holdreth were having the time of their lives, hipdeep in obliging specimens.

"I've never seen anything like it," Davison said for at least the fiftieth time, as he scooped up a small purplish squirrel-like creature and examined it curiously. The squirrel stared back, examining Davison just as curiously.

"Let's take some of these," Davison said. "I like them."

"Carry 'em on in, then," I said, shrugging. I didn't care which specimens they chose, so long as they filled up the storage hold quickly and let me blast off on schedule. I watched as Davison grabbed a pair of the squirrels and brought them into the ship.

Holdreth came over to me. He was carrying a sort of a dog with insect-faceted eyes and gleaming furless skin. "How's this one, Gus?"

"Fine," I said bleakly. "Wonderful."

He put the animal down—it didn't scamper away, just sat there smiling at us—and looked at me. He ran a hand through his fast-vanishing hair. "Listen, Gus, you've been gloomy all day. What's eating you?"

"I don't like this place," I said.

"Why? Just on general principles?"

"It's too *easy*, Clyde. Much too easy. These animals just flock around here waiting to be picked up."

Holdreth chuckled. "And you're used to a struggle, aren't you? You're just angry at us because we have it so simple here!"

"When I think of the trouble we went through just to get a pair of miserable vile-smelling anteaters, and—"

"Come off it, Gus. We'll load up in a hurry, if you like. But this place is a zoological gold mine!"

I shook my head. "I don't like it, Clyde. Not at all."

Holdreth laughed again and picked up his faceted-eyed dog. "Say, know where I can find another of these, Gus?"

"Right over there." I said, pointing. "By that tree. With its tongue hanging out. It's just waiting to be carried away."

Holdreth looked and smiled. "What do you know about that!" He snared his specimen and carried both of them inside.

I walked away to survey the grounds. The planet was too flatly incredible for me to accept on face value, without at least a look-see, despite the blithe way my two companions were snapping up specimens.

For one thing, animals just don't exist this way—in big miscellaneous quantities, living all together happily. I hadn't noticed more than a few of each kind, and there must have been five hundred different species, each one stranger-looking than the next. Nature doesn't work that way.

For another, they all seemed to be on friendly terms with one another, though they acknowledged the unofficial leadership of the giraffe-like creature. Nature doesn't work that way, either. I hadn't seen one quarrel between the animals yet. That argued that they were all herbivores, which didn't make sense ecologically.

I shrugged my shoulders and walked on.

Half an hour later, I knew a little more about the geography of our bonanza. We were on either an immense island or a peninsula of some sort, because I could see a huge body of water bordering the land some ten miles off. Our vicinity was fairly flat, except for a good-sized hill from which I could see the terrain.

There was a thick, heavily-wooded jungle not too far from the ship. The forest spread out all the way towards the water in one direction, but ended abruptly in the other. We had brought the ship down right at the edge of the clearing. Apparently most of the animals we saw lived in the jungle.

On the other side of our clearing was a low, broad plain that seemed to trail away into a desert in the distance; I could see an uninviting stretch of barren sand that contrasted strangely with the fertile jungle to my left. There was a small lake to the side. It was, I saw, the sort of country likely to attract a varied fauna, since there seemed to be every sort of habitat within a small area.

And the fauna! Although I'm a zoologist only by osmosis, picking up both my interest and my knowledge second-hand from Holdreth and Davison, I couldn't help but be astonished by the wealth of strange animals. They came in all different shapes and sizes, colors and odors, and the only thing they all had in common was their friendliness. During the course of my afternoon's wanderings a hundred animals must have come marching boldly right up to me, given me the once-over, and walked away. This included half a dozen kinds that I hadn't seen before, plus one of the eye-stalked, intelligent-looking giraffes and a furless dog. Again, I had the feeling that the giraffe seemed to be trying to communicate.

I didn't like it, I didn't like it at all.

I returned to our clearing, and saw Holdreth and Davison still buzzing madly around, trying to cram as many animals as they could into our hold.

"How's it going?" I asked.

"Hold's all full," Davison said. "We're busy making our alternate selections now." I saw him carrying out Holdreth's two furless dogs and picking up instead a pair of eight-legged penguinish things that uncomplainingly allowed themselves to be carried in. Holdreth was frowning unhappily.

"What do you want *those* for, Lee? Those dog-like ones seem much more interesting, don't you think?"

"No," Davison said. "I'd rather bring along these two. They're curious beasts, aren't they? Look at the muscular network that connects the—"

"Hold it, fellows," I said. I peered at the animal in Davison's hands and glanced up. "This *is* a curious beast," I said. "It's got eight legs."

"You becoming a zoologist?" Holdreth asked, amused.

"No—but I am getting puzzled. Why should this one have eight legs, some of the others here six, and some of the others only four?"

They looked at me blankly, with the scorn of professionals.

"I mean, there ought to be some sort of logic to evolution here, shouldn't there? On Earth we've developed a four-legged pattern of animal life; on Venus, they usually run to six legs. But have you ever seen an evolutionary hodgepodge like this place before?"

"There are stranger setups," Holdreth said. "The symbiotes on Sirius Three, the burrowers of Mizar—but you're right, Gus. This *is* a peculiar evolutionary dispersal. I think we ought to stay and investigate it fully."

Instantly I knew from the bright expression on Davison's face that I had blundered, had made things worse than ever. I decided to take a new tack.

"I don't agree," I said. "I think we ought to leave with what we've got, and come back with a larger expedition later."

Davison chuckled. "Come on, Gus, don't be silly! This is a chance of a lifetime for us—why should we call in the whole zoological department on it?"

I didn't want to tell them I was afraid of staying longer. I crossed my arms. "Lee, I'm the pilot of this ship, and you'll have to listen to me. The schedule calls for a brief stopover here, and we have to leave. Don't tell me I'm being silly."

"But you are, man! You're standing blindly in the path of scientific investigation, of—"

"Listen to me, Lee. Our food is calculated on a pretty narrow margin, to allow you fellows more room for storage. And this is strictly a collecting team. There's no provision for extended stays on any one planet. Unless you want to wind up eating your own specimens, I suggest you allow us to get out of here."

They were silent for a moment. Then Holdreth said, "I guess we can't argue with that, Lee. Let's listen to Gus and go back now. There's plenty of time to investigate this place later when we can take longer."

"But—oh, all right," Davison said reluctantly. He picked up the eight-legged penguins. "Let me stash these things in the hold, and we can leave." He looked strangely at me, as if I had done something criminal.

As he started into the ship, I called to him.

"What is it, Gus?"

"Look here, Lee. I don't *want* to pull you away from here. It's simply a matter of food," I lied, masking my nebulous suspicions.

"I know how it is, Gus." He turned and entered the ship.

I stood there thinking about nothing at all for a moment, then went inside myself to begin setting up the blastoff orbit.

I got as far as calculating the fuel expenditure when I noticed something. Feedwires were dangling crazily down from the control cabinet. Somebody had wrecked our drive mechanism, but thoroughly.

For a long moment, I stared stiffly at the sabotaged drive. Then I turned and headed into the storage hold.

"Davison?"

"What is it, Gus?"

"Come out here a second, will you?"

I waited, and a few minutes later he appeared, frowning impatiently. "What do you want, Gus? I'm busy and I—" His mouth dropped open. *"Look at the drive!"*

"You look at it," I snapped. "I'm sick. Go get Holdreth, on the double."

While he was gone I tinkered with the shattered mechanism. Once I had the cabinet panel off and could see the inside, I felt a little better; the drive wasn't damaged beyond repair, though it had been pretty well scrambled. Three or four days of hard work with a screwdriver and solderbeam might get the ship back into functioning order.

But that didn't make me any less angry. I heard Holdreth and Davison entering behind me, and I whirled to face them.

"All right, you idiots. Which one of you did this?"

They opened their mouths in protesting squawks at the same instant. I listened to them for a while, then said, "One at a time!"

"If you're implying that one of us deliberately sabotaged the ship," Holdreth said, "I want you to know—"

"I'm not implying anything. But the way it looks to me, you two decided you'd like to stay here a while longer to continue your investigations, and figured the easiest way of getting me to agree was to wreck the drive." I glared hotly at them. "Well, I've got news for you. I can fix this, and I can fix it in a couple of days. So go on—get about your business! Get all the zoologizing you can in, while you still have time. I—"

Davison laid a hand gently on my arm. "Gus," he said quietly, *we didn't do it.* Neither of us."

Suddenly all the anger drained out of me and was replaced by raw fear. I could see that Davison meant it.

"If you didn't do it, and Holdreth didn't do it, and I didn't do it—then who did?"

Davison shrugged.

"Maybe it's one of us who doesn't know he's doing it," I suggested. "Maybe—" I stopped. "Oh, that's nonsense. Hand me that tool-kit, will you, Lee?"

They left to tend to the animals, and I set to work on the repair job, dismissing all further speculations and suspicions from my mind, concentrating solely on joining Lead A to Input A and Transistor F to Potentiometer K, as indicated. It was slow, nerve-harrowing work, and by mealtime I had accomplished only the barest preliminaries. My fingers were starting to quiver from the strain of small-scale work, and I decided to give up the job for the day and get back to it tomorrow.

I slept uneasily, my nightmares punctuated by the moaning of the accursed anteaters and the occasional squeals, chuckles, bleats, and hisses of the various other creatures in the hold. It must have been four in the morning before I dropped off into a really sound sleep, and what was left of the night passed swiftly. The next thing I knew, hands were shaking me, and I was looking up into the pale, tense faces of Holdreth and Davison.

I pushed my sleep-stuck eyes open and blinked. "Huh? What's going on?"

Holdreth leaned down and shook me savagely. "Get up, Gus!"

I struggled to my feet slowly. "Hell of a thing to do, wake a fellow up in the middle of the—"

I found myself being propelled from my cabin and led down the corridor to the control room. Blearily, I followed where Holdreth pointed, and then I woke up in a hurry.

The drive was battered again. Someone—or *something*—had completely undone my repair job of the night before.

If there had been bickering among us, it stopped. This was past the category of a joke now; it couldn't be laughed off, and we found ourselves working together as a tight unit again, trying desperately to solve the puzzle before it was too late.

"Let's review the situation," Holdreth said, pacing nervously up and down the control cabin. "The drive has been sabotaged twice. None of us knows who did it, and on a conscious level each of us is convinced *he* didn't do it."

He paused. "That leaves us with two possibilities. Either, as Gus suggested, one of us is doing it unaware of it even himself, or someone else is doing it while we're not looking. Neither possibility is a very cheerful one."

"We can stay on guard, though," I said. "Here's what I propose: first, have one of us awake at all times—sleep in shifts, that is, with somebody guarding the drive until I get it fixed. Two—jettison all the animals aboard ship."

"*What?*"

"He's right," Davison said. "We don't know what we may have brought aboard. They don't seem to be intelligent, but we can't be sure. That purple-eyed baby giraffe, for instance—suppose he's been hypnotizing us into damaging the drive ourselves? How can we tell?"

"Oh, but—" Holdreth started to protest, then stopped and frowned soberly. "I suppose we'll have to admit the possibility," he said, obviously unhappy about the prospect of freeing our captives. "We'll empty out the hold, and you see if you can get the drive fixed. Maybe later we'll recapture them all, if nothing further develops."

We agreed to that, and Holdreth and Davison cleared the ship of its animal cargo while I set to work determinedly at the drive mechanism. By nightfall, I had managed to accomplish as much as I had the day before.

I sat up as watch the first shift, aboard the strangely quiet ship. I paced around the drive cabin, fighting the great temptation to doze off, and managed to last through until the time Holdreth arrived to relieve me.

Only—when he showed up, he gasped and pointed at the drive. It had been ripped apart a third time.

Now we had no excuse, no explanation. The expedition had turned into a nightmare.

I could only protest that I had remained awake my entire spell on duty, and that I had seen no one and no thing approach the drive panel. But that was hardly a satisfactory explanation, since it either cast guilt on me as the saboteur or implied that some unseen external power was repeatedly wrecking the drive. Neither hypothesis made sense, at least to me.

By now we had spent four days on the planet, and food was getting to be a major problem. My carefully budgeted flight schedule called for us to be two days out on our return journey to Earth by now. But we still were no closer to departure than we had been four days ago.

The animals continued to wander around outside, nosing up against the ship, examining it, almost fondling it, with those damned pseudo-giraffes staring soulfully at us always. The beasts were as friendly as ever, little knowing how the tension was growing within the hull. The three of us walked around like zombies, eyes bright and lips clamped. We were scared—all of us.

Something was keeping us from fixing the drive.

Something didn't want us to leave this planet.

I looked at the bland face of the purple-eyed giraffe staring through the viewport, and it stared mildly back at me. Around it was grouped the rest of the local fauna, the same incredible hodgepodge of improbable genera and species.

That night, the three of us stood guard in the control-room together. The drive was smashed anyway. The wires were soldered in so many places by now that the control panel was a mass of shining alloy, and I knew that a few more such sabotagings and it would be impossible to patch it together any more—if it wasn't so already.

The next night, I just didn't knock off. I continued soldering right on after dinner (and a pretty skimpy dinner it was, now that we were on close rations) and far on into the night.

By morning, it was as if I hadn't done a thing.

"I give up," I announced, surveying the damage. "I don't see any sense in ruining my nerves trying to fix a thing that won't stay fixed."

Holdreth nodded. He looked terribly pale. "We'll have to find some new approach."

"Yeah. Some new approach."

I yanked open the food closet and examined our stock. Even figuring in the synthetics we would have fed to the animals if we hadn't released them, we were low on food. We had overstayed even the safety margin. It would be a hungry trip back—if we ever did get back.

I clambered through the hatch and sprawled down on a big rock near the ship. One of the furless dogs came over and nuzzled in my shirt. Davison stepped to the hatch and called down to me.

"What are you doing out there, Gus?"

"Just getting a little fresh air. I'm sick of living aboard that ship." I scratched the dog behind his pointed ears, and looked around.

The animals had lost most of their curiosity about us, and didn't congregate the way they used to. They were meandering all over the plain, nibbling at little deposits of a white doughy substance. It precipitated every night. "Manna," we called it. All the animals seemed to live on it.

I folded my arms and leaned back.

We were getting to look awfully lean by the eighth day. I wasn't even trying to fix the ship any more; the hunger was starting to get me. But I saw Davison puttering around with my solderbeam.

"What are you doing?"

"I'm going to repair the drive," he said. "You don't want to, but we can't just sit around, you know." His nose was deep in my repair guide, and he was fumbling with the release on the solderbeam.

I shrugged. "Go ahead, if you want to." I didn't care what he did. All I cared about was the gaping emptiness in my stomach, and about the dimly grasped fact that somehow we were stuck here for good.

"Gus?"

"Yeah?"

"I think it's time I told you something. I've been eating the manna for four days. It's good. It's nourishing stuff."

"You've been eating—the manna? Something that grows on an alien world? You crazy?"

"What else can we do? Starve?"

I smiled feebly, admitting that he was right. From somewhere in the back of the ship came the sounds of Holdreth moving around. Holdreth had taken this thing worse than any of us. He had a family back on Earth, and he was beginning to realize that he wasn't ever going to see them again.

"Why don't you get Holdreth?" Davison suggested. "Go out there and stuff yourselves with the manna. You've got to eat something."

"Yeah. What can I lose?" Moving like a mechanical man, I headed towards Holdreth's cabin. We would go out and eat the manna and cease being hungry, one way or another.

"Clyde?" I called. "Clyde?"

I entered his cabin. He was sitting at his desk, shaking convulsively, staring at the two streams of blood that trickled in red spurts from his slashed wrists.

"Clyde!"

He made no protest as I dragged him towards the infirmary cabin and got tourniquets around his arms, cutting off the bleeding. He just stared dully ahead, sobbing.

I slapped him and he came around. He shook his head dizzily, as if he didn't know where he was.

"Easy, Clyde. Everything's all right."

"It's *not* all right," he said hollowly. "I'm still alive. Why didn't you let me die? Why didn't you—"

Davison entered the cabin. "What's been happening, Gus?"

"It's Clyde. The pressure's getting him. He tried to kill himself, but I think he's all right now. Get him something to eat, will you?"

We had Holdreth straightened around by evening. Davison gathered as much of the manna as he could find, and we held a feast.

"I wish we had nerve enough to kill some of the local fauna," Davison said. "Then we'd have a feast—steaks and everything!"

"The bacteria," Holdreth pointed out quietly. "We don't dare."

"I know. But it's a thought."

"No more thoughts," I said sharply. "Tomorrow morning we start work on the drive panel again. Maybe with some food in our bellies we'll be able to keep awake and see what's happening here."

Holdreth smiled. "Good. I can't wait to get out of this ship and back to a normal existence. God, I just can't wait!"

"Let's get some sleep," I said. "Tomorrow we'll give it another try. We'll get back," I said with a confidence I didn't feel.

The following morning I rose early and got my tool-kit. My head was clear, and I was trying to put the pieces together without much luck. I started towards the control cabin.

And stopped.

And looked out the viewport.

I went back and awoke Holdreth and Davison. "Take a look out the port," I said hoarsely.

They looked. They gaped.

"It looks just like my house," Holdreth said. "My house on Earth."

"With all the comforts of home inside, I'll bet." I walked forward uneasily and lowered myself through the hatch. "Let's go look at it."

We approached it, while the animals frolicked around us. The big giraffe came near and shook its head gravely. The house stood in the middle of the clearing, small and neat and freshly painted.

I saw it now. During the night, invisible hands had put it there. Had assembled and built a cosy little Earth-type house and dropped it next to our ship for us to live in.

"Just like my house," Holdreth repeated in wonderment.

"It should be," I said. "They grabbed the model from your mind, as soon as they found out we couldn't live on the ship indefinitely."

Holdreth and Davison asked as one, "What do you mean?"

"You mean you haven't figured this place out yet?" I licked my lips, getting myself used to the fact that I was going to spend the rest of my life here. "You mean you don't realize what this house is intended to be?"

They shook their heads, baffled. I glanced around, from the house to the useless ship to the jungle to the plain to the little pond. It all made sense now.

"They want to keep us happy," I said. "They know we weren't thriving aboard the ship, so they—they built us something a little more like home."

"*They?* The giraffes?"

"Forget the giraffes. They tried to warn us, but it's too late. They're intelligent beings, but they're prisoners just like us. I'm talking about the ones who run this place. The super-aliens who make us sabotage our own ship and not even know we're doing it, who stand someplace up there and gape at us. The ones who dredged together this motley assortment of beasts from all over the galaxy. Now we've been collected too. This whole damned place is just a zoo—a zoo for aliens so far ahead of us we don't dare dream what they're like."

I looked up at the shimmering blue-green sky, where invisible bars seemed to restrain us, and sank down dismally on the porch of our new home. I was resigned. There wasn't any sense in struggling against *them*.

I could see the neat little placard now:

EARTHMEN. NATIVE HABITAT, SOL III.

A MAN OF TALENT

*This story came into being at the first Milford Science Fiction Writers'
Conference in September, 1956: an astonishing assemblage of the great fig-
ures of the field, meeting for a week at a ramshackle vacation lodge in
Pennsylvania to share the problems and challenges of their profession.
James Blish, Damon Knight, and Judith Merril organized it; and the writers who gathered there included Theodore Sturgeon, Algis Budrys, Cyril
Kornbluth, Gordon R. Dickson, Fritz Leiber, Frederik Pohl, Lester del Rey,
L. Sprague de Camp, and just about everyone else who was anybody in the
world of 1950s science fiction. The very young Harlan Ellison was there,
too—he had sold maybe a dozen stories at that point—and so was I, by
some months even younger than Harlan. We were more or less the mascots
of the meeting, and the whipping-boys as well, Harlan catching hell for his
irrepressible brashness, and me because at the age of 21 I had sold reams
and reams of conscienceless rent-paying potboilers along with the somewhat better stories that I've chosen to reprint in this book (and which had
helped me to win the Hugo award for Most Promising New Writer that year,
just the week before Milford).*

*So I sat among my betters at Milford, listening to them speak of the
agonies of their art; and I, for whom writing was at that time no agony at
all, merely an exercise in discipline and concentration, felt abashed and
ultimately very troubled. I resolved, not to give up writing potboilers (for as
long as my landlord insisted on charging rent for my Manhattan apartment
I saw no harm in turning out stories that would help me to pay it) but to
reach for greater intensity in the stories that I took more seriously, my*

"real" science fiction. And after my return to New York, I tried my best to keep that resolution, at least for a while. "The Man With Talent," as the first version of this story was called, was written early in October, 1956, a few weeks after Milford—an attempt to grapple with the Milford experience in metaphorical form. Bob Lowndes paid me $75 for it—a premium rate then, believe it or not—and published it in the Winter, 1957 issue of Future Science Fiction. *A decade later, James Blish, one of the prime movers of the Milford meeting and a man famous for his harsh chastisement of poorly done science fiction, used it in an anthology about the future of art called* New Dreams This Morning, *an event which gave me such pleasure that I revised the story especially for the book and changed its title slightly. It is the revised version that I use here.*

———————

There was a scrap of a clipping that Emil Vilar carried about with him, a review of his first and only volume of poetry. Now, on this new world, he drew it out and read it for the ten-thousandth time. It was yellow with age, and the print was blurred, but that hardly mattered; the words were graven deep in Emil Vilar's memory.

> We welcome Emil Vilar both for his technical gifts and his breadth of understanding. He speaks with the authentic poetic voice. His book, certainly the most promising debut volume in many years, perhaps heralds the arrival of a major poet. Yet it must be doubted that Mr. Vilar will have the opportunity to fulfil this promise, working as he must in a world where such art as his is doomed to be stillborn. With the audience for poetry of any quality already nearly extinct, how can an Emil Vilar sustain and develop his talent?

Vilar had reddened with shame when the review appeared. He had known, inwardly, that it was the truth, that he had the stuff of a major poet within him, but he neither dared to take that resonant label upon himself nor welcomed another's saying it. But it had not mattered much. With or without the burden of that reputation, he had failed to find his following. It was not an age of poetry but of verse: the occasional ode, the snappy quatrain, the glorified limerick. The craft of poetry was nearly dead, the poet's function distorted. Practical matters, the immediately useful thing—they had triumphed on Earth. It was no century for the artist. A crowded, harried world could not afford such luxuries.

He had tried. For twenty years after, he had continued to write and to try. And finally he had admitted the truth of what the anonymous reviewer had said—and he had left Earth forever.

He looked up from the clipping at the landscape of his new world. He had selected it at random, from the thick volume of catalogued worlds in the library. Which world it was did not matter to him. All that mattered was that it was not Earth.

"Rigel Seven," he said aloud. The words were strange in his mouth, and he savored the interplay of the not-quite-assonant vowels of the two mild trochees that named his new home.

He was faintly disappointed, now that he was here, that he had picked a Terraformed planet. His motives had been clear enough at the start: he wanted a world as much like and as far from Earth as possible, where he could work in peace, unknown and undisturbed—where people would not plague him with their well-meant misinterpretations of his work, sting him with accusations of ivory-towerism or artistic irresponsibility, or call him any of the other names they had called him because he insisted on writing his poetry for himself and himself alone.

Earth didn't understand. Earth wanted him to be a rhymer, not a poet—and so Emil Vilar had quietly removed himself from the Terran scene. He had chosen a Terraformed planet as his new home. But as he looked at the gently sloping green hills and the familiar-seeming puffs of white fleece in the soft blue sky, he realized he had made one of his rare mistakes. How much richer his imagination would have been, he thought sadly, had he selected an Alienform world—one which had not yet been converted into a carbon copy of the mother planet. Here he had the same sky and the same clouds as on Earth; only the Sun was different, a hard, distant dot of incalculably ferocious intensity.

Well, he was here, and here he would stay. Carefully he folded his clipping and slid it into his wallet. Rigel Seven was as good a place as any, and any would be better than Earth.

The robot in the Earthside routing office had told him, with a smirk on its mirrored face, that he was the first emigrant to Rigel Seven in over five hundred years. That had been all right, too.

The planet had been settled eight hundred years earlier by sixteen wealthy Terran families, who had purchased it jointly as a private estate.

The conditions of the sale, of course, had been that the planet remained open to all comers for emigration, but that was a safe risk. The sky was full of stars, and each had its cluster of worlds; who would cross five hundred light-years to settle on Rigel Seven, when Sirius and Vega and Procyon and the Centauri stars beckoned just a few light-years from Earth?

Who but Emil Vilar, fleeing quietly from the world that would never understand him?

He had saved, in his fifty years, some five thousand dollars. That had nearly covered the transit fee. The rest had been supplied by his friends.

There had been six of them, men with faith in Emil Vilar. They had fought his going, but when they saw he was determined to go, they helped him. They contributed the needed thousand to see him through the journey, and they established a trust fund that would provide a monthly remittance for him for the rest of his life.

He took a deep breath. Rigel Seven was Terraformed, but they had left out the stink of Earth's air and the filth of her cities. The air was fresh and clear here. He smiled at the sight of his shadow, stretched mightily ahead of him over the grass.

For the first time in his memory, he felt happy.

The Rigel Seven spaceport was at the edge of a broad field that swept up the side of the hill in the distance like a green carpet. Farther back, on the hill, Vilar could see the shimmering paleness of a domed house. Someone was coming down the brown, winding path that led from the hill to the field.

He hefted his small suitcase and started to walk forward rapidly. The man met him in the middle of the field. He was tall and bronzed, shirtless, with long, rippling muscles lying flat and firm on his arms and chest. Vilar felt suddenly ashamed of his own dumpy body.

"You're the emigrant, aren't you?"

"I am Emil Vilar. The ship has just left me here."

"I know," the tall man said, grinning affably. "We saw it come down. It was quite a novelty for us. We don't get much traffic here, you know."

"I can imagine," Vilar said quietly. "Well, I shan't bother you much. I keep to myself most of the time."

"We have a place all ready for you. My name's Carpenter, by the way—Melbourne Hadley Carpenter. Come, I'll show you to your shack, and then you can come visit us later. We'll tell you how things work here."

"Work? But—I do not plan to participate in any communal activ—"

He paused, frowning, and shook his head gently. This was no time to spout a declaration of principles. "Never mind," he said. "Show me where I stay."

Carpenter led him back up the path to the foot of the hill, where there was a small shack looking upward at the great domed house.

"This is ideal," said Vilar. It was just what he had envisioned when he had made arrangements to live here.

"See you later," Carpenter told him, waved cheerily, and left. Vilar put a hand on the door-opener, broke the photonic circuit, and stepped in.

One bookcase, one bed, one closet, one dresser.

Ideal.

Vilar unpacked his single suitcase rapidly. It had been no struggle for him to break away from his Earthly possessions; he had been able to bring everything he owned and still make the fifty-pound mass limit of the subspace liner with ease.

First came the books, just eight of them. There was the slim blue-bound copy of *Poems,* by Emil Vilar (London, 2743, 61 pp.). After that, Pound's *Cantos,* the complete hundred and forty. Next came the King James Bible, *Swann's Way,* the complete Yeats, Davis's *On Historical Analysis* (both volumes in one), the plays of Cyril Tourneur, and the Greek Anthology. These were all Vilar had kept from a lifetime of reading, and he had added the most recent—the single volume of Proust—sixteen years before. Now he considered his library closed.

His meagre wardrobe followed, and he arrayed it in the closet and dresser with customary methodical precision. After that his linens and other household goods. Next the thin file envelope containing his poetic output since the 2743 volume. It was all unpublished, and the world had seen little of it.

Those works which had somehow passed muster and been shown to a few friends—those poems Vilar now regarded as tainted, though he kept them. Each seemed stained by the muddle-headed criticism it had inspired.

"A wonderful thing, Emil—but isn't it a shade too long?"

"Marvelous imagery, Emil. But when you bring in Dido, I think you're reaching too far for effect—"

"Splendid, but—"

"Magnificent, but—"

"Why all these tensions, Vilar? Why not relax the texture a trifle? If you had only—"

"Am I being too blunt in saying that I feel your work lately has been tending towards a dead end, a geometrical stasis that can only damage your standing? The failure of sensibility—"

He had listened patiently to each of them, digested their often conflicting critical views with dignity, and, finally, turned his back on the lot of them. They were chatterers. They made knowing noises, but what they really wanted to tell him was that his lines did not jingle enough. Retreating to Rigel Seven was the easiest solution. There had been no other way. Had he remained on Earth, he would have spent the rest of his days unchangingly, plagued by the cultists, the centre of a tiny, well-meaning circle of admirers who longed to share his gift, though they had no notion of the anguish they brought to its possessor. Better to be ignored, as he was by most of the world, than to have such a claque. So he had gone away.

He continued unpacking. He drew out two reams of paper: all he would need for the rest of his life. His pen. His notebook. He looked around. Everything was as it should be. The room was complete.

Vilar sat down at his desk and reached for a book. His hand lingered momentarily over his own little volume, quivered a bit, and moved on. He drew forth Yeats, then reconsidered and put him back. Fugitive lines from Eliot, whom he had long since memorized and so had not needed to bring with him, flickered through his mind:

…Gull against the wind, in the windy straits
Of Belle Isle, or running on the Horn.
White feathers in the snow, the Gulf claims,
And an old man driven by the Trades
To a sleepy corner.

Tenants of the house,
Thoughts of a dry brain in a dry season.

He worked, for most of the night, on a free fantasy based on the opening lines of *The Revenger's Tragedy*. Towards dawn, he rose, tore up the sheet, and blotted what he had written from his mind. He went outside on his tiny porch to watch the strange sun creep above the horizon of Rigel Seven. At this distance, bloated Rigel looked far smaller than

Sol—but the savage blaze of its hot blue-white light betrayed the alien star's true power.

Shortly after sunrise, Melbourne Hadley Carpenter returned.

"Have a good night?"

Vilar, rumpled-looking and red-eyed, nodded. "Excellent."

"Glad to hear it. Suppose you come up to the house now. My father's waiting to meet you, and so are all the others."

Vilar frowned suspiciously. "Why do they want to meet me?"

"Oh, just curiosity, I guess. You're the only one here who's not one of the Families, you know."

"I know," Vilar said, relieved. "You're sure you've never heard of me then?"

Carpenter shrugged. "How would we ever hear of you? We're completely out of touch with things, you know."

"True." One major worry was thereby avoided—he would be a complete stranger here, as he had hoped. A fresh start would be possible. The old man's brain was *not* dry; here in this sleepy corner, he could scale the greatest heights without attracting the clumsy attention that was so fatal to artistic endeavour.

He followed the tall young man up the hill and into the domed house. The lines of the building were clear and simple; in his amateur's way, Vilar approved of the architecture wholeheartedly. It had none of the falseness of Earth's current pseudo-archaism.

In the spacious central hall, an immense table had been set and at least fifty people sat around it. A tall man looking much like Melbourne Hadley Carpenter, but much older, with iron-grey hair and faintly stooping shoulders, rose from his seat at the head of the table.

"You're Emil Vilar," he said ringingly. "We're very happy to see you. I'm Theodore Hadley Carpenter, and this is my family."

Awed, Vilar nodded hesitantly. With a sweeping gesture of his hand, Theodore Hadley Carpenter indicated six almost identical younger men sitting to his right.

"My sons," he said.

Farther down the table were still younger men—this was the generation of Melbourne Hadley Carpenter, Vilar decided. "My grandsons," the patriarch said, confirming this.

"You have a very fine family, Mr Carpenter," Vilar said.

"One of the best, sir," Carpenter replied blandly. "Will you join us now for breakfast? We can talk afterwards."

Vilar had no objections, and took a vacant seat at the table. Breakfast proceeded—served, he noted, by pretty young girls who were probably Carpenter's granddaughters. There were no outsiders on this planet, no servants, no one who was not part of a Family.

Except me, he thought with wry amusement. *Always the outsider.*

Breakfast had been as efficiently Terraformed as the planet itself. Bacon and eggs, warm rolls, coffee—why, it was ludicrous to travel—what was it, five hundred and forty-five light years, untold trillions of miles?—and have warm rolls and coffee for breakfast. But people tend to cling, Vilar thought. What was the entire Terraforming project but a mighty whimper, a galaxy-shaking yawp of puny defiance (*barbaric* yawp, his well-stocked mind foot-noted automatically)? Man was progressively carving the worlds of space into the image of Earth, and eating rolls for breakfast.

Vilar considered the thought. Later, he knew, it would emerge concealed in the webwork of one of his poems, and still later he would see it there, and destroy the poem as a silly timebound polemic.

He sat back in his chair when he had finished eating. The table was cleared. Then, to his astonishment, old Carpenter clapped his hands and one of his look-alike sons fetched a musical instrument. It was stringed, the strings stretched tight over a graven sounding board. A *dulcimer,* Vilar thought in wonderment as the patriarch began to play, striking the strings with two carved ivory sticks.

The melody was a strange and complex one; the poet, who had a sound but far from detailed knowledge of musical theory, listened carefully. The short piece ended plaintively in the minor, coming to an abrupt halt with three descending thirds.

"My own composition," the old man said, in the silence that followed. "It's sometimes hard to get used to our music at first, but—"

"I thought it was fine," Vilar said shortly. He was anxious to finish this meal and return to work, and hoped there would be no further talk of performing.

He rose from his chair.

"Leaving so soon?" the old man asked. "Why, we haven't even talked."

"Talked? About what?"

Carpenter knotted his fingers together. "About your contribution to our group, of course. We can't happily let you stay with us and eat our food if you're not going to offer us anything, stranger. Come now—what do you do?"

"I'm a poet," Vilar said uneasily.

The old man chuckled. "A poet? Indeed, yes—but what do you *do?*"

"I don't understand you. If you mean what is my trade, I have none. I'm merely a poet."

"Grandfather means can you do anything else," whispered one of the younger Carpenters near him. "Of course, you're a poet—who ever said you wouldn't be?"

Vilar shook his head. "Nothing but a poet." It sounded like an indictment, self-spoken.

"We had hoped you were a medical man, or a bookbinder, or perhaps a blacksmith. Coming from Earth, as you were—who would have expected a *poet?* Why, we have poets aplenty here! Of all things for Earth to give us!"

Emil Vilar moistened his lips and fidgeted nervously. "I'm sorry to disappoint you," he said weakly, turning up the palms of his hands. "Terribly sorry."

The joke was on them, he thought later that morning. No wonder they had been so anxious to have him come. To them, Earth meant something rugged and harsh, strange and jagged. They had hoped to have the smooth rhythm of their life disrupted by the man from Earth.

Yes, the joke's on them, he decided. Instead of a blacksmith, they got Earth's last poet, her one and only poet. And Rigel Seven had plenty of those.

Emil Vilar looked up from his seat in the arboretum outside of the domed house. One of the tall grandsons—was it Melbourne Hadley Carpenter, or Theodore Hadley III, or one of the others?—stood near him.

"Grandfather would like to know if you would come inside now, Emil Vilar. He would like to see you alone."

"Very well," Vilar said. He rose and followed the tall young man inside and up the stairs to a richly panelled room in which sat the eldest of the Carpenter clan.

"Come in, please," the old man said gently.

Vilar took the seat offered him and waited tensely for old Carpenter to speak. At close range, he could see that the old man was ancient, but well-preserved even at a probable age of a hundred and fifty.

"You say you're a *poet*," Carpenter said, hitting the plosive sound fiercely. "Would you mind reading this, and giving me your honest opinion of it?"

Vilar took the proffered sheet of paper, as he had taken so many other amateur poetic attempts back on Earth, and read the poem very carefully. It was a villanelle, smoothly accomplished except for a slip in scansion in the third line of the quatrain. It was also shallow and completely lacking in poetic vision. For once, Vilar determined to be absolutely unsparing in his criticism.

"A pretty exercise," he said casually. "Neatly handled, except for this blunder in the next line to last." He indicated the blemish, and added, "Other than that, the work's totally devoid of value. It doesn't even have the virtue of being entertaining; its emptiness is merely offensive. Have I made myself clear?"

"You have," Carpenter said stiffly. "The verses were mine."

"You asked for honest criticism," Vilar reminded him.

"So I did—and I received it, perhaps. What of those paintings on the wall?"

They were abstracts, strikingly handled, in the neo-industrialist manner. "I'm not a painter, you realize," Vilar said haltingly. "But I'd say they were excellent—quite good, certainly."

"Those are mine, too," Carpenter said.

Vilar blinked in surprise. "You're very versatile, Mr Carpenter. Musician, composer, poet, painter—you hold all the arts at your command."

"Nothing unusual about it," Carpenter said. "Customary. A tenet of our society since the first settlers came here. Art's part of life, like breathing. We make no fuss about it. A man's got to have certain skills if he's to call himself civilized, and we develop them. Why set a few men aside as artists and canonize them? We've never let ourselves be mere spectators. We pride ourselves on our artistic ability—every last one of us. We are *all* poets, Mr Vilar. We all paint, we all play instruments, we all compose. And we regard it as unremarkable to do so."

"Whereas I'm limited to my one paltry art, is that it? I'm merely a poet?"

A sudden feeling of inferiority swept over him for the first time in ages. He had felt humble before—humble before Milton or Aeschylus, before Yeats or Shakespeare, as he struggled to equal their accomplishments, or even approach them. But there was a shade of difference between humility and inferiority. What he felt now was inadequacy, not merely as a poet, but as a person. For a man as self-assured as Vilar, it was a painful thing.

He looked up at old Carpenter.

"Will you excuse me?" he said, his voice strangely harsh and edgy.

Alone, in his shack, he stared at the sheet of paper, regretfully, and read the lines he had written:

Slippery shadows of daylight stand
Between each man and himself; each cries out,
But—

That was where they ended. He had just composed them—or so he had thought, at the moment. Now, five minutes later, he recognized them for what they were: lines from a poem he had composed in his youth and rightfully burned for the adolescent twaddle it was.

Where was his technique, his vaunted vowel sense, his intricate rhythms, and subtle verbal conflicts? He looked sadly at the clumsy nonsense his fear-numbed brain had dictated, and swept the sheet contemptuously to the floor.

Have I lost the gift?

It was a cold, soul-withering question, but it was followed hastily by another even more deadly: *Did I ever have the gift?*

But that was an easily answered question. There was the slim blue-bound volume, right over here—

The book was gone.

He stared at the quarter of an inch left vacant in the bookcase for a moment. The book had been taken. One of the Carpenters was evidently curious about his poetry.

Well, never mind, he thought, *I still carry the poems with me.*

To prove it, he recited "The Apples of Idun", one of the longest, and, to his mind, the best. When he was finished, his old confidence had returned. His gift had been no illusion.

But neither was the Carpenter family. And he could no longer stay here in their presence.

Dejectedly, he recalled the performance of the patriarch: with astonishing versatility, the old man flitted from one art form to the next—as did the others. There wasn't a man in the family who couldn't turn a verse, set his own song to music, perform the piece on one of a dozen instruments, and render a nonobjective interpretation of it in oils, to boot. Beside formidable talent of this sort, Vilar felt his own paltry gift fade into insignificance. Art was as natural to these people as breathing. They had been *bred* to it; no one wore the label "artist" on Rigel Seven, no specialist lurked in his private nook or category.

And Emil Vilar was aware that there was no place for him in a world of this sort. His talent was too ephemeral to survive among these genial philistines—for philistines they were, despite or perhaps because of their great range of abilities. They had no awareness that art was a sacred rite. To them it was an amusement, a pastime for gentlemen. Whatever they did, they did well, for they were trained toward excellence, but it was all on the same level of affable skilled amateurism. That was to be admired, certainly, more than the crude boorishness of Earth, but such an environment was also fatal to the real poetic fire.

These people were omniartistic—and omnivorous, too. They would devour Emil Vilar.

He took his suitcase from the closet and calmly began to pack. Returning to Earth was out of the question, but he would go somewhere, somewhere where life was more complex and art more highly valued.

"Why are you packing?" a resonant voice asked.

Vilar whirled. It was old Carpenter, standing in the doorway.

"I've decided to go. That's reason enough."

Carpenter smiled pleasantly. "Go? Where could you go? Back to Earth?"

"No—but anywhere away from here."

"You'll find the other fifteen Families much the same," the old man said. "Take my advice; stay here. We like you, Vilar. We don't want to lose you so soon."

Vilar was silent and motionless for a while. Then, without saying a word, he resumed packing.

Carpenter crossed the cabin quickly and put his hand on Vilar's arm. The old man's grip was surprisingly strong.

"Please," he said urgently. "Don't go."

Vilar loosened the grip and stepped away. "I can't stay here. I have to leave."

"But why?"

"*Because you're driving me crazy!*" Vilar shouted suddenly. It was the first time he had lost his temper in more than thirty years.

Quivering, he turned towards the older man. "You paint, you sing, you write, you compose. You do everything! And what of me? I'm a poet, nothing more. A *mere* poet. In this world that's like being a man with only one arm—someone to be pitied."

"But—"

"Let me finish," Vilar said. "Let me pass this information along to you: you're not artists, any one of you. You're artists-*manqué,* would-be artists, not-quite artists.

"Art's an ennobling thing—a gift, a talent. If everyone's talented, no talent exists. When gold lines the street, it's worth no more than dross. And so you people who are so proud of yourselves for many talents— why, you have none at all! Only skills."

Carpenter seemed to ignore Vilar's tirade. "Is that why you're leaving?" he asked.

"I'm—I'm—" Vilar paused, confused. "I'm leaving because I want to leave. Because I'm a real artist, and I know I am. I don't want to be polluted by the pretended art I see here. I have something real and wonderful, and I don't want to lose it. And I *will* lose it here."

"How wrong you are," Carpenter said. "In just that last, I mean. You do have a gift—and we need it. We want you to stay. Will you?"

"But you said this morning that I couldn't stay, not unless I brought something new to this place. And I haven't. What good is one more poet in a town full of them? Even," he added belligerently, "if that poet's worth all the rest in one?"

"You misunderstand," Carpenter said. "True, we need no more poets. But we need you. Vilar, *we need an audience!*"

Suddenly Emil Vilar understood. The joke was on him, after all. He had failed to see the real texture of life here, just as he had failed all these years to see his own role in human society. These people needed him, all right; what kind of army was it that had a thousand generals and no foot soldiers?

He started to laugh, slowly at first, then in violent upheaving gasps that brought tears to his eyes. After nearly a minute he grew silent again.

It was ideal, after all. So far as they were concerned, he had but a single talent: that of being an audience. Very well. They had no understanding of high art, and to them he was pitiful, useful only because of his limits. Good. Let them think that. Privately, he knew he was a poet, not an audience. But one had to pay a price in services rendered, in order to be a poet for one's self alone.

"I see," he said softly. "Very well, then. I'll be your audience."

He saw how the days to come would be. His value to them would be as a nonpainter, a noncomposer, an onlooker and critic. His private poetic endeavors would seem beneath contempt to them. Which was as he wanted it. The real artist was always alone, whether on Rigel Seven or in the midst of Earth's most teeming city. The audience might find him, but he must not fret about finding the audience. On Earth he had found no audience at first, and that had been all right, really; only when he had acquired the wrong kind of audience, a falsely knowing one, had he decided it was time to flee. A mistake, for the solace he sought was not to be had anywhere. Now he had come to a place that would neither reject him as a person nor meddle in his art, and he saw the conclusion that had escaped him before. It was senseless to flee again. He would be misunderstood anywhere; he saw now that it had always been pointless to go on from place to place in quest of the true environment of art. That environment was a myth, unattainable, unreal. Or, rather, that environment was within him, wherever he was. The wise thing was to hold his ground, play some useful role in society, and privately practice his art.

Alone among these gifted but complicated people, he could work out his artistic destiny on this strange and familiar planet without fear of the watchers. The Carpenters, that closed family group, hungered for spectators, for the love and appreciation of outsiders who would admire them for their attainments. Vilar did not need that.

"By the way," the old man said, smiling guiltily. "While you were in the park this morning, I took the liberty of borrowing *this.*" He reached inside his jacket and drew forth Vilar's collected poems.

"Oh? What did you think of them?" Vilar asked.

The patriarch frowned, fidgeted, coughed. "Ah—"

"An honest opinion," Vilar said. "As I gave this morning."

"Well, to be frank—two of my sons looked at them with me. And none of us could see any meaning or value in the lot, Vilar. I don't know where you got the idea you had any talent for poetry. You really don't, you know."

"I've often suspected that myself," Vilar said happily. He took the book and fondled it with satisfaction. Already he was envisioning a second volume—a volume that would appear in an edition of one, for his eyes alone.

ONE-WAY JOURNEY

Another of the new science-fiction magazines that sprang into being in the late 1950s, just in time to help me harness my unexpectedly vast productivity, was Infinity, *edited by a shrewd, owlish, pipe-smoking guy named Larry T. Shaw, who had been around science fiction for a long time as a reader, an agent, an editor, and even a (very occasional) writer. Shaw didn't have much in the way of an editorial budget to buy stories with, but he loved and understood science fiction, his taste was enlightened and perceptive, and he had close and long-standing friendships with many of the key figures of the New York science-fiction world of the 1940's and 1950's; so* Infinity, *for the three or four years it lasted, was a distinguished effort whose contents pages regularly bore the names of such top-level writers as Clifford D. Simak, Robert Sheckley, Isaac Asimov, James Blish, and Damon Knight. (Not to mention that of Harlan Ellison, who made his first sale there in the summer of 1955.)*

I was an eager contributor to Infinity *too, of course; I missed the first issue, but was in virtually every one thereafter. Shaw was willing to look at and often to buy many of the earnest, careful stories that I had written in my college days and had been unable to sell then. The first, in November of 1955, was "Hopper, "which I expanded a decade later into the novel* The Time Hoppers, *and other sales to his magazine followed steadily. "One-Way Journey," which I wrote in October, 1956—that highly sensitized immediately post-Milford period—was the fifth or sixth of them. I tried it first at Galaxy, since I believed that editor Horace Gold was fond of stories verging into psychopathology, but Gold found the story "too damned strong." He returned it with a rejection slip advising me that he wasn't as enthusiastic about psychiatric-case stories as I and a lot of other writers seemed to think, and wished I would turn to something else. "Why in hell compete with more people than you have to?" he asked me. "Leave these themes to them, where story literally battles story, like any other glut product. You've got other ideas. Let's see them." And so I did, with considerable success. But I took "One-Way Journey" over to Larry Shaw, who used it in the November, 1957 Infinity.*

Behind the comforting walls of Terra Import's headquarters on Kollidor, commander Leon Warshow was fumbling nervously with the psych reports on his mirror-bright desk. Commander Warshow was thinking about spaceman Matt Falk, and about himself. Commander Warshow was about to react very predictably.

Personnel Lieutenant Krisch had told him the story about Falk an hour before, and Warshow was doing the one thing expected of him: he was waiting for the boy, having sent for him, after a hasty conference with Cullinan, the *Magyar*'s saturnine psych officer.

An orderly buzzed and said, "Spaceman Falk to see you, sir."

"Have him wait a few minutes," Warshow said, speaking too quickly. "I'll buzz for him."

It was a tactical delay. Wondering why he, an officer, should be so tense before an interview with an enlisted man, Warshow riffled through the sheaf of records on Matt Falk. *Orphaned, 2543... Academy...two years' commercial service, military contract...injury en route to Kollidor...*

Appended were comprehensive medical reports on Falk's injury, and Dr. Sigstrom's okay. Also a disciplinary chart, very favorable, and a jaggle-edged psych contour, good.

Warshow depressed the buzzer. "Send in Falk," he said.

The photon beam clicked and the door swung back. Matt Falk entered and faced his commander stonily; Warshow glared back, studying the youngster as if he had never seen him before. Falk was just twenty-five, very tall and very blond, with wide, bunch-muscled shoulders and keen blue eyes. The scar along the left side of his face was almost completely invisible, but not even chemotherapeutic incubation had been able to restore the smooth evenness of the boy's jaw. Falk's face looked oddly lopsided; the unharmed right jaw sloped easily and handsomely up to the condyle, while the left still bore unseen but definitely present echoes of the boy's terrible shipboard accident.

"You want me, commander?"

"We're leaving Kollidor tomorrow, Matt," Warshow said quietly. "Lieutenant Krisch tells me you haven't returned to ship to pack your gear. Why?"

The jaw that had been ruined and rebuilt quivered slightly.

"*You* know, sir. I'm not going back to Earth, sir. I'm staying here… with Thetona."

There was a frozen silence. Then, with calculated cruelty, Warshow said, "You're really hipped on that flatface, eh?"

"Maybe so," Falk murmured. "That flatface. That gook. What of it?" His quiet voice was bitterly defiant.

Warshow tensed. He was trying to do the job delicately, without inflicting further psychopersonal damage on young Falk. To leave a psychotic crewman behind on an alien world was impossible—but to extract Falk forcibly from the binding webwork of associations that tied him to Kollidor would leave scars not only on crewman but on captain.

Perspiring, Warshow said, "You're an Earthman, Matt. Don't you—"

"Want to go home? No."

The commander grinned feebly. "You sound mighty permanent about that, son."

"I am," Falk said stiffly. "You know why I want to stay here. I *am* staying here. May I be excused now, sir?"

Warshow drummed on the desktop, hesitating for a moment, then nodded. "Permission granted, Mr Falk." There was little point in prolonging what he now saw had been a predeterminedly pointless interview.

He waited a few minutes after Falk had left. Then he switched on the communicator. "Send in Major Cullinan, please."

The beady-eyed psychman appeared almost instantly. "Well?"

"The boy's staying," Warshow said. "Complete and singleminded fixation. Go ahead—break it."

Cullinan shrugged. "We may have to leave him here, and that's all there is to it. Have you met the girl?"

"Kollidorian. Alien. Ugly as sin. I've seen her picture; he had it over his bunk until he moved out. And we *can't* leave him here, major."

Cullinan raised one bushy eyebrow quizzically. "We can try to bring Falk back, if you insist—but it won't work. Not without crippling him."

Warshow whistled idly, avoiding the psychman's stern gaze. "I insist," he said finally. "There's no alternative."

He snatched at the communicator.

"Lieutenant Krisch, please." A brief pause, then: "Krisch, Warshow. Tell the men that departure's been postponed four days. Have Molhaus refigure the orbits. Yes, four days. *Four.*"

Warshow hung up, glanced at the heaped Falk dossier on his desk, and scowled. Psych Officer Cullinan shook his head sadly, rubbing his growing bald spot.

"That's a drastic step, Leon."

"I know. But I'm not going to leave Falk behind." Warshow rose, eyed Cullinan uneasily, and added, "Care to come with me? I'm going down into Kollidor City."

"What for?"

"I want to talk with the girl," Warshow said.

Later, in the crazily twisting network of aimless streets that was the alien city, Warshow began to wish he had ordered Cullinan to come with him. As he made his way through the swarms of the placid, ugly, broad-faced Kollidorians, he regretted very much that he had gone alone.

What would he do, he wondered, when he finally did reach the flat where Falk and his Kollidorian girl were living? Warshow wasn't accustomed to handling himself in ground-borne interpersonal situations of this sort. He didn't know what to say to the girl. He thought he could handle Falk.

The relation of commander to crewman is that of parent to child, the Book said. Warshow grinned self-consciously.

He didn't feel very fatherly just now—more like a Dutch uncle, he thought.

He kept walking. Kollidor City spread out ahead of him like a tangled ball of twine coming unrolled in five directions at once; it seemed to have been laid down almost at random. But Warshow knew the city well. This was his third tour of duty to the Kollidor sector; three times he had brought cargo from Earth, three times waited while his ship was loaded with Kollidorian goods for export.

Overhead, the distant blue-white sun burnt brightly. Kollidor was the thirteenth planet in its system; it swung on a large arc nearly four billion miles from its blazing primary.

Warshow sniffled; it reminded him that he was due for his regular antipollen injection. He was already thoroughly protected, as was his crew, against most forms of alien disease likely to come his way on the trip.

But how do you protect someone like Falk? The commander had no quick answers for that. It wouldn't ordinarily seem necessary to inoculate spacemen against falling in love with bovine alien women, but—

"Good afternoon, Commander Warshow," a dry voice said suddenly.

Warshow glanced around, surprised and annoyed. The man who stood behind him was tall, thin, with hard, knobby cheekbones protruding grotesquely from parchmentlike chalk-white skin. Warshow recognized the genetic pattern, and the man. He was Domnik Kross, a trader from the quondam Terran colony of Rigel IX.

"Hello, Kross," Warshow said sullenly, and halted to let the other catch up.

"What brings you to the city, commander? I thought you were getting ready to pack up and flit away."

"We're—postponing four days," Warshow said.

"Oh? Got any leads worth telling about? Not that I care to—"

"Skip it, Kross." Warshow's voice was weary. "We've finished our trading for the season. You've got a clear field. Now leave me alone, yes?"

He started to walk faster, but the Rigelian, smiling bleakly, kept in step with him.

"You sound disturbed, commander."

Warshow glanced impatiently at the other, wishing he could unburden himself of the Rigelian's company. "I'm on a mission of top security value, Kross. Are you going to insist on accompanying me?"

Thin lips parted slyly in a cold grin. "Not at all, Commander Warshow. I simply thought I'd be civil and walk with you a way, just to swap the news. After all, if you're leaving in four days we're not really rivals any more, and—"

"Exactly," Warshow said.

"What's this about one of your crewmen living with a native?" Kross asked suddenly.

Warshow spun on his heel and glared up tensely. *"Nothing,"* he grated. "You hear that? There's nothing to it!"

Kross chuckled, and Warshow saw that he had decidedly lost a point in the deadly cold rivalry between Terran and Rigelian, between man and son of man. Genetic drift accounted for the Domnik Krosses—a little bit of chromosome looping on a colonized planet, a faint tincture of inbreeding over ten generations, and a new subspecies had appeared: an alien subspecies that bore little love for its progenitors.

They reached a complex fork in the street, and the commander impulsively turned to the left. Gratifyingly, he noticed that Kross was not following him.

"See you next year!" the Rigelian said.

Warshow responded with a noncommittal grunt and kept moving down the dirty street, happy to be rid of Kross so soon. The Rigelians, he thought, were nasty customers. They were forever jealous of the mother world and its people, forever anxious to outrace an Earthman to a profitable deal on a world such as Kollidor.

Because of Kross, Warshow reflected, *I'm going where I'm going now.* Pressure from the Rigelians forced Earthmen to keep up appearances throughout the galaxy. The Earthman's Burden, Terrans termed it unofficially. To leave a deserter behind on Kollidor would endanger Earth's prestige in the eyes of the entire universe—and the shrewd Rigelians would make sure the entire universe knew.

Warshow felt hemmed in. As he approached the flat where Falk said he was living, he felt cascades of perspiration tumbling stickily down his back.

"Yes, please?"

Warshow now stood at the door, a little appalled by the sight and the smell. A Kollidorian female faced him squarely.

Good God, he thought. *She's sure no beauty.*

"I'm...Commander Warshow," he said. "Of the *Magyar*. Matt's ship. May I come in?"

The sphincterlike mouth rippled into what Warshow supposed was a gracious smile. "Of course. I have hoped you would come. Matt has spoken so much of you."

She backed away from the door, and Warshow stepped inside. The pungent rankness of concentrated Kollidorian odor assaulted his nostrils. It was an unpainted two-room flat; beyond the room they were in,

Warshow saw another, slightly larger and sloppier, with kitchen facilities. Unwashed dishes lay heaped in the sink. To his surprise, he noticed an unmade bed in the far room…and another in the front one. *Single* beds. He frowned and turned to the girl.

She was nearly as tall as he was, and much broader. Her brown skin was drab and thick, looking more like hide than skin; her face was wide and plain, with two flat, unsparkling eyes, a grotesque bubble of a nose, and a many-lipped compound mouth. The girl wore a shapeless black frock that hung to her thick ankles. For all Warshow knew, she might be the pinnacle of Kollidorian beauty—but her charms scarcely seemed likely to arouse much desire in a normal Earthman.

"You're Thetona, is that right?"

"Yes, Commander Warshow." Voice dull and toneless, he noted.

"May I sit down?" he asked.

He was fencing tentatively, hemming around the situation without cutting towards it. He made a great business of taking a seat and crossing his legs fastidiously; the girl stared, cowlike, but remained standing.

An awkward silence followed; then the girl said, "You want Matt to go home with you, don't you?"

Warshow reddened and tightened his jaws angrily. "Yes. Our ship's leaving in four days. I came to get him."

"He isn't here," she said.

"I know. He's back at the base. He'll be home soon."

"You haven't done anything to him?" she asked, suddenly apprehensive.

He shook his head. "He's all right." After a moment Warshow glanced sharply at her and said, "He loves you, doesn't he?"

"Yes." But the answer seemed hesitant.

"And you love him?"

"Oh, yes," Thetona said warmly. "Certainly."

"I see." Warshow wet his lips. This was going to be difficult. "Suppose you tell me how you came to fall in love? I'm curious."

She smiled—at least, he assumed it was a smile. "I met him about two days after you Earthmen came for your visit. I was walking in the streets, and I saw him. He was sitting on the edge of the street, crying."

"*What?*"

Her flat eyes seemed to go misty. "Sitting there sobbing to himself. It was the first time I ever saw an Earthman like that—crying, I mean. I felt terribly sorry for him. I went over to talk to him. He was like a little lost boy."

Warshow looked up, astonished, and stared at the alien girl's placid face with total disbelief. In ten years of dealing with the Kollidorians, he had never gone too close to them; he had left personal contact mainly to others. But—

Dammit, the girl's almost human! Almost—

"Was he sick?" Warshow asked, his voice hoarse. "Why was he crying?"

"He was lonely," Thetona said serenely. "He was afraid. He was afraid of me, of you, of everyone. So I talked to him, there by the edge of the street, for many minutes. And then he asked to come home with me. I lived by myself, here. He came with me. And—he has been here since three days after that."

"And he plans to stay here permanently?" Warshow asked.

The wide head waggled affirmatively. "We are very fond of each other. He is lonely; he needs someone to—"

"That'll be enough," Falk's voice said suddenly.

Warshow whirled. Falk was standing in the doorway, his face bleak and grim. The scar on his face seemed to be inflamed, though Warshow was sure that was impossible.

"What are you doing here?" Falk asked.

"I came to visit Thetona," Warshow said mildly. "I didn't expect to have you return so soon."

"I know you didn't. I walked out when Cullinan started poking around me. Suppose you get out."

"You're talking to a superior officer," Warshow reminded him. "If I—"

"I resigned ten minutes ago," Falk snapped. "You're no superior of mine! Get out!"

Warshow stiffened. He looked appealingly at the alien girl, who put her thick six-fingered hand on Falk's shoulder and stroked his arm. Falk wriggled away.

"Don't," he said. "Well—are you leaving? Thetona and I want to be alone."

"Please go, Commander Warshow," the girl said softly. "Don't get him excited."

"Excited? Who's excited?" Falk roared. "I—"

Warshow sat impassively, evaluating and analyzing, ignoring for the moment what was happening.

Falk would have to be brought back to the ship for treatment. There was no alternative, Warshow saw. This strange relationship with the Kollidorian would have to be broken.

He stood up and raised one hand for silence. "Mr. Falk, let me speak."

"Go ahead. Speak quick, because I'm going to pitch you out of here in two minutes."

"I won't need two minutes," Warshow said. "I simply want to inform you that you're under arrest and that you're hereby directed to report back to the base at once, in my custody. If you refuse to come it will be necessary—"

The sentence went unfinished. Falk's eyes flared angrily, and he crossed the little room in three quick bounds. Towering over the much smaller Warshow, he grabbed the commander by the shoulders and shook him violently. "Get out!" he shrieked.

Warshow smiled apologetically, took one step backward, and slid his stunner from its place in his tunic. He gave Falk a quick, heavy jolt, and as the big man sagged towards the floor, Warshow grabbed him and eased him into a chair.

Thetona was crying. Great gobbets of amber liquid oozed from her eyes and trickled heartbreakingly down her coarse cheeks.

"Sorry," Warshow said. "It had to be done."

It had to be done.

It had to be done.

It *had* to be done.

Warshow paced the cabin, his weak eyes darting nervously from the bright row of rivets across the ceiling to the quiet grey walls to the sleeping form of Matt Falk, and finally to the waiting, glowering visage of Psych Officer Cullinan.

"Do you want to wake him?" Cullinan asked.

"No. Not yet." Warshow kept prowling restlessly, trying to square his actions within himself. A few more minutes passed. Finally Cullinan stepped out from behind the cot on which Falk lay, and took Warshow's arm.

"Leon, tell me what's eating you."

"Don't shrink *my* skull," Warshow burst out. Then, sorry, he shook his head. "I didn't mean that. You know I didn't."

"It's two hours since you brought him aboard the ship," Cullinan said. "Don't you think we ought to do something?"

"What can we do?" Warshow demanded. "Throw him back to that alien girl? Kill him? Maybe that's the best solution—let's stuff him in the converters and blast off."

Falk stirred. "Ray him again," Warshow said hollowly. "The stunning's wearing off."

Cullinan used his stunner, and Falk subsided. "We can't keep him asleep forever," the psychman said.

"No—we can't." Warshow knew time was growing short; in three days the revised departure date would arrive, and he didn't dare risk another postponement.

But if they left Falk behind, and if word got around that a crazy Earthman was loose on Kollidor, or that Earthmen went crazy at all—

And there was no answer to that.

"Therapy," Cullinan said quietly.

"There's no time for an analysis," Warshow pointed out immediately. "*Three days*—that's all."

"I didn't mean a full-scale job. But if we nail him with an amytal-derivative inhibitor drug, filter out his hostility to talking to us, and run him back along his memories, we might hit something that'll help us."

Warshow shuddered. "Mind dredging, eh?"

"Call it that," the psychman said. "But let's dredge whatever it is that's tipped his rocker, or it'll wreck us all. You, me—and that girl."

"You think we can find it?"

"We can try. No Earthman in his right mind would form a sexual relationship of this kind—or *any* sort of emotional bond with an alien creature. If we hit the thing that catapulted him into it, maybe we can break this obviously neurotic fixation and make him go willingly. Unless you're willing to leave him behind. I absolutely forbid dragging him away as he is."

"Of course not," Warshow agreed. He mopped away sweat and glanced over at Falk, who still dreamed away under the effects of the stunbeam. "It's worth a try. If you think you can break it, go ahead. I deliver him into thy hands."

The psychman smiled with surprising warmth. "It's the only way. Let's dig up what happened to him and show it to him. That should crack the shell."

"I hope so," Warshow said. "It's in your hands. Wake him up and get him talking. You know what to do."

A murky cloud of drug-laden air hung in the cabin as Cullinan concluded his preliminaries. Falk stirred and began to grope towards consciousness. Cullinan handed Warshow an ultrasonic injector filled with a clear, glittering liquid.

Just as Falk seemed to be ready to open his eyes, Cullinan leaned over him and began to talk, quietly, soothingly. Falk's troubled frown vanished, and he subsided.

"Give him the drug," Cullinan whispered. Warshow touched the injector hesitantly to Falk's tanned forearm. The ultrasonic hummed briefly, blurred into the skin. Warshow administered three cc. and retracted.

Falk moaned gently.

"It'll take a few minutes," Cullinan said.

The wall clock circled slowly. After a while, Falk's sleep-heavy eyelids fluttered. He opened his eyes and glanced up without apparent recognition of his surroundings.

"Hello, Matt. We're here to talk to you," Cullinan said. "Or rather, we want you to talk to us."

"Yes," Falk said.

"Let's begin with your mother, shall we? Tell us what you remember about your mother. Go back, now."

"My—mother?" The question seemed to puzzle Falk, and he remained silent for nearly a minute. Then he moistened his lips. "What do you want to know about her?"

"Tell us everything," Cullinan urged.

There was silence. Warshow found himself holding his breath.

Finally, Falk began to speak.

Warm. Cuddly. Hold me. Mamama.

I'm all alone. It's night, and I'm crying. There are pins in my leg where I slept on it, and the night air smells cold. I'm three years old, and I'm all alone.

Hold me, mama?

I hear mama coming up the stairs. We have an old house with stairs, near the spaceport where the big ships go *woosh!* There's the soft smell of mama holding me now. Mama's big and pink and soft. Daddy is pink too but he doesn't smell warm. Uncle is the same way.

Ah, ah, baby, she's saying. She's in the room now, and holding me tight. It's good. I'm getting very drowsy. In a minute or two I'll be asleep. I like my mama very much.

("Is that your earliest recollection of your mother?" Cullinan asked.)
("No. I guess there's an earlier one.")

Dark here. Dark and very warm, and wet, and nice. I'm not moving. I'm all alone here, and I don't know where I am. It's like floating in an ocean. A big ocean. The whole world's an ocean.

It's nice here, real nice. I'm not crying.

Now there's blue needles in the black around me. Colors...all kinds. Red and green and lemon-yellow, and I'm *moving!* There's pain and pushing, and—God!—it's getting cold. I'm choking! I'm hanging on, but I'm going to drown in the air out there! I'm—

("That'll be enough," Cullinan said hastily. To Warshow he explained, "Birth trauma. Nasty. No need to put him through it all over again." Warshow shivered a little and blotted his forehead.)

("Should I go on?" Falk asked.)

("Yes. Go on.")

I'm four, and it's raining *plunk-a plunk* outside. It looks like the whole world's turned grey. Mama and daddy are away, and I'm alone again. Uncle is downstairs. I don't know uncle really, but he seems to be here all the time. Mama and daddy are away a lot. Being alone is like a cold rainstorm. It rains a lot here.

I'm in my bed, thinking about mama. I want mama. Mama took the jet plane somewhere. When I'm big, I want to take jet planes somewhere too—someplace warm and bright where it doesn't rain.

Downstairs the phone rings, jingle-jingle. Inside my head I can see the screen starting to get bright and full of colors, and I try to picture mama's face in the middle of the screen. But I can't. I hear uncle's voice talking, low and mumbly. I decide I don't like uncle, and I start to cry.

Uncle's here, and he's telling me I'm too big to cry. That I shouldn't cry any more. I tell him I want mama.

Uncle makes a nasty-mouth, and I cry louder.

Hush, he tells me. Quiet, Matt. There, there, Matt boy.

He straightens my blankets, but I scrunch my legs up under me and mess them up again because I know it'll annoy him. I like to annoy him because he isn't mama or daddy. But this time he doesn't seem to get annoyed. He just tidies them up again, and he pats my forehead. There's sweat on his hands, and he gets it on me.

I want mama, I tell him.

He looks down at me for a long time. Then he tells me, mama's not coming back.

Not *ever,* I ask?

No, he says. Not ever.

I don't believe him, but I don't start crying, because I don't want him to know he can scare me. How about daddy, I say. Get him for me.

Daddy's not going to come back either, he tells me.

I don't believe you, I say. I don't like you, uncle. I hate you.

He shakes his head and coughs. You'd better learn to like me, he says. You don't have anybody else any more.

I don't understand him, but I don't like what he's saying. I kick the blankets off the bed, and he picks them up. I kick them off again, and he hits me.

Then he bends over quick and kisses me, but he doesn't smell right and I start to cry. Rain comes. I want mama, I yell, but mama never comes. Never at all.

(Falk fell silent for a moment and closed his eyes. "Was she dead?" Cullinan prodded.)

("She was dead," Falk said. "She and dad were killed in a fluke jet-liner accident, coming back from a holiday in Bangkok. I was four, then. My uncle raised me. We didn't get along, much, and when I was fourteen he put me in the Academy. I stayed there four years, took two years of graduate technique, then joined Terran Imports. Two-year hitch on Denufar, then transferred to Commander Warshow's ship *Magyar* where—where—")

(He stopped abruptly. Cullinan glanced at Warshow and said, "He's warmed up now, and we're ready to strike paydirt, to mangle a metaphor." To Falk, he said, "Tell us how you met Thetona.")

❋

I'm alone in Kollidor and wandering around alone. It's a big sprawling place with funny-looking conical houses and crazy streets, but deep down underneath I can see it's just like Earth. The people are people. They're pretty bizarre, but they've got one head and two arms and two legs, which makes them more like people than some of the aliens I've seen.

Warshow gave us an afternoon's liberty. I don't know why I've left the ship, but I'm here in the city alone. Alone. Dammit, *alone!*

The streets are paved, but the sidewalks aren't. Suddenly I'm very tired and I feel dizzy. I sit down at the edge of the sidewalk and put my head in my hands. The aliens just walk around me, like people in any big city would.

Mama, I think.

Then I think, *Where did that come from?*

And suddenly a great empty loneliness comes welling up from inside of me and spills out all over me, and I start to cry. I haven't cried—since—not in a long time. But now I cry, hoarse ratchety gasps and tears rolling down my face and dribbling into the corners of my mouth. Tears taste salty, I think. A little like raindrops.

My side starts to hurt where I had the accident aboard ship. It begins up near my ear and races like a blue flame down my body to my thigh, and it hurts like a devil. The doctors told me I wouldn't hurt any more. They lied.

I feel my aloneness like a sealed spacesuit around me, cutting me off from everyone. *Mama,* I think again. Part of me is saying, *act like a grownup,* but that part of me is getting quieter and quieter. I keep crying, and I want desperately to have my mother again. I realize now I never knew my mother at all, except for a few years long ago.

Then there's a musky, slightly sickening smell, and I know one of the aliens is near me. They're going to grab me by the scruff and haul me away like any weepy-eyed drunk in the public streets. Warshow will give me hell.

You're crying, Earthman, a warm voice says.

The Kollidorian language is kind of warm and liquid and easy to learn, but this sounds especially warm. I turn around, and there's this big native dame.

Yeah, I'm crying, I say, and look away. Her big hands clamp down on me and hang on, and I shiver a little. It feels funny to be handled by an alien woman.

She sits down next to me. You look very sad, she says.

I am, I tell her.

Why are you sad?

You'd never understand, I say. I turn my head away and feel tears start creeping out of my eyes, and she grabs me impulsively. I nearly retch from the smell of her, but in a minute or two I see it's sort of sweet and nice in a strange way.

She's wearing an outfit like a potato sack, and it smells pretty high. But she pulls my head against her big warm breasts and leaves it there.

What's your name, unhappy Earthman?

Falk, I say. Matthew Falk.

I'm Thetona, she says. I live alone. Are you lonely?

I don't know, I say. I really don't know.

But how can you not know if you're lonely? she asks.

She pulls my head up out of her bosom and our eyes come together. Real romantic. She's got eyes like tarnished half dollars. We look at each other, and she reaches out and pushes the tears out of my eyes.

She smiles. I think it's a smile. She has about thirty notches arranged in a circle under her nose, and that's a mouth. All the notches pucker. Behind them I see bright needly teeth.

I look up from her mouth to her eyes again, and this time they don't look tarnished so much. They're bright like the teeth, and deep and warm.

Warm. Her odor is warm. Everything about her is warm.

I start to cry again—compulsively, without knowing why, without knowing what the hell is happening to me. She seems to flicker, and I think I see a Terran woman sitting there cradling me. I blink. Nothing there but an ugly alien.

Only she's not ugly any more. She's warm and lovely, in a strange sort of way, and the part of me that disagrees is very tiny and tinny-sounding. I hear it yelling, *No,* and then it stops and winks out.

Something strange is exploding inside me. I let it explode. It bursts like a flower—a rose, or a violet, and that's what I smell instead of *her.*

I put my arms around her.

Do you want to come to my house, she asks.

Yes, yes, I say. Yes!

Abruptly, Falk stopped on the ringing affirmative, and his glazed eyes closed. Cullinan fired the stunner once, and the boy's taut body slumped.

"Well?" Warshow asked. His voice was dry and harsh. "I feel unclean after hearing that."

"You should," the psychman said. "It's one of the slimiest things I've uncovered yet. And you don't understand it, do you?"

The commander shook his head slowly. "No. Why'd he do it? He's in love with her—but *why?*"

Cullinan chuckled. "You'll see. But I want a couple of other people here when I yank it out. I want the girl, first of all—and I want Sigstrom."

"The doctor? What the hell for?"

"Because—if I'm right—he'll be very interested in hearing what comes out." Cullinan grinned enigmatically. "Let's give Falk a rest, eh? After all that talking, he needs it."

"So do I," Warshow said.

(Four people watched silently as Falk slipped into the drug-induced trance a second time. Warshow studied the face of the alien girl Thetona for some sign of the warmth Falk had spoken of. And yes, Warshow saw—it was there. Behind her sat Sigstrom, the *Magyar's* head medic. To his right, Cullinan. And lying on the cot in the far corner of the cabin, eyes open but unseeing, was Matt Falk.)

("Matt, can you hear me?" Cullinan asked. "I want you to back up a little...you're aboard ship now. The time is approximately one month ago. You're working in the converter section, you and Dave Murff, handling hot stuff. Got that?")

("Yes," Falk said. "I know what you mean.")

I'm in Converter Section AA, getting thorium out of hock to feed to the reactors; we've gotta keep the ship moving. Dave Murff's with me.

We make a good team on the waldoes.

We're running them now, picking up chunks of hot stuff and stowing them in the reactor bank. It's not easy to manipulate the remote-control mechanihands, but I'm not scared. This is my job, and I know how to do it.

I'm thinking about that bastard Warshow, though. Nothing particular against him, but he annoys me. Funny way he has of tensing up every time he has to order someone to do anything. Reminds me of my uncle. Yeah, my uncle. That's who I was trying to compare him with.

Don't much like Warshow. If he came in here now, maybe I'd tap him with the waldo—not much, just enough to sizzle his hide a little. Just for the hell of it: I always wanted to belt my uncle, just for the hell of it.

Hey, Murff yells. Get number two waldo back in alignment.

Don't worry, I say. "This isn't the first time I've handled these babies, lunkhead."

I'm shielded pretty well. But the air smells funny, as if the thorium's been ionizing it, and I wonder maybe something's wrong.

I swing number two waldo over and dump the thorium in the reactor. The green light pops on and tells me it's a square-on hit; the hot stuff is tumbling down into the reactor now and pushing out the neutrons like crazy.

Then Murff gives the signal and I dip into the storage and yank out some more hot stuff with number one waldo.

Hey, he yells again, and then number two waldo, the empty one, runs away from me.

The big arm is swinging in the air, and I see the little fingers of delicate jointed metal bones that so few seconds ago were hanging onto a chunk of red-hot Th-233. They seem to be clutching out for me.

I yell. God, I yell. Murff yells too as I lose control altogether, and he tries to get behind the control panel and grab the waldo handle. But I'm in the way, and I'm frozen so he can't do it. He ducks back and flattens himself on the floor as the big mechanical arm crashes through the shielding.

I can't move.

I stay there. The little fingers nick me on the left side of my jaw, and I scream. I'm on fire. The metal hand rakes down the side of my body, hardly touching me, and it's like a razor slicing through my flesh.

It's too painful even to feel. My nerves are canceling out. They won't deliver the messages to my brain.

And now the pain sweeps down on me. *Help! I'm burning! Help!*

("Stop there," Cullinan said sharply, and Falk's terrible screaming stopped. "Edit out the pain and keep going. What happens when you wake up?")

Voices. I hear them above me as I start to come out of the shroud of pain.

Radiation burns, a deep crackly voice is saying. It's Doc Sigstrom. The doc says, he's terribly burnt, Leon. I don't think he'll live.

Dammit, says another voice. That's Commander Warshow. He's got to live, Warshow says. I've never lost a man yet. Twenty years without losing anybody.

He took quite a roasting from that remote-control arm, a third voice says. It's Psych Officer Cullinan, I think. He lost control, Cullinan goes on. Very strange.

Yeah, I think. Very strange. I blanked out just a second, and that waldo seemed to come alive.

I feet the pain ripping up and down me. Half my head feels like it's missing, and my arm's being toasted. Where's the brimstone, I wonder.

Then Doc Sigstrom says, We'll try a nutrient bath.

What's that? Warshow asks.

New technique, the doc says. Chemotherapeutic incubation. Immersion in hormone solutions. They're using it on Earth in severe cases of type one radiation burns. I don't think it's ever been tried in space, but it ought to be. He'll be in free fall; gravity won't confuse things.

If it'll save him, Warshow says, I'm for it.

Then things fade. Time goes on—an eternity in hell, with the blazing pain racing up and back down my side. I hear people talking every now and then; feel myself being shifted from one place to another. Tubes are stuck in me to feed me. I wonder what I look like with half my body frizzled.

Suddenly, cool warmth. Yeah, it sounds funny. But it is warm and nourishing, and yet cool too, bathing me and taking the sting out of my body.

I don't try to open my eyes, but I know I'm surrounded by darkness. I'm totally immobile, in the midst of darkness, and yet I know that outside me the ship is racing on towards Kollidor, enclosing me, holding me.

I'm within the ship, rocking gently and securely. I'm within something within the ship. Wheels within wheels; doors inside doors. Chinese puzzle-box with me inside.

Soft fluid comes licking over me, nudging itself in where the tissue is torn and blasted and the flesh bubbled from heat. Caressing each individual cell, bathing my body organ by organ, I'm being repaired.

I float on an ocean and in an ocean. My body is healing rapidly. The pain ceases.

I'm not conscious of the passage of time at all. Minutes blend into minutes without joint; time flows unbreakingly, and I'm being lulled into a soft, unending existence. Happiness, I think. Security. Peace.

I like it here.

Around me, a globe of fluid. Around that, a striated webwork of metal. Around that, a spheroid spaceship, and around that a universe. Around that? I don't know, and I don't care. I'm safe here, where there's no pain, no fear.

Blackness. Total and utter blackness. Security equals blackness and softness and quiet. But then—

What are they doing?

What's happening?

Blue darts of light against the blackness, and now a swirl of colors. Green, red, yellow. Light bursts in and dazzles me. Smells, feels, noises.

The cradle is rocking. I'm moving.

No. They're pulling me. Out!

It's getting cold, and I can't breathe. I'm choking! I try to hang on, but they won't let go! They keep pulling me out, out, out into the world of fire and pain!

I struggle. I won't go. But it doesn't do any good. I'm out, finally.

I look around. Two blurry figures above me. I wipe my eyes and things come clear. Warshow and Sigstrom, that's who they are.

Sigstrom smiles and says, booming, "Well, he's healed wonderfully!"

A miracle, Warshow says. "A miracle."

I wobble. I want to fall, but I'm lying down already. They keep talking, and I start to cry in rage.

But there's no way back. It's over. All, all over. And I'm terribly alone.

Falk's voice died away suddenly. Warshow fought an impulse to get violently sick. His face felt cold and clammy, and he turned to look at the pale, nervous faces of Sigstrom and Cullinan. Behind them sat Thetona, expressionless.

Cullinan broke the long silence. "Leon, you heard the earlier session. Did you recognize what he was just telling us?"

"The birth trauma," Warshow said tonelessly.

"Obviously," Sigstrom said. The medic ran unshaking fingers through his heavy shock of white hair. "The chemotherapy…it was a womb for him. We put him back in the womb."

"And then we pulled him out," said Warshow. "We delivered him. And he went looking for a mother."

Cullinan nodded at Thetona. "He found one too."

Warshow licked his lips. "Well, now we have the answer. What do we do about it?"

"We play the whole thing to him on tapes. His conscious intellectual mind sees his relationship with Thetona for what it is—the neurotic grasping of a grown man forced into an artificial womb and searching for a mother. Once we've gotten that out of his basement and into the attic, so to speak, I think he'll be all right."

"But the ship was his mother," Warshow said. "That was where the incubation tank—the *womb*—was."

"The ship cast him out. You were an uncle-image, not a mother-substitute. He said so himself. He went looking elsewhere, and found Thetona. Let's give him the tapes."

Much later, Matt Falk faced the four of them in the cabin. He had heard his own voice rambling back over his lifetime. He *knew*, now.

There was a long silence when the last tape had played out, when Falk's voice had said, *"All, all over. And I'm terribly alone."*

The words seemed to hang in the room. Finally Falk said, "Thanks," in a cold, hard, tight, dead voice.

"Thanks?" Warshow repeated dully.

"Yes. Thanks for opening my eyes, for thoughtfully giving me a peek at what was behind my lid. Sure—*thanks.*" The boy's face was sullen, bitter.

"You understand why it was necessary, of course," Cullinan said. "Why we—"

"Yeah, I know why," Falk said. "And now I can go back to Earth with you, and your consciences are cleared." He glanced at Thetona, who was watching him with perturbed curiosity evident on her broad face. Falk shuddered lightly as his eyes met the alien girl's. Warshow caught the reaction and nodded. The therapy had been a success.

"I was happy," Falk said quietly. "Until you decided you *had* to take me back to Earth with you. So you ran me through a wringer and combed all the psychoses out of me, and—and—"

Thetona took two heavy steps towards him and put her arms on his shoulders. "No," he murmured, and wriggled away. "Can't you see it's over?"

"Matt—" Warshow said.

"Don't Matt me, cap'n! I'm out of my womb now, and back in your crew." He turned sad eyes on Warshow. "Thetona and I had something good and warm and beautiful, and you busted it up. It can't get put together again, either. Okay. I'm ready to go back to Earth, now."

He stalked out of the room without another word. Grey-faced, Warshow stared at Cullinan and at Thetona, and lowered his eyes.

He had fought to keep Matt Falk, and he had won—or had he? In fact, yes. But in spirit? Falk would never forgive him for this.

Warshow shrugged, remembering the book that said, *"The relation of commander to crewman is that of parent to child."*

Warshow would not allow Falk's sullen eyes to upset him any longer; it was only to be expected that the boy would be bitter.

No child ever really forgives the parent who casts him from the womb.

"Come on, Thetona," he said to the big, enigmatically frowning alien girl. "Come with me. I'll take you back down to the city."

SUNRISE ON MERCURY

The fine old custom of having writers construct stories around cover paint-
ings—now, I believe, probably extinct—brought "Sunrise On Mercury" into
existence in what was for me the hyperactive month of November, 1956. In
that vanished era, the pulp-magazine chains found it efficient and econom-
ical to print their covers in batches of four, well in advance of publication
date, which meant that there was usually no time to go through the process
of buying a story, farming it out to an artist to be illustrated,making plates
from the artist's painting, etc. Instead the artists would think up ideas for
illustrations—some sort of vivid and dramatic scene, often cheerfully
depicting some highly improbable event that was designed to tax a writer's
ingenuity to the limit—and it went to press right away, while some reliable
writer was hired to put that scene, by hook or by crook, into a story that
could be published to accompany it. It's a measure of how far I had come by
this time that I was already being given such assignments, here in the sec-
ond year of my career. But the editors knew I could be depended on to uti-
lize the illustration in some plausible way and to turn my cover story in on
time.

The editor for whom I did more of these than for any other was Robert
W. Lowndes of Science Fiction Stories *and* Future Science Fiction, *who*
had been a prominent figure in the science fiction field as reader, writer, and
editor for the past two decades. Bob Lowndes and I had become close
friends by now, despite an age difference of nearly twenty years. He was a
charming man, scholarly by nature, somewhat awkward and shy, and, since
we had many interests in common—among them, classical music, cats, and

the collecting of old science-fiction magazines—we swiftly took to each other. My wife and I began to be frequent weekend guests at Lowndes' small but pleasant country home about an hour's drive outside New York City; I explored his huge record collection, he and I argued amiably over our favorite stories and books, and I played with his cats. (And took a kitten home for Christmas in 1956.)

Soon after Randall Garrett had introduced me to him and I began regularly selling stories to his magazines, Lowndes started handing me two or three covers at once, commissioning me to write stories of five or six thousand words to accompany each one. The money wasn't much—a cent or occasionally a cent and a half a word on publication, cut-rate pay even in those days—but it was a guaranteed sale, and so speedy was I at turning out the stories that even at $60 for 6000 words, which is what I was paid for "Sunrise on Mercury," I did all right. ($60 for a day's pay was nothing contemptible in 1956.)

The cover that inspired this one, by the versatile and prolific Ed Emshwiller, showed the bleak landscape of Mercury with the sun rising ominously in the upper left-hand corner, a transparent plastic dome melting in Daliesque fashion in the upper right, and two harassed-looking men in spacesuits running for their lives below. Obviously something unexpected was going on, like sunrise happening a week ahead of schedule; so all I had to do was figure out a reason why that might occur, and I had my sixty bucks. The result, all things considered, wasn't half bad; and the story, which Lowndes used in the May, 1957 Science Fiction Stories, has been frequently anthologized over the past forty-plus years.

Nine million miles to the sunward of Mercury, with the *Leverrier* swinging into the series of spirals that would bring it down on the solar system's smallest world, Second Astrogator Lon Curtis decided to end his life.

Curtis had been lounging in a webfoam cradle waiting for the landing to be effected; his job in the operation was over, at least until the *Leverrier's* landing jacks touched Mercury's blistered surface. The ship's efficient sodium-coolant system negated the efforts of the swollen sun visible through the rear screen. For Curtis and his seven shipmates, no problems presented themselves; they had only to wait while the autopilot brought the ship down for man's second landing on Mercury.

Flight Commander Harry Ross was sitting near Curtis when he noticed the sudden momentary stiffening of the astrogator's jaws. Curtis abruptly reached for the control nozzle. From the spinnerets that had spun the webfoam came a quick green burst of dissolving fluorochrene; the cradle vanished. Curtis stood up.

"Going somewhere?" Ross asked.

Curtis's voice was harsh. "Just—just taking a walk."

Ross returned his attention to his microbook for a moment as Curtis walked away. There was the ratchety sound of a bulkhead dog being manipulated, and Ross felt a momentary chill as the cooler air of the superrefrigerated reactor compartment drifted in.

He punched a stud, turning the page. Then—

What the hell is he doing in the reactor compartment?

The autopilot would be controlling the fuel flow, handling it down to the milligram, in a way no human system could. The reactor was primed for the landing, the fuel was stoked, the compartment was dogged shut. No one—least of all a second astrogator—had any business going back there.

Ross had the foam cradle dissolved in an instant, and was on his feet a moment later. He dashed down the companionway and through the open bulkhead door into the coolness of the reactor compartment.

Curbs was standing by the converter door, toying with the release-tripper. As Ross approached, he saw the astrogator get the door open and put one foot to the chute that led downship to the nuclear pile.

"Curtis, you idiot! Get away from there! You'll kill us all!"

The astrogator turned, looked blankly at Ross for an instant, and drew up his other foot. Ross leaped.

He caught Curtis' booted foot in his hands, and despite a barrage of kicks from the astrogator's free boot, managed to drag Curtis off the chute. The astrogator tugged and pulled, attempting to break free. Ross saw the man's pale cheeks quivering. Curtis had cracked, but thoroughly.

Grunting, Ross yanked Curtis away from the yawning reactor chute and slammed the door shut. He dragged him out into the main section again and slapped him, hard.

"Why'd you want to do that? Don't you know what your mass would do to the ship if it got into the converter? You know the fuel intake's been calibrated already; 180 extra pounds and we'd arc right into the sun. What's wrong with you, Curtis?"

The astrogator fixed unshaking, unexpressive eyes on Ross. "I want to die," he said simply. "Why couldn't you let me die?"

He wanted to die. Ross shrugged, feeling a cold tremor run down his back. There was no guarding against this disease.

Just as aqualungers beneath the sea's surface suffered from *l'ivresse des grandes profondeurs*—rapture of the deeps—and knew no cure for the strange, depth-induced drunkenness that caused them to remove their breathing tubes fifty fathoms below, so did spacemen run the risk of this nameless malady, this inexplicable urge to self-destruction.

It struck anywhere. A repairman wielding a torch on a recalcitrant strut of an orbiting wheel might abruptly rip open his facemask and drink vacuum; a radioman rigging an antenna on the skin of his ship might suddenly cut his line, fire his directional pistol, and send himself drifting away. Or a second astrogator might decide to climb into the converter.

Psych Officer Spangler appeared, an expression of concern fixed on his smooth pink face. "Trouble?"

Ross nodded. "Curtis. Tried to jump into the fuel chute. He's got it, Doc."

Spangler rubbed his cheek and said: "They always pick the best times, dammit. It's swell having a psycho on a Mercury run."

"That's the way it is," Ross said wearily. "Better put him in stasis till we get home. I'd hate to have him running loose, looking for different ways of doing himself in."

"Why can't you let me die?" Curbs asked. His face was bleak. "Why'd you have to stop me?"

"Because, you lunatic, you'd have killed all the rest of us by your fool dive into the converter. Go walk out the airlock if you want to die—but don't take us with you."

Spangler glared warningly at him. "Harry—"

"Okay," Ross said. "Take him away."

The psychman led Curtis within. The astrogator would be given a tranquillizing injection and locked in an insoluble webfoam jacket for the rest of the journey. There was a chance he could be restored to sanity once they returned to Earth, but Ross knew that the astrogator would go straight for the nearest method of suicide the moment he was released aboard the ship.

Scowling, Ross turned away. A man spends his boyhood dreaming about space, he thought, spends four years at the Academy, and two more making dummy runs. Then he finally gets out where it counts and he cracks up. Curtis was an astrogation machine, not a normal human being; and he had just disqualified himself permanently from the only job he knew how to do.

Ross shivered, feeling chill despite the bloated bulk of the sun filling the rear screen. It could happen to anyone...even him. He thought of Curtis lying in a foam cradle somewhere in the back of the ship, blackly thinking over and over again, *I want to die,* while Doc Spangler muttered soothing things at him. A human being was really a frail form of life.

Death seemed to hang over the ship; the gloomy aura of Curtis's suicide-wish polluted the atmosphere.

Ross shook his head and punched down savagely on the signal to prepare for deceleration. Mercury's sharp globe bobbed up ahead. He spotted it through the front screen.

They were approaching the tiny planet middle-on. He could see the neat division now: the brightness of Sunside, that unapproachable inferno where zinc ran in rivers, and the icy blackness of Darkside, dull with its unlit plains of frozen CO_2.

Down the heart of the planet ran the Twilight Belt, that narrow area of not-cold and not-heat where Sunside and Darkside met to provide a thin band of barely tolerable territory, a ring nine thousand miles in circumference and ten or twenty miles wide.

The *Leverrier* plunged planetward. Ross allowed his jangled nerves to grow calm. The ship was in the hands of the autopilot; the orbit, of course, was precomputed, and the analogue banks in the drive were serenely following the taped program, bringing the ship towards its destination smack in the middle of—

My God!

Ross went cold from head to toe. The precomputed tape had been fed to the analogue banks—had been prepared by—had been entirely the work of—

Curtis.

A suicidal madman had worked out the *Leverrier's* landing program.

Ross began to shake. How easy it would have been, he thought, for death-bent Curtis to work out an orbit that would plant the *Leverrier* in a smoking river of molten lead—or in the mortuary chill of Darkside.

His false security vanished. There was no trusting the automatic pilot; they'd have to risk a manual landing.

Ross jabbed down on the communicator button. "I want Brainerd," he said hoarsely.

The first astrogator appeared a few seconds later, peering in curiously. "What goes, Captain?"

"We've just carted your assistant Curtis off to the pokey. He tried to jump into the converter."

Ross nodded. "Attempted suicide. I got to him in time. But in view of the circumstances, I think we'd better discard the tape you had him prepare and bring the ship down manually, yes?"

The first astrogator moistened his lips. "That sounds like a good idea."

"Damn right it is," Ross said, glowering.

As the ship touched down Ross thought, *Mercury is two hells in one.*

It was the cold, ice-bound kingdom of Dante's deepest pit—and it was also the brimstone empire of another conception. The two met, fire and frost, each hemisphere its own kind of hell.

He lifted his head and flicked a quick glance at the instrument panel above his deceleration cradle. The dials all checked: weight placement was proper, stability 100 per cent, external temperature a manageable 108°F, indicating they had made their descent a little to the sunward of the Twilight Belt's exact middle. It had been a sound landing.

He snapped on the communicator. "Brainerd?"

"All okay, Captain."

"Manual landing?"

"I had to," the astrogator said. "I ran a quick check on Curtis' tape, and it was all cockeyed. The way he had us coming in, we'd have grazed Mercury's orbit by a whisker and kept on going straight into the sun. Nice?"

"Very sweet," Ross said. "But don't be too hard on the kid. He didn't want to go psycho. Good landing, anyway. We seem to be pretty close to the center of the Twilight Belt, and that's where I feel most comfortable."

He broke the contact and unwebbed himself. Over the shipwide circuit he called all hands fore, double pronto.

The men got there quickly enough—Brainerd first, then Doc Spangler, followed by Accumulator Tech Krinsky and the three other crewmen. Ross waited until the entire group had assembled.

They were looking around curiously for Curtis. Crisply, Ross told them, "Astrogator Curtis is going to miss this meeting. He's aft in the psycho bin. Luckily, we can shift without him on this tour."

He waited until the implications of that statement had sunk in. The men seemed to adjust to it well enough, he thought: momentary expressions of dismay, shock, even horror quickly faded from their faces.

"All right," he said. "Schedule calls for us to put in some thirty-two hours of extravehicular activity on Mercury. Brainerd, how does that check with our location?"

The astrogator frowned and made some mental calculations. "Current position is a trifle to the sunward edge of the Twilight Belt; but as I figure it, the sun won't be high enough to put the Fahrenheit much above 120 for at least a week. Our suits can handle that temperature with ease."

"Good. Llewellyn, you and Falbridge break out the radar inflaters and get the tower set up as far to the east as you can go without getting roasted. Take the crawler, but be sure to keep an eye on the thermometer. We've only got one heatsuit, and that's for Krinsky."

Llewellyn, a thin, sunken-eyed spaceman, shifted uneasily. "How far to the east do you suggest, sir?"

"The Twilight Belt covers about a quarter of Mercury's surface," Ross said. "You've got a strip forty-seven degrees wide to move around in—but I don't suggest you go much more than twenty-five miles or so. It starts getting hot after that. And keeps going up."

Ross turned to Krinsky. In many ways the accumulator tech was the expedition's key man: it was his job to check the readings on the pair of solar accumulators that had been left here by the first expedition. He was to measure the amount of stress created by solar energies here, so close to the source of radiation, study force-lines operating in the strange magnetic field of the little world, and reprime the accumulators for further testing by the next expedition.

Krinsky was a tall, powerfully built man, the sort of man who could stand up to the crushing weight of a heatsuit almost cheerfully. The heatsuit was necessary for prolonged work in the Sunside zone, where the accumulators were mounted—and even a giant like Krinsky could stand the strain for only a few hours at a time.

"When Llewellyn and Falbridge have the radar tower set up, Krinsky, get into your heatsuit and be ready to move. As soon as we've got the accumulator station located, Dominic will drive you as far east as possible and drop you off. The rest is up to you. Watch your step. We'll be telemetering your readings, but we'd like to have you back alive."

"Yes, sir."

"That's about it," Ross said. "Let's get rolling."

Ross's own job was purely administrative—and as the men of his crew moved busily about their allotted tasks, he realized unhappily that he himself was condemned to temporary idleness. His function was that of overseer; like the conductor of a symphony orchestra, he played no instrument himself and was on hand mostly to keep the group moving in harmony towards the finish.

Everyone was in motion. Now he had only to wait.

Llewellyn and Falbridge departed, riding the segmented, thermo-resistant crawler that had traveled to Mercury in the belly of the *Leverrier*. Their job was simple: they were to erect the inflatable plastic radar tower out towards the sunward sector. The tower that the first expedition had left had long since librated into a Sunside zone and been liquefied; the plastic base and parabola, covered with a light reflective surface of aluminum, could hardly withstand the searing heat of Sunside.

Out there, it got up to 700° when the sun was at its closest. The eccentricities of Mercury's orbit accounted for considerable temperature variations on Sunside, but the thermometer never showed lower than 300° out there, even during aphelion. On Darkside, there was less of a temperature range; mostly the temperature hovered not far from absolute zero, and frozen drifts of heavy gases covered the surface of the land.

From where he stood, Ross could see neither Sunside nor Darkside. The Twilight Belt was nearly a thousand miles broad, and as the little planet dipped in its orbit the sun would first slide above the horizon, then slip back. For a twenty-mile strip through the heart of the Belt, the heat of Sunside and the cold of Darkside canceled out into a fairly stable, temperate climate; for five hundred miles on either side, the Twilight Belt gradually trickled towards the areas of extreme cold and raging heat.

It was a strange and forbidding planet. Humans could endure it for only a short time; it was worse than Mars, worse than the Moon. The sort of life capable of living permanently on Mercury was beyond Ross's powers of imagination. Standing outside the *Leverrier* in his spacesuit, he nudged the chin control that lowered a sheet of optical glass. He peered first towards Darkside, where he thought he saw a thin line of encroaching black—only illusion, he knew—and then towards Sunside.

In the distance, Llewellyn and Falbridge were erecting the spidery parabola that was the radar tower. He could see the clumsy shape outlined against the sky now—and behind it? A faint line of brightness rimming the bordering peaks? Illusion also, he knew. Brainerd had calculated that the sun's radiance would not be visible here for a week. And in a week's time they'd be back on Earth.

He turned to Krinsky. "The tower's nearly up. They'll be coming in with the crawler any minute. You'd better get ready to make your trip."

As the accumulator tech swung up the handholds and into the ship, Ross's thoughts turned to Curtis. The young astrogator had talked excitedly of seeing Mercury all the way out—and now that they were actually here, Curtis lay in a web of foam deep within the ship, moodily demanding the right to die.

Krinsky returned, now wearing the insulating bulk of the heatsuit over his standard rebreathing outfit. He looked more like a small tank than a man. "Is the crawler approaching, sir?"

"I'll check."

Ross adjusted the lensplate in his mask and narrowed his eyes. It seemed to him that the temperature had risen a little. Another illusion? He squinted into the distance.

His eyes picked out the radar tower far off towards Sunside. He gasped.

"Something the matter?" Krinsky asked.

"I'll say!" Ross squeezed his eyes tight shut and looked again. And—yes—the newly erected radar tower was drooping soggily and beginning to melt. He saw two tiny figures racing madly over the flat, pumice-covered ground to the silvery oblong that was the crawler. And—impossibly—the first glow of an unmistakable brightness was beginning to shimmer on the mountains behind the tower.

The sun was rising—a week ahead of schedule!

Ross ran back into the ship, followed by the lumbering figure of Krinsky. In the airlock, obliging mechanical hands descended to ease him out of his spacesuit; signaling to Krinsky to keep the heatsuit on, he dashed through into the main cabin.

"Brainerd? Brainerd! Where in hell are you?"

The senior astrogator appeared, looking puzzled. "What's up, Captain?"

"Look out the screen," Ross said in a strangled voice. "Look at the radar tower!"

"It's *melting*," Brainerd said, astonished. "But that's—that's—"

"I know. It's impossible." Ross glanced at the instrument panel. External temperature had risen to 112°—a jump of four degrees. And as he watched it glided up to 114°.

It would take a heat of at least 500° to melt the radar tower that way. Ross squinted at the screen and saw the crawler come swinging dizzily towards them: Llewellyn and Falbridge were still alive, then—though they probably had had a good cooking out there. The temperature outside the ship was up to 116°. It would probably be near 200° by the time the two men returned.

Angrily, Ross whirled to face the astrogator. "I thought you were bringing us down in the safety strip," he snapped. "Check your figures again and find out where the hell we *really* are. Then work out a blasting orbit, fast: That's the sun coming up over those hills."

The temperature had reached 120°. The ship's cooling system would be able to keep things under control and comfortable until about 250°; beyond that, there was danger of an overload. The crawler continued to draw near. It was probably hellish inside the little land car, Ross thought.

His mind weighed alternatives. If the external temperature went much over 250°, he would run the risk of wrecking the ship's cooling system by waiting for the two in the crawler to arrive. There was some play in the system, but not much. He decided he'd give them until it hit 275° to get back. If they didn't make it by then, he'd have to take off without them. It was foolish to try to save two lives at the risk of six. External temperature had hit 130°. Its rate of increase was jumping rapidly.

The ship's crew knew what was going on now. Without the need of direct orders from Ross, they were readying the *Leverrier* for an emergency blastoff.

The crawler inched forward. The two men weren't much more than ten miles away now; and at an average speed of forty miles an hour they'd be back within fifteen minutes. Outside the temperature was 133°. Long fingers of shimmering sunlight stretched towards them from the horizon.

Brainerd looked up from his calculation. "I can't work it. The damned figures don't come out."

"Huh?"

"I'm trying to compute our location—and I can't do the arithmetic. My head's all foggy."

What the hell. This was where a captain earned his pay, Ross thought. "Get out of the way," he said brusquely. "Let me do it."

He sat down at the desk and started figuring. He saw Brainerd's hasty notations scratched out everywhere. It was as if the astrogator had totally forgotten how to do his job.

Let's see, now. If we're—

He tapped out figures on the little calculator. But as he worked he saw that what he was doing made no sense. His mind felt bleary and strange; he couldn't seem to handle the elementary computations at all. Looking up, he said, "Tell Krinsky to get down there and make himself ready to help those men out of the crawler when they show up. They're probably half cooked."

Temperature 146°. He looked down at the calculator. Damn: it shouldn't be that hard to do simple trigonometry, should it?

Doc Spangler appeared. "I cut Curtis free," he announced. "He isn't safe during takeoff in that cradle."

From within came a steady mutter. "Just let me die…just let me die…"

"Tell him he's likely to get his wish," Ross murmured. "If I can't manage to work out a blastoff orbit we're all going to fry right here."

"How come you're doing it? What's the matter with Brainerd?"

"Choked up. Couldn't make sense of his own figures. And come to think of it, I'm not doing so well myself."

Fingers of fog seemed to wrap around his mind. He glanced at the dial. Temperature 152° outside. That gave the boys in the crawler 123° to get back here…or was it 321°? He was confused, utterly bewildered.

Doc Spangler looked peculiar too. The psych officer wore an odd frown. "I feel very lethargic suddenly," Spangler declared. "I know I really should get back to Curtis, but—"

The madman was keeping up a steady babble inside. The part of Ross's mind that still could think clearly realized that if left unattended Curtis was capable of doing almost anything.

Temperature 158°.

The crawler seemed to be getting nearer. On the horizon the radar tower was melting into a crazy shambles.

There was a shriek. "Curtis!" Ross yelled, his mind hurriedly returning to awareness. He ran aft, with Spangler close behind.

Too late.

Curtis lay on the floor in a bloody puddle. He had found a pair of shears somewhere.

Spangler bent. "He's dead."

"Dead. Of course." Ross's brain felt totally clear now. At the moment of Curtis' death the fog had lifted. Leaving Spangler to attend to the body, he returned to the astrogation desk and glanced through the calculations he had been doing. Worthless. An idiotic mess.

With icy clarity he started again, and this time succeeded in determining their location. They had come down better than three hundred miles sunward of where they had thought they were landing. The instruments hadn't lied—but someone's eyes had. The orbit that Brainerd had so solemnly assured him was a "safe" one was actually almost as deadly as the one Curtis had computed.

He looked outside. The crawler had almost reached the ship. Temperature 167° out there. There was plenty of time. They would make it with a few minutes to spare, thanks to the warning they had received from the melting radar tower.

But why had it happened? There was no answer to that.

Gigantic in his heatsuit, Krinsky brought Llewellyn and Falbridge aboard. They peeled out of their spacesuits and wobbled around unsteadily for a moment before they collapsed. They were as red as newly boiled lobsters.

"Heat prostration," Ross said. "Krinsky, get them into takeoff cradles. Dominic, you in your suit yet?"

The spaceman appeared at the airlock entrance and nodded.

"Good. Get down there and drive the crawler into the hold. We can't afford to leave it here. Double-quick, and then we're blasting off. Brainerd, that new orbit ready?"

"Yes, sir."

The thermometer grazed 200. The cooling system was beginning to suffer—but it would not have to endure much more agony. Within minutes the *Leverrier* was lifting from Mercury's surface—minutes ahead of the relentless advance of the sun. The ship swung into a parking orbit not far above the planet's surface.

As they hung there, catching their breaths, just one thing occupied Ross's mind: *why?* Why had Brainerd's orbit brought them down in a danger zone instead of the safety strip? Why had both he and Brainerd been unable to compute a blasting pattern, the simplest of elementary astrogation techniques? And why had Spangler's wits utterly failed him—just long enough to let the unhappy Curtis kill himself?

Ross could see the same question reflected on everyone's face: why?

He felt an itchy feeling at the base of his skull. And suddenly an image forced its way across his mind and he had the answer.

He saw a great pool of molten zinc, lying shimmering between two jagged crests somewhere on Sunside. It had been there thousands of years; it would be there thousands, perhaps millions, of years from now.

Its surface quivered. The sun's brightness upon the pool was intolerable even to the mind's eye.

Radiation beat down on the pool of zinc—the sun's radiation, hard and unending. And then a new radiation, an electromagnetic emanation in a different part of the spectrum, carrying a meaningful message:

I want to die.

The pool of zinc stirred fretfully with sudden impulses of helpfulness.

The vision passed as quickly as it came. Stunned, Ross looked up. The expressions on the six faces surrounding him confirmed what he could guess.

"You all felt it too," he said.

Spangler nodded, then Krinsky and the rest of them.

"Yes," Krinsky said. "What the devil was it?"

Brainerd turned to Spangler. "Are we all nuts, Doc?"

The psych officer shrugged. "Mass hallucination…collective hypnosis…"

"No, Doc." Ross leaned forward. "You know it as well as I do. That thing was real. It's down there, out on Sunside."

"What do you mean?"

"I mean that wasn't any hallucination we had. That's something alive down there—or as close to alive as anything on Mercury can be." Ross's hands were shaking. He forced them to subside. "We've stumbled over something very big," he said.

Spangler stirred uneasily. "Harry—"

"No, I'm not out of my head! Don't you see—that thing down there, whatever it is, is sensitive to our thoughts! It picked up Curtis' godawful caterwauling the way a radar set grabs electromagnetic waves. His were the strongest thoughts coming through; so it acted on them and did its damnedest to help Curtis get what he wanted."

"You mean by fogging our minds and deluding us into thinking we were in safe territory, when actually we were right near sunrise territory?"

"But why would it go to all that trouble?" Krinsky objected. "If it wanted to help poor Curtis kill himself, why didn't it just fix things so we came down right *in* Sunside. We'd cook a lot quicker that way."

"Originally it did," Ross said. "It helped Curtis set up a landing orbit that would have dumped us into the sun. But then it realized that the rest of us *didn't* want to die. It picked up the conflicting mental emanations of Curtis and the rest of us, and arranged things so that he'd die and we wouldn't." He shivered. "Once Curtis was out of the way, it acted to help the surviving crew members reach safety. If you'll remember, we were all thinking and moving a lot quicker the instant Curtis was dead."

"Damned if that's not so," Spangler said. "But—"

"What I want to know is, do we go back down?" Krinsky asked. "If that thing is what you say it is, I'm not so sure I want to go within reach of it again. Who knows what it might make us do this time?"

"It wants to help us," Ross said stubbornly. "It's not hostile. You aren't afraid of it, are you, Krinsky? I was counting on you to go out in the heatsuit and try to find it."

"Not me!"

Ross scowled. "But this is the first intelligent life-form man has ever found in the solar system. We can't just run away and hide." To Brainerd he said, "Set up an orbit that'll take us back down again—and this time put us down where we won't melt."

"I can't do it, sir," Brainerd said flatly.

"Can't?"

"Won't. I think the safest thing is for us to return to Earth at once."

"I'm ordering you."

"I'm sorry, sir."

Ross looked at Spangler. Llewellyn. Falbridge. Right around the circle. Fear was evident on every face. He knew what each of the men was thinking.

I don't want to go back to Mercury.

Six of them. One of him. And the helpful thing below.

They had outnumbered Curtis seven to one—but Curtis' mind had radiated an unmixed death-wish. Ross knew he could never generate enough strength of thought to counteract the fear-driven thoughts of the other six.

Mutiny.

Somehow he did not care to speak the word aloud. Sometimes there were cases where a superior officer might legitimately be removed from command for the common good, and this might be one. of them, he knew. But yet—

The thought of fleeing without even pausing to examine the creature below was intolerable to him. But there was only one ship, and either he or the six others would have to be denied.

Yet the pool had contrived to satisfy both the man who wished to die and those who wished to stay alive. Now, six wanted to return—but must the voice of the seventh be ignored?

You're not being fair to me, Ross thought, directing his angry outburst towards the planet below. *I want to see you. I want to study you. Don't let them drag me back to Earth so soon.*

When the *Leverrier* returned to Earth a week later, the six survivors of the Second Mercury Expedition all were able to describe in detail how a fierce death-wish had overtaken Second Astrogator Curtis and driven him to suicide. But not one of them could recall what had happened to Flight Commander Ross, or why the heatsuit had been left behind on Mercury.

WORLD OF A THOUSAND COLORS

As I said in the introduction to "The Silent Colony," many times in the early years of my career I would try on the style or technical approach of a writer I greatly admired, in order to find out, word by word, what the process of writing a story that I admired was like. Not that I ever matched the level of the writers whose modes I was adopting, of course—how could I have, back then? But it was a useful finger exercise all the same.

So here I am in my Jack Vance mode, back in November, 1956—a story written especially for W. W. Scott's new magazine, Super-Science *Fiction. I don't mean that I'm rewriting some particular Vance story—editors don't like you to do that—but that I'm dealing with my material in the manner of Vance, to get the hang of his remarkable flair for color and texture. I found it a voluptuous experience. W. W. Scott liked it, too, and gave me a nifty $120, which covered about three weeks' rent on my five-room apartment overlooking Manhattan's West End Avenue. (Try and rent a Manhattan apartment now, not just on West End Avenue but anywhere, for $150 a month!) Scottie ran the story in the June, 1957* Super Science.

When Jolvar Hollinrede discovered that the slim, pale young man opposite him was journeying to the World of a Thousand Colors to undergo the Test, he spied a glittering opportunity for himself. And in that moment was the slim, pale young man's fate set.

Hollinrede's lean fingers closed on the spun-fibre drinkflask. He peered across the burnished tabletop. "The *Test,* you say?"

The young man smiled diffidently. "Yes. I think I'm ready. I've waited years—and now's my big chance." He had had a little too much of the cloying liqueur he had been drinking; his eyes shone glassily, and his tongue was looser than it had any right to be.

"Few are called and fewer are chosen," Hollinrede mused. "Let me buy you another drink."

"No, I—"

"It will be an honor. Really. It's not every day I have a chance to buy a Testee a drink."

Hollinrede waved a jeweled hand and the servomech brought them two more drinkflasks. Lightly Hollinrede punctured one, slid it along the tabletop, kept the other in his hand unopened. "I don't believe I know your name," he said.

"Derveran Marti. I'm from Earth. You?"

"Jolvar Hollinrede. Likewise. I travel from world to world on business, which is what brings me to Niprion this day."

"What sort of business?"

"I trade in jewels," Hollinrede said, displaying the bright collection studding his fingers. They were all morphosims, not the originals, but only careful chemical analysis would reveal that. Hollinrede did not believe in exposing millions of credits' worth of merchandise to anyone who cared to lop off his hand.

"I was a clerk," Marti said. "But that's all far behind me. I'm on to the World of a Thousand Colors to take the Test! The Test!"

"The Test!" Hollinrede echoed. He lifted his unpunctured drinkflask in a gesture of salute, raised it to his lips, pretended to drain it. Across the table Derveran Marti coughed as the liqueur coursed down his throat. He looked up, smiling dizzily, and smacked his lips.

"When does your ship leave?" Hollinrede asked.

"Tomorrow midday. It's the *Star Climber.* I can't wait. This stopover at Niprion is making me fume with impatience."

"No doubt," Hollinrede agreed. "What say you to an afternoon of whist, to while away the time?"

An hour later Derveran Marti lay slumped over the inlaid cardtable in Hollinrede's hotel suite, still clutching a handful of waxy cards. Arms folded, Hollinrede surveyed the body.

They were about of a height, he and the dead man, and a chemo-therm mask would alter Hollinrede's face sufficiently to allow him to pass as Marti. He switched on the playback of the room's recorder to pick up the final fragments of their conversation.

"...care for another drink, Marti?"

"I guess I'd better not, old fellow. I'm getting kind of muzzy, you know. No, please don't pour it for me. I said I didn't want it, and—well, all right. Just a little one. There, that's enough. Thanks."

The tape was silent for a moment, then recorded the soft thump of Marti's body falling to the table as the quick-action poison unlatched his synapses. Smiling, Hollinrede switched the recorder to record and said, mimicking Marti, *"I guess I'd better not, old fellow. I'm getting kind of muzzy, you know."*

He activated the playback, listened critically to the sound of his voice, then listened to Marti's again for comparison. He was approach-ing the light, flexible quality of the dead man's voice. Several more attempts and he had it almost perfect. Producing a vocal homologizer, he ran off first Marti's voice, then his own pronouncing the same words.

The voices were alike to three decimal places. That would be good enough to fool the most sensitive detector; three places was the normal range of variation in any man's voice from day to day.

In terms of mass there was a trifling matter of some few grams which could easily be sweated off in the gymnasium the following morning. As for the dead man's gesture-complex, Hollinrede thought he could manage a fairly accurate imitation of Marti's manner of moving; he had studied the young clerk carefully for nearly four hours, and Hollinrede was a clever man.

When the preparations were finished, he stepped away and glanced at the mirror, taking a last look at his own face—the face he would not see again until he had taken the Test. He donned the mask. Jolvar Hollinrede became Derveran Marti.

Hollinrede extracted a length of cotton bulking from a drawer and wrapped it around Marti's body. He weighed the corpse, and added four milligrams more of cotton so that Marti would have precisely the mass Jolvar Hollinrede had had. He donned Marti's clothes finally, dressed the body in his own, and, smiling sadly at the convincing but worthless morphosim jewels on his fingers, transferred the rings to Marti's already-stiffening hands.

"Up with you," he grunted, and bundled the body across the room to the disposall.

"Farewell, old friend," he exclaimed feelingly, and hoisted Marti feet-first to the lip of the chute. He shoved, and the dead man vanished, slowly, gracefully, heading downward towards the omnivorous maw of the atomic converter buried in the deep levels of Stopover Planet Niprion.

Reflectively Hollinrede turned away from the disposall unit. He gathered up the cards, put away the liqueur, poured the remnant of the poisoned drink in the disposall chute.

An atomic converter was a wonderful thing, he thought pleasantly. By now the body of Marti had been efficiently reduced to its component molecules, and those were due for separation into atoms shortly after, and from atoms into subatomic particles. Within an hour the prime evidence to the crime would be nothing but so many protons, electrons, and neutrons—and there would be no way of telling which of the two men in the room had entered the chute, and which had remained alive.

Hollinrede activated the tape once more, rehearsed for the final time his version of Marti's voice, and checked it with the homologizer. Still three decimal places; that was good enough. He erased the tape.

Then, depressing the communicator stud, he said, "I wish to report a death."

A cold robot face appeared on the screen. "Yes?"

"Several minutes ago my host, Jolvar Hollinrede, passed on of an acute embolism. He requested immediate dissolution upon death and I wish to report that this has been carried out."

"Your name?"

"Derveran Marti. Testee."

"A Testee? You were the last to see the late Hollinrede alive?"

"That's right."

"Do you swear that all information you might give will be accurate and fully honest?"

"I so swear," Hollinrede said.

The inquest was brief and smooth. The word of a Testee goes without question; Hollinrede had reported the details of the meeting exactly as if he had been Marti, and after a check of the converter records revealed that a mass exactly equal to the late Hollinrede's had indeed been disposed of at precisely the instant witness claimed, the inquest was at its end. The verdict was natural death. Hollinrede told the officials that he had not known the late jeweltrader before that day, and had no interest in his property, whereupon they permitted him to depart.

Having died intestate, Hollinrede knew his property became that of the Galactic Government. But, as he pressed his hand, clad in its skintight chemotherm, against the doorplate of Derveran Marti's room, he told himself that it did not matter. Now he *was* Derveran Marti, Testee. And once he had taken and passed the Test, what would the loss of a few million credits in baubles matter to him?

Therefore it was with a light heart that the pseudo-Derveran Marti quitted his lodgings the next day and prepared to board the *Star Climber* for the voyage to the World of a Thousand Colors.

The clerk at the desk peered at him sympathetically as he pressed his fingers into the checkout plate, thereby erasing the impress from the doorplate upstairs.

"It was too bad about that old fellow dying on you yesterday, wasn't it, sir? I do hope it won't affect your Test result."

Hollinrede smiled blankly. "It was quite a shock to me when he died so suddenly. But my system has already recovered; I'm ready for the Test."

"Good luck to you, sir," the clerk said as Hollinrede left the hotel and stepped out on the flaring skyramp that led to the waiting ship.

The steward at the passenger hatch was collecting identiplates. Hollinrede handed his over casually. The steward inserted it tip-first in the computer near the door, and motioned for Hollinrede to step within the beam while his specifications were being automatically compared with those on the identiplate.

He waited, tensely. Finally the chattering of the machine stopped and a dry voice said, "Your identity is in order, Testee Derveran Marti. Proceed within."

"That means you're okay," the steward told him. "Yours is Compartment Eleven. It's a luxury job, you know. But you Testees deserve it. Best of luck, sir."

"Thanks," Hollinrede grinned. "I don't doubt I'll need it."

He moved up the ramp and into the ship. Compartment Eleven *was* a luxury job; Hollinrede, who had been a frugal man, whistled in amazement when he saw it. It was nearly eight feet high and almost twelve broad, totally private with an opaquer attached to the doorscope. Clinging curtains of ebony synthoid foam from Ravensmusk VIII had been draped lovingly over the walls, and the acceleration couch was trimmed in golden bryozone. The rank of Testee carried with it privileges that the late Derveran Marti certainly would never have mustered in private life—nor Jolvar Hollinrede either.

At 1143 the doorscope chimed; Hollinrede leaped from the soft couch a little too nervously and transluced the door. A crewman stood outside.

"Everything all right, sir? We blast in seventeen minutes."

"I'm fine," Hollinrede said. "Can't wait to get there. How long do you think it'll take?"

"Sorry sir. Not at liberty to reveal. But I wish you a pleasant trip, and should you lack for aught hesitate not to call on me."

Hollinrede smiled at the curiously archaic way the man had of expressing himself. "Never fear; I'll not hesitate. Many thanks." He opaqued the doorscope and resumed his seat.

At precisely 1200 the drive-engines of the *Star Climber* throbbed heavily; the pale green light over the door of Hollinrede's compartment glowed brightly for an instant, signaling the approaching blastoff. He sank down on the acceleration couch to wait.

A moment later came the push of acceleration, and then, as the gravshields took effect, the 7g escape force dwindled until Hollinrede felt comfortable again. He increased the angle of the couch in order to peer out the port.

The world of Niprion was vanishing rapidly in the background: already it was nothing but a mottled grey-and-gold ball swimming hazily in a puff of atmosphere. The sprawling metal structure that was the stopover hotel was invisible.

Somewhere back on Niprion, Hollinrede thought, the atoms that once had been Testee Derveran Marti were now feeding the plasma intake of a turbine or heating the inner shell of a reactor.

He let his mind dwell on the forthcoming Test. He knew little about it, really, considering he had been willing to take a man's life for a chance to compete. He knew the Test was administered once every five years to candidates chosen by Galaxywide search. The world where the Test was given was known only as the World of a Thousand Colors, and precisely where this world was no member of the general public was permitted to know.

As for the Test itself, by its very nature it was unknown to the Galaxy. For no winning Testee had ever returned from the World of a Thousand Colors. Some losers returned, their minds carefully wiped clean of any memories of the planet—but the winners never came back.

The Test's nature was unknown; the prize, inconceivable. All anyone knew was that the winners were granted the soul's utmost dream. Upon winning, one neither returned to his home world nor desired to return.

Naturally many men ignored the Test—it was something for "other people" to take part in. But millions, billions throughout the Galaxy competed in the preliminaries. And every five years, six or seven were chosen.

Jolvar Hollinrede was convinced he would succeed in the Test—but he had failed three times running in the preliminaries, and was thus permanently disqualified. The preliminaries were simple; they consisted merely of an intensive mental scanning. A flipflop circuit would flash YES or NO after that.

If YES, there were further scannings, until word was beamed through the Galaxy that the competitors for the year had been chosen.

Hollinrede stared moodily at the blackness of space. He had been eliminated unfairly, he felt; he coveted the unknown prize the Test offered, and felt bitter at having it denied him. When chance had thrown Testee Derveran Marti in his path, Hollinrede had leaped to take advantage of the opportunity.

And now he was on his way.

Surely, he thought, they would allow him to take the Test, even if he were discovered to be an impostor. And once he took it, he knew he would succeed. He had always succeeded in his endeavors. There was no reason for failure now.

Beneath the false mask of Derveran Marti, Hollinrede's face was tensely set. He dreamed of the Test and its winning—and of the end to the long years of wandering and toil.

The voice at the door said, "We're here, Testee Derveran. Please open up."

Hollinrede grunted, pulled himself up from the couch, threw open the door. Three dark-faced spacemen waited there for him.

"Where are we?" he asked nervously. "Is the trip over?"

"We have come to pilot you to the Test planet, sir," one of the space-men told him. "The *Star Climber* is in orbit around it, but will not make a landing itself. Will you follow us?"

"Very well," Hollinrede said.

They entered a lifeship, a slim grey tube barely thirty meters long, and fastened acceleration cradles. There were no ports. Hollinrede felt enclosed, hemmed in.

The lifeship began to slide noiselessly along the ejection channel, glided the entire length of the *Star Climber,* and burst out into space. A preset orbit was operating. Hollinrede clung to the acceleration cradle as the lifeship spun tightly inward towards a powerful gravitational field not far away.

The ship came to rest. Hollinrede lay motionless, flesh cold with nervousness, teeth chattering.

"Easy does it, sir. Up and out."

They lifted him and gently nudged him through a manifold com-pression lock. He moved forward on numb feet.

"Best of luck, sir!" an envious voice called behind him.

Then the lock clanged shut, and Hollinrede was on his own.

A riotous blaze of color swept down at him from every point of the compass.

He stood in the midst of what looked like a lunar crater; far in the distance on all sides was the massive upraised fissured surface of a ring-wall, and the ground beneath him was barren red-brown rock, crum-bling to pumice here and there but bare of vegetation.

In the sky was a solitary sun, a blazing Type A blue-white star. That sun alone was incapable of accounting for this flood of color.

Streamers of every hue seemed to sprout from the rocks, staining the ringwall olive-grey and brilliant cerise and dark, lustrous green. Pigments of every sort bathed the air; now it seemed to glow with cur-rents of luminous pink, now a flaming red, now a pulsing pure white.

His eyes adjusted slowly to the torrent of color. World of a Thousand Colors, they called this place? That was an underestimate. *Hundred thou-sand. Million. Billion.* Shades and near-shades mingled to form new colors.

"Are you Derveran Marti?" a voice asked.

Startled, Hollinrede looked around. It seemed as if a band of color had spoken: a swirling band of rich brown that spun tirelessly before him.

"Are you Derveran Marti?" the voice repeated, and Hollinrede saw that it had indeed come from the band of brown.

It seemed a desecration to utter the lie here on this world of awesome beauty, and he felt the temptation to claim his true identity. But the time for that was later.

"Yes," he said loudly. "I am Derveran Marti."

"Welcome, Derveran Marti. The Test will soon begin."

"Where?"

"Here."

"Right out here? Just like this?"

"Yes," the band of color replied. "Your fellow competitors are gathering."

Hollinrede narrowed his eyes and peered towards the far reaches of the ringwall. Yes; he saw tiny figures located at great distances from each other along the edge of the crater. One, two, three…there were seven all told, including himself. Seven, out of the whole Galaxy!

Each of the other six was attended by a dipping, bobbing blotch of color. Hollinrede noticed a squareshouldered giant from one of the Inner Worlds surrounded by a circlet of violent orange; to his immediate left was a sylphlike female, probably from one of the worlds of Dubhe, wearing only the revealing token garment of her people but shielded from inquisitive eyes by a robe of purest blue light. There were others; Hollinrede wished them well. He knew it was possible for all competitors to win, and now that he was about to attain his long-sought goal he held no malice for anyone. His mind was suffused with pity for the dead Derveran Marti, sacrificed that Jolvar Hollinrede might be in this place at this time.

"Derveran Marti," the voice said, "you have been chosen from among your fellow men to take part in the Test. This is an honor that comes to few; we of this world hope you appreciate the grace that has fallen upon you."

"I do," Hollinrede said humbly.

"We ourselves are winners of the prize you seek," the voice went on. "Some of us are members of the first expedition that found this world, eleven hundred years ago. As you see, life has unlimited duration in our present state of matter. Others of us have come more recently. The bank of pale purple moving above you to the left was a winner in the previous competition to this.

"We of the World of a Thousand Colors have a rare gift to offer: total harmony of mind. We exist divorced of body, as a stream of photons only. We live in perfect freedom and eternal delight. Once every five years we find it possible to increase our numbers by adding to our midst such throughout the Galaxy as we feel would desire to share our way of life—and whom we would feel happy to welcome to us."

"You mean," Hollinrede said shakily, "that all these beams of light— were once *people?*"

"They were that—until welcomed into us. Now they are men no more. This is the prize you have come to win."

"I see."

"You are not required to compete. Those who, after reaching our world, decide to remain in the material state, are returned to their home worlds with their memories cleared of what they have been told here and their minds free and happy to the end of their lives. Is this what you wish?"

Hollinrede was silent, letting his dazzled eyes take in the flamboyant sweep of color that illuminated the harsh, rocky world. Finally he said: "I will stay."

"Good. The Test will shortly begin."

Hollinrede saw the band of brown swoop away from him upward to rejoin its never-still comrades in the sky. He waited, standing stiffly, for something to happen.

Then this is what I killed a man for, he thought. His mind dwelled on the words of the band of brown.

Evidently many hundreds of years ago an exploratory expedition had come upon some unique natural phenomenon here at a far end of the universe. Perhaps it had been an accident, a stumbling into a pool of light perhaps, that had dematerialized them, turned them into bobbing immortal streaks of color. But that had been the beginning.

The entire Test system had been developed to allow others to enter this unique society, to leave the flesh behind and live on as pure energy. Hollinrede's fingers trembled; this was, he saw, something worth killing for!

He could see why some people might turn down the offer—those would be the few who cautiously would prefer to remain corporeal and so returned to their home worlds to live out their span.

But not me!

He faced upward and waited for the Test to begin. His shrewd mind was at the peak of its agility; he was prepared for anything they might throw at him. He wondered if anyone yet had come to the World of a Thousand Colors so determined to succeed.

Probably not. For most, the accolade was the result of luck—a mental scanning that turned up whatever mysterious qualities were acceptable to the people of this world. They did not have to *work* for their nomination. They did not have to kill for it.

But Hollinrede had clawed his way here—and he was determined to succeed.

He waited.

Finally the brown band descended from the mass of lambent color overhead and curled into a tight bowknot before him.

"The Test is about to begin, Jolvar Hollinrede."

Use of his own name startled him. In the past week he had so thoroughly associated his identity with that of Derveran Marti that he had scarcely let his actual name drift through his mind.

"So you know," he said.

"We have known since the moment you came. It is unfortunate; we would have wanted Derveran Marti among us. But now that you are here, we will test you on your own merits, Jolvar Hollinrede."

It was just as well that way, he thought. The pretense had to end sooner or later, and he was willing to stand or fall as himself rather. than under an assumed identity.

"Advance to the center of the crater, Jolvar Hollinrede," came the command from the brown band.

Leadenly Hollinrede walked forward. Squinting through the mist of color that hazed the view, he saw the other six competitors were doing the same. They would meet at the center.

"The Test is now under way," a new and deeper voice said.

Seven of them. Hollinrede looked around. There was the giant from the Inner World—Fondelfor, he saw now. Next to him, the near-nude sylph of Dubhe, and standing by her side, one diamond-faceted eye glittering in his forehead, a man of Alpheraz VII.

The selectors had cast their nets wide. Hollinrede saw another Terran, dark of skin and bright of eye; a being of Deneb IX, squat and muscular. The sixth Testee was a squirming globule from Spica's tenth world; the seventh was Jolvar Hollinrede, itinerant; home world, Terra.

Overhead hung a circular diadem of violet light. It explained the terms of the Test.

"Each of you will be awarded a characteristic color. It will project before you into the area you ring. Your object will be to blend your seven colors into one; when you have achieved this, you will be admitted into us."

"May I ask what the purpose of this is?" Hollinrede said coldly.

"The essence of our society is harmony—total harmony among us all, and inner harmony within those groups which were admitted at the same temporal juncture. Naturally if you seven are incapable even of this inner harmony, you will be incapable of the greater harmony of us all—and will be rejected."

Despite the impatient frowns of a few of his fellow contestants, Hollinrede said, "Therefore we're to be judged as a unit? An entity?"

"Yes and no," the voice replied. "And now the Test."

Hollinrede saw to his astonishment a color spurt from his arm and hang hovering before him—a pool of inky blackness deeper in hue than the dark of space. His first reaction was one of shock; then he realized that he could control the color, make it move.

He glanced around. Each of his companions similarly faced a hovering mass of color. The giant of Fondelfor controlled red; the girl of Dubhe, orange. The Alpherazian stared into a whirling bowl of deep yellow, the Terran green, the Spican radiant violet, the Denebian pearly grey.

Hollinrede stared at his globe of black. A voice above him seemed to whisper, *"Marti's color would have been blue. The spectrum has been violated."*

He shrugged away the words and sent his globe of black spinning into the area between the seven contestants ringed in a circle. At the same time each of the others directed his particular color inward.

The colors met. They clashed, pinwheeled, seemed to throw off sparks. They began to swirl in a hovering arc of radiance.

Hollinrede waited breathlessly, watching the others. His color of black seemed to stand in opposition to the other six. Red, orange, yellow, green, violet. The pearl-grey of the Denebian seemed to enfold the other colors warmly—all but Hollinrede's. The black hung apart.

To his surprise he saw the Dubhian girl's orange beginning to change hue. The girl herself stood stiffly, eyes closed, her body now bare. Sweat poured down her skin. And her orange hue began to shift towards the grey of the Denebian.

The others were following. One by one, as they achieved control over their Test color. First to follow was the Spican, then the Alpherazian.

Why can't I do that? Hollinrede thought wildly.

He strained to alter the color of his black, but it remained unchanged. The others were blending, now, swirling around; there was a predominantly grey cast, but it was not the grey of the Denebian but a different grey tending towards white. Impatiently he redoubled his efforts; it was necessary for the success of the group that he get his obstinate black to blend with the rest.

"The black remains aloof," someone said near him.

"We will fail if the black does not join us."

His streak of color now stood out boldly against the increasing milkiness of the others. None of the original colors were left now but his. Perspiration streamed down him; he realized that his was the only obstacle preventing the seven from passing the Test.

"The black still will not join us," a tense voice said.

Another said, "The black is a color of evil."

A third said, "Black is not a color at all. Black is the absence of color; white is the totality of color."

A fourth said, "Black is holding us from the white."

Hollinrede looked from one to the other in mute appeal. Veins stood out on his forehead from the effort, but the black remained unchanging. He could not blend it with the others.

From above came the voice of their examiner, suddenly accusing: "Black is the color of *murder.*"

The girl from Dubhe, lilting the ugly words lightly, repeated it. "Black is the color of murder."

"Can we permit a murderer among us?" asked the Denebian.

"The answer is self-evident," said the Spican, indicating the recalcitrant spear of black that marred the otherwise flawless globe of near-white in their midst.

"The murderer must be cast out ere the Test be passed," muttered the giant of Fondelfor. He broke from his position and moved menacingly towards Hollinrede.

"Look!" Hollinrede yelled desperately. "Look at the red!"

The giant's color had split from the grey and now darted wildly towards Hollinrede's black.

"This is the wrong way, then," the giant said, halting. "We must all join in it or we all fail."

"Keep away from me," Hollinrede said. "It's not my fault if—"

Then they were on him—four pairs of hands, two rough claws, two slick tentacles. Hollinrede felt himself being lifted aloft. He squirmed, tried to break from their grasp, but they held him up—

And dashed him down against the harsh rock floor.

He lay there, feeling his life seep out, knowing he had failed—and watched as they returned to form their circle once again. The black winked out of being.

As his eyes started to close, Hollinrede saw the six colors again blend into one. Now that the murderer had been cast from their midst, nothing barred the path of their harmony. Pearly grey shifted to purest white—the totality of color—and as the six merged into one, Hollinrede, with his dying glance, bitterly saw them take leave forever of their bodies and slip upward to join their brothers hovering brightly above.

WARM MAN

We come to January, 1957. My ledger entry for that month shows business as usual—seventeen stories, 85,000 words, and I was just warming up for the really productive times a couple of years down the line. How I did it, God only knows. These days I'm happy to manage two or three stories a year; that was a week's work for me in far-off unimaginable 1957.

A phenomenon, I was. And one who took notice of it was Anthony Boucher, the urbane and sophisticated editor of Fantasy and Science Fiction. *Tony, in his editorial capacity, was a collector at heart, who wanted one of everything for his superb magazine—including a story by this hypermanic kid from New York who seemed able to turn one out every hour. But Boucher wasn't going to relax his high standards simply for the sake of bagging me for his contents page; and so, although he told me in just about so many words that he'd be delighted to publish something of mine, he turned down the first few stories I sent him, offering great regrets and hope for the future. What I had to do in order to sell one to him, I told myself, was to break free of the pulp-magazine formulas that I had taken such trouble to master, and write something about and for adults. (Not so easy, when I was not much past twenty-one myself!) The specific genesis of "Warm Man" was a moment at that famous Milford Writers' Conference of September, 1956. During one workshop session Cyril Kornbluth had some sort of epiphany about his writing while a story of Damon Knight's was being discussed, and suddenly he cried out in a very loud voice, "Cold!" What that signified to him, I never knew; Algis Budrys, another writer present at that conference, told me long afterward that what he thought*

Kornbluth was saying was "Gold!", a reference to the editor of that name. (Knight did eventually sell that story to Gold.) Well, whether cold or Gold, Kornbluth's outcry set something working in me, something which surely had nothing at all to do with whatever had passed through Cyril's mind; in the story process that followed I turned "cold" to "warm" and out came, a few months later, this tale of psychic vampirism. I sent it to Boucher (who had been present at Milford also, I think) and by return mail across the continent came his expression of delight that I had broken the ice at last with him. He ran the story a few months later—the May 1957 issue—and put my name on the cover, a signal honor. Boucher was the best kind of editor— a demanding one, yes, but also the kind who is as pleased as you are that you have produced something he wants to publish. He (and a few others back then) helped to teach me the difficult lesson that quantity isn't as effective, in the long run, as quality. Which is demonstrated by this story's frequent reappearance in print over the span of more than three decades since it was written.

No one was ever quite sure just when Mr. Hallinan came to live in New Brewster. Lonny Dewitt, who ought to know, testified that Mr. Hallinan died on December 3, at 3:30 in the afternoon, but as for the day of his arrival no one could be nearly so precise.

It was simply that one day there was no one living in the unoccupied split-level on Melon Hill, and then the next *he* was there, seemingly having grown out of the woodwork during the night, ready and willing to spread his cheer and warmth throughout the whole of the small suburban community.

Daisy Moncrieff, New Brewster's ineffable hostess, was responsible for making the first overtures towards Mr. Hallinan. It was two days after she had first observed lights on in the Melon Hill place that she decided the time had come to scrutinize the newcomers, to determine their place in New Brewster society. Donning a light wrap, for it was a coolish October day, she left her house in the early forenoon and went on foot down Copperbeech Road to the Melon Hill turnoff, and then climbed the sloping hill till she reached the split-level.

The name was already on the mailbox: DAVIS HALLINAN. That probably meant they'd been living there a good deal longer than just two days, thought Mrs. Moncrieff; perhaps they'd be insulted by the tardiness of the invitation? She shrugged and used the doorknocker.

A tall man in early middle age appeared, smiling benignly. Mrs. Moncrieff was thus the first recipient of the uncanny warmth that Davis Hallinan was to radiate throughout New Brewster before his strange death. His eyes were deep and solemn, with warm lights shining in them; his hair was a dignified grey-white mane.

"Good morning," he said. His voice was deep, mellow.

"Good morning. I'm Mrs. Moncrieff—*Daisy* Moncrieff, from the big house on Copperbeech Road. You must be Mr. Hallinan. May I come in?"

"Ah—please, no, Mrs. Moncrieff. The place is still a chaos. Would you mind staying on the porch?"

He closed the door behind him—Mrs. Moncrieff later claimed that she had a fleeting view of the interior and saw unpainted walls and dust-covered bare floors—and drew one of the rusty porch chairs for her.

"Is your wife at home, Mr. Hallinan?"

"There's just me, I'm afraid. I live alone."

"Oh." Mrs. Moncrieff, discomforted, managed a grin nonetheless. In New Brewster everyone was married; the idea of a bachelor or a widower coming to settle there was strange, disconcerting...and just a little pleasant, she added, surprised at herself.

"My purpose in coming was to invite you to meet some of your new neighbors tonight—if you're free, that is. I'm having a cocktail party at my place about six, with dinner at seven. We'd be so happy if you came!"

His eyes twinkled gaily. "Certainly, Mrs. Moncrieff. I'm looking forward to it already."

The *ne plus ultra* of New Brewster society was impatiently assembled at the Moncrieff home shortly after 6, waiting to meet Mr. Hallinan, but it was not until 6:15 that he arrived. By then, thanks to Daisy Moncrieff's fearsome skill as a hostess, everyone present was equipped with a drink and a set of speculations about the mysterious bachelor on the hill.

"I'm sure he must be a writer," said Martha Weede to liverish Dudley Heyer. "Daisy says he's tall and distinguished and just *radiates* personality. He's probably here only for a few months—just long enough to get to know us all, and then he'll write a novel about us."

"Hmm. Yes," Heyer said. He was an advertising executive who commuted to Madison Avenue every morning; he had an ulcer, and was acutely aware of his role as a stereotype. "Yes, then he'll write a sizzling novel exposing suburban decadence, or a series of acid sketches for *The New Yorker.* I know the type."

Lys Erwin, looking desirable and just a bit disheveled after her third martini in thirty minutes, drifted by in time to overhear that. "You're *always* conscious of *types,* aren't you, darling? You and your grey flannel suit?"

Heyer fixed her with a baleful stare but found himself, as usual, unable to make an appropriate retort. He fumed away, smiled hello at quiet little Harold and Jane Dewitt, whom he pitied somewhat (their son Lonny, age 9, was a shy; sensitive child, a total misfit among his playmates), and confronted the bar, weighing the probability of a night of acute agony against the immediate desirability of a Manhattan.

But at that moment Daisy Moncrieff reappeared with Mr. Hallinan in tow, and conversation ceased abruptly throughout the parlor while the assembled guests stared at the newcomer. An instant later, conscious of their collective *faux pas,* the group began to chat again, and Daisy moved among her guests, introducing her prize.

"Dudley, this is Mr. Davis Hallinan. Mr. Hallinan, I want you to meet Dudley Heyer, one of the most talented men in New Brewster."

"Indeed? What do you do, Mr. Heyer?"

"I'm in advertising. But don't let them fool you; it doesn't take any talent at all. Just brass, nothing else. The desire to delude the public, and delude 'em good. But how about you? What line are you in?"

Mr. Hallinan ignored the question. "I've always thought advertising was a richly creative field, Mr. Heyer. But, of course, I've never really known at first hand—"

"Well, I have. And it's everything they say it is." Heyer felt his face reddening, as if he had had a drink or two. He was becoming talkative, and found Hallinan's presence oddly soothing. Leaning close to the newcomer, Heyer said, "Just between you and me, Hallinan, I'd give my whole bank account for a chance to stay home and write. Just write. I want to do a novel. But I don't have the guts; that's my trouble. I know that come Friday there's a $350 check waiting on my desk, and I don't dare give that up. So I keep writing my novel up here in my head, and it keeps eating me away down here in my gut. *Eating.*" He paused, conscious that he had said too much and that his eyes were glittering headily.

Hallinan wore a benign smile. "It's always sad to see talent hidden, Mr. Heyer. I wish you well."

Daisy Moncrieff appeared then, hooked an arm through Hallinan's, and led him away. Heyer, alone, stared down at the textured grey broadloom.

Now why did I tell him all that? he wondered. A minute after meeting Hallinan, he had unburdened his deepest woe to him—something he had not confided in anyone else in New Brewster, including his wife.

And yet—it had been a sort of catharsis, Heyer thought. Hallinan had calmly soaked up all his grief and inner agony, and left Heyer feeling drained and purified and warm.

Catharsis? Or a blood-letting? Heyer shrugged, then grinned and made his way to the bar to pour himself a Manhattan.

As usual, Lys and Leslie Erwin were at opposite ends of the parlor. Mrs. Moncrieff found Lys more easily, and introduced her to Mr. Hallinan.

Lys faced him unsteadily, and on a sudden impulse hitched her neckline higher. "Pleased to meet you, Mr Hallinan. I'd like you to meet my husband Leslie. *Leslie!* Come here, please?"

Leslie Erwin approached. He was twenty years older than his wife, and was generally known to wear the finest pair of horns in New Brewster—a magnificent spread of antlers that grew a new point or two almost every week.

"Les, this is Mr. Hallinan. Mr. Hallinan, meet my husband, Leslie."

Mr. Hallinan bowed courteously to both of them. "Happy to make your acquaintance."

"The same," Erwin said. "If you'll excuse me, now—"

"The louse," said Lys Erwin, when her husband had returned to his station at the bar. "He'd sooner cut his throat than spend two minutes next to me in public." She glared bitterly at Hallinan. "I don't deserve that kind of thing, do I?"

Mr. Hallinan frowned sympathetically. "Have you any children, Mrs. Erwin?"

"Hah! He'd never give me any—not with *my* reputation! You'll have to pardon me; I'm a little drunk."

"I understand, Mrs. Erwin."

"I know. Funny, but I hardly know you and I like you. You seem to *understand*. Really, I mean." She took his cuff hesitantly. "Just from looking at you, I can tell you're not judging me like all the others. I'm not really *bad,* am I? It's just that I get so *bored,* Mr. Hallinan."

"Boredom is a great curse," Mr. Hallinan observed.

"Damn right it is! And Leslie's no help—always reading his newspapers and talking to his brokers! But I can't help myself, believe me." She looked around wildly. "They're going to start talking about us in a minute, Mr. Hallinan. Every time I talk to someone new they start whispering. But promise me something—"

"If I can."

"Someday—someday soon—let's get together? I want to *talk* to you. God, I want to talk to someone—someone who understands why I'm the way I am. Will you?"

"Of course, Mrs. Erwin. Soon." Gently he detached her hand from his sleeve, held it tenderly for a moment, and released it. She smiled hopefully at him. He nodded.

"And now I must meet some of the other guests. A pleasure, Mrs. Erwin."

He drifted away, leaving Lys weaving shakily in the middle of the parlor. She drew in a deep breath and lowered her décolletage again.

At least there's one decent man in this town now, she thought. There was something *good* about Hallinan—good, and kind, and understanding.

Understanding. That's what I need. She wondered if she could manage to pay a visit to the house on Melon Hill tomorrow afternoon without arousing too much scandal.

Lys turned and saw thin-faced Aiken Muir staring at her slyly, with a clear-cut invitation on his face. She met his glance with a frigid, wordless *go to hell.*

Mr. Hallinan moved on, on through the party. And, gradually, the pattern of the party began to form. It took shape like a fine mosaic. By the time the cocktail hour was over and dinner was ready, an intricate, complex structure of interacting thoughts and responses had been built.

Mr. Hallinan, always drinkless, glided deftly from one New Brewsterite to the next, engaging each in conversation, drawing a few basic facts about the other's personality, smiling politely, moving on. Not until after he moved on did the person come to a dual realization: that Mr. Hallinan had said quite little, really, and that he had instilled a feeling of warmth and security in the other during their brief talk.

And thus while Mr. Hallinan learned from Martha Weede of her paralyzing envy of her husband's intelligence and of her fear of his scorn, Lys Erwin was able to remark to Dudley Heyer that Mr. Hallinan was a remarkably kind and understanding person. And Heyer, who had never been known to speak a kind word of anyone, for once agreed.

And later, while Mr. Hallinan was extracting from Leslie Erwin some of the pain his wife's manifold infidelities caused him, Martha Weede could tell Lys Erwin, "He's so gentle—why, he's almost like a saint!"

And while little Harold Dewitt poured out his fear that his silent 9-year-old son Lonny was in some way subnormal, Leslie Erwin, with a jaunty grin, remarked to Daisy Moncrieff, "That man must be a psychiatrist. Lord, he knows how to talk to a person. Inside of two minutes he had me telling him all my troubles. I feel better for it, too."

Mrs. Moncrieff nodded. "I know what you mean. This morning, when I went up to his place to invite him here, we talked a little while on his porch."

"Well," Erwin said, "if he's a psychiatrist he'll find plenty of business here. There isn't a person here riding around without a private monkey on his back. Take Heyer, over there—he didn't get that ulcer from happiness. That scatterbrain Martha Weede, too—married to a Columbia professor who can't imagine what to talk to her about. And my wife Lys is a very confused person too, of course."

"We all have our problems," Mrs. Moncrieff sighed. "But I feel much better since I spoke with Mr. Hallinan. Yes: *much* better."

Mr. Hallinan was now talking with Paul Jambell, the architect. Jambell, whose pretty young wife was in Springfield Hospital slowly dying of cancer. Mrs. Moncrieff could well imagine what Jambell and Mr. Hallinan were talking about.

Or rather, what Jambell was talking about—for Mr. Hallinan, she realized, did very little talking himself. But he was such a *wonderful* listener! She felt a pleasant glow, not entirely due to the cocktails. It was good to have someone like Mr. Hallinan in New Brewster, she thought. A man of his tact and dignity and warmth would be a definite asset.

When Lys Erwin woke—alone, for a change—the following morning, some of the past night's curious calmness had deserted her.

I have to talk to Mr. Hallinan, she thought.

She had resisted two implied, and one overt, attempts at seduction the night before, had come home, had managed even to be polite to her husband. And Leslie had been polite to her. It was most unusual.

"That Hallinan," he had said. "He's quite a guy."

"You talked to him too?"

"Yeah. Told him a lot. Too much, maybe. But I feel better for it."

"Odd," she had said. "So do I. He's a strange one, isn't he? Wandering around that party, soaking up everyone's aches. He must have had half the neuroses in New Brewster unloaded on his back last night."

"Didn't seem to depress him, though. More he talked to people, more cheerful and affable he got. And us, too. You look more relaxed than you've been in a month, Lys."

"I *feel* more relaxed. As if all the roughness and ugliness in me was drawn out."

And that was how it felt the next morning, too. Lys woke, blinked, looked at the empty bed across the room. Leslie was long since gone, on his way to the city. She knew she had to talk to Hallinan again. She hadn't got rid of it all. There was still some poison left inside her, something cold and chunky that would melt before Mr. Hallinan's warmth.

She dressed, impatiently brewed some coffee, and left the house. Down Copperbeech Road, past the Moncrieff house where Daisy and her stuffy husband Fred were busily emptying the ashtrays of the night before, down to Melon Hill and up the gentle slope to the split-level at the top.

Mr. Hallinan came to the door in a blue checked dressing gown. He looked slightly seedy, almost overhung, Lys thought. His dark eyes had puffy lids and a light stubble sprinkled his cheeks.

"Yes, Mrs. Erwin?"

"Oh—good morning, Mr. Hallinan. I—I came to see you. I hope I didn't disturb you—that is—"

"Quite all right, Mrs. Erwin." Instantly she was at ease. "But I'm afraid I'm really extremely tired after last night, and I fear I shouldn't be very good company just now."

"But you said you'd talk to me alone today. And—oh, there's so much more I want to tell you!"

A shadow of feeling—*pain? fear?* Lys wondered—crossed his face. "No," he said hastily. "No more—not just yet. I'll have to rest today. Would you mind coming back—well, say Wednesday?"

"Certainly, Mr. Hallinan. I wouldn't want to disturb you."

She turned away and stared down the hill, thinking: *He had too much of our troubles last night. He soaked them all up like a sponge, and today he's going to digest them—*

Oh, what am I thinking?

She reached the foot of the hill, brushed a couple of tears from her eyes, and walked home rapidly, feeling the October chill whistling around her.

And so the pattern of life in New Brewster developed. For the six weeks before his death, Mr. Hallinan was a fixture at any important community gathering, always dressed impeccably, always ready with his cheerful smile, always uncannily able to draw forth whatever secret hungers and terrors lurked in his neighbors' souls.

And invariably Mr. Hallinan would be unapproachable the day after these gatherings, would mildly but firmly turn away any callers. What he did, alone in the house on Melon Hill, no one knew. As the days passed, it occurred to all that no one knew much of anything about Mr. Hallinan. He knew *them* all right, knew the one night of adultery twenty years before that still racked Daisy Moncrieff, knew the acid pain that seared Dudley Heyer, the cold envy glittering in Martha Weede, the frustration and loneliness of Lys Erwin, her husband's shy anger at his own cuckoldry—he knew these things and many more, but none of them knew more of him than his name.

Still, he warmed their lives and took from them the burden of their griefs. If he chose to keep his own life hidden, they said, that was his privilege.

He took walks every day, through still-wooded New Brewster, and would wave and smile to the children, who would wave and smile back. Occasionally he would stop, chat with a sulking child, then move on, tall, erect, walking with a jaunty stride.

He was never known to set foot in either of New Brewster's two churches. Once Lora Harker, a mainstay of the New Brewster Presbyterian Church, took him to task for this at a dull dinner party given by the Weedes.

But Mr. Hallinan smiled mildly and said, "Some of us feel the need. Others do not."

And that ended the discussion.

Towards the end of November a few members of the community experienced an abrupt reversal of their feelings about Mr. Hallinan— weary, perhaps, of his constant empathy for their woes. The change in spirit was spearheaded by Dudley Heyer, Carl Weede, and several of the other men.

"I'm getting not to trust that guy," Heyer said. He knocked dottle vehemently from his pipe. "Always hanging around soaking up gossip, pulling out dirt—and what the hell for? What does *he* get out of it?"

"Maybe he's practicing to be a saint," Carl Weede remarked quietly. "Self-abnegation. The Buddhist Eightfold Path."

"The women all swear by him," said Leslie Erwin. "Lys hasn't been the same since he came here."

"*I'll* say she hasn't," said Aiken Muir wryly, and all of the men, even Erwin, laughed, getting the sharp thrust.

"All I know is I'm tired of having a father-confessor in our midst," Heyer said. "I think he's got a motive back of all his goody-goody warmness. When he's through pumping us he's going to write a book that'll put New Brewster on the map but good."

"You always suspect people of writing books," Muir said. *"Oh, that mine enemy would write a book...!"*

"Well, whatever his motives I'm getting annoyed. And that's why he hasn't been invited to the party we're giving on Monday night." Heyer glared at Fred Moncrieff as if expecting some dispute. "I've spoken to my wife about it, and she agrees. Just this once, dear Mr. Hallinan stays home."

It was strangely cold at the Heyers' party that Monday night. The usual people were there, all but Mr. Hallinan. The party was not a success. Some, unaware that Mr. Hallinan had not been invited, waited expectantly for the chance to talk to him, and managed to leave early when they discovered he was not to be there.

"We should have invited him," Ruth Heyer said after the last guest had left.

Heyer shook his head. "No. I'm glad we didn't."

"But that poor man, all alone on the hill while the bunch of us were here, cut off from us. You don't think he'll get insulted, do you? I mean, and cut us off from now on?"

"I don't care," Heyer said, scowling.

His attitude of mistrust towards Mr. Hallinan spread through the community. First the Muirs, then the Harkers, failed to invite him to

232

gatherings of theirs. He still took his usual afternoon walks, and those who met him observed a slightly strained expression on his face, though he still smiled gently and chatted easily enough, and made no bitter comments.

And on December 3, Wednesday, Roy Heyer, age 10, and Philip Moncrieff, age 9, set upon Lonny Dewitt, age 9, just outside the New Brewster Public School, just before Mr. Hallinan turned down the school lane on his stroll.

Lonny was a strange, silent boy, the despair of his parents and the bane of his classmates. He kept to himself, said little, nudged into corners and stayed there. People clucked their tongues when they saw him in the street.

Roy Heyer and Philip Moncrieff made up their minds they were going to make Lonny Dewitt say something, or else.

It was *or else*. They pummeled him and kicked him for a few minutes; then, seeing Mr. Hallinan approaching, they ran, leaving Lonny weeping silently on the flagstone steps outside the empty school.

Lonny looked up as the tall man drew near.

"They've been hitting you, haven't they? I see them running away now."

Lonny continued to cry. He was thinking, *There's something funny about this man. But he wants to help me. He wants to be kind to me.*

"You're Lonny Dewitt, I think. Why are you crying? Come, Lonny, stop crying! They didn't hurt you that much."

They didn't, Lonny said silently. *I like to cry.*

Mr. Hallinan was smiling cheerfully. "Tell me all about it. Something's bothering you, isn't it? Something big, that makes you feel all lumpy and sad inside. Tell me about it, Lonny, and maybe it'll go away." He took the boy's small cold hands in his own, and squeezed them.

"Don't want to talk," Lonny said.

"But I'm a friend. I want to help you."

Lonny peered close and saw suddenly that the tall man told the truth. He wanted to help Lonny. More than that: he *had* to help Lonny. Desperately. He was pleading. "Tell me what's troubling you," Mr. Hallinan said again.

OK, Lonny thought. *I'll tell you.*

And he lifted the floodgates. Nine years of repression and torment came rolling out in one roaring burst.

I'm alone and they hate me because I do things in my head and they never understood and they think I'm queer and they hate me I see them looking funny at me and they think funny things about me because I want to talk to them with my mind and they can only hear words and I hate them hate them hate hate hate—

Lonny stopped suddenly. He had let it all out, and now he felt better, cleansed of the poison he'd been carrying in him for years. But Mr. Hallinan looked funny. He was pale and white-faced, and he was staggering.

In alarm, Lonny extended his mind to the tall man. And got:

Too much. Much too much. Should never have gone near the boy. But the older ones wouldn't let me.

Irony: the compulsive empath overloaded and burned out by a compulsive sender who'd been bottled up.

...like grabbing a high-voltage wire...

...he was a sender, I was a receiver, but he was too strong...

And four last bitter words: *I...was...a...leech...*

"Please, Mr. Hallinan," Lonny said out loud. "Don't get sick. I want to tell you some more. Please, Mr. Hallinan."

Silence.

Lonny picked up a final lingering wordlessness, and knew he had found and lost the first one like himself. Mr. Hallinan's eyes closed and he fell forward on his face in the street. Lonny realized that it was over, that he and the people of New Brewster would never talk to Mr. Hallinan again. But just to make sure he bent and took Mr. Hallinan's limp wrist.

He let go quickly. The wrist was like a lump of ice. *Cold*—burningly cold. Lonny stared at the dead man for a moment or two.

"Why, it's dear Mr. Hallinan," a female voice said. "Is he—"

And feeling the loneliness return, Lonny began to cry softly again.

BLAZE OF GLORY

Horace Gold, the editor of Galaxy, *was another one back in that long-ago era who kept hammering away at my willingness to turn out anything, anything at all, for the sake of a ready paycheck. He knew I was a capable writer who was going to have a significant career; and so he yelled at me and yelled at me, and sent me one irate rejection slip after another, until I started to live up to his high expectations for me. I didn't always agree with his reactions to specific stories—he rejected some that I worked over as lovingly as I could, and felt were the best that I had in me—but his fundamental principle of pushing me to reach toward the highest possible level of achievement I could muster, and then to reach a little beyond that, eventually sank in.*

"Blaze of Glory" was the second story I sold him, in January, 1957. (The first, I think, which he bought while I was still in college in the spring of 1956, is best left where it is. It was a great thrill to sell it to him, and thus complete my sweep of the Big Three magazines, but the story itself now seems non-wonderful to me: like any editor, Horace had some weak spots as an editor, and that first story must have located one of them.) I'm pretty sure he was expecting even better fiction from me than this second one, too, and eventually I wrote some for him; but it must have showed him that I was at least starting to get the message, and my reward was a check for $150— something worth celebrating, back then. He published the story in the August, 1957 Galaxy.

They list John Murchison as one of the great heroes of space—a brave man and true, who willingly sacrificed himself to save his ship. He won his immortality on the way back from Shaula II.

One thing's wrong, though. He was brave, but he wasn't willing. He wasn't the self-sacrificing type. I'm inclined to think it was murder, or maybe execution. By remote control, you might say.

I guess they pick spaceship crews at random—say, by yanking a handful of cards from the big computer and throwing them up at the BuSpace roof. The ones that stick get picked. At least, that's the only way a man like Murchison could have been sent to Shaula II in the first place.

He was a spaceman of the old school, tall, bullnecked, coarse-featured, hard-swearing. He was a spaceman of a type that had never existed except in storytapes for the very young—the only kind Murchison was likely to have viewed. He was our chief signal officer.

Somewhere, he had picked up an awesome technical competence; he could handle any sort of communication device with supernatural ease. I once saw him tinker with a complex little Caphian artifact that had been buried for half a million years, and have it detecting the 21-centimeter "hydrogen song" within minutes. How he knew the little widget was a star-mapping device I will never understand.

But coupled with Murchison's extraordinary special skill was an irascibility, a self-centered inner moodiness flaring into seemingly unmotivated anger at unpredictable times, that made him a prime risk on a planet like Shaula II. There was something wrong with his circuit-breaker setup: you could never tell when he'd overload, start fizzing and sparking, and blow off a couple of megawatts of temper.

You must admit this is not the ideal sort of man to send to a world whose inhabitants are listed in the E-T Catalogue as *"wise, somewhat world-weary, exceedingly gentle, non-aggressive to an extreme degree and thus subject to exploitation. The Shaulans must be handled with great patience and forbearance, and should be given the respect due one of the galaxy's elder races."*

I had never been to Shaula II, but I had a sharp mental image of the Shaulans: melancholy old men pondering the whichness of the why and ready to fall apart at the first loud voice that caught them by surprise. So it caught me by surprise when the time came to affix my hancock to the roster of the *Felicific*, and I saw on the line above mine the scribbled words *Murchison, John F., Signalman First Class.*

I signed my name—*Loeb, Ernest T., Second Officer*—picked up my pay voucher, and walked away somewhat dizzily. I was thinking of the time I had seen Murchison, John F., giving a Denebolan frogman the beating of his life, for no particular reason at all. "All the rain here makes me sick" was all Murchison cared to say; the frogman lived and Big Jawn got an X on his psych report.

Now he was shipping out for Shaula? Well, maybe so…but my faith in the computer that makes up spaceship complements was seriously shaken.

We were the fourth or fifth expedition to Shaula II. The planet—second of seven in orbit round the brightest star in Scorpio's tail—was small and scrubby, but of great strategic importance as a lookout spot for that sector of the galaxy. The natives hadn't minded our intrusion, and so a military base had been established there after a little preliminary haggling.

The *Felicific* was a standard warp-conversion-drive ship holding thirty-six men. It had the usual crew of eight, plus a cargo of twenty-eight of Terra's finest, being sent out as replacements for the current staff of the base.

We blasted on 3 July 2530, a warmish day, made the conversion from ion-drive to warp-drive as soon as we were clear of the local system, and popped back into normal space three weeks later and two hundred light-years away. It was a routine trip in all respects.

With the warp-conversion drive, a ship is equipped to travel both long distances and short. It handles the long hops via subspace warp, and the short ones by good old standard ion-drive seat-of-the-spacesuit navigating. It's a good system, and the extra mass the double drive requires is more than compensated for by the saving in time and maneuverability.

The warp-drive part of the trip was pre-plotted and just about pre-traveled for us; no headaches *there*. But when we blurped back into the continuum about half a light-year from Shaula the human factor entered the situation. Meaning Murchison, of course.

It was his job to check and tend the network of telemetering systems that acted as the ship's eyes, to make sure the mass-detectors were operating, to smooth the bugs out of the communications channels between navigator and captain and drive-deck. In brief, he was the man who made it possible for us to land.

Every ship carried a spare signalman, just in case. In normal circumstances the spare never got much work. When the time came for the landing, Captain Knight buzzed me and told me to start lining up the men who would take part, and I signaled Murchison first.

His voice was a slow rasping drawl. "Yeah?"

"Second Officer Loeb. Prepare for landing, double-fast. Navigator Henrichs has the chart set up for you and he's waiting for your call."

There was a pause. Then: "I don't feel like it, Loeb."

It was my turn to pause. I shut my eyes, held my breath, and counted to three by fractions. Then I said, "Would you mind repeating that, Signalman Murchison?"

"Yes, sir. No, sir, I mean. Hell, Loeb, I'm fixing something. Why do you want to land now?"

"I don't make up the schedules," I said.

"Then who in blazes does? Tell him I'm busy!"

I turned down my phones' volume. "Busy doing what?"

"Busy doing nothing. Get off the line and I'll call Henrichs."

I sighed and broke contact. He'd just been ragging me. Once again, Murchison had been ornery for the sheer sake of being ornery. One of these days he was going to refuse to handle the landing entirely.

And that day, I told myself, is the day we'll crate him up and shove him through the disposal lock.

Murchison was a little island. He had his skills, and he applied them—when he felt like it. But only when he believed that he, Murchison, would profit. He never did anything unwillingly, because if he couldn't find it in himself to do it willingly he wouldn't do it at all. It was impossible to *make* him do something.

Unwisely, we tolerated it. But someday he would get a captain who didn't understand him, and he'd be slapped with a sentence of mutiny during a fit of temperament. For his sake, I hoped not. The penalty for mutiny in space is death.

With Murchison's cooperation gratefully accepted, we targeted on Shaula II, which was then at perihelion, and orbited it. Down in his little cubicle Murchison worked like a demon, taking charge of the ship's landing system in a tremendous way. He was a fantastic signalman when he wanted to be.

Later that day the spinning red ball that was Shaula II hung just ahead of us, close enough to let us see the three blobs of continents and the big, choppy hydrocarbon ocean that licked them smooth. The Terran base on Continent Three beamed as a landing-guide; Murchison picked it up, fed it through the computer bank to Navigator Henrichs, and we homed in for the landing.

The Terran base consisted of a couple of blockhouses, a sprawling barracks, and a good-sized radar parabola, all set in a ring out on an almost mathematically flat plain. Shaula II was a great world for plains; Columbus would have had the devil's time convincing people *this* world was round!

Murchison guided us to a glassy-looking area not far from the base, and we touched down. The *Felicific* creaked and groaned a little as the landing jacks absorbed its weight. Green lights went on all over the ship. We were free to go outside.

A welcoming committee was on hand: eight members of the base staff, clad in shorts and topees. Regulation uniforms went by the board on oven-hot Shaula II. The eight looked awfully happy to see us.

Coming over the flat sandy plain from the base were a dozen or so others, running, and behind them I could see even more. They were understandably glad we were here. Twenty-eight of them had spent a full year on Shaula II; they were eligible for their parity-program year's vacation.

There were some other—things—moving towards us. They moved slowly, with grace and dignity. I had expected to be impressed with the Shaulans, and I was.

They were erect bipeds about four feet tall, with long thin arms dangling to their knees; their grey skins were grainy and rough, and their dark eyes—they had three, arranged triangularly—were deepset and brooding. A fleshy sort of cowl or cobra-hood curled up from their necks to shield their round hairless skulls. The aliens were six in number, and the youngest-looking of them seemed ancient.

A brown-faced young man wearing shorts, topee, and tattooed stars stepped forward and said, "I'm General Gloster. I'm in charge here."

The Captain acknowledged his greeting. "Knight of the *Felicific*. We have your relief men with us."

"I sure as hell hope you do," Gloster said. "Be kind of silly to come all this way without them."

We all laughed a little over that. By now we were ringed in by at least fifty Earthmen, probably the entire base complement (we didn't rotate the entire base staff at once, of course), and the six aliens. The twenty-eight kids we had ferried here were looking around the place curiously, apprehensive about this hot, dry, flat planet that would be their home for the next sidereal year. The crew of the *Felicific* had gathered in a little knot near the ship. Most of them probably felt the way I did; they were glad we'd be on our way home in a couple of days.

Murchison was squinting at the six aliens. I wondered what he was thinking about.

The bunch of us traipsed back the half mile or so to the settlement; Gloster walked with Knight and myself, prattling volubly about the progress the base was making, and the twenty-eight newcomers mingled with the twenty-eight who were being relieved. Murchison walked by himself, kicking up puffs of red dust and scowling in his usual manner. The six aliens accompanied us at some distance.

"We keep building all the time," Gloster explained when we were within the compound. "Branching out, setting up new equipment, shoring up the old stuff: That radar parabola out there wasn't up, last replacement-trip."

I looked around. "The place looks fine, General." It was strange calling a man half my age *General,* but the Service sometimes works that way. "When do you plan to set up your telescope?"

"Next year, maybe." He glanced out the window at the featureless landscape. "We keep building all the time. It's the best way to stay sane on this world."

"How about the natives?" the Captain asked. "You have much contact with them?"

Gloster shrugged. "As much as they'll allow. They're a proud old race—pretty near dried up and dead now, just a handful of them left. But what a race they must have been once! What minds! What culture!"

I found Gloster's boyish enthusiasm discomforting. "Do you think we could meet one of the aliens before we go?" I asked.

"I'll see about it." Gloster picked up a phone. "McHenry? There any natives in the compound now? Good. Send him up, will you?"

Moments later one of the shorts-clad men appeared, hand in hand with an alien. At close range the Shaulan looked almost frighteningly old. A maze of wrinkles gullied its noseless face, running from the triple optics down to the dots of nostrils to the sagging, heavy-lipped mouth.

"This is Azga," Gloster said. "Azga, meet Captain Knight and Second Officer Loeb, of the *Felicific*."

The creature offered a wobbly sort of curtsey and said, in a deep, resonant, almost-human croak, "I am very humble indeed in your presence, Captain Knight and Second Officer Loeb."

Azga came out of the curtsey and the three eyes fixed on mine. I felt like squirming, but I stared back. It was like looking into a mirror that gave the wrong reflection.

Yet I enjoyed my proximity to the alien. There was something calm and wise and good about the grotesque creature; something relaxing, and terribly fragile. The rough grey skin looked like precious leather, and the hood over the skull appeared to shield it from worry and harm. A faint musty odor wandered through the room.

We looked at each other—Knight, and Gloster, and McHenry, and I—and we remained silent. Now that the Shaulan was here, what could we say? What new thing could we possibly tell the ancient creature?

I resisted an impulse to kneel. I was fumbling for words to express my emotion when the sharp buzz of the phone cut across the room.

Gloster nodded curtly to McHenry, who answered. The man listened for a moment. "Captain Knight, it's for you."

Puzzled, Knight took the receiver. He held it long enough to hear about three sentences and turned to me. "Loeb, get a landcar from someone in the compound and get back to the ship. Murchison's carrying on with one of the aliens."

I hotfooted down into the compound and spotted an enlisted man tooling up his landcar. I pulled rank and requisitioned it, and minutes later I was parking it outside the *Felicific* and was clambering hand-over-hand up the catwalk.

An excited-looking recruit stood at the open airlock

"Where's Murchison?" I asked.

"Down in the communicator cabin. He's got an alien in there with him. There's gonna be trouble."

I remembered Denebola, and Murchison kicking the stuffings out of a groaning frogman. I groaned a little myself, and dashed down the companionway.

The communications cabin was Murchison's *sanctum sanctorum,* a cubicle off the astro deck where he worked and kept control over the *Felicific*'s communications network. I yanked open the door and saw Murchison at the far end of the cabin holding a massive crescent wrench and glaring at a Shaulan facing him. The Shaulan had its back to me. It looked small and squat and helpless.

Murchison saw me as I entered. "Get out of here, Loeb. This isn't your affair."

"What's going on here?" I snapped.

"This alien snooping around. I'm gonna let him have it with the wrench."

"I meant no harm," the alien boomed sadly. "Mere philosophical interest in your strange machines, nothing more. If I have offended a folkway of yours I humbly apologize. It is not the way of my people to give offence."

I walked forward and took a position between them, making sure I wasn't within easy reach of Murchison's wrench. He was standing there with his nostrils spread, his eyes cold and hard, his breath pumping noisily. He was angry, and an angry Murchison was a frightening sight.

He took two heavy steps toward me. "I told you to get out. This is my cabin, Loeb. And neither you or any aliens got any business in it."

"Put down that wrench, Murchison. It's an order."

He laughed contemptuously. "Signalman First Class don't have to take orders from anyone but the Captain if he thinks the safety of the ship is jeopardized. And I do. There's a dangerous alien in here."

"Be reasonable," I said. "This Shaulan's not dangerous. He just wanted to look around. Just curious."

The wrench wiggled warningly. I wished I had a blaster with me, but I hadn't thought of bringing a weapon. The alien faced Murchison quite complacently, as if confident the signalman would never strike anything so old and delicate.

"You'd better leave," I said to the alien.

"No!" Murchison roared. He shoved me to one side and went after the Shaulan.

The alien stood there, waiting, as Murchison came on. I tried to drag the big man away, but there was no stopping him.

At least he didn't use the wrench. He let the big crescent slip clangingly to the floor and slapped the alien open-handed across its face. The Shaulan backed up a few feet. A trickle of bluish fluid worked its way along its mouth. Murchison raised his hand again. "Damned snooper! I'll teach you to poke in my cabin!" He hit the alien again.

This time the Shaulan folded up accordionwise and huddled on the floor. It focused those three deep solid-black eyes on Murchison reproachfully.

Murchison looked back. They stared at each other for a long, moment, until it seemed that their eyes were linked by an invisible cord. Then Murchison looked away.

"Get out of here," he muttered to the alien, and the Shaulan rose and departed, limping a little but still intact. Those aliens were more solid than they seemed.

"I guess you're going to put me in the brig," Murchison said to me. "Okay. I'll go quietly."

We didn't brig him, because there was nothing to be gained by that. I had seen the explosion coming right from the start. When you drop a lighted match into a tub of hydrazine, you don't punish the hydrazine for blowing up. And Murchison couldn't be blamed for what he did, either.

He got the silent treatment instead. The men at the base would have nothing to do with him whatsoever, because in their year on Shaula they had developed a respect for the aliens not far from worship, and any man who would actually use physical violence—well, he just wasn't worth wasting breath on.

The men of our crew gave him a wide berth too. He wandered among us, a tall, powerful figure with anger and loneliness stamped on his face, and he said nothing to any of us and no one said anything to him. Whenever he saw one of the aliens, he went far out of his way to avoid a meeting.

Murchison got another X on his psych report, and that second X meant he'd never be allowed to visit any world inhabited by intelligent life again. It was a BuSpace regulation, one of the many they have for the purpose of locking the barn door too late.

Three days went by this way on Shaula. On the fourth, we took aboard the twenty-eight departing men, said goodbye to Gloster and his staff and the twenty-eight we had ferried out to him, and—somewhat guiltily—goodbye to the Shaulans too.

The six of them showed up for our blastoff, including the somewhat battered one who had had the run-in with Murchison. They wished us well, gravely, without any sign of bitterness. For the hundredth time I was astonished by their patience, their wisdom, their understanding.

I held Azga's rough hand in mine and said goodbye. I told him for the first time what I had been wanting to say since our first meeting, how much I hoped we'd eventually reach the mental equilibrium and inner calm of the Shaulans. He smiled warmly at me, and I said goodbye again and entered the ship.

We ran the usual pre-blast checkups, and got ready for departure. Everything was working well; Murchison had none of his usual grumbles and complaints, and we were off the ground in record time.

A couple of days of ion-drive, three weeks of warp, two more of ion-drive deceleration, and we would be back on Earth.

The three weeks passed slowly, of course; when Earth lies ahead of you, time drags. But after the interminable greyness of warp came the sudden wrenching twist and the bright slippery *sliding* feeling as our Bohling generator threw us back into ordinary space.

I pushed down the communicator stud near my arm and heard the voice of Navigator Henrichs saying, "Murchison, give me the coordinates, will you?"

"Hold on," came Murchison's growl. "Patience, Sam. You'll get your coordinates as soon as I got 'em."

There was a pause; then Captain Knight said, "Murchison, what's holding up those coordinates? Where are we, anyway? Turn on the visiplates?"

"*Please,* Captain." Murchison's heavy voice was surprisingly polite. Then he ruined it. "Please, be good enough to shut up and let a man think."

"Murchison—" Knight sputtered, and stopped. We all knew one solid fact about our signalman: he did as he pleased. No one but no one coerced him into anything.

So we waited, spinning end-over-end somewhere in the vicinity of Earth, completely blind behind our wall of metal. Until Murchison chose to feed us some data, we had no way of bringing the ship down.

Three more minutes went by; then the private circuit Knight uses when he wants to talk to me alone lit up, and he said, "Loeb, go down to Communications and see what's holding Murchison up. We can't stay here forever."

"Yessir."

I pocketed a blaster—I hate making mistakes more than once—and left my cabin. I walked numbly to the companionway, turned to the left, hit the drophatch and found myself outside Murchison's door.

I knocked.

"Get away from here, Loeb!" Murchison bellowed from within.

I had forgotten that he had rigged a one-way vision circuit outside his door. I said, "Let me in, Murchison. Let me in or I'll come in blasting."

I heard a heavy sigh. "Come on in, then."

Nervously I pushed the door open and poked my head and the blaster snout in, half expecting Murchison to leap on me from above. But he was sitting at an equipment-jammed desk scribbling notes, which surprised me. I stood waiting for him to look up.

And finally he did. I gasped when I saw his face: drawn, harried, pale, tense. I had never seen an expression like that on Murchison's face before.

"What's going on?" I asked softly. "We're all waiting to get moving, and—"

He turned to face me squarely. "You want to know what's going on, Loeb? Well, listen: the ship's blind. None of the equipment is reading anything. No telemeter pickup, no visual, no nothing. *You* scrape up some coordinates, if you can."

We held a little meeting half an hour later, in the ship's Common Room. Murchison was there, and Knight, and myself, and Navigator Henrichs, and three representatives of the cargo.

"How did this happen?" Knight demanded.

Murchison shrugged. "It happened while we were in warp. We passed through something—magnetic field, maybe—and bollixed every instrument we have."

Knight glanced at Henrichs. "You ever hear of such a thing happening before?" He seemed to suspect Murchison of funny business.

But Henrichs shook his head. "No, Chief. And there's a good reason why, too. If this happens to a ship, the ship doesn't get back to tell about it."

He was right. With no contact at all with the outside, no information on location or orbits, there was no way to land the ship. And the radio, of course, was dead too; we couldn't even call for help.

Captain Knight looked grey-faced and very old. He asked worriedly, "What could have caused this thing?"

"No one knows what subspace conditions are like," Henrichs said. "It may have been a fluke magnetic field, as Murchison suggests. Or anything at all—an alien entity that swallowed our antennae, for all we know. The question's not what did it, Captain—it's how do we get back."

"Good point. Murchison, is there any chance you can repair the instruments?"

"No."

"Just like that—flat *no*? Hell, man, we've seen you do wonders with instruments on the blink before."

"*No,*" Murchison repeated stolidly. "I tried. I can't do a damned thing."

"That means we're finished, doesn't it?" asked Ramirez, one of our returnees. His voice was a little wild. "We might just as well have stayed on Shaula! At least we'd still be alive!"

"It looks pretty lousy," Henrichs admitted. The thin-faced navigator was frowning blackly. "We don't dare try a blind landing. There's nothing we can do. Nothing at all."

"There's *one* thing," Murchison said.

All eyes turned to him. "What?" Knight asked.

"Put a man in a spacesuit and anchor him to the skin of the ship. Have him guide us in by verbal instructions. It's a way, anyway."

"Pretty farfetched," Henrichs commented.

"Yes, dammit, but it's our only hope!" Murchison snapped. "Stick a man up there and let him talk us in."

"He'd incinerate once we hit Earth's atmosphere," I said. "We'd lose a man and still have to land blind."

Murchison puckered his thick lower lip. "You'll be able to judge the ship's height by hull temperature once you're that close. Besides, once the ship's inside the ionosphere you can use ordinary radio for the rest of the way down. The trick is to get *that* far."

"I think it's worth a try," Captain Knight said. "I guess we'll have to draw lots. Loeb, get some straws from the galley." His voice was grim.

"Never mind," Murchison said.

"Huh?"

"I said, never mind. Skip it. Forget about drawing straws. *I'll* go."

"Murchison—"

"*Skip it!*" he barked. "It's a failure in my department, so I'm going to go out there. I volunteer, get it? If anyone else wants to volunteer, I'll match him for it." He looked around at us. No one moved. "I don't hear any takers. I'll assume the job's mine." Sweat streamed down his face.

There was a startled silence, broken when Ramirez made the lousiest remark I've ever heard mortal man utter. "You're trying to make it up for hitting that defenseless Shaulan, eh, Murchison? Now you want to be a hero to even things up!"

If Murchison had killed him on the spot, I think we'd all have applauded. But the big man only turned to Ramirez and said quietly, "You're just as blind as the others. You don't know how rotten those defenseless Shaulans are, any of you. Or what they did to me." He spat. "You all make me sick. I'm going out there."

He turned and walked away...out, to get into his spacesuit and climb into the ship's skin.

Murchison's explicit instructions, relayed from the outside of the ship, allowed Henrichs to bring us in. It was quite a feat of teamwork.

At 50,000 feet above Earth, Murchison's voice suddenly cut out. We were able to pick up ground-to-ship radio by then and we taxied down. Later, they told us it seemed like a blazing candle was riding the ship's back. A bright, clear flame flared for a moment as we cleaved the atmosphere.

And I remember the look on Murchison's face as he left us to go out there. It was tense, bitter, strained—as if he were being *compelled* to go outside. As if he had no choice about volunteering for martyrdom.

I often wonder about that now. No one had ever made Murchison do anything he didn't want to do—until then.

We think of the Shaulans as gentle, meek, defenseless. Murchison crossed one of them, and he died. Gentle, meek, yes—but defenseless? Murchison didn't think so.

Maybe they whammied the ship and cursed Murchison with the urge to self-martyrdom, to punish him. Maybe. He never did trust them much.

It sort of tarnishes his glorious halo. But you know, sometimes I think Murchison was right about the Shaulans after all.

WHY?

I think this one might have pleased Horace too, or even Tony Boucher, if I had ever submitted it to them. But, like many of my stories at that time, it was written to order—for Bob Lowndes' Science Fiction Stories—around a cover painting, and I got a safe, easy $85 for it in March, 1957, half of what Galaxy would have paid for it if I had taken the risk of sending it there on a speculative basis instead of embodying my story idea in a sure-thing commission for Lowndes. (I should also point out, since we are dealing in alternative realities here, that I might never have had the idea for this story in the first place without the inspiration that Ed Emshwiller's vivid cover painting provided.)

"Why?" ran in Lowndes' November, 1957 issue. I have no notion how much it cost me in the long run to do these sold-in-advance stories for the lower-paying magazines instead of taking my chances on everything with the top-paying ones first. But at least the rent got paid on time every month, a fact which, as you surely must have gathered by now, was a matter of no trivial concern to me back in the early months of 1957, less than a year after my graduation from college.

And we left Capella XXII, after a six-month stay, and hopskipped across the galaxy to Dschubba, in the forehead of the Scorpion. And after the eight worlds of Dschubba had been seen and digested and recorded and classified, and after we had programmed all our material for transmission back to Earth, we moved on again, Brock and I.

We zeroed into warp and doublesqueaked into the star Pavo, which from Earth is seen to be the brightest star of the Peacock. And Pavo proved to be planetless, save for one ball of mud and methane a billion miles out; we chalked the mission off as unpromising, and moved on once again.

Brock was the coordinator; I, the fine-tooth man. He saw in patterns; I, in particulars. We had been teamed for eleven years. We had visited seventy-eight stars and one hundred sixty-three planets. The end was not quite in sight.

We hung in the greyness of warp, suspended neither in space nor in not-space, hovering in an interstice. Brock said, "I vote for Markab."

"Alpha Pegasi? No. I vote for Etamin."

But Gamma Draconis held little magic for him. He rubbed his angular hands through his tight-cropped hair and said, "The Wheel, then."

I nodded. "The Wheel."

The Wheel was our guide: not really a wheel so much as a map of the heavens in three dimensions, a lens of the galaxy, sprinkled brightly with stars. I pulled a switch; a beam of light lanced down from the ship's wall, needle-thin, playing against the Wheel. Brock seized the handle and imparted axial spin to the Wheel. Over and over for three, four, five rotations; then, stop. The light-beam stung Alphecca.

"Alphecca it will be," Brock said.

"Yes. Alphecca." I noted it in the log, and began setting up the coordinates on the drive. Brock was frowning uneasily.

"This failure to agree," he said. "This inability to decide on a matter so simple as our next destination—"

"Yes. Elucidate. Expound. Exegetize. What pattern do you see in that?"

Scowling he said, "Disagreement for the sake of disagreement is unhealthy. Conflict is valuable, but not for its own sake. It worries me."

"Perhaps we've been in space too long. Perhaps we should resign our commissions, leave the Exploratory Corps, return to Earth and settle there."

His face drained of blood. "No," he said. "No. No."

WHY?

We emerged from warp within humming-distance of Alphecca, a bright star orbited by four worlds. Brock was playing calculus at the time; driblets of sweat glossed his face at each integration. I peered through the thick quartz of the observation panel and counted planets.

"Four worlds," I said. "One, two, three, and four."

I looked at him. His unfleshy face was tight with pain. After nearly a minute he said, "Pick one."

"Me?"

"Pick one!"

"Alphecca II."

"All right. We'll land there. I won't contest the point, Hammond. I *want* to land on Alphecca II." He grinned at me—a bright-eyed wild grin that I found unpleasant. But I saw what he was doing. He was easing a stress-pattern between us, eliminating a source of conflict before the chafing friction exploded. When two men live in a spaceship eleven years, such things are necessary.

Calmly and untensely I took a reading on Alphecca II. I sighted us in and actuated the computer. This was the way a landing was effected; this was the way Brock and I had effected one hundred sixty-three landings. The ion-drive exploded into life.

We dropped "downward". Alphecca II rose to meet us as our slim pale-green needle of a ship dived tail-first towards the world below.

The landing was routine. I sketched out a big 164 on my chart, and we donned spacesuits to make our preliminary explorations. Brock paused a moment at the airlock, smoothing the purple cloth of his suit, adjusting his air-intake, tightening his belt cincture. The corners of his mouth twitched nervously. Within the head-globe he looked frightened, and very tired.

I said, "You're not well. Maybe we should postpone our first look-see."

"Maybe we should go back to Earth, Hammond. And live in a bee-hive and breathe filthy grey soup." His voice was edged with bitter reproach. "Let's go outside," he said. He turned away, face shadowed morosely, and touched the stud that peeled back the airlock hatch.

I followed him into the lock and down the elevator. He was silent, stiff, reserved. I wished I had his talent for glimpsing patterns: this mood of his had probably been a long time building.

But I saw no cause for it. After eleven years, I thought, I should know him almost as well as I do myself. Or better. But no easy answers came, and I followed him out onto the exit stage and dropped gently down.

Landing One Six Four was entering the exploratory stage.

The ground spread out far to the horizon, a dull orange in color, rough in texture, pebbly, thick of consistency. We saw a few trees, bare-trunked, bluish. Green vines swarmed over the ground, twisted and gnarled.

Otherwise, nothing.

"Another uninhabited planet," I said. "That makes one hundred eight out of the hundred sixty-four."

"Don't be premature. You can't judge a world by a few acres. Land at a pole; extrapolate utter barrenness. It's not a valid pattern. Not enough evidence."

I cut him short. "Here's one time when I perceive a pattern. I perceive that this world's uninhabited. It's too damned quiet."

Chuckling, Brock said, "I incline to agree. But remember Adhara XI."

I remembered Adhara XI: the small, sandy world far from its primary, which seemed nothing but endless yellow sand dunes, rolling westward round and round the planet. We had joked about the desert-world, dry and parched, inhabited only by the restless dunes. But after the report was written, after our data were codified and flung through subspace towards Earth, we found the oasis on the eastern continent, the tiny garden of green things and sweet air that so sharply was unlike the rest of Adhara XI. I remembered sleek scaly creatures slithering through the crystal lake, and an indolent old worm sleeping beneath a heavy-fruited tree.

"Adhara XI is probably swarming with Earth tourists," I said. "Now that our amended report is public knowledge. I often think we should have concealed the oasis from Earth, and. returned there ourselves when we grew tired of exploring the galaxy."

Brock's head snapped up sharply. He ripped a sprouting tip from a leathery vine and said, "*When* we grow tired? Hammond, aren't you tired already? Eleven years, a hundred sixty-four worlds?"

Now I saw the pattern taking fairly clear shape. I shook my head, throttling the conversation. "Let's get down the data, Brock. We can talk later."

We proceeded with the measurements of our particular sector of Alphecca II. We nailed down the dry vital statistics, bracketing them off so Earth could enter the neat figures in its giant catalogue of explored worlds.

GRAVITY—1.02 E.

ATMOSPHERIC CONSTITUTION—ammonia/carbon dioxide

WHY?

Type ab7, unbreathable
ESTIMATED PLANETARY DIAMETER—.87 E.
INTELLIGENT LIFE—*none*
We filled out the standard tests, took the standard soil samples. Exploration had become a smooth mechanical routine.

Our first tour lasted three hours. We wandered over the slowly rising hills, with the spaceship always at our backs, and Alphecca high behind us. The dry soil crunched unpleasantly beneath our heavy boots.

Conversation was at a minimum. Brock and I rarely spoke when it was not absolutely necessary—and when we did speak, it was to let a tight, tense remark escape confinement, not to communicate anything. We shared too many silent memories. Eleven years and one hundred sixty-four planets. All Brock had to do was say *"Fomalhaut"*, or I *"Theta Eridani"*, and a train of associations and memories was set off in whose depths we could browse silently for hours and hours.

Alphecca II did not promise to be as memorable as those worlds. There would be nothing here to match the fantastic moonrise of Fomalhaut VI, the five hundred mirror-bright moons in stately procession through the sky, each glinting in a different hue. That moonrise had overwhelmed us four years ago, and remained yet bright. Alphecca II, dead world that it was, or rather world not yet alive, would leave no marks on our memories.

But bitterness was rising in Brock. I saw the pattern forming; I saw the question bubbling up through the layers of his mind, ready to be asked.

And on the fourth day, he let it be asked. After four days on Alphecca II, four days of staring at the grotesque twisted green shapes of the angular sprawling vines, four days of watching the lethargic fission of the pond protozoa who seemed to be the world's only animal life, Brock suddenly looked up at me.

He asked the shattering question that should never be asked.
"Why?" he said.

Eleven years and a hundred sixty-four worlds earlier, the seeds of that unanswered question had been sown. I was fresh out of the Academy, twenty-three, a tall, sharp-nosed boy with what some said was an irritatingly precise way of looking at things.

I should say that I bitterly resented being told I was coldly precise. People accused me of Teutonic heaviness. A girl I once had known said that to me, after a notably unsuccessful romance had come trailing to a halt. I recall turning to her, glaring at the light dusting of freckles across her nose, and telling her, "I have no Teutonic blood whatsoever. If you'll take the trouble to think of the probable Scandinavian derivation of my name—"

She slapped me.

Shortly after that, I met Brock—Brock, who at twenty-four was already the Brock I would know at thirty-five, harsh of face and voice, dark of complexion, with an expression of nervous wariness registering in his blue-black eyes always and ever. Brock never accused me of Teutonicism; he laughed when I cited some minor detail from memory, but the laugh was one of respect.

We were both Academy graduates; we both were restless. It showed in Brock's face, and I don't doubt it showed in mine. Earth was small and dirty and crowded, and each night the stars, those bright enough to glint through the haze and brightness of the cities, seemed to mock at us.

Brock and I gravitated naturally together. We shared a room in Appalachia North, we shared a library planchet, we shared reading tapes and music-discs and occasionally lovers. And eight weeks after my twenty-third birthday, seven weeks before Brock's twenty-fourth, we hailed a cab and invested our last four coins in a trip downtown to the Administration of External Exploration.

There, we spoke to a bland-faced, smiling man with one leg prosthetic—he boasted of it—and his left hand a waxy synthetic one. "I got that way on Sirius VI," he told us. "But I'm an exception. Most of the exploration teams keep going for years and years, and nothing ever happens to them. McKees and Haugmuth have been out twenty-three years now. That's the record. We hear from them, every few months or so. They keep on going, farther and farther out."

Brock nodded. "Good. Give us the forms."

He signed first. I added my name below, finishing with a flourish. I stacked the triplicate forms neatly together and shoved them back at the half-synthetic recruiter.

"Excellent. Excellent. Welcome to the Corps."

He shook our hands, giving the hairy-knuckled right hand to Brock, the waxy left to me. I gripped it tightly, wondering if he could feel my grip.

Three days later we were in space, bound outward. In all the time since the original idea had sprung up unvoiced between us, neither Brock nor myself had paused to ask the damnable question.

Why?

We had joined the Corps. We had renounced Earth. Motive, unstated. Or unknown. We let the matter lie dormant between us for eleven years, through a procession of strange and then less strange worlds.

Until Brock's agony broke forth to the surface. He destroyed eleven years of numb peace with one half-whispered syllable, there in the ship's lab our fourth morning on Alphecca II.

I looked at him for perhaps thirty seconds. Moistening my lips, I said, "What do you mean, Brock?"

"You know what I mean." The flat declarative tone was one of simple truth. "The one thing we haven't been asking ourselves all these years, because we knew we didn't have an answer for it and we *like* to have answers for things. Why are we here, on Alphecca II—with a hundred sixty-three visited worlds behind us?"

I shrugged. "You didn't have to start this, Brock." Outside the sun was climbing towards noon height, but I felt cold and dry, as if the ammonia atmosphere were seeping into the ship. It wasn't.

"No," he said. "I didn't have to start this. I could have let it fester for another eleven years. But it came popping out, and I want to settle it. We left Earth because we didn't like it there. Agreed?"

I nodded.

"But that's not *why* enough," he persisted. "Why do we explore? Why do we keep running from planet to planet, from one crazy airless ball to the next, out here where there are no people and no cities? Green crabs on Rigel V, sand-fish on Caph. Dammit, Hammond, what are we looking for?"

Very calmly I said, "Ourselves, maybe?"

His face crinkled scornfully. "Foggy-eyed and imprecise, and you know it. We're not looking for ourselves out here. We're trying to *lose* ourselves. Eh?"

"No!"

"Admit it!"

I stared through the quartz window at the stiff, almost wooden vines that covered the pebbly ground. They seemed to be moving faintly, to be stretching their rigid bodies in a contraction of some sort. In a dull, tired voice, Brock said, "We left Earth because we couldn't cope with it. It was too crowded and too dirty for sensitive shrinking souls like us. We had the choice of withdrawing into shells and huddling there for eighty or ninety years, or else pulling up and leaving for space. We left. There's no society out here, just each other."

"We've adjusted to each other," I pointed out.

"So? Does that mean we could fit into Earth society? Would you want to go back? Remember the team—McKees and Haugmuth, is it?—who spent thirty-three years in space and came back. They were catatonic eight minutes after landing, the report said."

"Let me give you a simpler *why*," I ventured. "Why did you start griping all of a sudden? Why couldn't you hold it in?"

"That's not a simpler *why*. It's part of the same one. I came to an answer, and I didn't like it. I got the answer that we were out here because we couldn't make the grade on Earth."

"No!"

He smiled apologetically. "No? All right, then. Give me another answer. I want an answer, Hammond. I need one, now."

I pointed to the synthesizer. "Why don't you have a drink instead?"

"That comes later," he said sombrely. "After I've given up trying to find out."

The stippling of fine details was becoming a sharp-focus picture. Brock—self-reliant Brock, self-contained, self-sufficient—had come to the end of his self-sufficiency. He had looked too deeply beneath the surface.

"At the age of eight," I began, "I asked my father what was outside the universe. That is, defining the universe as That Which Contains Everything, could there possibly be something or someplace outside its bounds? He looked at me for a minute or two, then laughed and told me not to worry about it. But I did worry about it. I stayed up half the night worrying about it, and my head hurt by morning. I never found out what was outside the universe."

"The universe is infinite," said Brock moodily. "Recurving in on itself, topologically—"

"Maybe. But I worried over it. I worried over First Cause. I worried all through my adolescence. Then I stopped worrying."

He smiled acidly. "You became a vegetable. You rooted yourself in the mud of your own ignorance, and decided not to pull loose because it was too painful. Am I right, Hammond?"

"No. I joined the Exploratory Corps."

I dreamed, that night, as I swung in my hammock. It was a vivid and unpleasant dream, which stayed with me well into the following morning as a sort of misshapen reality that had attached itself to me in the night.

I had been a long time falling asleep. Brock had brooded most of the day, and a long hike over the bleak tundra had done little to improve his mood. Towards nightfall he dialed a few drinks, inserted a disc of Sibelius in his ear, and sat staring glumly at the darkening sky outside the ship. Alphecca II was moonless. The night was the black of space, but the atmosphere blurred the neighboring stars.

I remember drifting off into a semisleep: a half-somnolence in which I was aware of Brock's harsh breathing to my left, but yet in which I had no volition, no control over my limbs. And after that state came sleep, and with it dreams.

The dream must have grown from Brock's bitter remark of earlier: *You became a vegetable. You rooted yourself in the mud of your own ignorance.*

I accepted the statement literally. Suddenly I *was* a vegetable, possessed of all my former faculties, but rooted in the soil.

Rooted.

Straining for freedom, straining to break away, caught eternally by my legs, thinking, thinking...

Never to move, except for a certain thrashing of the upper limbs.

Rooted.

I writhed, longed to get as far as the rocky hill beyond, only as far as the next yard, the next inch. But I had lost all motility. It was as if my legs were grasped in a mighty trap, and, without pain, without torment, I was bound to the earth.

I woke, finally, damp with perspiration. In his hammock, Brock slept, seemingly peacefully. I considered waking him and telling him of the nightmare, but decided against it. I tried to return to sleep.

At length, I slept.

Dreamlessly.

The preset alarm throbbed at 0700; dawn had preceded us by nearly an hour.

Brock was up first; I sensed him moving about even as I stirred towards wakefulness. Still caught up in the strange unreal reality of my nightmare, I wondered on a conscious level if today would be like yesterday—if Brock, obsessed by his sudden thirst for an answer, would continue to brood and sulk.

I hoped not. It would mean the end of our team if Brock cracked up; after eleven years, I was not anxious for a new partner.

"Hammond? You up yet?"

His voice had lost the edgy quality of yesterday, but there was something new and subliminally frightening in it.

Yawning, I said, "Just about. Dial breakfast for me, will you?"

"I did already. But get out of the sack and come look at this."

I lurched from the hammock, shook my head to clear it, and started forward.

"Where are you?"

"Second level," he said. "At the window. Come take a look."

I climbed the spiral catwalk to the viewing-station; Brock stood with his back towards me, looking out. As I drew near I said, "I had the strangest dream last night—"

"The hell with that. Look."

At first I didn't notice anything strange. The bright-colored landscape looked unchanged, the pebbly orange soil, the dark blue trees, the tangle of green vines, the murk of the morning atmosphere. But then I saw I had been looking too far from home.

Writhing up the side of the window, just barely visible to the right, was a gnarled knobby green rope. Rope? No. It was one of the vines.

"They're all over the ship," Brock said. "I've checked all the ports. During the night the damned things must have come crawling up the side of the ship like so many snakes and wrapped themselves around us. I guess they figure we're here to stay, and they can use us as bracing-posts the way they do those trees."

I stared with mixed repugnance and fascination at the hard bark of the vine, at the tiny suckers that held it fast to the smooth skin of our ship.

"That's funny," I said. "It's sort of an attack by extra-terrestrial monsters, isn't it?"

We suited up and went outside to have a look at the "attackers". At a distance of a hundred yards, the ship looked weirdly bemired. Its graceful lines were broken by the winding fingers of the vine, spiraling up its sleek sides from a thick parent stem on the ground. Other shoots of the vine sprawled near us, clutching futilely at us as we moved among them.

I was reminded of my dream. Somewhat hesitantly I told Brock about it.

Why?

He laughed. "Rooted, eh? You were dreaming *that* while those vines were busy wrapping themselves around the ship. Significant?"

"Perhaps." I eyed the tough vines speculatively. "Maybe we'd better move the ship. If much more of that stuff gets around it, we may not be able to blast off at all."

Brock knelt and flexed a shoot of vine. "The ship could be completely cocooned in this stuff and we'd still be able to take oft," he said. "A spacedrive wields a devil of a lot of thrust. We'll manage."

And *whick!*

A tapering finger of the vine arched suddenly and whipped around Brock's middle. *Whick! Whick!*

Like animated rope, like a bark-covered serpent, it curled about him. I drew back, staring. He seemed half amused, half perplexed.

"The thing's got pull, all right," he said. He was smiling lopsidedly, annoyed at having let so simple a thing as a vine interfere with his freedom of motion. But then he winced in obvious pain.

"—Tightening," he gasped.

The vine contracted muscularly; it skittered two or three feet towards the tree from which its parent stock sprang, and Brock was jerked suddenly off balance. As the corded arm of the vine yanked him backward he began to topple, poising for what seemed like seconds on his left foot, right jutting awkwardly in the air, arms clawing for balance.

Then he fell.

I was at his side in a moment, carefully avoiding the innocent looking vine-tips to right and left. I planted my foot on the trailing vine that held Brock. I levered downward and grabbed the tip where it bound his waist. I pulled; Brock pushed.

The vine yielded.

"It's giving," he grunted. "A little more."

"Maybe I'd better go back for the blaster," I said.

"No. No telling what this thing may do while you're gone. Cut me in two, maybe. Pull!"

I pulled. The vine struggled against our combined strength, writhed, twisted. But gradually we prevailed. It curled upward, loosened, went limp. Finally it drooped away, leaving Brock in liberty.

He got up slowly, rubbing his waist.

"Hurt?"

"Just the surprise," he said. "Tropistic reaction on the plant's part; I must have triggered some hormone chain to make it do that." He eyed the now quiescent vine with respect.

"It's not the first time we've been attacked," I said. "Alpheraz III——"

"Yes."

I hadn't even needed to mention it. Alpheraz III had been a hellish jungle planet; the image in his mind, as it was in mine, was undoubtedly that of a tawny beast the size of a goat held in the inexorable grip of some stocky-trunked plant, rising in the air, vanishing into a waiting mouth of the carnivorous tree—

—and moments later a second tendril dragging me aloft, and only a hasty blaster-shot by Brock keeping me from being a plant's dinner.

We returned to the ship, entering the hatch a few feet from one of the vines that now encrusted it. Brock unsuited; the vine had left a red, raw line about his waist.

"The plant tried," I said.

"To kill me?"

"No. To move on. To get going. To see what was behind the next hill."

He frowned and said, "What are you talking about?"

"I'm not so sure, yet. I'm not good at seeing patterns. But it's taking shape. I'm getting it now, Brock. I'm getting it all. I'm getting your answer!"

He massaged his stomach. "Go ahead," he said. "Think it out loud."

"I'm putting it together out of my dream and out of the things you said and out of the vines down there." I walked slowly about the cabin. "Those plants—they're stuck there, aren't they? They grow in a certain place and that's where they remain. Maybe they wiggle a little, and maybe they writhe, but that's the size of it."

"They can grow long."

"Sure. But not infinitely long. They can't grow long enough to reach another planet. They're rooted, Brock. Their condition is permanently fixed. Brock, suppose those plants had brains?"

"I don't think this has anything to do with—"

"It does," I said. "Just assume those plants were intelligent. They want to go. They're stuck. So one of them lashes out in fury at you. *Jealous* fury."

He nodded, seeing it clearly now. "Sure. We don't have roots. We can go places. We can visit a hundred sixty-four worlds and walk all over them."

"That's your answer, Brock. There's the *why* you were looking for." I took a deep breath. "You know why we go out to explore? Not because we're running away. Not because there's some inner compulsion driving us to coast from planet to planet. Uh-uh. It's because we *can* do it. That's all the why you need. We explore because it's possible for us to explore."

Some of the harshness faded from his face. "We're special," he said. "We can move. It's the privilege of humanity. The thing that makes us *us*."

I didn't need to say any more. After eleven years, we don't need to vocalize every thought. But we had it, now: the special uniqueness that those clutching vines down there envied so much. Motility.

We left Alphecca II finally, and moved on. We did the other worlds of the system and headed outward, far out this time, as much of a hop as we could make. And we moved on from there to the next sun, and from there to the next, and onward.

We took a souvenir with us from Alphecca II though. When we blasted off, the vine that had wrapped itself round the ship gripped us so tightly that it wasn't shaken loose by the impact of blastoff. It remained hugging us as we thrust into space, dangling, roots and all. We finally got tired of looking at it, and Brock went out in a spacesuit to chop it away from the ship. He gave a push, imparted velocity to it, and the vine went drifting off sunward.

If had achieved its goal: it had left its home world. But it had died in the attempt. And that was the difference, we thought, all the difference in the universe, as we headed outward and outward, across the boundless gulfs to the next world we would visit.

THE OUTBREEDERS

This, on the other hand, was a story that I did take a chance with. Fat lot of good it did me. I wrote it in May, 1957, thought that it was a cut above my usual level of work at that time, and with high hopes tried it on Horace Gold and John Campbell and maybe even Tony Boucher. They all swiftly handed it back to me. And so I took it over to Hans Stefan Santesson at Fantastic Universe, *who accepted it that October, giving me (not very swiftly) $55 for it, and published it (in an equally leisurely way) in the issue of September, 1959.*

For some reason that I'm not able to remember the story appeared there under the highly Protestant pseudonym of "Calvin M. Knox." Randall Garrett had dreamed up that byline for me in 1955, at a time when I had not yet sold a story to John W. Campbell under my own name, as a way of getting around Campbell's supposed anti-Semitism; according to Garrett, Campbell was reputed to dislike seeing Jewish names in his magazine. I had been using it sporadically ever since, both for Campbell's Astounding *and elsewhere. (Campbell, who had never displayed the slightest sign of anti-Semitism in his professional and personal dealings with me, found the whole notion pretty amusing, when around 1960 I finally explained the reason for the creation of the pen name to him, and reminded me that a certain Isaac Asimov had been appearing regularly on his contents page for two decades. He had also regularly published the work of such notorious non-Aryans as Alfred Bester and C. M. Kornbluth, and, in an earlier era, that of Nathan Schachner and Donald A. Wollheim.)*

Why the Knox byline was used for this one, I can't say: certainly I was glad to lurk behind some pseudonym when I was producing "Tyrants of the

Purple Void," or whatever, for one of the trashier magazines, but this story always seemed a charming one to me, and I would have had no reason to want to conceal my authorship of it—other than, perhaps, that my own name was being seen with such embarrassing frequency in every magazine of the era that it seemed best to hide some of my output behind false whiskers rather than let the public know I was really as prolific as in fact I was. Prolific writers are often mistrusted: people wonder how anything written so quickly can be worth reading. (But you damned well had to be prolific when stories you wrote in the spring of 1957 earned you $55 minus your agent's commission, payable two years after acceptance, as this one did.)

The week before his wedding, Ryly Baille went alone into the wild forests that separated Baille lands from those of the Clingert clan. The lonely journey was a prenuptial tradition among the Bailles; his people expected him to return with body toughened by exertion, mind sharp and clear from solitary meditation. No one at all expected him to meet and fall in love with a Clingert girl.

He left early on a Threeday morning; nine Bailles saw him off. Old Fredrog, the Baille Clanfather, wished him well. Minton, Ryly's own father, clasped him by the hand for a long, awkward moment. Three of his patrilineal cousins offered their best wishes. And Davud, his dearest friend and closest phenotype-brother, slapped him affectionately.

Ryly said good-bye also to his mother, to the Clanmother, and to Hella, his betrothed. He shouldered his bow and quiver, hitched up his hiking trousers, and grinned nervously. Overhead, Thomas, the yellow primary sun, was rising high; later in the day the blue companion, Doris, would join her husband in the sky. It was a warm spring morning.

Ryly surveyed the little group: six tall, blond-haired, blue-eyed men, three tall, red-haired, hazel-eyed women. Perfect examples all of Baille-norm, and therefore the highest representatives of evolution.

"So long, all," he said, smiling. There was nothing else to say. He turned and headed off into the chattering forest. His long legs carried him easily down the well-worn path. Tradition required him to follow the main path until noon, when the second sun would enter the sky; then, wherever he might be, he was to veer sharply from the road and hew his own way through the vegetation for the rest of the journey.

He would be gone three days, two nights. On the third evening he would turn back, returning by morning to claim his bride.

He thought of Hella as he walked. She was a fine girl; he was happy Clanfather had allotted her to him. Not that she was prettier than any of the other current eligibles—they were all more or less equal. But Hella had a certain bright sparkle, a way of smiling, that Ryly thought he could grow to like.

Thomas was climbing now towards his noon height; the forest grew warm. A bright-colored, web-winged lizard sprang squawking from a tree to the left of the path and fluttered in a brief clumsy arc over Ryly's head. He notched an arrow and brought the lizard down—his first kill of the trip. Tucking three red pinlike tail feathers in his belt, he moved on.

At noon the first blue rays of Doris mingled with the yellow of Thomas. The moment had come. Ryly knelt to mutter a short prayer in memory of those two pioneering Bailles who had come to The World so many generations ago to found the clan, and swung off to the right, cutting between the fuzzy grey boles of two towering sweetfruit trees. He incised his name on the forestward side of one tree as a guide-sign for his return, and entered the unknown part of the forest.

He walked till he was hungry; then he killed an unwary bouncer, skinned, cooked, and ate the meaty rodent, and bathed in a crystal-bright stream at the edge of an evergreen thicket. When darkness came, he camped near an upjutting cliff, and for a long time lay on his back, staring up at the four gleaming little moons, telling himself the old clan legends until he fell asleep.

The following morning was without event; he covered many miles, carefully leaving trail-marks behind. And shortly before Dorisrise he met the girl.

It was really an accident. He had sighted the yellow dorsal spines of a wabbler protruding a couple of inches over the top of a thick hedge, and decided the wabbler's horns would be as good a trophy as any to bring back to Hella. He strung his bow and waited for the beast to lift its one vulnerable spot, the eye, into view.

After a moment the wabbler's head appeared, top-heavy with the weight of the spreading snout-horns. Ryly fingered his bowstring and targeted on the bloodshot eye.

His aim was false; the arrow thwacked hard against the scalelike black leather of the wabbler's domed skull, hung—penetrating the skin for an instant—and dropped away. The wabbler snorted in surprise and anger and set off, crashing noisily through the underbrush, undulating wildly as its vast flippers slammed the ground.

Ryly gave chase. He strung his bow on the run, as he followed the trail of the big herbivore. Somewhere ahead a waterfall rumbled; the wabbler evidently intended to make an aquatic getaway. Ryly broke into a clearing—and saw the girl standing next to the wabbler, patting its muscular withers and murmuring soothing sounds. She glared up at Ryly as he appeared.

For a moment he hardly recognized her as human. She was slim and dark-haired, with great black eyes, a tiny tilted nose, full lips. She wore a brightly colored saronglike affair of some batik cloth; it left her tanned legs bare. And she was almost a foot shorter than Ryly; Baille women rarely dipped below five-ten in height.

"Did you shoot at this animal?" she demanded suddenly.

Ryly had difficulty understanding her; the words seemed to be in his language, but the vowels sounded all wrong, the consonants not harsh enough.

"I did," he said. "I didn't know he was your pet."

"*Pet!* The wabblers aren't pets. They're sacred. Are you a Baille?"

Taken aback by the abrupt question, Ryly sputtered a moment before nodding.

"I thought so. I'm Joanne Clingert. What are you doing on Clingert territory?"

"So that's it," Ryly said slowly. He stared at her as if she had just crawled out from under a lichen-crusted rock. "You're a *Clingert*. That explains things."

"Explains what?"

"The way you look, the way you talk, the way you…" He moved hesitantly closer, looking down at her. She looked very angry, but behind the anger shone something else—

A sparkle, maybe. A brightness.

Ryly shuddered. The Clingerts were dreaded alien beings of a terrible ugliness, or so Clanfather had constantly reiterated. Well, maybe so. But, then, *this* Clingert could hardly be typical. She seemed so delicate and lovely, quite unlike the rawboned, athletic Baille women.

A blue shaft of light broke through the saw-toothed leaves of the trees and shattered on the Clingert's brow. Almost as a reflex, Ryly sank to his knees to pray.

"Why are you doing that?" the Clingert asked.

"It's Dorisrise! Don't you pray at Dorisrise?"

She glanced upward at the blue sun now orbiting the yellow primary. "That's only Secundus that just rose. What did you call it—*Doris?*"

Ryly concluded his prayer and rose. "Of course. And there's Thomas next to her."

"Hmm. We call them Primus and Secundus. But I suppose it's not surprising that the Bailles and Clingerts would have different names for the suns. Thomas and Doris…that's nice. Named for the original Bailles?"

Ryly nodded. "And I guess Primus and Secundus founded the Clingerts?"

She laughed—a brittle tinkling sound that bounced prettily back from the curtain of trees. "No, hardly. Jarl and Bess were our founders. *Primus* and *Secundus* only mean first and second, in Latin."

"Latin? What's that? I—"

Ryly shut his mouth, suddenly. A cold tremor of delayed alarm passed through him. He stared at the Clingert in horror.

"Is something wrong?" the Clingert asked. "You look so pale."

"We're talking to each other," Ryly said. "We're holding a nice little conversation. Very friendly, and all."

She looked indignant. "Is anything wrong with that?"

"Yes," Ryly said glumly. "I'm supposed to hate you."

They walked together to the place where the waterfall cascaded in a bright foaming tumble down the mountainside, and they talked. And Ryly discovered that Clingerts were not quite so frightening as he had been led to believe.

His wanderings had brought him close to Clingert territory; Joanne had been but an hour from home when she had met him. But he nervously declined an offer to come to the Clingert settlement with her. That would be carrying things much too far.

After a while the Clingert said, "Do you hate me yet?"

"I don't think I'm going to hate you," Ryly told her. "I think I like you. And particularly every time I think of Hella—"

"Hella?" The Clingert's eyes flashed angrily.

"The Baille who was my betrothed." He accented the *was*. "Clanfather gave her to me last month. We were supposed to be married when I returned to the settlement. I thought I was looking forward to it too. Until—until—"

A wabbler mooed somewhere deeper in the forest. Ryly stared help-lessly at the Clingert, realizing now what was happening to him.

He was falling in love with the Clingert.

Ever since the days when Thomas and Doris Baille first came to The World, Baille and Clingert had kept firm boundaries. Baille had mated only with Baille. And now—

Ryly shook his head sadly. In the blue-and-gold brilliance of the afternoon, this Clingert seemed infinitely more desirable to him than any Baille woman ever had.

She touched his hand gently. "You're very quiet. You're not at all like the Clingert men."

"I guess I'm not. What are they like?"

She made a little face. "Much shorter than you are, with ugly straight dark hair and black eyes. Their muscles bunch up in knots when they draw bows; your arms are long and lean. And Clingert men get bald at a very young age." Her hand lightly ruffled his Baille-yellow hair. "Do Bailles lose their hair young?"

"Bailles never get bald. Clanfather's hair is still as yellow as mine, and he's past fifty." Ryly fell silent again, thinking of Clanfather and what he would say if he knew what had taken place out here.

Not since the days when Thomas cast the first Clingert from his sight has this happened, he would probably intone in a deep, sententious voice.

Ryly remembered a time far away in his childhood when a Baille woman had birthed a dark-haired son. Clanfather had driven child and parents out into the forest, and there other Bailles had stoned them. Ryly was not anxious to share that fate. But yet—

He scrambled to his feet. The Clingert looked at him in alarm. "Where are you going?" she asked.

"Back. To the Baille settlement."

There was a moment of silence between them. Finally Ryly took a deep breath and said, "I'll return. Meet me at this place three days from now, at Dorisrise—I mean, when Secundus rises. Will you be here?"

Uneasiness glimmered in her dark eyes. "Yes," she said.

He reached the familiar Baille territory near nightfall the next day, having covered the outlying ground as rapidly as he could and with as few stops along the way as possible. He ducked back onto the main road around the time of Thomasset on Fiveday. He had had little difficulty in locating the tree that bore his name in its bark. Only the blue sun shone now, and it was low above the horizon; the moons were beginning their procession across the twilight-dimmed sky.

Ryly stole into the settlement on the back road. That route brought him past the crude little cabin which Thomas had built with his own hands as a place for Doris and himself to live, long ago when the first Baille had tumbled out of the sky and settled on The World. Ryly quivered a little as he passed the dingy old shrine; the sort of betrayal he was contemplating did not come easy to him.

Above all, he did not want to be seen. Not until he had spoken with his phenotype-brother Davud.

A cat mewled. Ryly ducked into the concealing darkness of a vine bower and waited. A stiff-necked old man passed by: Clanfather. Ryly held his breath until the old one had entered the Clan house; he slipped out of his shelter, then padded silently across the main courtyard, and ran into the open archway that led to Davud's cabin.

The light was on. Davud was inside, drowsing in a chair. Ryly tip-toed through the rear door. He sprang across the room in four big-bounds and clapped his hands over Davud's mouth before the other had fully come awake.

"It's me—Ryly. I'm back."

"*Mmph!*"

"Keep quiet and don't make any loud noises. I don't want people to find out I'm here yet."

He stepped back. Davud rubbed his lips and said, "What in Thomas' name made you want to scare me like that? For a second I thought it was a Clingert raid."

Ryly winced. He stared intently at Davud, wondering if it was safe to tell him. Davud, of all the Bailles, was closest to him in physique and in attitude, which was the reason Clanfather had designated them phenotype-brothers even though they had different parents. Among the Bailles, actual parentage meant little, since genetically every clan member was virtually identical to every other.

He and Davud were uncannily alike, though: both standing six-three, the Baille-norm height, both with the same twist to their unruly blond hair, the same sharpness of nose, and the same thinness of earlobe.

He poured a beaker of thick yellow bryophyte wine and sipped it slowly to steady his nerves. "I have to talk to you, Davud. Something very important has happened to me."

Ignoring that, Davud said, "You weren't supposed to come back until tomorrow morning. I saw Hella around Thomasset, and she said she couldn't wait to see you again." Davud grinned. "I told her I was enough like you to do, but she wouldn't listen to the idea."

"Don't talk about Hella. Listen to me, Davud. I went into Clingert territory on my trip. I met a Clingert girl. I...love her...I think."

Davud was on his feet in an instant, facing Ryly, brow to brow, chin to chin. His nostrils were quivering. "What did you just say?"

Very quietly Ryly repeated his words.

"I thought that was it," Davud muttered. "Ryly, are you out of your head? Marry a Clingert? That *filth?*"

"But you haven't seen—"

"I don't need to see. You know the old stories of how the first Clingert quarreled with Thomas until Thomas was forced to drive him away. You know what sort of creatures the Clingerts are. How can you possibly—"

"Love one? Davud, you don't know how easy it is. The Baille girls are so damned big and brawny! Joanne is—well, you'd have to see her to know. The fact that Thomas and the first Clingert had some silly quarrel hundreds of years ago—"

Davud's face was a white mask of indignation. *"Ryly!* Get hold of yourself! You're talking nonsense, man—absolute nonsense. Baille and Clingert must never breed. Would you want to pollute our line with theirs?"

"Yes." Defiantly.

"You're mad, then. But why did you come back here to tell me about all this? Why didn't you simply stay with your Clingert?"

"I wanted someone to know. Someone I could trust—like you."

"You made a mistake in that case," Davud said. "I'm going to tell Clanfather the whole story, and when they stone you I'll be glad to take part. That's what they did the last time this happened, fifteen years ago, if you remember. When Luri Baille had a baby that looked like a Clingert. The line has to be kept pure."

"Why?"

"It—it has to, that's all," Davud said weakly. As Ryly started to walk out, he added, "Hey! Where do you think you're going?"

"Back to the forest," Ryly said in a bitter voice. "I promised her I'd be back. I should never have come here in the first place." He was shaking and perspiring heavily; somewhat to his own surprise he realized that by this conversation he had effectively cut himself off from the Bailles forever.

"You're not going, Ryly. I won't let you."

Davud grabbed Ryly's collar, but he pulled away. "Don't try to stop me, Davud."

Without replying, Davud gripped the fleshy part of his arm. Calmly Ryly pivoted and smashed his fist into the face that was so much like his own. Davud blinked, half believing, and started to mutter something. Ryly quickly jerked his arm free and hit Davud a second time. Davud sagged to the floor.

Ryly stood poised indecisively for a second, watching with some astonishment the flow of blood from his phenotype-brother's broken nose. Then he turned and dashed through the doorway, out into the dark courtyard, and ran as hard as he could for the forest road.

He listened for the shouts of pursuers but could hear none yet. He wondered if perhaps he had hit Davud too hard.

Ryly spent an uneasy night in the forest not too far from the edge of the Baille territory; when morning came, he struck out at a rapid pace for the Baille-Clingert border. Joanne would be at the waterfall by Dorisrise—he hoped. For an instant he considered what would become of him if she had been playing him false, but he reached no answer. Could he return to the Bailles and marry Hella after all? He didn't think so.

The day grew warmer as he half trotted through the forest, following the series of trail-marks he had left to guide himself. When he reached the trysting place, it was not yet Dorisrise; Thomas alone was in the sky. Ryly sat by the water's edge and splashed himself to clean away the sweat of travel.

He heard footsteps. He looked up, hoping it might be Joanne. But it was Davud who appeared.

"So you followed me?"

Davud nodded. "I had to, Ryly."

"And I suppose you brought the whole tribe behind you, all of them foaming at the mouth and ready to stone me." Ryly sighed. "I guess I didn't hit you hard enough, then. You woke up too soon."

Davud's nose was swollen and slightly askew. He said, "I came alone. I want to try to talk you out of this crazy thing, Ryly. Nobody else knows about it yet."

"Good. Now you go back and forget anything I said to you last night."

"I can't do that," Davud said. "I can't let you mate with a—a *Clingert*. I came to bring you back to Baille land with me."

Ryly clenched his fists. He had no desire to fight with his phenotype-brother a second time, but if Davud was going to insist—

"Get away from me, Davud. Go back alone."

It was almost Dorisrise time, now. Ryly hoped he would be able to get Davud out of the way before Joanne reached their rendezvous. But Davud was shaking his head stubbornly. "Baille and Clingert shall not breed. Thomas set that law down for us in the beginning, and it can never be broken. It is—"

He stopped, jaw sagging, and pointed. Slowly Ryly turned. The first rays of Doris glinted blue in the flowing waterfall, and Joanne stood behind him.

"Which of you is Ryly?" she asked plaintively.

Ryly unfroze first. "I am," he said. "This is my phenotype-brother Davud. He came with me to—meet you. Davud, this is Joanne."

"Is *this* a Clingert?" Davud asked slowly. "But—but—Clanfather always said they were *ugly!* And—"

Joanne laughed, her special Clingert sort of laugh that Ryly had already grown to love. "He seems stunned. Just as stunned as you were, three days ago. Do all of you Bailles think we're ogres?"

Davud sat down heavily on a rotting stump. His face was very pale by the light of the double suns; he was shaking his head reflectively and seemed to be talking quietly to himself. At length he said, "All right. I apologize, Ryly. Now I see what you were talking about. *Now* I see!"

There was an overenthusiastic note in Davud's tone of voice that irked Ryly, but he refrained from voicing any annoyance. "What about Thomas and his laws now, Davud?" he said. "Now that you've seen a Clingert?"

"I take everything back," Davud murmured. "Everything."

Ryly glanced from his phenotype-brother to Joanne. "I guess we have his blessing; then. If—if you're willing to become an outcast from the Clingerts, that is."

Now it was Joanne's turn to look startled. "Outcast? For fulfilling the aim of the first Clingert?"

"What's that?"

"You mean you don't know?"

Ryly shook his head. "I don't have the faintest idea of what you're talking about."

"When it all started," she said patiently. "When the spaceship exploded and the Clingerts and Bailles were thrown free and landed on The World, hundreds of years ago, Jarl Clingert wanted to interbreed, but Thomas Baille wouldn't have any of it. He wanted to keep his line pure. So there hasn't been very much contact between Clingert and Baille since then, ever since the time the first Baille threatened without provocation to kill Jarl Clingert if he came within ten miles of—"

"Hold it," Ryly said. "It was Clingert who tried to kill Thomas Baille and marry Doris, but Thomas drove him off and—"

"No," said Joanne. "You've got it all backward. It was *Baille's* fault that—"

"Let's discuss ancient history some other time," Davud interjected suddenly. There was a curiously pained expression on his face. "Ryly, do you mind if I talk to you alone a moment?"

"Why—all right," Ryly said, surprised.

They drew a few feet farther away, and Ryly said, "Well? What do you think of her?"

"That's what I want to talk to you about," Davud whispered harshly. "I think she's far and away above the Baille women. She's so—*different*. Gentle but not weak, small but not flimsy—"

"I knew you'd like her, Davud."

"Not *like*," Davud groaned. "Love. I love her too, Ryly."

It came like a blow across the face. Ryly's eyes widened and stared into the equally blue ones of his phenotype-brother. The Baille genes had been duplicated perfectly among them, it seemed. In every respect.

"You can't mean that," Ryly said.

"I do. Dammit, I do. How can I help it?"

"We can't *both* have her, Davud. And I think I have priority. I—"

Davud gasped and seized him suddenly, spinning him around. Ryly looked, shut his eyes, touched his fingers lightly to his eyelids, and looked again. The mirage was still there. It was no illusion.

He saw two Joannes.

"Ryly? Davud? Meet Melena. Melena Clingert."

"Is she—your sister?" Ryly asked hoarsely. The two Clingerts were, at this distance, identical.

"My cousin," Joanne said. "I don't have any sisters." She grinned. "Melena was hiding near the far side of the waterfall. I brought her along to have a peek at Ryly."

Ryly and his phenotype-brother exchanged astonished glances.

"Of course," Ryly said softly. "We Bailles all look alike; why shouldn't the Clingerts? Three hundred years of inbreeding. Lord, they must all be identical!"

"More or less," Joanne said. "There are some minor variations but not many. Most of the unfixed genes in the clan were lost generations ago. As probably happened in your clan too. This was the thing that Jarl Clingert wanted to avoid, but when Thomas Baille refused to—"

"It was Clingert's treacherous ways that caused the whole thing," Ryly snapped. "Let's get that straight right now. Why, it's common knowledge!"

"Among whom? Among the Bailles, that's who—whom!" Joanne's eyes were blazing again, with the fury Ryly loved so much to see. "But why don't you listen to the Clingert side of the story for a change? You Bailles were always like that, shutting your ears to anything important. You—" She stopped in mid-breath. Very quietly she said, "I'm sorry, Ryly."

"It was my fault. I started the whole thing."

"No," she said, shaking her head. "I did, when I brought up the topic of—"

He smiled and touched a finger lightly to her lips. "Look," he said.

She looked. Davud and Melena had drawn to one side, standing on a moist, moss-covered patch of ground within the field of spray and foam of the waterfall. They were talking softly. It wasn't difficult to see by their faces what the topic of discussion was.

"We'll have to forget about ancient history now," Joanne said. "Forget all about what happened between Jarl Clingert and Thomas Baille four centuries ago."

Ryly took her hand. "We'll go somewhere else on The World," he said. "Start all over, build a new settlement. Just the four of us. And maybe we can recruit some others, if I can lure a few Bailles out here to meet Clingerts."

"And vice versa. The Clingert men hate the Bailles now too, you know. But that can stop. We'll breed the feuding out."

Ryly looked over at Davud and Melena, then back at Joanne. Everything looked incredibly lovely at that moment—the angular red leaves of the overhanging trees, the white spray of the falls, prismatically colored blue and gold by the sunlight, the quiet green clouds drifting above. He wanted to fix that moment in his mind forever.

He smiled. His mind was still full of insidious Clanfather-instilled legends of the early days on The World as seen through Baille eyes. But he could start forgetting them now.

Soon there would be a third clan on The World—a hybrid clan, both fair and dark, both short and tall.

And someday his descendants would be spinning legends about *him,* and how he had helped to found the clan, back in the misty time-shrouded days of the remote past.

THE MAN WHO NEVER FORGOT

One of the most useful tools a writer can have is a retentive memory. Names, places, dates, bits of esoteric information, the look and feel of an object, the color of the sky over Paris one summer afternoon in 1957—the more detail you can summon up at the twitch of a synapse, the richer and more meaningful your fiction becomes. My memory isn't what it once was, but it's still pretty sharp, and once upon a time it was truly extraordinary, the kind of trick memory that can tell you not only where to find a certain fact but on which side of the page it's located. That kind of memory has disadvantages as well as advantages, though—nobody likes a smartass, and the kid who's always right is the one who always gets chased around the block by the ones who are always wrong. So there's more than a tincture of autobiographical feeling in this otherwise purely fictional piece.

I wrote it in June of the preternaturally fertile year of 1957 and sent it to Anthony Boucher, who bought it with gratifying rapidity and used it in the February, 1958 issue of Fantasy and Science Fiction. *Glancing through it now, I'm startled to see how strongly it foreshadows a much better known work of mine that deals with the hidden drawbacks of superior mental powers—the novel* Dying Inside, *which I would write fifteen years later.*

He saw the girl waiting in line outside a big Los Angeles movie house, on a mildly foggy Tuesday morning. She was slim and pale, barely five-three, with stringy flaxen hair, and she was alone. He remembered her, of course.

He knew it would be a mistake, but he crossed the street anyway and walked up along the theater line to where she stood.

"Hello," he said.

She turned, stared at him blankly, flicked the tip of her tongue out for an instant over her lips. "I don't believe I—"

"Tom Niles," he said. "Pasadena, New Year's Day, 1955. You sat next to me. Ohio State 20, Southern Cal 7. You don't remember?"

"A football game? But I hardly ever—I mean—I'm sorry, mister. I—"

Someone else in the line moved forward towards him with a tight hard scowl on his face. Niles knew when he was beaten. He smiled apologetically and said, "I'm sorry, miss. I guess I made a mistake. I took you for someone I knew—a Miss Bette Torrance. Excuse me."

And he strode rapidly away. He had not gone more than ten feet when he heard the little surprised gasp and the "But I *am* Bette Torrance!"—but he kept going.

I should know better after twenty-eight years, he thought bitterly. *But I forget the most basic fact—that even though I remember people, they don't necessarily remember me—*

He walked wearily to the corner, turned right, and started down a new street, one whose shops were totally unfamiliar to him and which, therefore, he had never seen before. His mind, stimulated to its normal pitch of activity by the incident outside the theater, spewed up a host of tangential memories like the good machine it was: *1 Jan. 1955. Rose Bowl Pasadena California Seat G126; warm day, high humidity, arrived in stadium 12.03 P.M., PST. Came alone. Girl in next seat wearing blue cotton dress, white oxfords, carrying Southern Cal pennant. Talked to her. Name Bette Torrance, senior at Southern Cal, government major. Had a date for the game but he came down with flu symptoms night before, insisted she see game anyway. Seat on other side of her empty. Bought her a hot dog, $.20 (no mustard)—*

There was more, much more. Niles forced it back down. There was the virtually stenographic report of their conversation all that day:

("...I hope we win. I saw the last Bowl game we won, two years ago..."

278

"...Yes, that was 1953. Southern Cal 7, Wisconsin 0...and two straight wins in 1944-45 over Washington and Tennessee..."

"...Gosh, you know a lot about football! What did you do, memorize the record book?")

And the old memories. The jeering yell of freckled Joe Merritt that warm April day in 1937—*who are you, Einstein?* And Buddy Call saying acidly on 8 November 1939, *Here comes Tommy Niles, the human adding machine. Get him!* And then the bright stinging pain of a snowball landing just below his left clavicle, the pain that he could summon up as easily as any of the other pain-memories he carried with him. He winced and closed his eyes suddenly, as if struck by the icy pellet here on a Los Angeles street on a foggy Tuesday morning.

They didn't call him the human adding machine any more. Now it was the human tape recorder; the derisive terms had to keep pace with the passing decades. Only Niles himself remained unchanging, The Boy With The Brain Like A Sponge grown up into The Man With The Brain Like A Sponge, still cursed with the same terrible gift.

His data-cluttered mind ached. He saw a diminutive yellow sports car parked on the far side of the street, recognized it by its make and model and color and licence number as the car belonging to Leslie F. Marshall, twenty-six, blond hair, blue eyes, television actor with the following credits—

Wincing, Niles applied the cutoff circuit and blotted out the upwelling data. He had met Marshall once, six months ago, at a party given by a mutual friend—an erstwhile mutual friend; Niles found it difficult to keep friends for long. He had spoken with the actor for perhaps ten minutes and had added that much more baggage to his mind.

It was time to move on, Niles decided. He had been in Los Angeles ten months. The burden of accumulated memories was getting too heavy; he was greeting too many people who had long since forgotten him (*curse my John Q. Average build, 5 feet 9, 163 pounds, brownish hair, brownish eyes, no unduly prominent physical features, no distinguishing scars except those inside,* he thought). He contemplated returning to San Francisco, and decided against it. He had been there only a year ago; Pasadena, two years ago; the time had come, he realized, for another eastward jaunt.

Back and forth across the face of America goes Thomas Richard Niles, Der fliegende Holländer, the Wandering Jew, the Ghost of Christmas Past, the Human Tape Recorder. He smiled at a newsboy who had sold him a copy of the *Examiner* on 13 May past, got the usual blank stare in return, and headed for the nearest bus terminal.

For Niles the long journey had begun on 11 October 1929, in the small Ohio town of Lowry Bridge. He was third of three children, born of seemingly normal parents, Henry Niles (b. 1896), Mary Niles (b. 1899). His older brother and sister had shown no extraordinary manifestations. Tom had.

It began as soon as he was old enough to form words; a neighbor woman on the front porch peered into the house where he was playing, and remarked to his mother, "Look how *big* he's getting, Mary!"

He was less than a year old. He had replied, in virtually the same tone of voice, *"Look how* big *he's getting, Mary!"* It caused a sensation, even though it was only mimicry, not even speech.

He spent his first twelve years in Lowry Bridge, Ohio. In later years, he often wondered how he had been able to last there so long.

He began school at the age of four, because there was no keeping him back; his classmates were five and six, vastly superior to him in physical coordination, vastly inferior in everything else. He could read. He could even write, after a fashion, though his babyish muscles tired easily from holding a pen. And he could remember.

He remembered everything. He remembered his parents' quarrels and repeated the exact words of them to anyone who cared to listen, until his father whipped him and threatened to kill him if he ever did *that* again. He remembered that too. He remembered the lies his brother and sister told, and took great pains to set the record straight. He learned eventually not to do that, either. He remembered things people had said, and corrected them when they later deviated from their earlier statements.

He remembered everything.

He read a textbook once and it stayed with him. When the teacher asked a question based on the day's assignment, Tommy Niles' skinny arm was in the air long before the others had even really assimilated the question. After a while, his teacher made it clear to him that he could *not* answer every question, whether he had the answer first or not; there were twenty other pupils in the class. The other pupils in the class made that abundantly clear to him, after school.

He won the verse-learning contest in Sunday school. Barry Harman had studied for weeks in hopes of winning the catcher's mitt his father had promised him if he finished first—but when it was Tommy Niles' turn to recite, he began with *In the beginning God created the heaven and the earth,* continued through *Thus the heavens and the earth were finished, and all the host of them,* headed on into *Now the serpent was more subtle than any beast of the field which the Lord God had made,* and presumably would have continued clear through Genesis, Exodus, and on to Joshua if the dazed proctor hadn't shut him up and declared him the winner. Barry Harman didn't get his glove; Tommy Niles got a black eye instead.

He began to realize he was different. It took time to make the discovery that other people were always forgetting things, and that instead of admiring him for what he could do they hated him for it. It was difficult for a boy of eight, even Tommy Niles, to understand why they hated him, but eventually he did find out, and then he started learning how to hide his gift.

Through his ninth and tenth years he practiced being normal, and almost succeeded; the after-school beatings stopped, and he managed to get a few Bs on his report cards at last, instead of straight rows of A. He was growing up; he was learning to pretend. Neighbors heaved sighs of relief, now that that terrible Niles boy was no longer doing all those crazy things.

But inwardly he was the same as ever. And he realized he'd have to leave Lowry Bridge soon.

He knew everyone too well. He would catch them in lies ten times a week, even Mr. Lawrence, the minister, who once turned down an invitation to pay a social call to the Nileses one night, saying, "I really have to get down to work and write my sermon for Sunday," when only three days before Tommy had heard him say to Miss Emery, the church secretary, that he had had a sudden burst of inspiration and had written three sermons all at one sitting, and now he'd have some free time for the rest of the month.

Even Mr. Lawrence lied, then. And he was the best of them. As for the others—

Tommy waited until he was twelve; he was big for his age by then and figured he could take care of himself. He borrowed twenty dollars from the supposedly secret cashbox in the back of the kitchen cupboard (his mother had mentioned its existence five years before, in Tommy's hearing) and tiptoed out of the house at three in the morning. He caught the night freight for Chillicothe, and was on his way.

There were thirty people on the bus out of Los Angeles. Niles sat alone in the back, by the seat just over the rear wheel. He knew four of the people in the bus by name—but he was confident they had forgotten who he was by now, and so he kept to himself.

It was an awkward business. If you said hello to someone who had forgotten you, they thought you were a troublemaker or a panhandler. And if you passed someone by, thinking he had forgotten you, and he hadn't—well, then you were a snob. Niles swung between both those poles five times a day. He'd see someone, such as that girl Bette Torrance, and get a cold, unrecognizing stare; or he'd go by someone else, believing the other person did not remember him but walking rapidly just in case he did, and there would be the angry, "Well! Who the blazes do you think you are!" floating after him as he retreated.

Now he sat alone, bouncing up and down with each revolution of the wheel, with the one suitcase containing his property thumping constantly against the baggage rack over his head. That was one advantage of his talent: he could travel light. He didn't need to keep books, once he had read them, and there wasn't much point in amassing belongings of any other sort either; they became overfamiliar and dull too soon.

He eyed the road signs. They were well into Nevada by now. The old, wearisome retreat was on.

He could never stay in the same city too long. He had to move on to new territory, to some new place where he had no old memories, where no one knew him, where he knew no one. In the sixteen years since he had left home, he'd covered a lot of ground.

He remembered the jobs he had held.

He had been a proofreader for a Chicago publishing firm, once. He did the jobs of two men. The way proofreading usually worked, one man read the copy from the manuscript, the other checked it against the galleys. Niles had a simpler method: he would scan the manuscript once, thereby memorizing it, and then merely check the galley for discrepancies. It brought him fifty dollars a week for a while, before the time came to move along.

He once held a job as a sideshow freak in a traveling carnie that made a regular Alabama-Mississippi-Georgia circuit. Niles had really been low on cash, then. He remembered how he had gotten the job: by buttonholing the carnie boss and demanding a tryout. "Read me anything—anything at all! I can remember it!" The boss had been skeptical, and didn't see any use for such an act anyway, but finally gave in when Niles practically fainted of malnutrition in his office. The boss read him an editorial from a Mississippi county weekly, and when he was through Niles recited it back, word perfect. He got the job, at fifteen dollars a week plus meals, and sat in a little booth under a sign that said The Human Tape Recorder. People read or said things to him, and he repeated them. It was dull work; sometimes the things they said to him were filthy, and most of the time they couldn't even remember what they had said to him a minute later. He stayed with the show four weeks, and when he left no one missed him much.

The bus rolled on into the fogbound night.

There had been other jobs: good jobs, bad jobs. None of them had lasted very long. There had been some girls too, but none of *them* had lasted too long. They had all, even those he had tried to conceal it from, found out about his special ability, and soon after that they had left. No one could stay with a man who never forgot, who could always dredge yesterday's foibles out of the reservoir that was his mind and hurl them unanswerably into the open. And the man with the perfect memory could never live long among imperfect human beings.

To forgive is to forget, he thought. The memory of old insults and quarrels fades, and a relationship starts anew. But for him there could be no forgetting, and hence little forgiving.

He closed his eyes after a little while and leaned back against the hard leather cushion of his seat. The steady rhythm of the bus lulled him to sleep. In sleep, his mind could rest; he found ease from memory. He never dreamed.

In Salt Lake City he paid his fare, left the bus, suitcase in hand, and set out in the first direction he faced. He had not wanted to go any farther east on that bus. His cash reserve was only sixty-three dollars now, and he had to make it last. He found a job as a dishwasher in a downtown restaurant, held it long enough to accumulate a hundred dollars, and moved out again, this time hitchhiking to Cheyenne. He stayed there a month and took a night bus to Denver, and when he left Denver it was to go to Wichita.

Wichita to Des Moines to Minneapolis, Minneapolis to Milwaukee, then down through Illinois, carefully avoiding Chicago, and on to Indianapolis. It was an old story for him, this traveling. Gloomily he celebrated his twenty-ninth birthday alone in an Indianapolis rooming house on a drizzly October day, and for the purpose of brightening the occasion, summoned up his old memories of his fourth birthday party in 1933...one of the few unalloyedly happy days of his life.

They were all there, all his playmates, and his parents, and his brother Hank, looking gravely important at the age of eight, and his sister Marian, and there were candles and favors and punch and cake. Mrs Heinsohn from next door stopped in and said, "He looks like a regular little man," and his parents beamed at him, and everyone sang and had a good time. And afterwards, when the last game had been played, the last present opened, when the boys and girls had waved good-bye and disappeared up the street, the grownups sat around and talked of the new president and the many strange things that were happening in the country, and little Tommy sat in the middle of the floor, listening and recording everything and glowing warmly, because somehow during the whole afternoon no one had said or done anything cruel to him. He was happy that day, and he went to bed still happy.

Niles ran through the party twice, like an old movie he loved well; the print never grew frayed, the registration always remained as clear and sharp as ever. He could taste the sweet tang of the punch, he could relive the warmth of that day when through some accident the others had allowed him a little happiness.

Finally he let the brightness of the party fade, and once again he was in Indianapolis on a grey, bleak afternoon, alone in an eight-dollar-a-week furnished room.

Happy birthday to me, he thought bitterly. *Happy birthday.*

He stared at the blotchy green wall with the cheap Corot print hung slightly askew. I could have been something special, he brooded, one of the wonders of the world. Instead I'm a skulking freak who lives in dingy third-floor back rooms, and I don't dare let the world know what I can do.

He scooped into his memory and came up with the Toscanini performance of Beethoven's Ninth he had heard in Carnegie Hall once while he was in New York. It was infinitely better than the later performance Toscanini had approved for recording, yet no microphones had taken it down; the blazing performance was as far beyond recapture as a flame five minutes snuffed, except in one man's mind. Niles had it all: the majestic downcrash of the tympani, the resonant, perspiring basso bringing forth the great melody of the finale, even the french-horn bobble that must have enraged the maestro so, the infuriating cough from the dress circle at the gentlest moment of the adagio, the sharp pinching of Niles' shoes as he leaned forward in his seat—

He had it all, in highest fidelity.

He arrived in the small town on a moonless night three months later, a cold, crisp January evening, when the wintry wind swept in from the north, cutting through his thin clothing and making the suitcase an almost impossible burden for his numb, gloveless hand. He had not meant to come to this place, but he had run short of cash in Kentucky, and there had been no helping it. He was on his way to New York, where he could live in anonymity for months unbothered, and where he knew his rudeness would go unnoticed if he happened to snub someone on the street or if he greeted someone who had forgotten him.

But New York was still hundreds of miles away, and it might have been millions on this January night. He saw a sign: BAR. He forced himself forward towards the sputtering neon; he wasn't ordinarily a drinker, but he needed the warmth of alcohol inside him now, and perhaps the barkeep would need a man to help out, or could at least rent him a room for what little he had in his pockets.

There were five men in the bar when he reached it. They looked like truck drivers. Niles dropped his valise to the left of the door, rubbed his stiff hands together, exhaled a white cloud. The bartender grinned jovially at him.

"Cold enough for you out there?"

Niles managed a grin. "I wasn't sweating much. Let me have something warming. Double shot of bourbon, maybe."

That would be ninety cents. He had $7.34.

He nursed the drink when it came, sipped it slowly, let it roll down his gullet. He thought of the summer he had been stranded for a week in Washington, a solid week of 97-degree temperature and 97-per cent humidity, and the vivid memory helped to ease away some of the psychological effects of the coldness.

He relaxed; he warmed. Behind him came the penetrating sound of argument.

"—I tell you Joe Louis beat Schmeling to a pulp the second time! Kayoed him in the first round!"

"You're nuts! Louis just barely got him down in a fifteen-round decision, the second bout."

"Seems to me—"

"I'll put money on it. Ten bucks says it was a decision in fifteen, mac."

Sounds of confident chuckles. "I wouldn't want to take your money so easy, pal. Everyone knows it was a knockout in one."

"Ten bucks, I said."

Niles turned to see what was happening. Two of the truck drivers, burly men in dark pea jackets, stood nose to nose. Automatically the thought came: *Louis knocked Max Schmeling out in the first round at Yankee Stadium, New York, 22 June 1938.* Niles had never been much of a sports fan, and particularly disliked boxing—but he had once glanced at an almanac page cataloguing Joe Louis' title fights, and the data had, of course remained.

He watched detachedly as the bigger of the two truck drivers angrily slapped a ten-dollar bill down on the bar; the other matched it. Then the first glanced up at the barkeep and said. "Okay, bud. You're a shrewd guy. Who's right about the second Louis-Schmeling fight?"

The barkeep was a blank-faced cipher of a man, middle-aged, balding, with mild, empty eyes. He chewed at his lip a moment, shrugged, fidgeted, finally said, "Kinda hard for me to remember. That musta been twenty-five years ago."

Twenty, Niles thought.

"Lessee now," the bartender went on. "Seems to me I remember—yeah, sure. It went the full fifteen, and the judges gave it to Louis. I seem to remember a big stink being made over it; the papers said Joe should've killed him a lot faster'n that."

A triumphant grin appeared on the bigger driver's face. He deftly pocketed both bills.

The other man grimaced and howled, "Hey! You two fixed this thing up beforehand! I know damn well that Louis kayoed the German in one."

"You heard what the man said. The money's mine."

"No," Niles said suddenly, in a quiet voice that seemed to carry halfway across the bar. *Keep your mouth shut,* he told himself frantically. *This is none of your business. Stay out of it!*

But it was too late.

"What you say?" asked the one who'd dropped the ten-spot.

"I say you're being rooked. Louis won the fight in one round, like you say. 22 June 1938, Yankee Stadium. The barkeep's thinking of the Arturo Godoy fight. That went the full fifteen in 1940. February 9."

"There—told you! Gimme back my money!"

But the other driver ignored the cry and turned to face Niles. He was a cold-faced, heavy-set man, and his fists were starting to clench. "Smart man, eh? Boxing expert?"

"I just didn't want to see anybody get cheated," Niles said stubbornly. He knew what was coming now. The truck driver was weaving drunkenly towards him; the barkeep was yelling, the other patrons backing away.

The first punch caught Niles in the ribs; he grunted and staggered back, only to be grabbed by the throat and slapped three times. Dimly he heard a voice saying, "Hey, let go the guy! He didn't mean anything! You want to kill him?"

A volley of blows doubled him up; a knuckle swelled his right eyelid, a fist crashed stunningly into his left shoulder. He spun, wobbled uncertainly, knowing that his mind would permanently record every moment of this agony.

Through half-closed eyes he saw them pulling the enraged driver off him; the man writhed in the grip of three others, aimed a last desperate kick at Niles' stomach and grazed a rib, and finally was subdued.

Niles stood alone in the middle of the floor, forcing himself to stay upright, trying to shake off the sudden pain that drilled through him in a dozen places.

"You all right?" a solicitous voice asked. "Hell, those guys play rough. You oughtn't mix up with them."

"I'm all right," Niles said hollowly. "Just...let me...catch my breath."

"Here. Sit down. Have a drink. It'll fix you up."

"No," Niles said. *I can't stay here. I have to get moving.* "I'll be all right," he muttered unconvincingly. He picked up his suitcase, wrapped his coat tight about him, and left the bar, step by step by step.

He got fifteen feet before the pain became unbearable. He crumpled suddenly and fell forward on his face in the dark, feeling the cold iron-hard frozen turf against his cheek, and struggled unsuccessfully to get up. He lay there, remembering all the various pains of his life, the beatings, the cruelty, and when the weight of memory became too much to bear he blanked out.

The bed was warm, the sheets clean and fresh and soft. Niles woke slowly, feeling a temporary sensation of disorientation, and then his infallible memory supplied the data on his blackout in the snow and he realized he was in a hospital.

He tried to open his eyes; one was swollen shut, but he managed to get the other's lids apart. He was in a small hospital room—no shining metropolitan hospital pavilion, but a small country clinic with ginger-bread molding on the walls and homey lace curtains, through which afternoon sunlight was entering.

So he had been found and brought to a hospital. That was good. He could have easily died out there in the snow; but someone had stumbled over him and brought him in. That was a novelty, that someone had both-ered to help him; the treatment he had received in the bar last night—was it last night?—was more typical of the world's attitude towards him. In twenty-nine years he had somehow failed to learn adequate concealment, camouflage and every day he suffered the consequences. It was so hard for him to remember, he who remembered everything else, that the other people were not like him, and hated him for what he was.

Gingerly he felt his side. There didn't seem to be any broken ribs— just bruises. A day or so of rest and they would probably discharge him and let him move on.

A cheerful voice said, "Oh, you're awake, Mr. Niles. Feeling better now? I'll brew some tea for you."

He looked up and felt a sudden sharp pang. She was a nurse—twen-ty-two, twenty-three, new at the job perhaps, with a flowing tumble of curling blonde hair and wide, clear blue eyes. She was smiling, and it seemed to Niles it was not merely a professional smile. "I'm Miss Carroll, your day nurse. Everything okay?"

"Fine," Niles said hesitantly. "Where am I?"

"Central County General Hospital. You were brought in late last night—apparently you'd been beaten up and left by the road out on Route 32. It's a lucky thing Mark McKenzie was walking his dog, Mr. Niles." She looked at him gravely. "You remember last night, don't you? I mean—the shock—amnesia—"

Niles chuckled. "That's the last ailment in the world I'd be afraid of," he said. "I'm Thomas Richard Niles, and I remember pretty well what happened. How badly am I damaged?"

"Superficial bruises, mild shock and exposure, slight case of frost-bite," she summed up. "You'll live. Dr. Hammond'll give you a full checkup a little later, after you've eaten. Let me bring you some tea."

Niles watched the trim figure vanish into the hallway.

She was certainly an attractive girl, he thought, fresh-eyed, alert...*alive.*

Old cliche: patient falling for his nurse. But she's not for me, I'm afraid.

Abruptly the door opened and the nurse reentered, bearing a little enameled tea tray. "You'll never guess! I have a surprise for you, Mr. Niles. A visitor. Your mother."

"My moth—"

"She saw the little notice about you in the county paper. She's waiting outside, and she told me she hasn't seen you in seventeen years. Would you like me to send her in now?"

"I guess so," Niles said, in a dry, feathery voice.

A second time the nurse departed. *My God,* Niles thought! *If I had known I was this close to home—*

I should have stayed out of Ohio altogether.

The last person he wanted to see was his mother. He began to tremble under the covers. The oldest and most terrible of his memories came bursting up from the dark compartment of his mind where he thought he had imprisoned it forever. The sudden emergence from warmth into coolness, from darkness to light, the jarring slap of a heavy hand on his buttocks, the searing pain of knowing that his security was ended, that from now on he would be alive, and therefore miserable—

The memory of the agonized birth-shriek sounded in his mind. He could never forget being born. And his mother was, he thought, the one person of all he could never forgive, since she had given him forth into the life he hated. He dreaded the moment when—

"Hello, Tom. It's been a long time."

Seventeen years had faded her, had carved lines in her face and made the cheeks more baggy, the blue eyes less bright, the brown hair a mousy grey. She was smiling. And to his own astonishment Niles was able to smile back.

"Mother."

"I read about it in the paper. It said a man of about thirty was found just outside town with papers bearing the name Thomas R. Niles, and he was taken to Central County General Hospital. So I came over, just to make sure—and it *was* you."

A lie drifted to the surface of his mind, but it was a kind lie, and he said it: "I was on my way back home to see you. Hitchhiking. But I ran into a little trouble en route."

"I'm glad you decided to come back, Tom. It's been so lonely, ever since your father died, and of course Hank was married, and Marian too—it's good to see you again. I thought I never would."

He lay back, perplexed, wondering why the upwelling flood of hatred did not come. He felt only warmth towards her. He was glad to see her.

"How has it been—all these years, Tom? You haven't had it easy. I can see. I see it all over your face."

"It hasn't been easy," he said. "You know why I ran away?"

She nodded. "Because of the way you are. That thing about your mind—never forgetting. I knew. Your grandfather had it too, you know."

"My grandfather—but—"

"You got it from him. I never did tell you, I guess. He didn't get along too well with any of us. He left my mother when I was a little girl, and I never knew where he went. So I always knew you'd go away the way he did. Only you came back. Are you married?"

He shook his head.

"Time you got started, then, Tom. You're near thirty."

The door opened, and an efficient-looking doctor appeared. "Afraid your time's up, Mrs. Niles. You'll be able to see him again later. I have to check him over, now that he's awake."

"Of course, doctor." She smiled at him, then at Niles. "I'll see you later, Tom."

"Sure, mother."

Niles lay back, frowning, as the doctor poked at him here and there. *I didn't hate her.* A growing wonderment rose in him, and he realized he should have come home long ago. He had changed, inside, without even knowing it.

Running away was the first stage in growing up, and a necessary one. But coming back came later, and that was the mark of maturity. He was back. And suddenly he saw he had been terribly foolish all his bitter adult life.

He had a gift, a great gift, an awesome gift. It had been too big for him until now. Self-pitying, self-tormented, he had refused to allow for the shortcomings of the forgetful people about him, and had paid the price of their hatred. But he couldn't keep running away forever. The time would have to come for him to grow big enough to contain his gift, to learn to live with it instead of moaning in dramatic, self-inflicted anguish.

And now was the time. It was long overdue.

His grandfather had had the gift; they had never told him that. So it was genetically transmissible. He could marry, have children, and they, too, would never forget.

It was his duty not to let his gift die with him. Others of his kind, less sensitive, less thin-skinned, would come after and they, too, would know how to recall a Beethoven symphony or a decade-old wisp of conversation. For the first time since that fourth birthday party he felt a hesitant flicker of happiness. The days of running were ended; he was home again. *If I learn to live with others, maybe they'll be able to live with me.*

He saw the things he yet needed: a wife, a home, children—

"—a couple of days' rest, plenty of hot liquids, and you'll be as good as new, Mr. Niles," the doctor was saying. "Is there anything you'd like me to bring you now?"

"Yes," Niles said. "Just send in the nurse, will you? Miss Carroll, I mean."

The doctor grinned and left. Niles waited expectantly, exulting in his new self. He switched on Act Three of *Die Meistersinger* as a kind of jubilant backdrop music in his mind, and let the warmth sweep up over him. When she entered the room he was smiling and wondering how to begin saying what he wanted to say.

THERE WAS AN OLD WOMAN

Here—as in "Songs of Summer"—you see me moving away from the cautious generic s-f-magazine style that I stuck to most of the time in these very commercial-minded early years, and attempting something a little more challenging. It was written in November, 1957, accepted a few months later by Larry Shaw of Infinity, *and published in that fine magazine's final issue, that of November, 1958 (in which I had two other stories under pseudonyms and a book review column, accounting for 75 of that issue's 130 pages by myself).* Infinity *was already struggling, as were many of the other lesser science-fiction magazines, when Shaw accepted the story. My ledger indicates that I finally got paid—$65—a couple of months after publication, and I suspect I didn't have an easy time collecting.*

The theme of multiple extra utero *birth was sufficiently interesting to me that I would use it again, in a very different way, eight years later, in my novel* Thorns, *the first significant book of my literary maturity.*

———————

Since I was raised from earliest infancy to undertake the historian's calling, and since it is now certain that I shall never claim that profession as my own, it seems fitting that I perform my first and last act as a historian.

I shall write the history of that strange and unique woman, the mother of my thirty brothers and myself, Miss Donna Mitchell.

She was a person of extraordinary strength and vision, our mother. I remember her vividly, seeing her with all her sons gathered round her in our secluded Wisconsin farmhouse on the first night of summer, after we had returned to her from every part of the country for our summer's vacation. One-and-thirty strapping sons, each one of us six feet one inch tall, with a shock of unruly yellow hair and keen, clear blue eyes, each one of us healthy, strong, well nourished, each one of us twenty-one years and fourteen days old—one-and-thirty identical brothers.

Oh, there were differences between us, but only we and she could perceive them. To outsiders, we were identical; which was why, to outsiders, we took care never to appear together in groups. We ourselves knew the differences, for we had lived with them so long.

I knew my brother Leonard's cheekmole—the right cheek it was, setting him off from Jonas, whose left cheek was marked with a fly-speck. I knew the faint tilt of Peter's chin, the slight oversharpness of Dewey's nose, the florid tint of Donald's skin. I recognized Paul by his pendulous earlobes, Charles by his squint, Noel by the puckering of his lower lip. David had a blue-stubbled face, Mark flaring nostrils, Claude thick brows.

Yes, there were differences. We rarely confused one with another. It was second nature for me to distinguish Edward from Albert, George from Philip, Frederick from Stephen. And Mother never confused us.

She was a regal woman, nearly six feet in height, who even in middle age had retained straightness of posture and majesty of bearing. Her eyes, like ours, were blue; her hair, she told us, had once been golden like ours. Her voice was a deep, mellow contralto; rich, firm, commanding, the voice of a strong woman. She had been professor of biochemistry at some Eastern university (she never told us which one, hating its name so) and we all knew by heart the story of her bitter life and of our own strange birth.

"I had a theory," she would say. "It wasn't an orthodox theory, and it made people angry to think about it, so of course they threw me out. But I didn't care. In many ways that was the most fortunate day of my life."

"Tell us about it, Mother," Philip would invariably ask. He was destined to be a playwright; he enjoyed the repetition of the story whenever we were together.

She said:

"I had a theory. I believed that environment controlled personality, that given the same set of healthy genes any number of different adults could be shaped from the raw material. I had a plan for testing it—but when I told them, they discharged me. Luckily, I had married a wealthy if superficial-minded executive, who had suffered a fatal coronary attack the year before. I was independently wealthy, thanks to him, and free to pursue independent research, thanks to my university discharge. So I came to Wisconsin and began my great project."

We knew the rest of the story by heart, as a sort of litany.

We knew how she had bought a huge, rambling farm in the flat green country of central Wisconsin, a farm far from prying eyes. Then, how on a hot summer afternoon she had gone forth to the farm land nearby, and found a field hand, tall and brawny, and to his great surprise seduced him in the field where he worked.

And then the story of that single miraculous zygote, which our mother had extracted from her body and carefully nurtured in special nutrient tanks, irradiating it and freezing it and irritating it and dosing it with hormones until, exasperated, it subdivided into thirty-two, each one of which developed independently into a complete embryo.

Embryo grew into foetus, and foetus into child, in Mother's ingenious artificial wombs. One of the thirty-two died before birth of accidental narcosis; the remainder survived, thirty-one identical males sprung from the same egg, to become us.

With the formidable energy that typified her, Mother singlehandedly nursed thirty-one baby boys; we thrived, we grew. And then the most crucial stage of the experiment began. We were differentiated at the age of eighteen months, each given his own room, his own particular toys, his own special books later on. Each of us was slated for a different profession. It was the ultimate proof of her theory. Genetically identical, physically identical except for the minor changes time had worked on our individual bodies, we would nevertheless seek out different fields of employment.

She worked out the assignments at random, she said. Philip was to be a playwright, Noel a novelist, Donald a doctor. Astronomy was Allan's goal, Barry's, biology, Albert's the stage. George was to be a concert pianist, Claude a composer, Leonard a member of the bar, Dewey a dentist. Mark was to be an athlete; David, a diplomat. Journalism waited for Jonas, poetry for Peter, painting for Paul.

Edward would become an engineer, Saul a soldier, Charles a statesman; Stephen would go to sea. Martin was aimed for chemistry,

Raymond for physics, James for high finance. Ronald would be a librarian, Robert a bookkeeper, John a priest, Douglas a teacher. Anthony was to be a literary critic, William an architect, Frederick an airplane pilot. For Richard was reserved a life of crime; as for myself, Harold, I was to devote my energies to the study and writing of history.

This was my mother's plan. Let me tell of my own childhood and adolescence, to illustrate its workings.

My first recollections are of books. I had a room on the second floor of our big house. Martin's room was to my left, and in later years I would regret it, for the air was always heavy with the stink of his chemical experiments. To my right was Noel, whose precocious typewriter sometimes pounded all night as he worked on his endless first novel.

But those manifestations came later. I remember waking one morning to find that during the night a bookcase had been placed in my room, and in it a single book—Hendrik Willem van Loon's *The Story of Mankind*. I was four, almost five, then; thanks to Mother's intensive training we were all capable readers by that age, and I puzzled over the big type, learning of the exploits of Charlemagne and Richard the Lionhearted and staring at the squiggly scratches that were van Loon's illustrations.

Other books followed, in years to come. H. G. Wells's *Outline of History*, which fascinated and repelled me at the same time. Toynbee, in the Somervell abridgement, and later, when I had entered adolescence, the complete and unabridged edition. Churchill, and his flowing periods and ringing prose. Sandburg's poetic and massive life of Lincoln; Wedgwood on the Thirty Years' War; Will Durant, in six or seven blocklike volumes.

I read these books, and where I did not understand I read on anyway, knowing I would come back to that page in some year to come and bring new understanding to it. Mother helped, and guided, and chivvied. A sense of the panorama of man's vast achievement sprang up in me. To join the roll of mankind's chroniclers seemed the only possible end for my existence.

Each summer from my fourteenth to my seventeenth, I traveled—alone, of course, since Mother wanted to build self-reliance in us. I visited the great historical places of the United States: Washington, DC, Mount Vernon, Williamsburg, Bull Run, Gettysburg. A sense of the past rose in me.

Those summers were my only opportunities for contact with strangers, since during the year and especially during the long snow-bound winters we stayed on the farm, a tight family unit. We never went to public school; obviously, it was impossible to enroll us, en masse, without arousing the curiosity my mother wished to avoid.

Instead, she tutored us privately, giving us care and attention that no professional teacher could possibly have supplied. And we grew older, diverging towards our professions like branching limbs of a tree.

As a future historian, of course, I took it upon myself to observe the changes in my own society, which was bounded by the acreage of our farm. I made notes on the progress of my brothers, keeping my note-books well hidden, and also on the changes time was working on Mother. She stood up surprisingly well, considering the astonishing burden she had taken upon herself. Formidable was the best word to use in describing her.

We grew into adolescence. By this time Martin had an imposing chemical laboratory in his room; Leonard harangued us all on legal fine points, and Anthony pored over Proust and Kafka, delivering startling critical interpretations. Our house was a beehive of industry constantly, and I don't remember being bored for more than three consecutive seconds, at any time. There were always distractions: Claude and George jostling for room on the piano bench while they played Claude's four-hand sonata, Mark hurling a baseball through a front window, Peter declaiming a sequence of shocking sonnets during our communal dinner.

We fought, of course, since we were healthy individualists with sound bodies. Mother encouraged it; Saturday afternoon was wrestling time, and we pitted our growing strengths against one another.

Mother was always the dominant figure, striding tall and erect around the farm, calling to us in her familiar boom, assigning us chores, meeting with us privately. Somehow she had the knack of making each of us think we were the favorite child, the one in whose future she was most deeply interested of all. It was false, of course; though once Jonas unkindly assert-ed that Barry must be her real favorite, because he, like her, was a biologist.

I doubted it. I had learned much about people through my constant reading, and I knew that Mother was something extraordinary—a fanatic, if you like, or merely a woman driven by an inner demon, but still and all a person of overwhelming intellectual drive and conviction, whose will to know the truth had led her to undertake this fantastic experiment in biology and human breeding.

I knew that no woman of that sort could stoop to petty favoritism. Mother was unique. Perhaps, had she been born a man, she would have changed the entire course of human development.

When we were seventeen, she called us all together round the big table in the common room of our rambling home. She waited, needing to clear her throat only once in order to cut the hum of conversation.

"Sons," she said, and the echo rang through the entire first floor of the house. "Sons, the time has come for you to leave the farm."

We were stunned, even those of us who were expecting it. But she explained, and we understood, and we did not quarrel.

One could not become a doctor or a chemist or a novelist or even a historian in a total vacuum. One had to enter the world. And one needed certain professional qualifications.

We were going to college.

Not all of us, of course. Robert was to be a bookkeeper; he would go to business school. Mark had developed, through years of practice, into a superb right-handed pitcher, and he was to go to Milwaukee for a major-league tryout. Claude and George, aspiring composer and aspiring pianist, would attend an Eastern conservatory together, posing as twins.

The rest of us were to attend colleges, and those who were to go on to professions such as medicine or chemistry would plan to attend professional schools afterwards. Mother believed a college education was essential, even to a poet or a painter or a novelist.

Only one of us was not sent to any accredited institution. He was Richard, who was to be our criminal. Already he had made several sallies into the surrounding towns and cities, returning a few days or a few weeks later with money or jewels and with a guilty grin on his face. He was simply to be turned loose into the school of Life, and Mother warned him never to get caught.

As for me, I was sent to Princeton and enrolled as a liberal-arts student. Since, like my brothers, I was privately educated, I had no diplomas or similar records to show them, and they had to give me an equivalency examination in their place. Evidently I did quite well, for I was immediately accepted. I wired Mother, who sent a check for $3,000 to cover my first year's tuition and expenses.

I enrolled as a history major; among my first-year courses were Medieval English Constitutional History and the Survey of Western Historical Currents; naturally, my marks were the highest in the class in both cases. I worked diligently and even with a sort of frenzied fury. My other courses, in the sciences or in the arts, I devoted no more nor no less time to than was necessary, but history was my ruling passion.

At least, through my first two semesters of college.

June came, and final exams, and then I returned to Wisconsin, where Mother was waiting. It was 21 June when I returned; since not all colleges end their spring semester simultaneously, some of my brothers had been home for more than a week, others had not yet arrived. Richard had sent word that he was in Los Angeles, and would be with us after the first of July. Mark had signed a baseball contract and was pitching for a team in New Mexico, and he, too, would not be with us.

The summer passed rapidly.

We spent it as we had in the old days before college, sharing our individual specialities, talking, meeting regularly and privately with Mother to discuss the goals that still lay ahead. Except for Claude and George, we had scattered in different directions, no two of us at the same school.

I returned to Princeton that fall for my sophomore year. It passed, and I made the homeward journey again, and in the fall traveled once more eastward. The junior year went by likewise.

And I began to detect signs of a curious change in my inward self. It was a change I did not dare mention to Mother on those July days when I met with her in her room near the library. I did not tell my brothers, either. I kept my knowledge to myself, brooding over it, wondering why it was that this thing should happen to me, why I should be singled out.

For I was discovering that the study of history bored me utterly and completely.

The spirit of rebellion grew in me during my final year in college. My marks had been excellent; I had achieved Phi Beta Kappa and several graduate schools were interested in having me continue my studies with them. But I had been speaking to a few chosen friends (none of whom knew my bizarre family background, of course) and my values had been slowly shifting.

I realized that I had mined history as deeply as I ever cared to. Waking and sleeping, for more than fifteen years, I had pondered Waterloo and Bunker Hill, considered the personalities of Cromwell and James II, held imaginary conversations with Jefferson and Augustus Caesar and Charles Martel. And I was bored with it.

It began to become evident to others, eventually. One day during my final semester a friend asked me, "Is there something worrying you, Harry?"

I shook my head quickly—too quickly. "No," I said. "Why? Do I look worried?"

"You look worse than worried. You look obsessed."

We laughed about it, and finally we went down to the student center and had a few beers, and before long my tongue had loosened a little.

I said, "There *is* something worrying me. And you know what it is? I'm afraid I won't live up to the standards my family set for me."

Guffaws greeted me. "Come off it, Harry! Phi Beta in your junior year, top class standing, a brilliant career in history ahead of you—what do they want from you, blood?"

I chuckled and gulped my beer and mumbled something innocuous, but inside I was curdling.

Everything I was, I owed to Mother. She made me what I am. But I was played out as a student of history; I was the family failure, the goat, the rotten egg. Raymond still wrestled gleefully with nuclear physics, with Heisenberg and Schrödinger and the others. Mark gloried in his fast ball and his slider and his curve. Paul daubed canvas merrily in his Greenwich Village flat near NYU, and even Robert seemed to take delight in keeping books.

Only I had failed. History had become repugnant to me. I was in rebellion against it. I would disappoint my mother, become the butt of my brothers' scorn, and live in despair, hating the profession of historian and fitted by training for nothing else.

I was graduated from Princeton summa cum laude, a few days after my twenty-first birthday. I wired Mother that I was on my way home, and bought train tickets.

It was a long and grueling journey to Wisconsin. I spent my time thinking, trying to choose between the unpleasant alternatives that faced me.

I could attempt duplicity, telling my mother I was still studying history, while actually preparing myself for some more attractive profession—the law, perhaps.

I could confess to her at once my failure of purpose, ask her forgiveness for disappointing her and flawing her grand scheme, and try to begin afresh in another field.

Or I could forge ahead with history, compelling myself grimly to take an interest, cramping and paining myself so that my mother's design would be complete.

None of them seemed desirable paths to take. I brooded over it, and was weary and apprehensive by the time I arrived at our farm.

The first of my brothers I saw was Mark. He sat on the front porch of the big house, reading a book which I recognized at once and with some surprise as Volume I of Churchill. He looked up at me and smiled feebly.

I frowned. "I didn't expect to find *you* here, Mark. According to the local sports pages the Braves are playing on the Coast this week. How come you're not with them?"

His voice was a low murmur. "Because they gave me my release," he said.

"What?"

He nodded. "I'm washed up at twenty-one. They made me a free agent; that means I can hook up with any team that wants me."

"And you're just taking a little rest before offering yourself around?"

He shook his head. "I'm through. Kaput. Harry, I just can't stand baseball. It's a silly, stupid game. You know how many times I had to stand out there in baggy knickers and throw a bit of horsehide at some jerk with a club in his paws? A hundred, hundred-fifty times a game, every four days. For what? What the hell does it all mean? Why should I bother?"

There was a strange gleam in his eyes. I said, "Have you told Mother?"

"I don't dare! She thinks I'm on leave or something. Harry, how can I tell her—"

"I know." Briefly, I told him of my own disenchantment with history. We were mutually delighted to learn that we were not alone in our affliction. I picked up my suitcases, scrambled up the steps, and went inside.

Dewey was cleaning up the common room as I passed through. He nodded hello glumly. I said, "How's the tooth trade?"

He whirled and glared at me viciously.

"Something wrong?" I asked.

"I've been accepted by four dental schools, Harry."

"Is that any cause for misery?"

He let the broom drop, walked over to me, and whispered, "I'll murder you if you tell Mother this. But the thought of spending my life poking around in foul-smelling oral cavities sickens me. Sickens."

"But I thought—"

"Yeah. You thought. You've got it soft; you just need to dig books out of the library and rearrange what they say and call it new research. I have to drill and clean and fill and plug and—" He stopped. "Harry, I'll kill you if you breathe a word of this. I don't want Mother to know that I didn't come out the way she wanted."

I repeated what I had said to Mark—and told him about Mark, for good measure. Then I made my way upstairs to my old room. I felt a burden lifting from me; I was not alone. At least two of my brothers felt the same way. I wondered how many more were at last rebelling against the disciplines of a lifetime.

Poor Mother, I thought! Poor Mother!

Our first family council of the summer was held that night. Stephen and Saul were the last to arrive, Stephen resplendent in his Annapolis garb, Saul crisp looking and stiff-backed from West Point. Mother had worked hard to wangle appointments for those two.

We sat around the big table and chatted. The first phase of our lives, Mother told us, had ended. Now, our preliminary educations were complete, and we would undertake the final step towards our professions— those of us who had not already entered them.

Mother looked radiant that evening, tall, energetic, her white hair cropped mannishly short, as she sat about the table with her thirty-one strapping sons. I envied and pitied her: envied her for the sweet serenity of her life, which had proceeded so inexorably and without swerving towards the goal of her experiment, and pitied her for the disillusioning that awaited her.

For Mark and Dewey and I were not the only failures in the crop.

I had made discreet inquiries during the day. I learned that Anthony found literary criticism to be a fraud and a sham, that Paul knew clearly he had no talent as a painter (and, also, that very few of his contemporaries did either), that Robert bitterly resented a career of bookkeeping, that piano playing hurt George's fingers, that Claude had had difficulty with his composing because he was tone deaf, that the journalistic grind was too strenuous for Jonas, that John longed to quit the seminarial life because he had no calling, that Albert hated the uncertain Bohemianism of an actor's life—

We circulated, all of us raising for the first time the question that had sprouted in our minds during the past several years. I made the astonishing discovery that not one of Donna Mitchell's sons cared for the career that had been chosen for him.

The experiment had been a resounding flop.

Late that evening, after Mother had gone to bed, we remained together, discussing our predicament. How could we tell her? How could we destroy her life's work? And yet, how could we compel ourselves to lives of unending drudgery?

Robert wanted to study engineering; Barry, to write. I realized I cared much more for law than for history, while Leonard longed to exchange law for the physical sciences. James, our banker-manque, much preferred politics. And so it went, with Richard (who claimed five robberies, a rape, and innumerable picked pockets) pouring out his desire to settle down and live within the law as an honest farmer.

It was pathetic.

Summing up the problem in his neat forensic way, Leonard said, "Here's our dilemma: Do we all keep quiet about this and ruin our lives, or do we speak up and ruin Mother's experiment?"

"I think we ought to continue as is, for the time being," Saul said. "Perhaps Mother will die in the next year or two. We can start over then."

"Perhaps she *doesn't* die?" Edward wanted to know. "She's tough as nails. She may last another twenty or thirty or even forty years."

"And we're past twenty-one already," remarked Raymond. "If we hang on too long at what we're doing, it'll be too late to change. You can't start studying for a new profession when you're thirty-five."

"Maybe we'll get to *like* what we're doing by then," suggested David hopefully. "Diplomatic service isn't as bad as all that, and I'd say—"

"What about me?" Paul yelped. "I can't paint and I know I can't paint. I've got nothing but starvation ahead of me unless I wise up and get into business in a hurry. You want me to keep messing up good white canvas the rest of my life?"

"It won't work," said Barry in a doleful voice. "We'll have to tell her."

Douglas shook his head. "We can't do that. You know just what she'll do. She'll bring down the umpteen volumes of notes she's made on this experiment, and ask us if we're going to let it all come to naught."

"He's right," Albert said. "I can picture the scene now. The big organ-pipe voice blasting us for our lack of faith, the accusations of ingratitude—"

"Ingratitude?" William shouted. "She twisted us and pushed us and molded us without asking our permission. Hell, she *created* us with her laboratory tricks. But that didn't give her the right to make zombies out of us."

"Still," Martin said, "we can't just go to her and tell her that it's all over. The shock would kill her."

"Well?" Richard asked in the silence that followed. "What's wrong with that?"

For a moment, no one spoke. The house was quiet; we heard footsteps descending the stairs. We froze.

Mother appeared, an imperial figure even in her old housecoat. "You boys are kicking up too much of a racket down here," she boomed. "I know you're glad to see each other again after a year, but I need my sleep."

She turned and strode upstairs again. We heard her bedroom door slam shut. For an instant we were all ten-year-olds again, diligently studying our books for fear of Mother's displeasure.

I moistened my lips. "Well?" I asked. "I call for a vote on Richard's suggestion."

Martin, as a chemist, prepared the drink, using Donald's medical advice as his guide. Saul, Stephen, and Raymond dug a grave, in the woods at the back of our property. Douglas and Mark built the coffin.

Richard, ending his criminal career with a murder to which we were all accessories before the fact, carried the fatal beverage upstairs to Mother the next morning, and persuaded her to sip it. One sip was all that was necessary; Martin had done his work well.

Leonard offered us a legal opinion: It was justifiable homicide. We placed the body in its coffin and carried it out across the fields. Richard, Peter, Jonas and Charles were her pallbearers; the others of us followed in their path.

We lowered the body into the ground and John said a few words over her. Then, slowly, we closed over the grave and replaced the sod, and began the walk back to the house.

"She died happy," Anthony said. "She never suspected the size of her failure." It was her epitaph.

As our banker, James supervised the division of her assets, which were considerable, into thirty-one equal parts. Noel composed a short figment of prose which we agreed summed up our sentiments.

We left the farm that night, scattering in every direction, anxious to begin life. All that went before was a dream from which we now awakened. We agreed to meet at the farm each year, on the anniversary of her death, in memory of the woman who had so painstakingly divided a zygote into thirty-two viable cells, and who had spent a score of years conducting an experiment based on a theory that had proved to be utterly false.

We felt no regret, no qualm. We had done what needed to be done, and on that last day some of us had finally functioned in the professions for which Mother had intended us.

I, too. My first and last work of history will be this, an account of Mother and her experiment, which records the beginning and the end of her work. And now it is complete.

THE IRON CHANCELLOR

Nothing very serious or lofty here, just a slick, well-made story somewhat in the Henry Kuttner vein. (He was one of my early idols, a clever, prolific, technically proficient writer who died in 1958 at the age of 44. I never knew him personally but I followed his stories eagerly in the magazines when I was in my teens—they appeared under a host of pseudonyms, but we ferreted them all out—and later studied them with ferocious concentration to pry loose their secrets). It dates from December, 1957; Horace Gold, who had a weakness himself for the Kuttner sort of light comedy with a grim twist, quickly bought it without giving me a particularly hard time and printed it in the May, 1958 issue of Galaxy.

It has had a healthy post-publication life in anthologies—most conspicuously in a bizarre volume edited by a couple of good friends of mine, Martin H. Greenberg and George R. R. Martin, called The Science Fiction Weight-Loss Book. *It's been optioned a couple of times for television, too, but so far has never been produced.*

The Carmichaels were a pretty plump family, to begin with. Not one of the four of them couldn't stand to shed quite a few pounds. And there happened to be a superspecial on roboservitors at one of the Miracle Mile roboshops—40% off on the 2061 model, with adjustable caloric-intake monitors.

Sam Carmichael liked the idea of having his food prepared and served by a robot who would keep one beady solenoid eye on the collective family waistline. He squinted speculatively at the glossy display model, absentmindedly slipped his thumbs beneath his elastobelt to knead his paunch, and said, "How much?"

The salesman flashed a brilliant and probably synthetic grin. "Only two thousand nine hundred ninety-five, sir. That includes free service contract for the first five years. Only two hundred credits down and up to forty months to pay."

Carmichael frowned, thinking of his bank balance. Then he thought of his wife's figure, and of his daughter's endless yammering about her need to diet. Besides, Jemima, their old robocook, was shabby and gear-stripped, and made a miserable showing when other company executives visited them for dinner.

"I'll take it," he said.

"Care to trade in your old robocook, sir? Liberal trade-in allowances—"

"I have a '43 Madison." Carmichael wondered if he should mention its bad arm libration and serious fuel-feed overflow, but decided that would be carrying candidness too far.

"Well—ah—I guess we could allow you fifty credits on a '43, sir. Seventy-five, maybe, if the recipe bank is still in good condition."

"Excellent condition." That part was honest—the family had never let even one recipe wear out. "You could send a man down to look her over."

"Oh, no need to do that, sir. We'll take your word. Seventy-five, then? And delivery of the new model by this evening?"

"Done," Carmichael said. He was glad to get the pathetic old '43 out of the house at any cost.

He signed the purchase order cheerfully, pocketed the facsim and handed over ten crisp twenty-credit vouchers. He could almost feel the roll of fat melting from him now, as he eyed the magnificent '61 roboservitor that would shortly be his.

The time was only 1810 hours when he left the shop, got into his car and punched out the coordinates for home. The whole transaction had taken less than ten minutes. Carmichael, a second-level executive at Normandy Trust, prided himself both on his good business sense and his ability to come quickly to a firm decision.

Fifteen minutes later, his car deposited him at the front entrance of their totally detached self-powered suburban home in the fashionable

Westley subdivision. The car obediently took itself around back to the garage, while Carmichael stood in the scanner field until the door opened. Clyde, the robutler, came scuttling hastily up, took his hat and cloak, and handed him a Martini.

Carmichael beamed appreciatively. "Well done, thou good and faithful servant!"

He took a healthy sip and headed towards the living room to greet his wife, son and daughter. Pleasant gin-induced warmth filtered through him. The robutler was ancient and due for replacement as soon as the budget could stand the charge, but Carmichael realized he would miss the clanking old heap.

"You're late, dear," Ethel Carmichael said as he appeared. "Dinner's been ready for ten minutes. Jemima's so annoyed her cathodes are clicking."

"Jemima's cathodes fail to interest me," Carmichael said evenly. "Good evening, dear. Myra. Joey. I'm late because I stopped off at Marhew's on my way home."

His son blinked. "The robot place, Dad?"

"Precisely. I bought a '61 roboservitor to replace old Jemima and her sputtering cathodes. The new model has," Carmichael added, eyeing his son's adolescent bulkiness and the rather-more-than-ample figures of his wife and daughter, "some very special attachments."

They dined well that night, on Jemima's favorite Tuesday dinner menu—shrimp cocktail, fumet of gumbo chervil, breast of chicken with creamed potatoes and asparagus, delicious plum tarts for dessert, and coffee. Carmichael felt pleasantly bloated when he had finished, and gestured to Clyde for a snifter of his favorite afterdinner digestive aid, VSOP Cognac. He leaned back, warm, replete, able easily to ignore the blustery November winds outside.

A pleasing electroluminescence suffused the dining room with pink—this year, the experts thought pink improved digestion—and the heating filaments embedded in the wall glowed cozily as they delivered the BTUs. This was the hour of relaxation in the Carmichael household.

"Dad," Joey began hesitantly, "about that canoe trip next weekend—"

Carmichael folded his hands across his stomach and nodded. "You can go, I suppose. Only be careful. If I find out you didn't use the equilibriator this time—"

The door chime sounded. Carmichael lifted an eyebrow and swivelled in his chair.

"Who is it, Clyde?"

"He gives his name as Robinson, sir. Of Robinson Robotics, he said. He has a bulky package to deliver."

"It must be that new robocook, Father!" Myra Carmichael exclaimed.

"I guess it is. Show him in, Clyde."

Robinson turned out to be a red-faced, efficient-looking little man in greasy green overalls and a plaid pullover-coat, who looked disapprovingly at the robutler and strode into the Carmichael living room.

He was followed by a lumbering object about seven feet high, mounted on a pair of rolltreads and swathed completely in quilted rags.

"Got him all wrapped up against the cold, Mr. Carmichael. Lot of delicate circuitry in that job. You ought to be proud of him."

"Clyde, help Mr. Robinson unpack the new robocook," Carmichael said.

"That's okay—I can manage it. And it's *not* a robocook, by the way. It's called a roboservitor now. Fancy price, fancy name."

Carmichael heard his wife mutter, "Sam, how much—"

He scowled at her. "Very reasonable, Ethel. Don't worry so much."

He stepped back to admire the roboservitor as it emerged from the quilted swaddling. It was big, all right, with a massive barrel of a chest—robotic controls are always housed in the chest, not in the relatively tiny head—and a gleaming mirror-keen finish that accented its sleekness and newness. Carmichael felt the satisfying glow of pride in ownership. Somehow it seemed to him that he had done something noble and lordly in buying this magnificent robot.

Robinson finished the unpacking job and, standing on tiptoes, opened the robot's chest panel. He unclipped a thick instruction manual and handed it to Carmichael, who stared at the tome uneasily.

"Don't fret about that, Mr. Carmichael. This robot's no trouble to handle. The book's just part of the trimming. Come here a minute."

Carmichael peered into the robot's innards. Pointing, Robinson said, "Here's the recipe bank—biggest and best ever designed. Of course it's possible to tape in any of your favorite family recipes, if they're not already there. Just hook up your old robocook to the integrator circuit and feed 'em in. I'll take care of that before I leave."

"And what about the—ah—special features?"

"The reducing monitors, you mean? Right over here. See? You just tape in the names of the members of the family and their present and desired weights, and the roboservitor takes care of the rest. Computes caloric intake, adjusts menus, and everything else."

Carmichael grinned at his wife. "Told you I was going to do something about our weight, Ethel. No more dieting for you, Myra—the robot does all the work." Catching a sour look on his son's face, he added, "And you're not so lean yourself, Buster."

"I don't think there'll be any trouble," Robinson said buoyantly. "But if there is, just buzz for me. I handle service and delivery for Marhew Stores in this area."

"Right."

"Now if you'll get me your obsolete robocook, I'll transfer the family recipes before I cart it away on the trade-in deal."

There was a momentary tingle of nostalgia and regret when Robinson left, half an hour later, taking old Jemima with him. Carmichael had almost come to think of the battered '43 Madison as a member of the family. After all, he had bought her sixteen years before, only a couple of years after his marriage.

But she—it, he corrected in annoyance—was only a robot, and robots became obsolete. Besides, Jemima probably suffered all the aches and pains of a robot's old age and would be happier dismantled. Carmichael blotted Jemima from his mind.

The four of them spent most of the rest of that evening discovering things about their new roboservitor. Carmichael drew up a table of their weights (himself, 192; Ethel, 145; Myra, 139; Joey, 189) and the amount they proposed to weigh in three months' time (himself, 180; Ethel, 125;. Myra, 120; Joey, 175). Carmichael then let his son, who prided himself on his knowledge of practical robotics, integrate the figures and feed them to the robot's programming bank.

"You wish this schedule to take effect immediately?" the roboservitor queried in a deep, mellow bass.

Startled, Carmichael said, "T-tomorrow morning, at breakfast. We might as well start right away."

"He speaks well, doesn't he?" Ethel asked.

"He sure does," Joey said. "Jemima always stammered and squeaked, and all she could say was, 'Dinner is serrved' and 'Be careful, sirr, the soup plate is very warrm.'"

Carmichael smiled. He noticed his daughter admiring the robot's bulky frame and sleek bronze limbs, and thought resignedly that a seventeen-year-old girl could find the strangest sorts of love objects. But he was happy to see that they were all evidently pleased with the robot. Even with the discount and the trade-in, it *had* been a little on the costly side.

But it would be worth it.

Carmichael slept soundly and woke early, anticipating the first breakfast under the new regime. He still felt pleased with himself.

Dieting had always been such a nuisance, he thought—but, on the other hand, he had never enjoyed the sensation of an annoying roll of fat pushing outward against his elastobelt. He exercised sporadically, but it did little good, and he never had the initiative to keep a rigorous dieting campaign going for long. Now, though, with the mathematics of reducing done effortlessly for him, all the calculating and cooking being handled by the new robot—now, for the first time since he had been Joey's age, he could look forward to being slim and trim once again.

He dressed, showered and hastily depilated. It was 0730. Breakfast was ready.

Ethel and the children were already at the table when he arrived. Ethel and Myra were munching toast; Joey was peering at a bowl of milkless dry cereal, next to which stood a full glass of milk. Carmichael sat down.

"Your toast, sir," the roboservitor murmured.

Carmichael stared at the single slice. It had already been buttered for him, and the butter had evidently been measured out with a micrometer. The robot proceeded to hand him a cup of black coffee.

He groped for the cream and sugar. They weren't anywhere on the table. The other members of his family were regarding him strangely, and they were curiously, suspiciously silent.

"I like cream and sugar in my coffee," he said to the hovering roboservitor. "Didn't you find that in Jemima's old recipe bank?"

"Of course, sir. But you must learn to drink your coffee without such things, if you wish to lose weight."

Carmichael chuckled. Somehow he had not expected the regimen to be quite like this—quite so, well, Spartan. "Oh, yes. Of course. Ah—are the eggs ready yet?" He considered a day incomplete unless he began it with soft-boiled eggs.

"Sorry, no, sir. On Mondays, Wednesdays and Fridays, breakfast is to consist of toast and black coffee only, except for Master Joey, who gets cereal, fruit juice and milk."

"I—see."

Well, he had asked for it. He shrugged and took a bite of the toast. He sipped the coffee; it tasted like river mud, but he tried not to make a face.

Joey seemed to be going about the business of eating his cereal rather oddly, Carmichael noticed next. "Why don't you pour that glass of milk *into* the cereal?" he asked. "Won't it taste better that way?"

"Sure it will. But Bismarck says I won't get another glass if I do, so I'm eating it this way."

"Bismarck?"

Joey grinned. "It's the name of a famous nineteenth-century German dictator. They called him the Iron Chancellor." He jerked his head towards the kitchen, to which the roboservitor had silently retreated. "Pretty good name for him, eh?"

"No," said Carmichael. "It's silly."

"It has a certain ring of truth, though," Ethel remarked.

Carmichael did not reply. He finished his toast and coffee somewhat glumly and signaled Clyde to get the car out of the garage. He felt depressed—dieting didn't seem to be so effortless after all, even with the new robot.

As he walked towards the door, the robot glided around him and handed him a small printed slip of paper. Carmichael stared at it. It said:

FRUIT JUICE
LETTUCE-TOMATO SALAD
(ONE) HARD-BOILED EGG
BLACK COFFEE

"What's this thing?"

"You are the only member of this family group who will not be eating three meals a day under my personal supervision. This is your luncheon menu. Please adhere to it," the robot said smoothly.

Repressing a sputter, Carmichael said, "Yes—yes. Of course."

He pocketed the menu and made his way uncertainly to the waiting car.

He was faithful to the robot's orders at lunchtime that day; even though he was beginning to develop resistance to the idea that had seemed so appealing only the night before, he was willing, at least, to give it a try.

But something prompted him to stay away from the restaurant where Normandy Trust employees usually lunched, and where there were human waiters to smirk at him and fellow executives to ask prying questions.

He ate instead at a cheap robocafeteria two blocks to the north. He slipped in surreptitiously with his collar turned up, punched out his order (it cost him less than a credit altogether) and wolfed it down. He still was hungry when he had finished, but he compelled himself to return loyally to the office.

He wondered how long he was going to be able to keep up this iron self-control. Not very long, he realized dolefully. And if anyone from the company caught him eating at a robocafeteria, he'd be a laughing stock. Someone of executive status just *didn't* eat lunch by himself in mechanized cafeterias.

By the time he had finished his day's work, his stomach felt knotted and pleated. His hand was shaky as he punched out his destination on the car's autopanel, and he was thankful that it took less than an hour to get home from the office. Soon, he thought, he'd be tasting food again. Soon. Soon. He switched on the roof-mounted video, leaned back in the recliner and tried to relax as the car bore him homeward.

He was in for a surprise, though, when he stepped through the safety field into his home. Clyde was waiting as always, and, as always, took his hat and cloak. And, as always, Carmichael reached out for the cocktail that Clyde prepared nightly to welcome him home.

There was no cocktail.

"Are we out of gin, Clyde?"

"No, sir."

"How come no drink, then?"

The robot's rubberized metallic features seemed to droop. "Because, sir, a Martini's caloric content is inordinately high. Gin is rated at a hundred calories per ounce and—"

"Oh, no. You too!"

"Pardon, sir. The new roboservitor has altered my responsive circuits to comply with the regulations now in force in this household."

Carmichael felt his fingers starting to tremble. "Clyde, you've been my butler for almost twenty years."

"Yes, sir."

"You always make my drinks for me. You mix the best Martinis in the Western Hemisphere."

"Thank you, sir."

"And you're going to mix one for me right now! That's a direct order!"

314

"Sir! I—" The robutler staggered wildly and nearly careened into Carmichael. It seemed to have lost all control over its gyro-balance; it clutched agonizedly at its chest panel and started to sag.

Hastily, Carmichael barked, "Order countermanded! Clyde, are you all right?"

Slowly, and with a creak, the robot straightened up. It looked dangerously close to an overload. "Your direct order set up a first-level conflict in me, sir," Clyde whispered faintly. "I—came close to burning out just then, sir. May—may I be excused?"

"Of course. Sorry, Clyde." Carmichael balled his fists. There was such a thing as going too far! The roboservitor—Bismarck—had obviously placed on Clyde a flat prohibition against serving liquor to him. Reducing or no reducing, there were *limits*.

Carmichael strode angrily towards the kitchen.

His wife met him halfway. "I didn't hear you come in, Sam. I want to talk to you about—"

"Later. Where's that robot?"

"In the kitchen, I imagine. It's almost dinnertime."

He brushed past her and swept on into the kitchen, where Bismarck was moving efficiently from electrostove to magnetic worktable. The robot swivelled as Carmichael entered.

"Did you have a good day, sir?"

"No! I'm hungry!"

"The first days of a diet are always the most difficult, Mr. Carmichael. But your body will adjust to the reduction in food intake before long."

"I'm sure of that. But what's this business of tinkering with Clyde?"

"The butler insisted on preparing an alcoholic drink for you. I was forced to adjust his programming. From now on, sir, you may indulge in cocktails on Tuesdays, Thursdays, and Saturdays. I beg to be excused from further discussion now, sir. The meal is almost ready."

Poor Clyde! Carmichael thought. *And poor me!* He gnashed his teeth impotently a few times, then gave up and turned away from the glistening, overbearing roboservitor. A light gleamed on the side of the robot's head, indicating that he had shut off his audio circuits and was totally engaged in his task.

Dinner consisted of steak and peas, followed by black coffee. The steak was rare; Carmichael preferred it well done. But Bismarck—the name was beginning to take hold—had had all the latest dietetic theories taped into him, and rare meat it was.

After the robot had cleared the table and tidied up the kitchen, it retired to its storage place in the basement, which gave the Carmichael family a chance to speak openly to each other for the first time that evening.

"Lord!" Ethel snorted. "Sam, I don't object to losing weight, but if we're going to be *tyrannized* in our own home—"

"Mom's right," Joey put in. "It doesn't seem fair for that thing to feed us whatever it pleases. And I didn't like the way it messed around with Clyde's circuits."

Carmichael spread his hands. "I'm not happy about it either. But we have to give it a try. We can always make readjustments in the programming if it turns out to be necessary."

"But how long are we going to keep this up?" Myra wanted to know. "I had three meals in this house today and I'm starved!"

"Me, too," Joey said. He elbowed himself from his chair and looked around. "Bismarck's downstairs. I'm going to get a slice of lemon pie while the coast is clear."

"No!" Carmichael thundered.

"No?"

"There's no sense in my spending three thousand credits on a dietary robot if you're going to cheat, Joey. I forbid you to have any pie."

"But, Dad, I'm hungry! I'm a growing boy! I'm—"

"You're sixteen years old, and if you grow much more, you won't fit inside the house," Carmichael snapped, looking up at his six-foot-one son.

"Sam, we can't starve the boy," Ethel protested. "If he wants pie, let him have some. You're carrying this reducing fetish too far."

Carmichael considered that. Perhaps, he thought, I *am* being a little oversevere. And the thought of lemon pie was a tempting one. He was pretty hungry himself.

"All right," he said with feigned reluctance. "I guess a bit of pie won't wreck the plan. In fact, I suppose I'll have some myself. Joey, why don't you—"

"Begging your pardon," a purring voice said behind him. Carmichael jumped half an inch. It was the robot, Bismarck. "It would be most unfortunate if you were to have pie now, Mr. Carmichael. My calculations are very precise."

Carmichael saw the angry gleam in his son's eye, but the robot seemed extraordinarily big at that moment, and it happened to stand between him and the kitchen.

He sighed weakly. "Let's forget the lemon pie, Joey."

After two full days of the Bismarckian diet, Carmichael discovered that his inner resources of will power were beginning to crumble. On the third day he tossed away the printed lunchtime diet and went out irresponsibly with MacDougal and Hennessey for a six-course lunch, complete with cocktails. It seemed to him that he hadn't tasted real food since the robot arrived.

That night, he was able to tolerate the seven-hundred-calorie dinner without any inward grumblings, being still well lined with lunch. But Ethel and Myra and Joey were increasingly irritable. It seemed that the robot had usurped Ethel's job of handling the daily marketing and had stocked in nothing but a huge supply of healthy low-calorie foods. The larder now bulged with wheat germ, protein bread, irrigated salmon, and other hitherto unfamiliar items. Myra had taken up biting her nails; Joey's mood was one of black sullen brooding, and Carmichael knew how that could lead to trouble quickly with a sixteen-year-old.

After the meager dinner, he ordered Bismarck to go to the basement and stay there until summoned.

The robot said, "I must advise you, sir, that I will detect indulgence in any forbidden foods in my absence and adjust for it in the next meals."

"You have my word," Carmichael said, thinking it was indeed queer to have to pledge on your honor to your own robot. He waited until the massive servitor had vanished below; then he turned to Joey and said, "Get the instruction manual, boy."

Joey grinned in understanding. Ethel said, "Sam, what are you going to do?"

Carmichael patted his shrunken waistline. "I'm going to take a can opener to that creature and adjust his programming. He's overdoing this diet business. Joey, have you found the instructions on how to reprogram the robot?"

"Page 167. I'll get the tool kit, Dad."

"Right." Carmichael turned to the robutler, who was standing by dumbly, in his usual forward-stooping posture of expectancy. "Clyde, go down below and tell Bismarck we want him right away."

Moments later, the two robots appeared. Carmichael said to the roboservitor, "I'm afraid it's necessary for us to change your program. We've overestimated our capacity for losing weight."

"I beg you to reconsider, sir. Extra weight is harmful to every vital organ in the body. I plead with you to maintain my scheduling unaltered."

317

"I'd rather cut my own throat. Joey, inactivate him and do your stuff."

Grinning fiercely, the boy stepped forward and pressed the stud that opened the robot's ribcage. A frightening assortment of gears, cams and translucent cables became visible inside the robot. With a small wrench in one hand and the open instruction book in the other, Joey prepared to make the necessary changes, while Carmichael held his breath and a pall of silence descended on the living room. Even old Clyde leaned forward to have a better view.

Joey muttered, "Lever F, with the yellow indicia, is to be advanced one notch...umm. Now twist Dial B9 to the left, thereby opening the taping compartment and—oops!"

Carmichael heard the clang of a wrench and saw the bright flare of sparks; Joey leaped back, cursing with surprisingly mature skill. Ethel and Myra gasped simultaneously.

"What happened?" four voices—Clyde's coming in last—demanded.

"Dropped the damn wrench," Joey said. "I guess I shorted out something in there."

The robot's eyes were whirling satanically and its voice box was emitting an awesome twelve-cycle rumble. The great metal creature stood stiffly in the middle of the living room; with brusque gestures of its big hands, it slammed shut the open chest plates.

"We'd better call Mr. Robinson," Ethel said worriedly. "A short-circuited robot is likely to explode, or worse."

"We should have called Robinson in the first place," Carmichael murmured bitterly. "It's my fault for letting Joey tinker with an expensive and delicate mechanism like that. Myra, get me the card Mr. Robinson left."

"Gee, Dad, this is the first time I've ever had anything like that go wrong," Joey insisted. "I didn't know—"

"You're darned right you didn't know." Carmichael took the card from his daughter and started towards the phone. "I hope we can reach him at this hour. If we can't—"

Suddenly Carmichael felt cold fingers prying the card from his hand. He was so startled he relinquished it without a struggle. He watched as Bismarck efficiently ripped it into little fragments and shoved them into a wall disposal unit.

The robot said, "There will be no further meddling with my program tapes." Its voice was deep and strangely harsh.

"What—"

"Mr. Carmichael, today you violated the program I set down for you. My perceptors reveal that you consumed an amount far in excess of your daily lunchtime requirement."

"Sam, what—"

"Quiet, Ethel. Bismarck, I order you to shut yourself off at once."

"My apologies, sir. I cannot serve you if I am shut off."

"I don't want you to serve me. You're out of order. I want you to remain still until I can phone the repairman and get him to service you."

Then he remembered the card that had gone into the disposal unit. He felt a faint tremor of apprehension.

"You took Robinson's card and destroyed it."

"Further alteration of my circuits would be detrimental to the Carmichael family," said the robot. "I cannot permit you to summon the repairman."

"Don't get him angry, Dad," Joey warned. "I'll call the police. I'll be back in—"

"You will remain within this house," the robot said. Moving with impressive speed on its oiled treads, it crossed the room, blocking the door, and reached far above its head to activate the impassable privacy field that protected the house. Carmichael watched, aghast, as the inexorable robotic fingers twisted and manipulated the field controls.

"I have now reversed the polarity of the house privacy field," the robot announced. "Since you are obviously not to be trusted to keep to the diet I prescribe, I cannot allow you to leave the premises. You will remain within and continue to obey my beneficial advice."

Calmly, he uprooted the telephone. Next the windows were opaqued and the stud broken off. Finally, the robot seized the instruction book from Joey's numbed hands and shoved it into the disposal unit.

"Breakfast will be served at the usual time," Bismarck said mildly. "For optimum purposes of health, you are all to be asleep by 2300 hours. I shall leave you now, until morning. Good night."

Carmichael did not sleep well that night, nor did he eat well the next day. He awoke late, for one thing—well past nine. He discovered that someone, obviously Bismarck, had neatly canceled out the impulses from the housebrain that woke him at seven each morning.

The breakfast menu was toast and black coffee. Carmichael ate disgruntledly, not speaking, indicating by brusque scowls that he did not want to be spoken to. After the miserable meal had been cleared away, he surreptitiously tiptoed to the front door in his dressing gown, and darted a hand towards the handle.

The door refused to budge. He pushed until sweat dribbled down his face. He heard Ethel whisper warningly, "Sam—" and a moment later cool metallic fingers gently disengaged him from the door.

Bismarck said, "I beg your pardon, sir. The door will not open. I explained this last night."

Carmichael gazed sourly at the gimmicked control box of the privacy field. The robot had them utterly hemmed in. The reversed privacy field made it impossible for them to leave the house; it cast a sphere of force around the entire detached dwelling. In theory, the field could be penetrated from outside, but nobody was likely to come calling without an invitation. Not here in Westley. It wasn't one of those neighborly subdivisions where everybody knew everybody else. Carmichael had picked it for that reason.

"Damn you," he growled, "you can't hold us *prisoners* in here!"

"My intent is only to help you," said the robot, in a mechanical yet dedicated voice. "My function is to supervise your diet. Since you will not obey willingly, obedience must be enforced—for your own good."

Carmichael scowled and walked away. The worst part of it was that the roboservitor sounded so *sincere!*

Trapped. The phone connection was severed. The windows were darkened. Somehow, Joey's attempt at repairs had resulted in a short circuit of the robot's obedience filters, and had also exaggeratedly stimulated its sense of function. Now Bismarck was determined to make them lose weight if it had to kill them to do so.

And that seemed very likely.

Blockaded, the Carmichael family met in a huddled little group to whisper plans for a counterattack. Clyde stood watch, but the robutler seemed to be in a state of general shock since the demonstration of the servitor-robot's independent capacity for action, and Carmichael now regarded him as undependable.

"He's got the kitchen walled off with some kind of electronic-based force web," Joey said. "He must have built it during the night. I tried to sneak in and scrounge some food, and got nothing but a flat nose for trying."

"I know," Carmichael said sadly. "He built the same sort of doohickey around the bar. Three hundred credits of good booze in there and I can't even grab the handle!"

"This is no time to worry about drinking," Ethel said morosely. "We'll be skeletons any day."

"It isn't *that* bad, Mom!" Joey said.

"Yes, it is!" cried Myra. "I've lost five pounds in four days!"

"Is that so terrible?"

"I'm wasting away," she sobbed. "My figure—it's vanishing! And—"

"Quiet," Carmichael whispered. "Bismarck's coming!"

The robot emerged from the kitchen, passing through the force barrier as if it had been a cobweb. It seemed to have effect on humans only, Carmichael thought. "Lunch will be served in eight minutes," it said obsequiously, and returned to its lair.

Carmichael glanced at his watch. The time was 1230 hours. "Probably down at the office they're wondering where I am," he said. "I haven't missed a day's work in years."

"They won't care," Ethel said. "An executive isn't required to account for every day off he takes, you know."

"But they'll worry after three or four days, won't they?" Myra asked. "Maybe they'll try to phone—or even send a rescue mission!"

From the kitchen, Bismarck said coldly, "There will be no danger of that. While you slept this morning, I notified your place of employment that you were resigning."

Carmichael gasped. Then, recovering, he said: "You're lying! The phone's cut off—and you never would have risked leaving the house, even if we were asleep!"

"I communicated with them via a microwave generator I constructed with the aid of your son's reference books last night," Bismarck replied. "Clyde reluctantly supplied me with the number. I also phoned your bank and instructed them to handle for you all such matters as tax payments, investment decisions, etc. To forestall difficulties, let me add that a force web will prevent access on your part to the electronic equipment in the basement. I will be able to conduct such communication with the outside world as will be necessary for your welfare, Mr. Carmichael. You need have no worries on that score."

"No," Carmichael echoed hollowly. "No worries."

He turned to Joey. "We've got to get out of here. Are you sure there's no way of disconnecting the privacy field?"

"He's got one of his force fields rigged around the control box. I can't even get near the thing."

"If only we had an iceman, or an oilman, the way the old-time hous-es did," Ethel said bitterly. "He'd show up and come inside and probably he'd know how to shut the field off. But not here. Oh, no. We've got a shiny chrome-plated cryostat in the basement that dishes out lots of liq-uid helium to run the fancy cryotronic super-cooled power plant that gives us heat and light, and we have enough food in the freezer to last for at least a decade or two, and so we can live like this for years, a neat little self-contained island in the middle of civilization, with nobody bothering us, nobody wondering about us, with Sam Carmichael's pet robot to feed us whenever and as little as it pleases—"

There was a cutting edge to her voice that was dangerously close to hysteria.

"Ethel, please," said Carmichael.

"Please what? Please keep quiet? Please stay calm? Sam, we're *pris-oners* in here!"

"I know. You don't have to raise your voice."

"Maybe if I do, someone will hear us and come get us out," she replied more coolly.

"It's four hundred feet to the next home, dear. And in the seven years we've lived here, we've had about two visits from our neighbors. We paid a stiff price for seclusion and now we're paying a stiffer one. But please keep under control, Ethel."

"Don't worry, Mom. I'll figure a way out of this," Joey said reassuringly.

In one corner of the living room, Myra was sobbing quietly to her-self, blotching her makeup. Carmichael felt a faintly claustrophobic quiver. The house was big, three levels and twelve rooms, but even so he could get tired of it very quickly.

"Luncheon is served," the roboservitor announced in booming tones.

And tired of lettuce-and-tomato lunches, too, Carmichael added silently; as he shepherded his family towards the dining room for their meager midday meal.

"You have to do *something* about this, Sam," Ethel Carmichael said on the third day of their imprisonment.

He glared at her. "Have to, eh? And just what am I supposed to do?"

"Daddy, don't get excited," Myra said.

He whirled on her. "Don't tell me what I should or shouldn't do!"

"She can't help it, dear. We're all a little overwrought. After all, cooped up here—"

"I know. Like lambs in a pen," he finished acidly. "Except that we're not being fattened for slaughter. We're—being *thinned,* and for our own alleged good!"

Carmichael subsided gloomily. Toast-and-black-coffee, lettuce-and-tomato, rare-steak-and-peas. Bismarck's channels seemed to have frozen permanently at that daily menu.

But what could he do?

Contact with the outside world was impossible. The robot had erected a bastion in the basement from which he conducted such little business with the world as the Carmichael family had. Generally, they were self-sufficient. And Bismarck's force fields ensured the impossibility of any attempts to disconnect the outer sheath, break into the basement, or even get at the food supply or the liquor. It was all very neat, and the four of them were fast approaching a state of starvation.

"Sam?"

He lifted his head wearily. "What is it, Ethel?"

"Myra had an idea before. Tell him, Myra."

"Oh, it would never work," Myra said demurely.

"Tell him!"

"Well—Dad, you *could* try to turn Bismarck off."

"Huh?" Carmichael grunted.

"I mean if you or Joey could distract him somehow, then Joey or you could open him up again and—"

"No," Carmichael snapped. "That thing's seven feet tall and weighs three hundred pounds. If you think *I'm* going to wrestle with it—"

"We could let Clyde try," Ethel suggested.

Carmichael shook his head vehemently. "The carnage would be frightful."

Joey said, "Dad, it may be our only hope."

"You too?" Carmichael asked.

He took a deep breath. He felt himself speared by two deadly feminine glances, and he knew there was no hope but to try it. Resignedly, he pushed himself to his feet and said, "Okay. Clyde, go call Bismarck. Joey, I'll try to hang on to his arms while you open up his chest. Yank anything you can."

"Be careful," Ethel warned. "If there's an explosion—"

"If there's an explosion, we're all free," Carmichael said testily. He turned to see the broad figure of the roboservitor standing at the entrance to the living room.

"May I be of service, sir?"

"You may," Carmichael said. "We're having a little debate here and we want your evidence. It's a matter of defannizing the poozlestan and—*Joey, open him up!*"

Carmichael grabbed for the robot's arms, trying to hold them without getting hurled across the room, while his son clawed frantically at the stud that opened the robot's innards. Carmichael anticipated immediate destruction—but, to his surprise, he found himself slipping as he tried to grasp the thick arms.

"Dad, it's no use. I—he—"

Carmichael found himself abruptly four feet off the ground. He heard Ethel and Myra scream and Clyde's "*Do* be careful, sir."

Bismarck was carrying them across the room, gently, cradling him in one giant arm and Joey in the other. It set them down on the couch and stood back.

"Such an attempt is highly dangerous," Bismarck said reprovingly. "It puts me in danger of harming you physically. Please avoid any such acts in the future."

Carmichael stared broodingly at his son. "Did you have the same trouble I did?"

Joey nodded. "I couldn't get within an inch of his skin. It stands to reason, though. He's built one of those damned force screens around himself, too!"

Carmichael groaned. He did not look at his wife and his children. Physical attack on Bismarck was now out of the question. He began to feel as if he had been condemned to life imprisonment—and that his stay in durance vile would not be extremely prolonged.

In the upstairs bathroom, six days after the beginning of the blockade, Sam Carmichael stared at his haggard fleshless face in the mirror before wearily climbing on the scale.

He weighed 180 pounds.

He had lost twelve pounds in less than two weeks. He was fast becoming a quivering wreck.

A thought occurred to him as he stared at the wavering needle on the scale, and sudden elation spread over him. He dashed downstairs. Ethel was doggedly crocheting in the living room; Joey and Myra were playing cards grimly, desperately now, after six solid days of gin rummy and honeymoon bridge.

"Where's that robot?" Carmichael roared. "Come out here!"

"In the kitchen," Ethel said tonelessly.

"Bismarck! Bismarck!" Carmichael roared. "Come out here!"

The robot appeared. "How may I serve you, sir?"

"Damn you, scan me with your superpower receptors and tell me how much I weigh!"

After a pause, the robot said gravely, "One hundred seventy-nine pounds eleven ounces, Mr. Carmichael."

"Yes! Yes! And the original program I had taped into you was supposed to reduce me from 192 to 180," Carmichael crowed triumphantly. "So I'm finished with you, as long as I don't gain any more weight. And so are the rest of us, I'll bet. Ethel! Myra! Joey! Upstairs and weigh yourselves!"

But the robot regarded him with a doleful glare and said, "Sir, I find no record within me of any limitation on your reduction of weight."

"*What?*"

"I have checked my tapes fully. I have a record of an order causing weight reduction, but that tape does not appear to specify a *terminus ad quem.*"

Carmichael exhaled and took three staggering steps backward. His legs wobbled; he felt Joey supporting him. He mumbled, "But I thought—I'm sure we did—I *know* we instructed you—"

Hunger gnawed at his flesh. Joey said softly, "Dad, probably that part of his tape was erased when he short-circuited."

"Oh," Carmichael said numbly.

He tottered into the living room and collapsed heavily in what had once been his favorite armchair. It wasn't any more. The entire house had become odious to him. He longed to see the sunlight again, to see trees and grass, even to see that excrescence of an ultramodern house that the left-hand neighbors had erected.

But now that would be impossible. He had hoped, for a few minutes at least, that the robot would release them from dietary bondage when the original goal was shown to be accomplished. Evidently that was to be denied him. He giggled, then began to laugh.

"What's so funny, dear?" Ethel asked. She had lost her earlier tendencies to hysteria, and after long days of complex crocheting now regarded the universe with quiet resignation.

"Funny? The fact that I weigh 180 now. I'm lean, trim, fit as a fiddle. Next month I'll weigh 170. Then 160. Then finally about 88 pounds or so. We'll all shrivel up. Bismarck will starve us to death."

"Don't worry, Dad. We're going to get out of this."

Somehow Joey's brash boyish confidence sounded forced now. Carmichael shook his head. "We won't. We'll never get out. And Bismarck's going to reduce us *ad infinitum*. He's got no *terminus ad quem!*"

"What's he saying?" Myra asked.

"It's Latin," Joey explained. "But listen, Dad—I have an idea that I think will work." He lowered his voice. "I'm going to try to adjust Clyde, see? If I can get a sort of multiphase vibrating effect in his neural pathway, maybe I can slip him through the reversed privacy field. He can go get help, find someone who can shut the field off. There's an article on multiphase generators in last month's *Popular Electromagnetics* and it's in my room upstairs. I—"

His voice died away. Carmichael, who had been listening with the air of a condemned man hearing his reprieve, said impatiently, "Well? Go on. Tell me more."

"Didn't you hear that, Dad?"

"Hear what?"

"The front door. I thought I heard it open just now."

"We're all cracking up," Carmichael said dully. He cursed the salesman at Marhew, he cursed the inventor of cryotronic robots, he cursed the day he had first felt ashamed of good old Jemima and resolved to replace her with a new model.

"I hope I'm not intruding, Mr. Carmichael," a new voice said apologetically.

Carmichael blinked and looked up. A wiry, ruddy-cheeked figure in a heavy peajacket had materialized in the middle of the living room. He was clutching a green metal toolbox in one gloved hand. He was Robinson, the robot repairman.

Carmichael asked hoarsely, "How did you get in?"

"Through the front door. I could see a light on inside, but nobody answered the doorbell when I rang, so I stepped in. Your doorbell's out of order. I thought I'd tell you. I know it's rude—"

"Don't apologize," Carmichael muttered. "We're delighted to see you."

"I was in the neighborhood, you see, and I figured I'd drop in and see how things were working out with your new robot," Robinson said.

Carmichael told him crisply and precisely and quickly. "So we've been prisoners in here for six days," he finished. "And your robot is gradually starving us to death. We can't hold out much longer."

The smile abruptly left Robinson's cheery face. "I *thought* you all looked rather unhealthy. Oh, damn, now there'll be an investigation and all kinds of trouble. But at least I can end your imprisonment."

He opened his toolbox and selected a tubular instrument eight inches long, with a glass bulb at one end and a trigger attachment at the other. "Force-field damper," he explained. He pointed it at the control box of the privacy field and nodded in satisfaction. "There. Great little gadget. That neutralizes the effects of what the robot did and you're no longer blockaded. And now, if you'll produce the robot—"

Carmichael sent Clyde off to get Bismarck. The robutler returned a few moments later, followed by the looming roboservitor. Robinson grinned gaily, pointed the neutralizer at Bismarck and squeezed. The robot froze in midglide, emitting a brief squeak.

"There. That should immobilize him. Let's have a look in that chassis now."

The repairman quickly opened Bismarck's chest and, producing a pocket flash, peered around in the complex interior of the servomechanism, making occasional clucking inaudible comments.

Overwhelmed with relief, Carmichael shakily made his way to a seat. Free! Free at last! His mouth watered at the thought of the meals he was going to have in the next few days. Potatoes and Martinis and warm buttered rolls and all the other forbidden foods!

"Fascinating," Robinson said, half to himself. "The obedience filters are completely shorted out, and the purpose nodes were somehow soldered together by the momentary high-voltage arc. I've never seen anything quite like this, you know."

"Neither had we," Carmichael said hollowly.

"Really, though—this is an utterly new breakthrough in robotic science! If we can reproduce this effect, it means we can build self-willed robots—and think of what that means to science!"

"We know already," Ethel said.

"I'd love to watch what happens when the power source is operating," Robinson went on. "For instance, is that feedback loop really negative or—"

"No!" five voices shrieked at once—with Clyde, as usual, coming in last.

It was too late. The entire event had taken no more than a tenth of a second. Robinson had squeezed his neutralizer trigger again, activating Bismarck—and in one quick swoop the roboservitor seized neutralizer and toolbox from the stunned repairman, activated the privacy field once again, and exultantly crushed the fragile neutralizer between two mighty fingers.

Robinson stammered, "But—but—"

"This attempt at interfering with the well-being of the Carmichael family was ill advised," Bismarck said severely. He peered into the toolbox, found a second neutralizer and neatly reduced it to junk. He clanged shut his chest plates.

Robinson turned and streaked for the door, forgetting the reactivated privacy field. He bounced back hard, spinning wildly around. Carmichael rose from his seat just in time to catch him.

There was a panicky, trapped look on the repairman's face. Carmichael was no longer able to share the emotion; inwardly he was numb, totally resigned, not minded for further struggle.

"He—he moved, so *fast!*" Robinson burst out.

"He did indeed," Carmichael said tranquilly. He patted his hollow stomach and sighed gently. "Luckily, we have an unoccupied guest bedroom for you, Mr. Robinson. Welcome to our happy little home. I hope you like toast and black coffee for breakfast."

OZYMANDIAS

The same November 1958 issue of Larry Shaw's Infinity *that contained "There Was An Old Woman" included this one also, under the pseudonym of "Ivar Jorgenson," a name which really belonged to a writer named Paul W. Fairman but through complicated maneuverings, which are described thoroughly in my collection* In the Beginning, *had become attached to me. (Attached to the point where a really dreadful novel by Fairman that was published under the Jorgenson byline, or rather "Jorgensen," as he preferred to spell it, is occasionally presented to me at a science-fiction convention to be autographed. I always decline to take credit for it on the grounds that it wasn't my work, and I hope they believe me.) "Ozymandias" was one of—good God—eighteen short stories and magazine articles that I turned out in January, 1958. And not the worst of them, either. My lifelong preoccupation with archaeology again shows through here.*

The planet had been dead about a million years. That was our first impression, as our ship orbited down to its sere brown surface, and as it happened our first impression turned out to be right. There had been a civilization here once—but Earth had swung around Sol ten-to-the-sixth times since the last living being of this world had drawn breath.

"A dead planet," Colonel Mattern exclaimed bitterly. "Nothing here that's of any use. We might as well pack up and move on."

It was hardly surprising that Mattern would feel that way. In urging

329

a quick departure and an immediate removal to some world of greater utilitarian value, Mattern was, after all, only serving the best interests of his employers. His employers were the General Staff of the Armed Forces of the United States of America. They expected Mattern and his half of the crew to produce results, and by way of results they meant new weapons and military alliances. They hadn't tossed in 70 per cent of the budget for this trip just to sponsor a lot of archaeological putterings.

But lucky for *our* half of the outfit—the archaeological putterers' half—Mattern did not have an absolute voice in the affairs of the outfit. Perhaps the General Staff had kicked in for 70 per cent of our budget, but the cautious men of the military's Public Liaison branch had seen to it that we had at least some rights.

Dr. Leopold, head of the non-military segment of the expedition, said brusquely, "Sorry, Mattern, but I'll have to apply the limiting clause here."

Mattern started to sputter. "But—"

"But nothing, Mattern. We're here. We've spent a good chunk of American cash in getting here. I insist that we spend the minimum time allotted for scientific research, as long as we *are* here."

Mattern scowled, looking down at the table, supporting his chin on his thumbs and digging the rest of his fingers in hard back of his jawbone. He was annoyed, but he was smart enough to know he didn't have much of a case to make against Leopold.

The rest of us—four archaeologists and seven military men; they outnumbered us a trifle—watched eagerly as our superiors battled. My eyes strayed through the porthole and I looked at the dry windblown plain, marked here and there with the stumps of what might have been massive monuments millennia ago.

Mattern said bleakly, "The world is of utterly no strategic consequence. Why, it's so old that even the vestiges of civilization have turned to dust!"

"Nevertheless, I reserve the right granted to me to explore any world we land on, for a period of at least one hundred sixty-eight hours," Leopold returned implacably.

Exasperated, Mattern burst out, "Dammit, *why*? Just to spite me? Just to prove the innate intellectual superiority of the scientist to the man of war?"

"Mattern, I'm not injecting personalities into this."

"I'd like to know what you *are* doing, then? Here we are on a world that's obviously useless to me and probably just as useless to you. Yet you stick me on a technicality and force me to waste a week here. Why, if not out of spite?"

"We've made only the most superficial reconnaissance so far," Leopold, said. "For all we know this place may be the answer to many questions of galactic history. It may even be a treasure-trove of super-bombs, for all—"

"Pretty damned likely!" Mattern exploded. He glared around the conference room, fixing each of the scientific members of the committee with a baleful stare. He was making it quite clear that he was trapped into a wasteful expense of time by our foggy-eyed desire for Knowledge.

Useless knowledge. Not good hard practical knowledge of the kind *he* valued.

"All right," he said finally. "I've protested and I've lost, Leopold. You're within your rights in insisting on remaining here one week. But you'd damned well better be ready to blast off when your time's up!"

It had been foregone all along, of course. The charter of our expedition was explicit on the matter. We had been sent out to comb a stretch of worlds near the Galactic Rim that had already been brushed over hastily by a survey mission.

The surveyors had been looking simply for signs of life, and, finding none, they had moved on. We were entrusted with the task of investigating in detail. Some of the planets in the group had been inhabited once, the surveyors had reported. None bore present life.

Our job was to comb through the assigned worlds with diligence. Leopold, leading our group, had the task of doing pure archaeological research on the dead civilizations; Mattern and his men had the more immediately practical job of looking for fissionable material, leftover alien weapons, possible sources of lithium or tritium for fusion, and other such militarily useful things. You could argue that in a strictly pragmatic sense our segment of the group was just dead weight, carted along for the ride at great expense, and you would be right.

But the public temper over the last few hundred years in America had frowned on purely military expeditions. And so, as a sop to the nation's conscience, five archaeologists, of little empirical consequence so far as national security mattered, were tacked onto the expedition.

Us.

Mattern made it quite clear at the outset that *his* boys were the Really Important members of the expedition, and that we were simply ballast. In a way, we had to agree. Tension was mounting once again on our sadly disunited planet; there was no telling when the Other Hemisphere would rouse from its quiescence of a hundred years and decide to plunge once more into space. If anything of military value lay out here, we knew we had to find it before They did.

The good old armaments race. Hi-ho! The old space stories used to talk about expeditions from Earth. Well, we *were* from Earth, abstractly speaking—but in actuality we were from America, period. Global unity was as much of a pipedream as it had been three hundred years earlier, in the remote and primitive chemical-rocket era of space travel. Amen. End of sermon. We got to work.

The planet had no name, and we didn't give it one; a special commission of what was laughably termed the United Nations Organization was working on the problem of assigning names to the hundreds of worlds of the galaxy, using the old idea of borrowing from ancient Terran mythologies in analogy to the Mercury-Venus-Mars nomenclature of our own system.

Probably they would end up saddling this world with something like Thoth or Bel-Marduk or perhaps Avalokitesvara. We knew it simply as Planet Four of the system belonging to a yellow-white FS IV Procyonoid sun, Revised HD Catalogue # 170861.

It was roughly Earthtype, with a diameter of 6100 miles, a gravity index of .93, a mean temperature of 45 degrees F. with a daily fluctuation range of about ten degrees, and a thin, nasty atmosphere composed mostly of carbon dioxide with wisps of helium and hydrogen and the barest smidgeon of oxygen. Quite possibly the air had been breathable by humanoid life millions of years ago—but that was millions of years ago. We took good care to practice our breathing-mask drills before we ventured out of the ship.

The sun, as noted, was an FS IV and fairly hot, but Planet Four was a hundred eighty-five million miles away from it at perihelion, and a good deal further when it was at the other swing of its rather eccentric orbit; the good old Keplerian ellipse took quite a bit of punishment in this system. Planet Four reminded me in many ways of Mars—except that Mars, of course, had never known intelligent life of any kind, at least none that had troubled to leave a hint of its existence, while this planet had obviously had a flourishing civilization at a time when Pithecanthropus was Earth's noblest being.

In any event, once we had thrashed out the matter of whether or not we were going to stay here or pull up and head for the next planet on our schedule, the five of us set to work. We knew we had only a week—Mattern would never grant us an extension unless we came up with something good enough to change his mind, which was improbable—and we wanted to get as much done in that week as possible. With the sky as full of worlds as it is, this planet might never be visited by Earth scientists again.

Mattern and his men served notice right away that they were going to help us, but reluctantly and minimally. We unlimbered the three small halftracks carried aboard ship and got them into functioning order. We stowed our gear—cameras, picks and shovels, camel's-hair brushes—and donned our breathing-masks, and Mattern's men helped us get the halftracks out of the ship and pointed in the right direction.

Then they stood back and waited for us to shove off.

"Don't any of you plan to accompany us?" Leopold asked. The half-tracks each held up to four men.

Mattern shook his head. "You fellows go out by yourselves today and let us know what you find. We can make better use of the time filing and catching up on back log entries."

I saw Leopold start to scowl. Mattern was being openly contemptuous; the least he could do was have his men make a token search for fissionable or fusionable matter! But Leopold swallowed down his anger.

"Okay," he said. "You do that. If we come across any raw veins of plutonium I'll radio back."

"Sure," Mattern said. "Thanks for the favor. Let me know if you find a brass mine, too." He laughed harshly. "Raw plutonium! I half believe you're serious!"

We had worked out a rough sketch of the area, and we split up into three units. Leopold, alone, headed straight due west, towards the dry riverbed we had spotted from the air. He intended to check alluvial deposits, I guess.

Marshall and Webster, sharing one halftrack, struck out to the hilly country southeast of our landing point. A substantial city appeared to be buried under the sand there. Gerhardt and I, in the other vehicle, made off to the north, where we hoped to find remnants of yet another city. It was a bleak, windy day; the endless sand that covered this world mounted into little dunes before us, and the wind picked up handfuls and tossed it against the plastic dome that covered our truck. Underneath the steel cleats of our tractor-belt, there was a steady crunch-crunch of metal coming down on sand that hadn't been disturbed in millennia.

Neither of us spoke for a while. Then Gerhardt said, "I hope the ship's still there when we get back to the base."

Frowning, I turned to look at him as I drove. Gerhardt had always been an enigma: a small scrunchy guy with untidy brown hair flapping in his eyes, eyes that were set a little too close together. He had a degree from the University of Kansas and had put in some time on their field staff with distinction, or so his references said.

I said, "What the hell do you mean?"

"I don't trust Mattern. He hates us."

"He doesn't. Mattern's no villain—just a fellow who wants to do his job and go home. But what do you mean, the ship not being there?"

"He'll blast off without us. You see the way he sent us all out into the desert and kept his own men back. I tell you, he'll strand us here!"

I snorted. "Don't be a paranoid. Mattern won't do anything of the sort."

"He thinks we're dead weight on the expedition," Gerhardt insisted. "What better way to get rid of us?"

The halftrack breasted a hump in the desert. I kept wishing a vulture would squeal somewhere, but there was not even that. Life had left this world ages ago. I said, "Mattern doesn't have much use for us, sure. But would he blast off and leave three perfectly good halftracks behind? Would he?"

It was a good point. Gerhardt grunted agreement after a while. Mattern would never toss equipment away, though he might not have such scruples about five surplus archaeologists.

We rode along silently for a while longer. By now we had covered twenty miles through this utterly barren land. As far as I could see, we might just as well have stayed at the ship. At least there we had a surface lie of building foundations.

But another ten miles and we came across our city. It seemed to be of linear form, no more than half a mile wide and stretching out as far as we could see—maybe six or seven hundred miles; if we had time, we would check the dimensions from the air.

Of course it wasn't much of a city. The sand had pretty well covered everything, but we could see foundations jutting up here and there, weathered lumps of structural concrete and reinforced metal. We got out and unpacked the power-shovel.

An hour later, we were sticky with sweat under our thin spacesuits and we had succeeded in transferring a few thousand cubic yards of soil from the ground to an area a dozen yards away. We had dug one devil of a big hole in the ground.

And we had nothing.

Nothing. Not an artifact, not a skull, not a yellowed tooth. No spoons, no knives, no baby-rattles.

Nothing.

The foundations of some of the buildings had endured, though whittled down to stumps by a million years of sand and wind and rain. But nothing else of this civilization had survived. Mattern, in his scorn, had been right, I admitted ruefully: this planet was as useless to us as it was to them. Weathered foundations could tell us little except that there had once been a civilization here. An imaginative palaeontologist can reconstruct a dinosaur from a fragment of a thighbone, can sketch out a presentable saurian with only a fossilized ischium to guide him. But could we extrapolate a culture, a code of laws, a technology, a philosophy, from bare weathered building foundations?

Not very likely.

We moved on and dug somewhere else half a mile away, hoping at least to unearth one tangible remnant of the civilization that had been. But time had done its work; we were lucky to have the building foundations. All else was gone.

"*Boundless and bare, the lone and level sands stretch far away,*" I muttered.

Gerhardt looked up from his digging. "Eh? What's that?" he demanded.

"Shelley," I told him.

"Oh. Him."

He went back to digging.

Late in the afternoon we finally decided to call it quits and head back to the base. We had been in the field for seven hours and had nothing to show for it except a few hundred feet of tridim films of building foundations.

The sun was beginning to set; Planet Four had a thirty-five hour day, and it was coming to its end. The sky, always somber, was darkening now. There was no moon. Planet Four had no satellites. It seemed a bit unfair; Three and Five of the system each had four moons, while around the massive gas giant that was Eight a cluster of thirteen moonlets whirled.

We wheeled round and headed back, taking an alternate route three miles east of the one we had used on the way out, in case we might spot something. It was a forlorn hope, though.

Six miles along our journey, the truck radio came to life. The dry, testy voice of Dr. Leopold reached us:

"Calling Trucks Two and Three. Two and Three, do you read me? Come in, Two and Three."

Gerhardt was driving. I reached across his knee to key in the response channel and said, "Anderson and Gerhardt in Number Three, sir. We read you."

A moment later, somewhat more faintly, came the sound of Number Two keying into the three-way channel, and I heard Marshall saying, "Marshall and Webster in Two, Dr. Leopold. Is something wrong?"

"I've found something," Leopold said.

From the way Marshall exclaimed *"Really!"* I knew that Truck Number Two had had no better luck than we. I said, "That makes one of us, then."

"You've had no luck, Anderson?"

"Not a scrap. Not a potsherd."

"How about you, Marshall?"

"Check. Scattered signs of a city, but nothing of archaeological value, sir."

I heard Leopold chuckle before he said, "Well, I've found something. It's a little too heavy for me to manage by myself. I want both outfits to come out here and take a look at it."

"What is it, sir?" Marshall and I asked simultaneously, in just about the same words.

But Leopold was fond of playing the Man of Mystery. He said, "You'll see when you get here. Take down my coordinates and get a move on. I want to be back at the base by nightfall."

Shrugging, we changed course to head for Leopold's location. He was about seventeen miles southwest of us, it seemed. Marshall and Webster had an equally long trip to make; they were sharply southeast of Leopold's position.

The sky was fairly dark when we arrived at what Leopold had computed as his coordinates. The headlamps of the halftrack lit up the desert for nearly a mile, and at first there was no sign of anyone or anything. Then I spotted Leopold's halftrack parked off to the east, and from the south Gerhardt saw the lights of the third truck rolling towards us.

We reached Leopold at about the same time. He was not alone. There was an—object—with him.

"Greetings, gentlemen." He had a smug grin on his whiskery face. "I seem to have made a find."

He stepped back and, as if drawing an imaginary curtain, let us take a peek at his find. I frowned in surprise and puzzlement. Standing in the sand behind Leopold's halftrack was something that looked very much like a robot.

It was tall, seven feet or more, and vaguely humanoid; that is, it had arms extending from its shoulders, a head on those shoulders, and legs. The head was furnished with receptor plates where eyes, ears, and mouth would be on humans. There were no other openings. The robot's body was massive and squarish, with sloping shoulders, and its dark metal skin was pitted and corroded as by the workings of the elements over uncountable centuries.

It was buried up to its knees in sand. Leopold, still grinning smugly (and understandably proud of his find) said, "Say something to us, robot."

From the mouth-receptors came a clanking sound, the gnashing of—what? Gears?—and a voice came forth, oddly high-pitched but audible. The words were alien and were spoken in a slippery singsong kind of inflection. I felt a chill go quivering down my back.

"It understands what you say?" Gerhardt questioned.

"I don't think so," Leopold said. "Not yet, anyway. But when I address it directly, it starts spouting. I think it's a kind of—well, guide to the ruins, so to speak. Built by the ancients to provide information to passersby; only it seems to have survived the ancients and their monuments as well."

I studied the thing. It *did* look incredibly old—and sturdy; it was so massively solid that it might indeed have outlasted every other vestige of civilization on this planet. It had stopped talking, now, and was simply staring ahead. Suddenly it wheeled ponderously on its base, swung an arm up to take in the landscape nearby, and started speaking again.

I could almost put the words in its mouth: "—*and over here we have the ruins of the Parthenon, chief temple of Athena on the Acropolis. Completed in the year 438 B.C., it was partially destroyed by an explosion in 1687 while in use as a powder magazine by the Turks—*"

"It *does* seem to be a sort of a guide," Webster remarked. "I get the definite feeling that we're being given an historical narration now, all about the wondrous monuments that must have been on this site once."

"If only we could understand what it's saying!" Marshall exclaimed.

"We can try to decipher the language somehow," Leopold said. "Anyway, it's a magnificent find, isn't it? And—"

I began to laugh suddenly. Leopold, offended, glared at me and said, "May I ask what's so funny, Dr. Anderson?"

"Ozymandias!" I said, when I had subsided a bit. "It's a natural! Ozymandias!"

"I'm afraid I don't—"

"Listen to him," I said. "It's as if he was built and put here for those who follow after, to explain to us the glories of the race that built the cities. Only the cities are gone, and the robot is still here! Doesn't he seem to be saying, '*Look on my works, ye Mighty, and despair*'?"

"'*Nothing beside remains,*'" Webster quoted. "It's apt. Builders and cities all gone, but the poor robot doesn't know it, and delivers his spiel nonetheless. Yes. We ought to call him Ozymandias!"

Gerhardt said, "What shall we do with it?"

"You say you couldn't budge it?" Webster asked Leopold.

"It weighs five or six hundred pounds. It can move of its own volition, but I couldn't move it myself."

"Maybe the five of us—" Webster suggested.

"No," Leopold said. An odd smile crossed his face. "We will leave it here."

"What?"

"Only temporarily," he added. "We'll save it—as a sort, of surprise for Mattern. We'll spring it on him the final day, letting him think all along that this planet was worthless. He can rib us all he wants—but when it's time to go, we'll produce our prize!"

"You think it's safe to leave it out here?" Gerhardt asked.

"Nobody's going to steal it," Marshall said.

"And it won't melt in the rain," Webster added.

"But—suppose it walks away?" Gerhardt demanded. "It can do that, can't it?"

Leopold said, "Of course. But where would it go? It will remain where it is, I think. If it moves, we can always trace it with the radar. Back to the base, now; it grows late."

We climbed back into our halftracks. The robot, silent once again, planted knee-deep in the sand, outlined against the darkening sky, swivelled to face us and lifted one thick arm in a kind of salute.

"Remember," Leopold warned us as we left. "Not one word about this to Mattern!"

At the base that night, Colonel Mattern and his seven aides were remarkably curious about our day's activities. They tried to make it seem as if they were taking a sincere interest in our work, but it was perfectly obvious to us that they were simply goading us into telling them what they had anticipated—that we had found absolutely nothing. This was the response they got, since Leopold forbade mentioning Ozymandias. Aside from the robot, the truth was that we had found nothing, and when they learned of this they smiled knowingly, as if saying that had we listened to them in the first place we would all be back on Earth seven days earlier, with no loss.

The following morning after breakfast Mattern announced that he was sending out a squad to look for fissionable materials, unless we objected.

"We'll only need one of the halftracks," he said. "That leaves two for you. You don't mind, do you?"

"We can get along with two," Leopold replied a little sourly. "Just so you keep out of our territory."

"Which is?"

Instead of telling him, Leopold merely said, "We've adequately examined the area to the southeast of here, and found nothing of note. It won't matter to us if your geological equipment chews the place up."

Mattern nodded, eyeing Leopold curiously as if the obvious concealment of our place of operations had aroused suspicions. I wondered whether it was wise to conceal information from Mattern. Well, Leopold wanted to play his little game, I thought; and one way to keep Mattern from seeing Ozymandias was not to tell him where we would be working.

"I thought you said this planet was useless from your viewpoint, Colonel," I remarked.

Mattern stared at me. "I'm sure of it. But it would be idiotic of me not to have a look, wouldn't it—as long as we're spending the time here anyway?"

I had to admit that he was right. "Do you expect to find anything, though?"

He shrugged. "No fissionables, certainly. It's a safe bet that everything radioactive on *this* planet has long since decomposed. But there's always the possibility of lithium, you know."

"Or pure tritium," Leopold said acidly. Mattern merely laughed, and made no reply.

Half an hour later we were bound westward again to the point where we had left Ozymandias. Gerhardt, Webster, and I rode together in one halftrack, and Leopold and Marshall occupied the other. The third, with two of Mattern's men and the prospecting equipment, ventured off to the southeast towards the area Marshall and Webster had fruitlessly combed the day before.

Ozymandias was where we had left him, with the sun coming up behind him and glowing round his sides. I wondered how many sunrises he had seen. Billions, perhaps.

We parked the halftracks not far from the robot and approached, Webster filming him in the bright light of morning. A wind was whistling down from the north, kicking up eddies in the sand.

"Ozymandias have remain here," the robot said as we drew near.

In English.

For a moment we didn't realize what had happened, but what followed afterwards was a five-man quadruple-take. While we gabbled in confusion the robot said, "Ozymandias decipher the language somehow. Seem to be a sort of guide."

"Why—he's parroting fragments from our conversation yesterday," Marshall said.

"I don't think he's parroting," I said. "The words form coherent concepts. He's *talking* to us!"

"Built by the ancients to provide information to passersby," Ozymandias said.

"Ozymandias!" Leopold said. "Do you speak English?"

The response was a clicking noise, followed moments later by, "Ozymandias understand. Not have words enough. Talk more."

The five of us trembled with common excitement. It was apparent now what had happened, and the happening was nothing short of incredible. Ozymandias had listened patiently to everything we had said the night before; then, after we had gone, he had applied his million-year-old mind to the problem of organizing our sounds into sense, and somehow had succeeded. Now it was merely a matter of feeding vocabulary to the creature and letting him assimilate the new words. We had a walking and talking Rosetta Stone!

Two hours flew by so rapidly we hardly noticed their passing. We tossed words at Ozymandias as fast as we could, defining them when possible to aid him in relating them to the others already engraved on his mind.

By the end of that time he could hold a passable conversation with us. He ripped his legs free of the sand that had bound them for centuries—and, serving the function for which he had been built millennia ago, he took us on a guided tour of the civilization that had been and had built him.

Ozymandias was a fabulous storehouse of archaeological data. We could mine him for years.

His people, he told us, had called themselves the Thaiquens (or so it sounded)—had lived and thrived for three hundred thousand local years, and in the declining days of their history had built him, as indestructible guide to their indestructible cities. But the cities had crumbled, and Ozymandias alone remained—bearing with him memories of what had been.

"This was the city of Durab. In its day it held eight million people. Where I stand now was the temple of Decamon, sixteen hundred feet of your measurement high. It faced the Street of the Winds—"

"The Eleventh Dynasty was begun by the accession to the Presidium of Chonnigar IV, in the eighteen thousandth year of the city. It was in the reign of this dynasty that the neighboring planets first were reached—"

"The Library of Durab was on this spot. It boasted fourteen million volumes. None exist today. Long after the builders had gone, I spent time reading the books of the Library and they are memorized within me—"

"The Plague struck down nine thousand a day for more than a year, in that time—"

It went on and on, a cyclopean newsreel, growing in detail as Ozymandias absorbed our comments and added new words to his vocabulary. We followed the robot as he wheeled his way through the desert, our recorders gobbling in each word, our minds numbed and dazed by the magnitude of our find. In this single robot lay waiting to be tapped the totality of a culture that had lasted three hundred thousand years! We could mine Ozymandias the rest of our lives, and still not exhaust the fund of data implanted in his all-encompassing mind.

When, finally, we ripped ourselves away and, leaving Ozymandias in the desert, returned to the base, we were full to bursting. Never in the history of our science had such a find been vouchsafed: a complete record, accessible and translated for us.

We agreed to conceal our find from Mattern once again. But, like small boys newly given a toy of great value, we found it hard to hide our feelings. Although we said nothing explicit, our overexcited manner certainly must have hinted to Mattern that we had not had as fruitless a day as we had claimed.

That, and Leopold's refusal to tell him exactly where we had been working during the day, must have aroused Mattern's suspicions. In any event, during the night as we lay in bed I heard the sound of halftracks rumbling off into the desert; and the following morning, when we entered the messhall for breakfast, Mattern and his men, unshaven and untidy, turned to look at us with peculiar vindictive gleams in their eyes.

Mattern said, "Good morning, gentlemen. We've been waiting for some time for you to arise."

"It's no later than usual, is it?" Leopold asked.

"Not at all. But my men and I have been up all night. We—ah—did a bit of archaeological prospecting while you slept." The Colonel leaned forward, fingering his rumpled lapels, and said, "Dr. Leopold, for what reason did you choose to conceal from me the fact that you had discovered an object of extreme strategic importance?"

"What do you mean?" Leopold demanded—with a quiver taking the authority out of his voice.

"I mean," said Mattern quietly, "the robot you named Ozymandias. Just why did you decide not to tell me about it?"

"I had every intention of doing so before our departure," Leopold said.

Mattern shrugged. "Be that as it may. You concealed the existence of your find. But your manner last night led us to investigate the area—and since the detectors showed a metal object some twenty miles to the west, we headed that way. Ozymandias was quite surprised to learn that there were other Earthmen here."

There was a moment of crackling silence. Then Leopold said, "I'll have to ask you not to meddle with that robot, Colonel Mattern. I apologize for having neglected to tell you of it—I didn't think you were quite so interested in our work—but now I must insist you and your men keep away from it."

"Oh?" Mattern said crisply. "Why?"

"Because it's an archaeological treasure-trove, Colonel. I can't begin to stress its value to us. Your men might perform some casual experiment with it and short circuit its memory channels, or something like that. And so I'll have to assert the rights of the archaeological group of this expedition. I'll have to declare Ozymandias part of our preserve, and off bounds for you."

Mattern's voice suddenly hardened. "Sorry, Dr. Leopold. You can't invoke that now."

"Why not?"

"Because Ozymandias is part of *our* preserve. And off bounds for you, Doctor."

I thought Leopold would have an apoplectic fit right there in the messhall. He stiffened and went white and strode awkwardly across the room towards Mattern. He choked out a question, inaudible to me.

Mattern replied, "Security, Doctor. Ozymandias is of military use. Accordingly we've brought him to the ship and placed him in sealed quarters, under top-level wraps. With the power entrusted to me for such emergencies, I'm declaring this expedition ended. We return to Earth at once with Ozymandias."

Leopold's eyes bugged. He looked at us for support, but we said nothing. Finally, incredulously, he said, "He's—of military use?"

"Of course. He's a storehouse of data on the ancient Thaiquen weapons. We've already learned things from him that are unbelievable in their scope. Why do you think this planet is bare of life, Dr. Leopold? Not even a blade of grass? A million years won't do that. But a super-weapon *will*. The Thaiquens developed that weapon. And others, too. Weapons that can make your hair curl. And Ozymandias knows every detail of them. Do you think we can waste time letting you people fool with that robot, when he's loaded with military information that can make America totally impregnable? Sorry, Doctor. Ozymandias is your find, but he belongs to us. And we're taking him back to Earth."

Again the room was silent. Leopold looked at me, at Webster, at Marshall, at Gerhardt. There was nothing that could be said.

This was basically a militaristic mission. Sure, a few archaeologists had been tacked onto the crew, but fundamentally it was Mattern's men and not

Leopold's who were important. We weren't out here so much to increase the fund of general knowledge as to find new weapons and new sources of strategic materials for possible use against the Other Hemisphere.

And new weapons had been found. New, undreamed-of weapons, product of a science that had endured for three hundred thousand years. All locked up in Ozymandias' imperishable skull.

In a harsh voice Leopold said, "Very well, Colonel. I can't stop you, I suppose."

He turned and shuffled out without touching his food, a broken, beaten, suddenly very old man.

I felt sick.

Mattern had insisted the planet was useless and that stopping here was a waste of time; Leopold had disagreed, and Leopold had turned out to be right. We had found something of great value.

We had found a machine that could spew forth new and awesome recipes for death. We held in our hands the sum and essence of the Thaiquen science—the science that had culminated in magnificent weapons, weapons so superb they had succeeded in destroying all life on this world. And now we had access to those weapons. Dead by their own hand, the Thaiquens had thoughtfully left us a heritage of death.

Grey-faced, I rose from the table and went to my cabin. I wasn't hungry now.

"We'll be blasting off in an hour," Mattern said behind me as I left. "Get your things in order."

I hardly heard him. I was thinking of the deadly cargo we carried, the robot so eager to disgorge its fund of data. I was thinking what would happen when our scientists back on Earth began learning from Ozymandias.

The works of the Thaiquens now were ours. I thought of the poet's lines: *"Look on my works, ye Mighty—and despair."*

COUNTERPART

By May of 1958 I had been, by my own reckoning, a professional science-fiction writer for nearly three years, dating from the time in June, 1955, when Randall Garrett and I began collaborating in the mass production of short stories. In those three years I had accomplished all sorts of things far beyond my wildest adolescent fantasies. I had sold several hundred stories to every magazine in the business from the top (Astounding, Galaxy, Fantasy & Science Fiction *to the bottom* (Bob Lowndes' various half-cent-a-word-on-publication titles.) *I had won the Hugo for Most Promising New Author. My income was considerable and I no longer fretted over how I was going to pay next month's rent on that elegant apartment on West End Avenue. Indeed, in the summer of 1957 we had splurged on the first of what would be many European journeys for me, a trip to England and France, and within another year or two we were regularly flying down to the West Indies for an annual February holiday also. I developed a taste for good food and fine wines and began to explore New York's best restaurants. It was a pretty startling life for someone not yet two years out of college.*

Then, too, I had swiftly found a place for myself in the bustling science-fiction social scene of the era, when nearly everybody of any importance in science fiction, except for a few Californians, lived in and around New York City: though I was much younger than everybody else, I moved freely through that dazzling group, readily accepted as a friend by such writers as James Blish, Isaac Asimov, Robert Sheckley, Lester del Rey, Frederik Pohl, Algis Budrys, Damon Knight, Phil Klass ("William Tenn"), Avram Davidson, Theodore Sturgeon, Cyril Kornbluth, Harry Harrison, and many more. One part of me, the star-struck boy who had been reading the fiction of these people since his teens, could hardly cease marveling at the ease with which I had won acceptance within that group; but on some other level I had come to terms with the fact that I was now one of them, the youngest of the s-f pros but a pro nevertheless, and that this was what my life was going to be like thenceforth. And, though most of them are gone by now, I have maintained my friendships with some of those people for more than half a century.

An aspect of that life that was growing increasingly troublesome to me, however, was the sense that my new friends in the professional s-f community privately deplored the ease with which I moved between the world of seriously conceived science fiction and that of absolute hackwork. Many of them had churned out a bit of hackery now and then when financial pressures required it—Blish and Knight, for example, had written sports stories for Lowndes' pulp magazines, though they knew next to nothing about sports, and del Rey had written for every kind of pulp there was. But there was a prevailing attitude in the whole crowd that science fiction was something special, a field apart, that it was a kind of holy cause which one should serve to the best of one's writing abilities. If money troubles arrived, getting a real-world job was preferable to turning out hackwork. (Blish was a public-relations man for a pharmaceuticals company, Kornbluth worked for a press service, Pohl, Budrys, and Harrison had held various kinds of editorial jobs, and even Asimov was only a part-time writer, then, who was still on the faculty of Boston University.) I alone had never held any sort of real-world job, and had never had a thought of getting one. By and large, I preferred to write science fiction of the sort that such splendid writers as Sturgeon, Blish, Budrys, and Kornbluth were renowned for; but when the unpaid bills began to mount, I would cheerfully and unhesitatingly turn out whatever some pulp-magazine editor wanted me to write, be it a two-part serial about blue Mercurians and green Martians, or a horror story in which slavering monsters rampaged through Times Square. And few of the others had been so cheerfully and openly opportunistic about writing s-f.

Whatever reservations my friends in the science-fiction community had about that, they kept them to themselves, so far as I could perceive. They could see, after all, how well I was living—the restaurants, the fine apartment, the trips to Europe—and they couldn't very well tell me that I ought to give up such things for the sake of artistic purity and resign myself to the sort of difficult lives of constant financial uncertainty that most of them lived. Only the most outspoken of them—Lester del Rey, who always said what he believed and paid no heed to the consequences, and Fred Pohl, another who always expressed himself straightforwardly—ever criticized me to my face for writing all that junk, both of them arguing that there was more commercial benefit in the long run in taking the high road rather than the low. Who, they said, was ever going to reprint that blue-Mercurian stuff in an anthology, or want it expanded into a novel? I'd get my penny a word for the hackwork and all those stories would sink at once into oblivion, they told me, whereas the best science fiction went through one incarnation after another, and I had to admit that there was some logic in that.

I didn't crave the monastic austerity of the truly devoted science-fiction writer's impoverished life, though, and I still had no interest in taking a part-time job. But as I moved along through my twenties I did begin to feel that it was time for me to start distancing myself from some of that opportunism. At the beginning of my career, neither my writing skills nor my experience of the world had been sufficient to let me compete at the highest levels of the s-f field, but that was starting not to be true any longer. Though still not a convert to the ideal of starving for my art, I began to think that if I needed to write rent-payers, I should do them under pseudonyms for markets outside science fiction—men's magazines, crime-fiction magazines, true confessions, whatever—and, when writing science fiction, try to write with all the ability at my command instead of fulfilling some harried pulp-magazine editor's need for quickly confected formula merchandise.

This feeling, which I had sensed in its first inchoate form at the Milford Writers' Conference of September, 1956, began to crystallize in me at a party at Harlan Ellison's Manhattan apartment in the summer of 1957, shortly before Harlan's departure for military service. I was chatting with Algis Budrys and Cyril Kornbluth, two science-fiction writers who had never compromised their ideals despite pressing financial problems. Kornbluth's health wasn't good—he was to die the following year at 34— and his children had medical problems too. Budrys, just a few years older than I was, had two small children already and a third on the way. They took outside jobs to supplement their modest writing incomes; I, childless and healthy, financed my taste for high living by writing about blue-skinned Mercurians. Though neither of them said a word to me about any of that, I readily imagined that I felt their silent disapproval. And I went home in a seriously troubled mood that afternoon, experiencing something that was not exactly guilt, nor shame, but, at the minimum, a kind of deep uncertainty. I had become a science-fiction writer because I loved science fiction; I had wanted nothing more than to make myself a member of the community of science-fiction writers; and now, having achieved that, I was writing, most of the time, far below the level of my own abilities. Well, I was who I was and I had written what I had written for what had seemed to me to be good and proper reasons, but if what I had hoped was to leave my mark on science fiction—and that was true—then I had to ask myself whether this was the mark I wanted to leave. Out of this inner crisis, this deep restlessness of the summer of 1957 and the months that followed, came a resolution to put as much distance as I could between myself and the sort of facile, even cynical work that I had been doing so much of the time. One of the first products of that change of attitude was the long story that follows here, "Counterpart," which I wrote in May, 1958. It is not, God knows, the equal of the kind of material that Theodore Sturgeon, Fritz Leiber, or Cyril Kornbluth were writing at that time. But neither is it a simpleminded slambang adventure story. As I had in my teens with "Road to Nightfall," but only rarely since, I attempted to populate a science-fiction scenario with realistic characters facing realistic dilemmas, and to tell the story with as much intensity as I could summon. My hope was, I suppose, to sell it to Horace Gold's Galaxy, which from its inception in 1950 had made a specialty of this kind of science fiction. But, as I had seen again and again, Horace, although he often excoriated me for taking the easy way out in my fiction, somehow never wanted to buy my serious stories, only my frivolous ones. John Campbell, now entering the long twilight of his great editorial career, didn't want it either: he seemed to want only stories that reflected his own ideas, at this time. As I matured, I found myself less and less able to write fiction that suited his ideological needs, and his path and mine were about to diverge forever. Nor could I sell the story to the third of the top magazines, Fantasy & Science Fiction, where Robert P. Mills had replaced Anthony Boucher as editor. Tony might well have bought the story, but Mills did not, and suddenly, with many of the other science-fiction magazines now shutting down as a distribution crisis struck magazine publishing, I found myself out of markets for it. So much, I thought, for artistic integrity! In January, 1959, I took the story over to Hans Stefan Santesson of Fantastic Universe, who had published my equally hard-to-sell "Road to Nightfall" a few months before. Hans accepted it gladly enough, and ran it in his October, 1959 issue.

But soon Fantastic Universe would disappear too. By the end of 1959, only about half a dozen science-fiction magazines would remain, a vastly shrunken market indeed for free-lance writers. All the action-adventure s-f magazines for which I had done my hackery were swept away overnight, *but so were most of the outlets for science fiction of a more serious kind. I had, it seemed, chosen a very poor moment to set out on the high road toward artistic integrity.*

Mark Jenner delivered the play's final line with as much force as he could muster, and the curtain dropped like a shroud, cutting off stage from audience. Jenner gasped for breath and fashioned a warm smile for his face to wear. The other six members of the cast left the wings and arranged themselves around him, and the curtain rose again for the calls. A trickle of applause crossed the footlights.

This is it, Jenner thought. *We're through.*

He bowed graciously, peering beyond the glare of the foots to count the house. The theater was about three quarters full—but half the people out there were free-riders, pulled in by the management just to give the house a semblance of fullness. And how many of the others were discount-ticket purchasers? Probably, Jenner thought as the curtain dropped again, there were no more than fifty legitimate customers in the house. And so another play went down the drain. A savage voice within him barked mockingly, telling him that it was his fault, that he no longer had what it took to hold an audience, that he lacked the subtle magnetism needed to pull people out of their homes and into the theater.

There would be no more curtain calls. Tiredly, Jenner walked off into the wings and saw Dan Hall, the producer, standing there. Abruptly the tinsel glamor of curtain calls faded. There could be only one reason why Hall was here now, and the dour, sallow cast of the producer's pudgy face left no doubt in Jenner's mind. Closing notices would be posted tonight. Tomorrow, Mark Jenner would be back to living off capital again and waiting out his days.

"Mark…"

Jenner stopped. Hall had reached out to touch his arm. "Evening, Dan. How goes it?"

"Bad."

"The receipts?"

Hall chuckled dryly. "What receipts? We had a houseful of unemployed actors sitting out there on passes; and the advance sale for tomorrow night is about eleven bucks' worth."

"There isn't going to be any tomorrow night, is there, Dan?" Jenner asked leadenly.

Hall did not answer. Marie Haas, the ingenue, radiant in the sparkling gown that looked so immodest on so young a girl, glided toward them. She wrapped one arm around the rotund producer, one around Jenner. On stage, the hands were busy pulling the set apart.

"Big house tonight, wasn't it?" she twittered.

"I was just telling Mark," Hall said. "Most of those people were unemployed actors here on passes."

"And," Jenner added, "there are seven more unemployed actors here on this stage right now."

"No!" Marie cried.

Jenner tried to smile. It was rough on a girl of nineteen to lose her first big play after a ten-day run; but, he thought, it was rougher on a forty-year-old ex-star. It wasn't so long ago, he told himself, that the name Mark Jenner on a marquee meant an automatic season's run. *Lovely to Look At,* opened October 16, 1973, ran 630 performances. *Lorelei,* opened December 9, 1977, ran 713 performances. *Girl of the Dawn,* opened February 7, 1981, ran 583 performances. *Misty Isle,* opened March 6, 1989—ran ten performances. Jenner peered wearily at the producer. The rest of the cast had gathered round, now, half of them still in war paint and costume. As the star, Jenner had the right to ask the question. He asked it.

"We're through, aren't we, Dan?"

Hall nodded slowly. "The theater owner told me tonight that we're below the minimum draw. He's exercising option and throwing us out; he wants to rent the place for video. We're through, all right."

Jenner climbed methodically out of his costume, removed his makeup, cocked a sardonic eye on the spangled star on the door of his dressing cubicle, and left the theater. He had arranged to meet his old friend Walt Hollis after the show for a drink. Hollis was an electrician, currently handling the lights for one of the other Broadway shows—one of the hits. They had agreed to meet in a bar Jenner liked, on Forty-ninth Street off Sixth Avenue.

The bar was a doggedly old-fashioned one, without any of the strippers currently the mode in depuritanized New York, without B-girls, without synthetics, without video. Jenner felt particularly grateful for that last omission.

He sat slumped in the booth, a big, rumpled-looking man just beginning to get fleshy, and gripped the martini in one of his huge hands. He needed the cold drink to unwind the knot of tension in his stomach. Once, acting had unwound it for him; now, an evening on the stage wound it only a little tighter.

"What is it I've lost, Holly?" he demanded. His voice was the familiar crackling baritone of old; automatically, he projected it too far.

The man opposite him frowned, as though he were sagging under the burden of knowing that he was Mark Jenner's oldest and possibly last friend. "You've lost a job, for one thing," Walt Hollis said lightly.

Jenner scowled. "I don't mean that. I mean—why have I lost what I once had? Why have I gone downhill instead of up? I ought to be at the peak of my acting career now; instead, I'm a has-been at forty. Was I just a flash in the pan, then, back in the seventies?"

"No. You had talent."

"Then why did I lose it?"

"You didn't," Hollis said calmly. He took a deep sip of his gin and tonic, leaned back, stared at his much bigger companion. "You didn't lose anything. You just didn't gain."

"I don't understand."

"Yes, you do," Hollis said. His thumbs squeezed against his aching eyeballs for a moment. He had had this conversation with Jenner too often, in the past five years. Jenner simply did not listen. "Acting isn't the easiest profession in the world, Mark. Lord knows I don't have to tell you that. But what you've never grasped is that acting has toughened up tremendously since the days you broke in. And you've remained right at the same level you hit at the start of your career."

Jenner tightened his lips. He felt cold and curiously alone even in this crowded midtown bar.

"I used to be a star," he said.

"*Used* to be. Look, Mark, these days you need something colossal to drag people out of their warm homes and into a Broadway theater. Homes are too comfortable; the streets are too risky. You never can tell when you'll get mugged if you step out after dark. So you don't step out. You stay home."

"People come out to see that British play, the one with what's-his-name in it," Jenner pointed out.

"With Bert Tylor? Of course they do. Tylor has what it takes to get people into a theater."

"And I don't, is that it?" Jenner fought to keep the crispness out of his voice.

Hollis nodded slowly. "You don't have it, Mark. Not any more."

"And what is this—this magic something-or-other that I lack?"

"It's empathy," Hollis said. "The power to get yourself across the footlights, to set up a two-way flow, to get those people in the audience so damned involved in what you're saying that it turns into part of themselves."

Jenner glowered at the small man. "You're not telling me anything I don't know. All you did just now was to define what any actor has to do."

Hollis shook his head. "It's more than that, now. Now you need special help—techniques for reaching the soul of the fellow in the six-buck seat. I've been offering you these techniques for almost a year, but you've been too damned stubborn to listen to me—too proud to admit a gadget could help you."

"I had a part lined up," Jenner said in a weak voice. "Last May Dan Hall came to me, said he was doing a play that looked good for me, and was I interested? Hell, sure I was interested. I hadn't worked for two years; I was supposed to be box-office poison. But Dan signed me."

Hollis said, "And you rehearsed all summer, and half the fall. And played the sticks half the winter while that poor hapless devil of a playwright tried to fix up the play you were killing, Mark."

Jenner sucked in his breath sharply. He began to say something, then throttled it. He shook his head slowly like a bull at bay. "Go on, Holly. I have this coming to me. Don't pull the punches."

The small man said thinly, "You weren't putting that play across the footlights, Mark. So when it finally got to New York it opened in March and closed in March. Okay. You had all the rope you needed, and you sure hanged yourself! Where do you go from here?"

"Nowhere. I'm at the bottom of the heap now."

"You still have a chance," Hollis said. He leaned forward and seemed to be hanging on Jenner's words like an anxious chickenhawk. "I can help you. I've been telling you that for a year."

"I don't want my mind tinkered with."

"You could have your name up in lights again, live in a Fifth Avenue penthouse. You could get back all the things you used to have, before—before you started to slide."

Jenner stared at the little man's pale, unlined face as if Hollis were nothing but a pane of glass, and as if all the secrets of the universe were inscribed on the back of the booth behind him. In a low voice Jenner said, "I won't get *everything* back. Fame, maybe. Money, maybe. But not everything."

"You didn't need to make your wife run away from you," Hollis said with deliberate cruelty. "But maybe you could make her want to come back."

"Would *I* want her back?"

"That's up to you. I can't answer all your questions for you. What time is it?"

"One-fifteen a.m. The morning papers will be out soon. Maybe they'll mention the closing of *Misty Isle*. Maybe there'll be a sticky little paragraph about how Mark Jenner has helped to kill another good play."

"Forget all that," Hollis said sharply. "Stop brooding about the past. You're going to start everything over tonight."

Jenner looked up, surprised. "When did I agree to let you monkey with me, Holly?"

"You didn't. But what else can you do, now?"

The surprise widened on Jenner's face. He looked down and stared at the formica tabletop until the pattern blurred before his eyes. Hollis was right, Jenner realized numbly. There was nothing else to do now, no place else to go, no more ships to come in.

"Okay," Jenner said in a harsh, throaty voice. "You win. Let's get out of here."

They took the Bronx undertube to Hollis' Riverdale home. Jenner kept a car stored in a Fifty-ninth Street garage, but four martinis in little more than an hour and a half had left him too wobbly to drive, and Hollis did not have a license. At half past one in the morning, the tube was crowded; Jenner and Hollis sat in one of the middle cars, and Jenner was bitterly amused to note that nobody seemed to recognize him, or at least no one cared to come over and say, "Pardon me, but are you really…"

In the old days, Jenner recalled, his agents had forbade him strictly to enter the subways. They didn't even have the undertubes then. But if the Mark Jenner of 1977 had entered a subway, he would have been ripped apart, Orpheus-like, by the autograph hunters. Now, he was just another big man with a martini-glaze on his face.

Hollis remained silent all through the twenty-minute trip, and that forced Jenner back on his own inner resources. It was not pleasant for him to have to listen to the output of his own mind for twenty minutes. There were too many memories rising to confront him.

❋

He could remember the tall, gawky teen-age Ohio boy who had overnight turned into the tall, confident New Yorker of twenty-one, back in '70. The School of Dramatic Arts; the wide-eyed hours of discovering Ibsen and Chekhov and Pirandello; the big break, the lead in *Right You Are* at a small off-Broadway house, with a big-name Broadway mogul happening to come to the dingy little second-story theater to see young Jenner's mordant, incisive Laudisi.

The following autumn, a bit part in a short-lived comedy, thanks to that lucky break. Then some television work; after that, a longer part in a serious drama. Finally, in the spring of 1973, an offer to play the juvenile lead in a bit of froth called *Lovely to Look At*. Jenner was twenty-four and obscure when the show opened, that fall; when it closed, two years later, he was famous. He owned two Cadillacs, lived in a penthouse apartment, gave away vintage champagne the way other men handed out cigarettes. In 1976, while out in Hollywood doing the film version of *Lovely*, he unexpectedly married dazzling, bosomy, much-publicized, twenty-year-old Helene Bryan, current queen of the movie colony. Experts predicted that the fabulous Jenner would weary of the pneumatic blonde within months; but Helene turned out to have unexpected depth, wearing a real personality behind her sleek personality mask. In the end it was she who wearied of a down-slipping, bitterly irascible, and incipiently alcoholic Jenner, eleven years later. Eleven years, Jenner thought! They seemed like a week, and the two years of separation a lifetime.

Jenner thought back on the successes. Two years of *Lorelei;* a year and nine months of *Girl of the Dawn;* then the ill-starred turkey, *Hullaballoo;* and finally his last big hit, *Bachelor Lady,* which ran a year—October 1982 to September 1983. After that, almost overnight, people stopped coming to see Mark Jenner act; he had lost his hold. In the season of 1986-87 he appeared in no less than three plays, the longest-lived of which held the boards for five weeks. Somewhere along the line, he had lost his magic. He had also lost Helene, in that dreadful spring of 1987 when she returned to California to stay.

And somewhere along the line, Jenner realized he had lost the eager young man who loved Ibsen and Chekhov and Pirandello. As a professional, he had specialized almost exclusively in frothy romantic confections. That was unintentional; it was simply that he could never resist a producer waving a fat contract. It wouldn't have mattered, much, except that he kept up contact with Walt Hollis, one of the first people he had met when he came to New York, and Hollis served to remind Jenner of the Pirandello days.

Hollis had never been an actor. He was a lighting technician in the old days, and a lighting technician he still was, the best of his craft—a slim, mousy little man who looked no older at fifty than he had at thirty. Hollis had been more than a mere electrician, though. He was a theoretician, a student of the acting technique, a graduate engineer as well. He tinkered with gadgets, and sometimes he told Jenner about them. Jenner listened with open ears, never retaining a thing.

Two years ago, Hollis had told him of something new he was developing—a technique that might be able to turn any man with a bit of acting skill into a Barrymore, into an Olivier. Jenner had laughed. In that year, '87, his main concern had been to show the world how self-sufficient he was in the face of adversity. He was not going to grasp at any electronic straws, oh no! That would be admitting he was in trouble!

Well, he was in trouble. And as *Misty Isle* sank rapidly into limbo under a fierce critical barrage, Jenner bleakly realized he could sink no lower himself. Now was the time at last to listen to Hollis. Now was the time to clutch at any offer of salvation. *Now.*

"We're here," Hollis said, breaking a twenty-minute silence. "Watch your step getting out. You don't want to trip and mash up your pretty profile."

In the twenty years he had known Walt Hollis, Jenner had been inside the little man's home no more than a dozen times, and not at all in the last decade. It was a tidy little place, four small rooms, overfastidiously neat. Bookshelves lined the walls—an odd assortment of books, half literary, half technical. Hollis lived by himself; he had never married. That had made it hard for Jenner to see him socially very often; Helene had hated to visit bachelors.

Now Jenner allowed himself to be deposited in a comfortable armchair, while Hollis, ever tense, paced the worn broadloom carpet in front of him. Jenner felt completely helpless. Hollis was his last hope.

Hollis said, "Mark, I'm going to be ruthlessly frank in everything I say to you from tonight on. You aren't going to like the things I say. If you get annoyed, blow off steam. It'll do you good."

"I won't get annoyed," Jenner said tonelessly. "There isn't a thing you could say about me that wouldn't be true."

"You will get annoyed—so annoyed that you'll want to punch me in the face." Hollis grinned shyly. "I hope you'll be able to control that. You've got me by fifty or sixty pounds."

He paced back and forth. Jenner watched him. For twenty years, Mark Jenner had felt a sort of pity for Hollis, for the timid and retiring electrician whose only pleasure seemed to be in helping others. Sure, Hollis made good pay, and he was the best in his business. But for all that, he was just a backstage flunky. Now he was much more than that; he was Jenner's last hope.

Hollis said, "You're going to have to withdraw from your regular activities completely for six months or so, Mark. Give up your room. Move in here with me until the treatment's finished. Then we'll see what we can do about getting you back on Broadway. It may not be easy—but if things work the way I think they'll work, you'll be climbing straight for the stratosphere the month I'm done with you."

"I'll be satisfied just to work regularly. Suppose you tell me what you're going to do to me."

Hollis spun around and jabbed the air with a forefinger. "First let's talk about your past. You were a big hit once, Mark, then you started slipping. Now you're nowhere. Okay: *Why* did it happen?"

"Yeah. You tell me. Why?"

"It happened," Hollis said, "because you failed to adapt to the changing times. You never developed the kind of emotional charge that an actor needs now, if he's going to reach his audience. You stayed put, worshiping the good old status quo. You acted in the 1973 way for fifteen years, but by 1987 it wasn't good enough for the public or for the critics."

"Especially the critics," Jenner growled. "They crucified me!"

"The critics are paid to slap down anything that isn't what the public would consider good entertainment," Hollis said thinly. "You can't blame them; you have to blame yourself. You had an early success, and you stuck at that level until you were left behind."

Jenner nodded gravely. "Okay, Holly. Let's say I frittered away my talent. I'd rather think that than that I never had any talent in the first place. How can you help me?"

Hollis paused in his nervous march and came to light like a fretful butterfly, on a backless wooden chair. "I once explained my technique to you, and you nodded all through it, but I could see you weren't listening. You'll have to listen to me now, Mark, or I can't help you."

"I'm listening."

"I hope so. Briefly, what I'm going to do is put you through a sort of lay analysis…"

"I've *been* analyzed!"

"Keep quiet and listen for a change," Hollis said with a vigor Jenner had never heard him display before. "You'll be put through a sort of lay analysis, under deep narcohypnosis. What I want, actually, is a taped autobiography, going as deep into your life as I can dredge."

"Are you qualified to do this sort of thing?" Jenner asked.

"I'm qualified to build the machine and ask the questions. The psychiatric angle I've researched as thoroughly as possible. The rest comes out of you, until we have the tape."

"Okay," Jenner said. "So what do you do with this tape biography of me?"

"I put it aside," Hollis said. "Then I take another tape, put you under hypnosis again, and feed the *new* tape *into* you. The new tape will be one that I've taken from some other person. It'll be carefully expurgated to keep you from knowing the other person's identity, but you'll get a deep whiff of his personality. Then I take *your* tape and pipe it into the man who made the other one."

Jenner frowned, not comprehending. "I don't get this. Who's the other person? You?"

"Of course not. He'll be a man you never met. You won't ever see him; you won't ever know who he is. But you'll know what kind of food he likes and why; what he thinks when he's in bed with his wife; how he feels on a hot, sweaty summer day; what he felt like the first time he kissed a girl. You'll remember his getting whopped for stealing cigarettes from his father, and you'll remember his college graduation day. You'll have all his memories, hopes, dreams, fears. He'll have yours."

Jenner squinted and tried to figure out what the little man was heading toward. "What good will all that do—to peek into each other's minds?"

Hollis smiled. "When you build up a character on stage, you mine him out of yourself—out of your own perceptions and reactions and experiences. You take the playwright's bare lines, and you flesh them

out by interpreting words as action, words as expression, words as car-
riers of emotion. If you're a good actor—which means if you have
enough inner resource to swing the trick—you convince the audience
that you are the man the program says you are. If not, you get a job selling popcorn in front of the theater."

"So…"

Hollis swept right on. "So this way you'll have two sets of emotions
and experiences to build on. You can synthesize them into a portrayal
that no actor can begin to give." Hollis locked his thin hands together
over one knee and bent forward, his mild face bright with enthusiasm
now. "Besides, you'll have the advantage of being inside another man's
skull, knowing what makes him tick; it'll give you a perspective you
can't possibly have now. Combining his memories with yours, it'll be
that much easier for you to get inside the audience's collective skull too,
Mark. You see the picture now? You follow what I'm driving at?"

"I think so," Jenner said heavily. With awkwardly deliberate
motions he pulled a cigarette out of Hollis' pack on the table, and lit it.
Jenner did not actually smoke; he valued his throat too highly. But now
he needed something to do with his hands, and the cigarette-lighting
ritual provided it. "But tell me this—what does this other fellow get out
of having *my* tape pumped into him?"

"He's a politician," Hollis said. "By which I mean a man who's in
public life. He wants to run for a high office. He's a capable man, but
with your talent for projection, combined with his own inner drive, he's
sure to win."

"You mean you have the other man picked out already?"

"He's been picked out and waiting for nearly a year. I told him I
would get a great actor to serve as the counterweight on this little see-
saw. He's been waiting. I had you in mind, but it took this flop tonight
to make you come around. You *will* go along with this, won't you?"

Jenner shut his eyes for a moment and drew the burning smoke
deep into his lungs. He felt like gagging. He was drained of all strength;
if Hollis had snapped off the light, he would have fallen asleep on the
spot, clothes and all.

He said, after a moment, "So, I'll be taking another man into my
head with me. And that supposedly will make me a star again. Ah—
have you ever tried this stunt before?"

"You and he will be the first subjects," Hollis confessed.

"And you're confident nothing will go wrong?"

"I'm not confident at all," Hollis said quietly. "It *ought* to work; but it might make both of you gibbering lunatics instead."

"And still you're ready to try this on me?" Jenner asked.

"I wouldn't want you going into it without a warning. But the odds are good in favor of a successful outcome; otherwise I wouldn't dream of asking you to play along with me."

Jenner stubbed out his half-smoked cigarette. He glanced around at the books on the shelves, at the single painting, at the austere furniture. "How long will it take?"

"About six months. I have to edit two tapes, don't forget. And we can't do all the work overnight."

"Will it cost me anything?"

Hollis laughed. "Mark, I'd pay *you* to do this if you wanted me to. I want to help you—and to see if my theories were right."

"I hope they are." Jenner stood up, coming to his full height, squaring his shoulders, trying to play the role of a successful actor even now, when he was nothing but a hollow has-been. "Okay," he said in the resonant Jenner tones. "I commit myself into thy hands, Holly. I've lost everything else a man can lose; I guess it doesn't matter much if I lose my mind."

Jenner woke up in the middle of the next afternoon. He had been asleep for thirteen hours, and he had needed it. Hollis was gone, having left a note explaining that he had to attend a rehearsal in Manhattan and would be back about five. Jenner dressed slowly, remembering the conversation of the night before, realizing that he had effectively pledged his soul to the unmephisthophelean Hollis.

He turned Hollis' sheet of notepaper over and scrawled his own note: *"Going downtown to settle my affairs. Will return later tonight."* He took the undertube back to Manhattan, taxied from the tube station to his hotel, and checked out, settling his bill with cash. For two years he had lived in a twenty-dollar-a-week room in a midtown hotel, with no more personal property than he needed. Most of his possessions had been in storage since the breakup with Helene in '87; he kept hardly enough in the hotel room to fill a single suitcase.

He packed up and left. Dragging the suitcase that contained three changes of clothing, his makeup kit, his useless script for *Misty Isle,* and the 1986-89 volume of his scrapbook, Jenner set out for the tube station again. It was five-thirty. If he made good connections, he could reach Hollis' place a little after six. And that gave him time for a little bit of fortification first.

He stopped at a Lexington Avenue bar and had two martinis. On the third drink he shifted to gibsons. By the fourth, he had acquired a slatternly-looking bar girl with thick orange lipstick; he bought her the requested rye and soda, had one himself, then went into the washroom and got sick. When he came out, the girl was gone. Shrugging, Jenner wandered to another bar and had two more martinis, this time successfully keeping them down. A hundred yards up the block, he had another gibson.

He reached Hollis' place at half past ten, sober enough to walk on his own steam but too drunk to remember what he had done with his suitcase. He kept insisting that Hollis call the police and have them search for the grip, but Hollis merely smiled amiably and ignored him, leading him to the bedroom and putting him to bed. A moment before he fell asleep, Jenner reflected that it was just as well he had lost the suitcase. With it, he had lost his pitiful press clippings of the last four years, as well as his makeup kit and his final script. Now he could shed his past with alacrity; he had no albatrosses slung around his neck.

He woke up at nine the next morning, feeling unaccountably clear-headed and cheerful. The smell of frying bacon reached his nostrils. From the kitchen, Hollis yelled, "Go take a quick shower. Breakfast'll be ready when you come out."

They breakfasted in silence. At twenty of ten, they finished their coffee. Hollis said quietly, "All right, Mark. Are you ready to begin?"

Walt Hollis had rigged an experimental laboratory in his fourth room and he installed Jenner in the middle of it. The room was no more than twelve by fifteen, and it seemed to Jenner that there was an enormous amount of equipment in it. He himself sat in a comfortable chair in the center of the room, facing a diabolically complex bit of apparatus with fluorescent light rings and half a dozen theatrical gelatins to provide a shifting pattern of illuminated color. There was a big tape recorder in the room, with a fifteen-inch reel primed and loaded. There were instruments that Jenner simply could not identify at all; he had no technical background, and he merely classified them as "electronic" and let it go at that.

The room's window had been carefully curtained off; the door frame was lined with felt. When Hollis chose, he could plunge the room into total darkness. Jenner felt an irrational twinge of fear. Obscurely, the machine facing him reminded him of a dentist's drill, an instrument he had always feared and hated. But this drill would bite deep into his mind.

"I won't be in the room with you," Hollis said. "I'll be monitoring from outside. Any time you want me, just raise your right hand and I'll come in. Okay?"

"Okay," Jenner muttered.

"First I've got a pill for you, Mark. Proclorperazine. It's an ataractic."

"A tranquilizer?"

"Call it that; it's just to ease your nerves. You're very tense right now, you know. You're afraid of what I'm going to do."

"Damned right I'm afraid. But you don't see me getting up and running out!"

"Of course not," Hollis said. "Here. Take it."

While Jenner swallowed the pill, Hollis busily rolled up the actor's sleeve and swabbed his arm with alcohol. Jenner watched, already relaxing, as Hollis readied a glittering hypodermic.

"This is the hypnosis-inducing drug, Mark."

"Sodium pentothal? Amytal?"

"Of that family of ego-depressants, yes." Hollis deftly discharged the syringe's contents into one of Jenner's veins. "I've had medical help in preparing this project," he said. "Sit back. Stretch your feet out. Relax, Mark."

Jenner relaxed. He was vaguely conscious of Hollis' final reassuring pat on the shoulder, of the fact that the small man had left the room, that the room had gone dark. He heard a faint hum that might have come either from the tape recorder or from the strange apparatus in the middle of the room.

Colored lights began to play on him. Wheels of bright plastic whirled before his eyes. Jenner stared, fascinated, feeling his tension drain away. All he had to do was relax. Rest. Everything would be all right. Relax.

"Can you hear me, Mark?"

"I hear you."

"Good. Do you feel any discomfort?"

"No discomfort."

"Fine. Listen to me, Mark."

"I'm listening."

"I mean *really* listening, now. Listening with your brain and not just your ears. Are you listening to me, Mark?"

"I'm listening."

"Excellent. This is what I want you to do for me, Mark. I want you to go back and think about your life. Then I want you to tell me all about yourself. Everything. From the beginning."

Spring, 1953. Mark Jenner was four years old. Mark Jenner's brother Tom had reached the ninth of the twelve years he was to have. Tom Jenner had been fighting, against his mother's express orders, and he had been knocked down and bruised.

Mark Jenner stared up at his older brother. Tom's cheek was scraped and bloody, and one side of his mouth was starting to swell puffily.

"Mama's gonna murder you," Mark chortled. "Said you wasn't supposed to fight."

"Wasn't fighting," Tom said.

"I saw you! You picked on Mickey Swenson, and he knocked you down and made your face all bloody!"

"You wouldn't tell mama that, would you?" Tom asked in a low voice. "If she asked you what happened to me, I mean."

Mark blinked. "If she asked, I'd have to tell."

"No," Tom said. His still-pudgy hands gripped Mark's shoulders painfully. "We're gonna go inside. I'm gonna tell mama I tripped on a stone and fell down."

"But you were *fighting!* With Mickey Swenson."

"We don't have to tell mama that. We can tell her something else— make up a story."

"But…"

"All you have to do is say I fell down, that I wasn't fighting with anybody. And I'll give you a nickel. Okay?"

Mark looked puzzled. How could he tell mama something that was not true? It seemed easy enough. All he had to do was move his mouth and the sounds would come out. It seemed important to Tom. Already Mark was beginning to believe that Tom had really fallen, that there had been no fight.

They trooped into the house, the dirty little boy and the dirty littler one. Mrs. Jenner appeared, looming high over both of them, her hands upraised at the sight of her eldest son's battered face.

"Tom! What happened!"

Before Tom could reply, Mark said gravely, "Tom tripped on a stone. He fell down and hurt himself."

"Oh! You poor dear—does it hurt?"

As Mrs. Jenner trooped Tom off to the bathroom for repairs, Mark Jenner, four years old, experienced a curious warm sensation of pride. He had told his first conscious lie. He had spoken something that was not the truth, had done it deliberately with the hope of a reward. He did not know it then, but his career as an actor had begun auspiciously.

Spring, 1966. Mark Jenner was seventeen, a junior at Noah Webster High School, Massilon, Ohio. He was six feet one and weighed 152 pounds. He was carrying the schoolbooks of Joanne Lauritszon, sixteen years eight months old. The Mark Jenner of 1989 saw her for what she was: a raw, newly fledged female with a padded chest and a shrill voice. The Mark Jenner of 1966 saw her as Aphrodite.

It took all his skill to work the conversation to the subject of the forthcoming junior prom. It took all his courage to invite the girl who walked at his side.

It took all his strength to endure her as she said, "But I've *got* a prom date already, Mark. I'm going with Nat Hospers."

"Oh—yes, of course. Sorry. I should have figured it out myself."

And he handed her back her books and ran stumbling away, cursing himself for his awkwardness, cursing Hospers for his car and his football-player muscles and his aplomb with girls. Mark had saved up for months for the prom; he had vowed he would die of grief if Joanne refused him. Somehow, he did not die.

Autumn, 1976. Hollywood. Mark Jenner was twenty-seven, rugged-looking and tanned, drawing three thousand dollars a week during the filming of *Lovely to Look At.* He sat at the best table in Hollywood's most exclusive nightclub, and opposite him, resplendent in her ermine wrap, sat the queen of filmland, Helene Bryan, lovely, moist-lipped, high-bosomed, that month blazoned on the covers of a hundred magazines in near nudity. She was twenty. She had been a coltish ten-year-old, interested only in dolls and frills, the year Mark Jenner had first thought he had fallen in love. Now he had fallen in love with her, with this $250,000-a-year goddess of sexuality.

An earlier Mark Jenner might have drawn back timidly from such a radiant beauty, but the Mark Jenner of 1976 was afraid of no one, of nothing. He smiled at the blonde girl in the ermine wrap.

He said, "Helene, will you marry me?"

"Of course, darling! Of course!"

Spring, 1987. Mark Jenner was thirty-eight. *Three Days in Marrakesh* had played nine days on Broadway. The night that closing notices went up, Mark Jenner pub-crawled until 3 a.m. The sour taste of cheap tap beer was in his mouth as he staggered home, feeling the ache in his feet and the soreness in his soul. He had not even bothered to remove the gray makeup from his hair. With it, he looked sixty years old, and right now he felt sixty, not thirty-eight. He wondered if Helene would be asleep.

Helene was not asleep; Helene was up, and packing. She wore a simple cotton dress and no makeup at all, and for once she looked her thirty-one years, instead of seeming to be in her late teens or very early twenties. She had the suitcase nearly full. Jenner had been expecting this for a long time, and now that it had come he was hardly surprised. He was too numb to react emotionally. He dropped heavily on the bed and watched her pack.

"The show closed tonight," he said.

"I know. Holly phoned and told me all about it, at midnight."

"I'm sorry I came home late. I stopped to condole with a few friends."

The brisk packing motions continued unabated. "It doesn't matter."

"Helene..."

"I'm just taking this one suitcase, Mark. I'll wire you my new address when I'm in Los Angeles, and you can ship the rest of my things out to me."

"Divorce?"

"Separation. I can't watch you this way any more, Mark."

He smiled. "No. It isn't fun to watch a man fall apart, I guess. Goodbye, Helene."

He was too drained of energy to care to make a scene. She finished packing, locked the suitcase, and went into the study to make a phone call. Then she left, without saying good-bye. Jenner sat smiling stupidly for a while after the door slammed, slowly getting used to the fact that it was all over at last. He rose, went to the sideboard, poured himself a highball glass of gin. He gulped it. He cried.

Late winter, 1989. Mark Jenner was forty years old. He sat in a special chair in Walt Hollis' apartment while lights played on his tranquil face…

It was three months and many miles of mylar tape before Hollis was satisfied. Jenner had gone through a two-hour session each morning, reminiscing with unhesitating frankness. It had not been like the analysis at all; the analysis had not been successful because he had lied to the analyst frequently and well, digging up bits of old parts and offering them as his personal experiences, out of perverse and no doubt psychotic motivations.

This was different. He was drugged; he spewed forth his genuine past, and when the session was over he had no recollection of what he had said. Hollis never told him. Sometimes Jenner would ask, as he drowned his grogginess in a postsession cup of coffee, but Hollis would never reply.

From ten to twelve every day, Jenner recorded. From one to three, Hollis cloistered himself in the little room and edited the tapes. From three to six every day, Jenner was banished from the house while his counterpart in the project occupied the little room. Jenner never got so much as a glimpse of the other.

When the three months had elapsed, when Jenner had finally surrendered as much of his past life as he could yield, when Hollis had edited the formless stream of consciousness into a continuous, consecutive, and intelligible pattern, the time came to enter the second stage of the process.

Now there were new drugs, new patterns of light, new responses. Jenner did not speak; he listened. His subconscious lay open, receptive, absorbing all that reached it and locking it in for permanent possession.

And slowly, the personality of a man formed in Jenner's mind, embedding itself deep in layers of consciousness previously private, inextricably meshing itself with the web of memories that was Mark Jenner.

This man was like Jenner in many ways. He was physically commanding; his voice had the ring of authority, and people listened when he spoke. But as Jenner watched the man's life shape itself from day to day, from year to compressed and edited year, he realized the difference. The other had chosen to be personally dominating as well. He, Jenner, had sacrificed his personality in order to be able to don many masks. A politician or a statesman must thrust his ego forward; an actor must bury his.

The other man, Jenner's mind told him, was forty-two years old. A severe attack of colitis five years back was the only serious illness he had had. He stood six feet one and a half, weighed 190 pounds, was mildly hyperthyroid metabolically, and never slept more than five hours a night.

He had a law degree from a major university—Hollis had edited the school's identity out. He had been married twice, divorcing his first wife on grounds of her adultery, and he had two children by his second wife, who regarded him with the awe one usually reserves for a paternal parent. He had been an assistant district attorney and had schemed for his superior's disgrace; eventually he had succeeded to the post himself, and had consciously been involved in the judicial murder of an innocent man.

Despite this, he thought of himself, by and large, as liberal and enlightened. He had served two terms in the Congress of the United States, representing an important eastern state. He hoped to be elected to the Senate in the 1990 elections. Consulting an almanac, Jenner discovered that many eastern states would be electing senators in 1990: Delaware, Georgia, Kentucky, Maine, Massachusetts, Mississippi, New Hampshire, New Jersey, Rhode Island, South Carolina, Tennessee, Virginia, West Virginia. About all Jenner learned from that was that his man was not officially an inhabitant of New York, Pennsylvania, or Connecticut.

Before the three months ended, Jenner knew the other man's soul nearly as well as he knew his own, or perhaps better. He understood the pattern of childhood snubs and paternal goadings that had driven him toward public life. He knew how the other had struggled to overcome his shyness. He knew how it had been when the other had first had a woman; he knew, for the first time in his life, what it was like to be a father.

The other man in Jenner's head was a "good" man, dedicated and intelligent; but yet, he stood revealed as a liar, a cheat, a hypocrite, even indirectly a murderer. Jenner realized with sudden icy clarity that any human being's mind would yield the same muck of hidden desires and repressed, half-acknowledged atrocities.

The man's memories were faceless; Jenner supplied faces. In the theater of his imagination, he built a backdrop for the other's childhood, supplied an image for parents and first wife and second wife and children and friends. Day by day the pattern grew; after ninety days, Jenner had a second self. He had a double well of memories. His fund of experiences was multiplied factorially; he could now judge the agonies of one adolescence against another, now could evaluate one man's striving against another's, now could compare two broken marriages and could vicariously know the joys of an almost-successful one. He knew the other's mind the way no man before had ever known another's mind. Not even Hollis, editing the tapes, could become the other man in the way Jenner, drugged and receptive, had become.

When the last tape had been funneled into Jenner's skull, when the picture was complete, Jenner knew the experiment had been a success. Now he had the inner drive he had lacked before; now he could reach out into the audience and squeeze a man's heart. He had always had the technical equipment of a great actor. Now he had the soul of one.

He wondered frequently about the other man and decided to keep his eye on the coming senatorial campaign in the East. He wanted desperately to know who was the man who bore in his brain all of Mark Jenner's triumphs and disappointments, all the cowardices and vanities and ambitions that made him human.

He *had* to know, but he postponed the search; at the moment, returning to the stage was more important.

The show was called *No Roses for Larrabee*. It was about an aging video star named Jack Larrabee, who skids down to obscurity and then fights his way back up. It had appeared the previous fall as a ninety-minute video show; movie rights had already been sold, but it was due for a Broadway fling first. The author was a plump kid named Harrell, who had written three previous triple-threat dramas. Harrell had half a million dollars in the bank, fifty thousand more in his mattress at his Connecticut villa, and maintained psychoanalysts on both coasts.

Casting was scheduled to start on October 20. The play had already been booked into the Odeon for a February opening, which meant a truncated pre-Broadway tour. Advance sales were piling up. It was generally assumed in the trade that the title role would be played by the man who had created it for the video version, ex-hoofer Lloyd Lane.

On October 10, Mark Jenner phoned his agent for the first time in six months. The conversation was brief. Jenner said, "I've been away, having some special treatments. I feel a lot better now. I want you to get me a reading for the stage version of Larrabee. Yeah, that's right. I want the lead."

Jenner didn't care what strings his agent had to pull to get the reading. He wasn't interested in the behind-the-scenes maneuvering. Six days later, he got a phone call from the play's producer, J. Carlton Vincennes. Vincennes was skeptical, but he was willing to take a look, anyway. Jenner was invited to come down for a reading on the twentieth.

On the twentieth, Jenner read for the part of Jack Larrabee. There were only five other people in the room—Vincennes; Harrell, the playwright; Donovan, the director; Lloyd Lane; and an actor named Goldstone who was there to try out for the secondary lead. Jenner picked up the part cold, riffled through it for a few minutes, and started to read it as if he were giving his maiden speech on the floor of the Senate. He put the words across as if he had a pipeline into the subconscious minds of his five auditors. He did things with vowel shadings and with facial expressions that he had never dared to do before, and this was only improvisation as he went. He wasn't just Mark Jenner, has-been, now; he was Mark Jenner plus someone else, and the combined output was overpowering.

After twenty minutes he tired and broke off the reading. He looked at the five faces. Four registered varying degrees of amazed pleasure and disbelief; the fifth belonged to Lloyd Lane. Lane was pale and sweat-beaded with the knowledge that he had just lost a leading role, and with it the hefty Hollywood contract that was sure to follow the Broadway one.

Two days later Jenner signed a run-of-the-show contract with Vincennes. A squib appeared in the theatrical columns the day after that:

Mark Jenner will be making a Broadway comeback in the J. C. Vincennes production of No Roses for Larrabee. *The famed matinee idol of the seventies has been absent from the stage for nearly a year. His last local appearance was in the ill-starred* Misty Isle, *which saw ten performances last March. Jenner reportedly has spent the cast season recovering from a nervous breakdown.*

Rehearsals were strange. Jenner had always been a good study, and so he knew his lines flat by the fourth or fifth run-through. The other actors were still shambling through their parts mechanically, muttering from their scripts, while Jenner was *acting*—projecting at them, putting his character across. After a while, the disparity became less noticeable. The cast came to life, responding to the vigor of Jenner's portrayal. When they started working out in the empty theater, there were always a few dozen witnesses to the rehearsal. Backers came, and other directors, theatrical people in general, all attracted by the rumors of Jenner's incandescent performance.

And it *was* incandescent. Not only because the part was so close to his own story, either; an actor playing an autobiographical role can easily slip into maudlin sogginess. For Jenner the part was both autobiographical and external. He interpreted it with his double mind, with the mind of a tired actor and with the mind of a potential senator on the way up. The two personalities crossbred; Jenner's performance tugged at the heart. Advance sales piled up until record figures began to dance across the ledger pages.

They opened in New Haven on the tenth of February to a packed house and rave reviews. Ten days later was the Broadway opening, right on schedule; neither driving snow nor pelting rain kept the tuxedo-and-mink crowd away from the opening-night festivities. A little electric crackle of tension hung in the air in the theater. Jenner felt utterly calm. *This is it,* he told himself. *The chips are down. The voters are going to the polls...*

The curtain rose, and Jenner-as-Larrabee shuffled on stage and disgorged his first mumbled lines; he got his response and came across clearer the second time, still a bent figure with hollow cheeks and sad eyes, and the part began to take hold of him. Jack Larrabee grew before the audience's eyes. By nine o'clock, he was as real as any flesh-and-blood person. Jenner was putting him across; the playwright's words were turning to gold.

The first-act curtain line was a pianissimo; Jenner gave it and dropped to his knees, then listened to the drumroll of applause welling up out of the ten-dollar seats. The second-act clincher was the outcry of a baffled, doomed man, and Jenner was baffled and doomed as he wrenched the line out of him. The audience roared as the curtain cascaded down. Jenner drew the final line of the play too—a triumphal, ringing asseveration of joy and redemption that filled the big house like a trumpet call. Then the curtain was dropping, and rising again; and dropping and rising and dropping and rising, while a thunder of applause pounded at his temples; and he knew he had reached them, reached them deeply, reached them so deep they had sprung up from their own jaded weariness to acclaim him.

There was a cast party later that night, much later, in the big Broadway restaurant where such parties are traditionally given. Vincennes was there belligerently waving the reviews from the early editions. The word had gone out: Jenner was back, and Jenner was magnificent. Lloyd Lane came up to him—Jenner's understudy, now. He looked shell-shocked. He said, "God, Mark, I watched the whole thing from the wings. I've never seen anything like it. You really *were* Larrabee out there, weren't you?"

Looking at this man he had elbowed aside, Jenner felt a twinge of guilt, and redness rose to his cheeks. Then the other mind intervened, the ruthless mind of the nameless politician, and Jenner realized that Lane had deserved to be pushed aside. A better actor simply had supplanted him. But there were tears in the corners of Lane's eyes.

Someone rushed up to Jenner with a gaudy magnum of champagne, and there was a *pop!* and then the champagne started to flow. Jenner, who had not had anything to drink for months, gratefully accepted the bubbling glass. Within, he kept icy control over himself. This was his night of triumph. He would drink, but he would not get drunk.

He drank. Vapid showgirls clawed through the circle of well-wishers around him to offer their meaningless congratulations. Flashbulbs glittered in his eyes. Men who had not spoken a civil word to him in five years pumped his hand. Within, Jenner felt a core of melancholy. Helene was not here; Walt Hollis—to whom he owned all this—was not here. Nor was his counterpart, the man whose mind he wore.

Champagne slid easily down his gullet. His smile grew broader. A bald-headed man named Feldstein clinked glasses with him and said,

"You must really be relishing this night, Mark. You had it coming, all right. How does it feel to be a success again?"

Jenner grinned warmly. The champagne within him loosened the words, and they drifted easily up through his lips. "It's wonderful. I want to thank everyone who supported me in this campaign. I want to assure them that their trust in me will be amply repaid when I reach Washington."

"Hah! Great sense of humor, Mark. Wotta fellow!" And the bald-headed man turned away, laughing. It was good that he turned away at that moment—for if he had continued to face Mark Jenner, he would have had to witness the look of dismay and terror that came over Jenner's suddenly transformed, suddenly horror-stricken face.

The play was a success, of course. It became one of those plays that everybody simply *had* to see, and everyone saw it. It promised to run for at least two seasons, which was extraordinary for a nonmusical play.

But night after night in the hotel suite Mark Jenner had rented, he wrestled with the same problem:

Who am I?

The words that had first slipped out the night of the cast party now recurred in different forms almost every day. Phantom memories obsessed him; in his dreams, women he had never known came to reminisce with him about the misdeeds of a summer afternoon. He missed the children he had never fathered—the boy who was seven, and the girl who was four. He found himself reading the front pages of newspapers, scanning the Washington news, though always before he had turned first to the theatrical pages. He detected traces of pomposity in some of his sentences.

He knew what was happening. Walt Hollis had done the job too well; the other mind was encroaching on his own, intertwining, enmeshing, ingesting. There were blurred moments in the dark of the night when Jenner forgot his own name, and temporarily nameless, dreamed the dreams the other man should have dreamed.

And, no doubt, it was the same way with the other, whoever he was. Jenner realized bleakly that a strange compulsion bound him. He lay under a geas; he had to find his counterpart, the man who shared his mind. He had to know who he was.

He asked Hollis.

Hollis had come to him in the lavish hotel suite on the sixth day after *Larrabee's* opening. The little man approached Jenner diffidently, almost as if he were upset by the magnitude of his own experiment's success.

"I guess it worked," Hollis said.

Jenner grinned expansively. "That it did, Holly! When I'm up there on the stage I have the strength I never knew I could have. Have you seen the play?"

"Yes. The third night. I was—impressed."

"Damn right you were impressed," Jenner said. "You should be, watching your Frankenstein monster in action up there. Your golem." There was nothing bitter in Jenner's tone; he was being genially sardonic.

But Hollis went pale. "Don't talk about it that way."

"True, isn't it?"

"Don't—don't ever refer to yourself that way, Mark. It isn't right."

Jenner shrugged. Then casually, he interjected a new theme. "My alter ego—the chap you matched up with me—how's *he* doing?"

"Coming along all right," Hollis said quietly.

"Just—all right?"

"In his profession it takes time for results to become apparent. But he's building up strength, lining up an organization. I saw him yesterday, and he said he's very hopeful for the future."

"For the Senate race, you mean?"

Hollis looked past Jenner's left shoulder. "Perhaps."

Jenner scowled. "Holly—tell me his name."

"I can't do that."

"I have to know it, Holly! Please!"

"Mark, one of the terms of our agreement..."

"To hell with our agreement! Will you tell me or won't you?"

The small man looked even smaller now. He seemed to be shivering. He rose, backed toward the door of Jenner's suite. His hand fumbled for the opener button.

"Where are you going?" Jenner demanded.

"Away. I don't dare let you keep asking me about him. You're too convincing. And you mustn't make me tell you. You mustn't find out who he is. Not ever."

"Holly! Come back here! *Holly!*"

The door slammed. Jenner stood in the middle of the room staring at it, slowly shaking his head. Hollis had bolted like a frightened hare. *He was afraid of me,* Jenner realized. *Afraid I'd make him talk.*

"All right," Jenner said out loud, softly. "If you won't tell me, I'll have to find out for myself."

It took him ten days to find out. Ten days in which he delivered eleven sterling performances in *No Roses for Larrabee,* ten days in which he felt the increasing encroachment of the stranger in his mind, ten days it which Mark Jenner and the stranger blurred even closer together. Or the seventh of those ten days, he received a phone call from Helene long distance. He stared at her tired face in the tiny screen and remembered how like a new-blown rose she had looked on the morning after their wedding, in Acapulco, and he listened to her strangely subdued voice.

"…visiting New York again in a few weeks. Mind if I stop up to see you, Mark? After all, we're still legally married, you know."

He smiled and made an empty reply. "Be glad to see you, Helene. For old times' sake."

"And of course I want to see the play. Can I get seats easily?"

"If you try hard enough, you can scrape up a seat in the balcony for fifty bucks," he said. "But I'm allotted a few ducats for each show. Let me know the night, and I'll put a couple away for you."

"One's enough," she said quietly.

He grinned at her, and they made a bit of small talk, and they hung up. She was obviously angling for a reconciliation. Well, he wasn't so sure he'd take her back. From what he'd heard, she had done a good bit of sleeping around in the past three years, and she was thirty-four now. A successful man like Mark Jenner might reasonably be expected to take a second wife, a girl in her twenties, someone more decorative than Helene was now. After all, the other had married again, and he had done it only because his first wife did not mix well with the party bigwigs—not primarily because she had been cheating on him.

Three days later, Jenner knew the identity of the nameless man in his mind.

It was not really hard to find out. Jenner hired a research consultant to do some work for him. What he wanted, Jenner explained, was a list of members of the House of Representatives who fulfilled the following qualifications: they had to be in their early forties, more than six feet tall, residents of an eastern state, married, divorced, and married again, with two children by the second wife. They had to be in their second term in the House, and had to be considered likely prospects for a higher political post in the near future. These were the facts Hollis had allowed him to retain. Jenner hoped they would be enough.

A few hours later, he had the answer he was hoping for. Only one man, of all the 475 representatives in the one hundredth Congress, fit all of the qualifications. He was Representative Clifford T. Norton, Republican, of the Fifth District of Massachusetts.

A little more research filled in some of Representative Norton's background. His first wife had been named Betty, the second Phyllis. His children's names were Clifford Junior and Karen. He had gone to Yale as an undergraduate, then to Harvard Law, thereby building up loyalties at both schools. He had been elected to the House in '86 after a distinguished career as district attorney, and he had been returned by a larger plurality in the '88 elections. His term of office expired in January of 1991. He hoped to move into the other wing of the Capitol immediately, as junior senator from Massachusetts. In recent months, according to the morgue file Jenner's man consulted, Norton had shown sudden brilliance and persuasiveness on the House floor.

It figured. Now Norton was a politician with the mind of an actor grafted to his own. The combination couldn't miss, Jenner thought.

Jenner felt an odd narcissistic fascination for this man with whom he was a brain-brother; he wanted anxiously to meet Norton. He wondered whether Norton had managed to uncover the identity of the actor whose tape Hollis had crossed with his own; and, Jenner wondered, if Norton *did* know, was he proud to share the memories of Broadway's renascent idol?

It was the last week in March 1990. Congress was home for its Easter recess. No doubt, Representative Norton was making ample use of his new oratorical powers among the home folks, as he began his drive toward the Senate seat. On a rainy Tuesday afternoon Jenner put through a long-distance phone call to Representative Norton at his Massachusetts office. Jenner had to give his name to a secretary before Norton would come to the phone.

Norton's voice was deep and rich, like Jenner's own. He did not use a visual circuit on his phone. He said, "Hello there, Jenner. I was wondering when you were going to call me."

"You knew about me, then?"

"Of course I knew! As soon as that play opened and I read the reviews, I knew you were the one!"

They arranged a meeting for two the following afternoon, at the home of Walt Hollis in Riverdale. Hollis had once given Jenner a key, and somehow Jenner had kept it. And he knew Hollis would not be home until five that afternoon, which gave them three hours to talk.

That night, Jenner phoned the theater and let the stage manager know that he was indisposed. The stage manager pleaded, but Jenner stood on his contractual rights. That evening Lloyd Lane played the part of Jack Larrabee, to the dismay of the disgruntled and disappointed audience. Jenner spent the evening pacing through the five rooms of his suite, clenching his hands, glorying masochistically in the turmoil and hatred bubbling inside him. He counted the hours of the sleepless night. In the morning, he breakfasted late, read till noon, paced the floor till half past one, and took the undertube to Hollis' place.

He used the key to let himself in. There was no sign of Norton. Jenner seated himself in Hollis' neat-as-a-pin living room and waited, thinking that it was utterly beyond toleration that another man should walk the earth privy to the inmost thoughts of Mark Jenner.

At two-fifteen, the doorbell rang. Jenner activated the scanner. The face in the lambent visual field was dark, strong chinned, square, powerful. Jenner opened the door and stood face to face with the only man in the universe who knew that the nine-year-old Mark Jenner had eaten a live angleworm on a dare. Clifford Norton stared levelly at the only man in the universe who knew what he had done to twelve-year-old Marian Simms in her father's garage, twenty-nine years ago.

The two big men faced each other for a long moment in the vestibule of Hollis' apartment. They maintained civil smiles. They both breathed deeply. In Jenner's mind, thoughts whirled wildly, and he knew Norton well enough to be aware that Norton was planning strategy too.

Then the stasis broke.

The animal growl of hatred burst from Jenner's lips first, but a moment later Norton was roaring too, and the two men crashed heavily together in the middle of the floor. They clinched, and one of Norton's legs snaked between Jenner's, tumbling him over; Norton dropped on top of him, but Jenner sidled out from under and slammed his elbow into the pit of Norton's stomach.

Norton gasped. He lashed out with groping hands and caught Jenner's throat. His hands tightened, while Jenner tugged and finally dragged Norton's fingers from his throat. He sucked in breath. His knee rose, going for Norton's groin. The two men writhed on the floor like raging lions, each trying to cripple and damage the other, each hoping to land a crushing blow, each trying ultimately to kill the other.

It lasted only a few moments. They separated with no spoken word and came separately to their feet. They stared at each other once again, now flushed and bruised, their neat suits rumpled, their shirttails out.

"We're acting like fools," Norton said. "Or like little boys."

"We couldn't help ourselves," Jenner said. "It was a natural thing for us to fight. We leaped at each other like men trying to catch their own shadows."

They sat down, Jenner in Hollis' chair, Norton on the couch across the room. For more than a minute, the only sound was that of heavy breathing. Jenner's heart pounded furiously. He hadn't engaged in physical combat in twenty-five years.

"I didn't think it would be this way, exactly," Norton said. "There are times when I wake up and I think I'm you. Angling for a tryout, quarreling with your wife, hitting the bottle."

"And times when I remember prosecuting an innocent man for murder and winning the case," Jenner said.

Norton's face darkened. "And I remember eating a live worm..."

"And I remember a scared twelve-year-old girl cornered in a garage..."

Again they fell silent, both of them slumped over, bearing the burden of each other's pasts. Norton said, "We should never have done this. Come here, and met."

"I had to see you."

"And I had to see you."

"We can't ever see each other again," said Jenner. "It's either got to be murder or a truce between us. Those few minutes when we were fighting—I actually wanted to kill you, Norton. To see you go blue in the face and die."

Norton nodded. "I had the same feeling. Neither of us can really bear the idea that someone else knows him inside and out, even though it's done us so much good in so many ways. I'll get the Senate, all right. And maybe the White House in another six years."

"And I'm back on the stage. I'll get my wife back, if I want her. Everything I lost. Yes," Jenner said. "It's worth sharing your mind. But

376

we can't ever meet again. We're each a small part of each other, and the hatred's too strong. I guess it's self-hatred, really. But we might—we might lose control of ourselves, the way we did just now."

The front door opened suddenly. Walt Hollis stood in the vestibule, a small pinched-faced man with narrow shoulders and a myopic squint. And, just now, a dazed expression on his face.

"You two—how did you get here—why…"

"I still had a key," Jenner said. "I called Norton and invited him down to meet me here. We didn't expect you back so early."

Hollis' mouth worked spasmodically for ten seconds before the words came. "You should never have met each other. The traumatic effects—possible dangers…"

"We've already had a good brawl," Norton said. "But we won't any more. We've declared a truce."

He crossed the room and forced himself to smile at Jenner. Jenner summoned his craft and made his face show genial conviviality, though within all was loathing. They shook hands.

"We aren't going to see each other ever again," Jenner explained. "Norton's going to be president, and I'm going to win undying fame in the theater. And each of us will owe our accomplishments to the other."

"And to you, Hollis," Norton added.

"Maybe Norton and I will keep in touch by mail," Jenner said. "Drop each other little notes, suggestions. An actor can help a politician. A politician can help an actor. Call it long-range symbiosis, Holly. The two of us ought to go places, thanks to you."

Jenner glanced at Norton, and this time the smile that was exchanged was a sincere one. There was no need for words between them. They walked past the numb Hollis and into the small laboratory room and methodically smashed the equipment. If Hollis were to put someone else through this treatment, Jenner thought, the competition might be a problem. He and Norton wanted no further competition in their chosen fields.

They returned to the living room and gravely said good-bye to Hollis. Jenner was calm inside, now, at last. He and Norton departed, going their separate ways once they reached the street. Jenner knew he would never see Norton again. It was just as well; he would have to live with Norton's memories for the rest of his life.

Hollis surveyed the wreckage of his lab with a stony heart. He felt cold and apprehensive. This was the reward of his labors, this was what he got for trying to help. But he should have realized it. After all, he had edited the tapes for both of them. He knew what they were. He carried the burden of both souls in his own small heart. He knew what they had done, and he knew what they were capable of doing, now that the errors of one sanctioned the errors of the other.

Tiredly, Hollis closed the laboratory door, cutting off the sight of the wreckage. He thought of Jenner and Norton and wondered when they would realize that he knew all their secrets.

He wondered how long Jenner and Norton would let him live.

DELIVERY GUARANTEED

However high-minded my thoughts about writing science fiction might have been getting in 1957 and 1958, I was still not yet above writing stories around cover paintings at editorial request, which I saw (and still see) as a harmless virtuoso exercise rather than as any kind of display of venality. The cover artists who were involved in such projects liked to set cunning traps for the writers by handing them truly perplexing images, and it was always an interesting challenge to come up with a story idea that managed to be worthwhile in its own right while still fulfilling the mandate laid down by the depicted scene. Some very fine writers (Isaac Asimov, Algis Budrys, and Clifford D. Simak among them) had written some excellent stories via this back-to-front method, and one of the masterpieces of the science-fiction short story, James Blish's "Common Time," had resulted from just such an assignment. So it was with great delight that I wrote a dozen or more cover stories for Bob Lowndes' two magazines, Future *and* Science Fiction Stories, *and I hesitated not at all when Lowndes handed me a photostat of an Ed Emshwiller painting showing a man and a woman in spacesuits aboard a log raft that was zipping along through the asteroid belt propelled by a small rocket engine. I wrote the story the next day—it was August, 1958—and Lowndes featured it in the February, 1959* Science Fiction Stories. *This would, in fact, be the last cover story I would do for him, because with their next issues both his magazines dropped cover paintings entirely, for reasons of economy, and soon after that they would cease to exist at all. At some point in 1958 the American News Company, the main distributor (and financial backer) for nearly all of the science-fiction magazines for which I wrote, went abruptly out of business, and all of those magazines instantly vanished. With their disappearance, the thing that I had set out to do in 1955, and which I had actually succeeded at for the past three years—to earn my living as a full-time science-fiction writer—was no longer possible to achieve. Perhaps Robert A. Heinlein and Ray Bradbury, who stood at the very summit of the field, might be able still to manage it, Heinlein by writing lucrative novels for young readers, Bradbury by publishing stories in the high-paying slick magazines. But the rest of us, competing for the few available slots on the contents pages of the handful of surviving science-fiction magazines, were left high and dry. The juvenile-oriented hack markets were gone, and so were most of markets for science fiction of a more adult kind. Certainly neither the Heinlein option nor the Bradbury one was open to me, at my current level of skill. I remember taking a long, anguished walk through the streets of Manhattan on a summer evening in 1958, pondering my future as a writer. On the one hand, I still was wrestling with that unfocused yearning to enhance my standing in the science-fiction world, preferably by writing ambitious novels for the top book publishers, who at that time were Doubleday (in hardcover) and Ballantine (in paperback). But on the other, I had never written a major novel, only young-adult titles and short adventure tales for Don Wollheim's Ace Books, and I had little confidence that I would be able to shoulder my way into either of those two important publishing houses, which then could pick and choose from the novels of the best writers in the field: Heinlein, Asimov, Blish, Sturgeon, Clarke, Anderson, Simak, Pohl, Wyndham, and so on and on. And I still had an expensive life-style to support: that apartment on West End Avenue, those trips to the West Indies and Europe. It might be a better idea, I thought, to abandon science fiction entirely, or almost so, and earn the bulk of my living from the multitude of high-paying men's magazines and other general-interest publications that still existed and were in constant need of material. But I came home from that walk determined to give science fiction one last try, and began to sketch out a novel that I hoped would greatly exceed in power and scope anything I had written up till then, with the hope that it would land me a place on Doubleday's elite list. I finished it in October, 1958; it was called* The Seed of Earth; *my agent took it to Doubleday, and Doubleday quickly turned it down. They didn't think it was a particularly awful book—or a particularly great one—but in any case they were publishing just one book a month of science fiction, and, as I had anticipated, were too busy doing Heinlein and Asimov and Simak to have room on the list for me. The next stop was*

Ballantine, and, instead of relying on my agent, I took the manuscript to Betty Ballantine, the company's co-owner and editor, myself. I had a long and friendly chat with her, told her all about my ambitions and yearnings, and went away thinking that she might very well want to publish me. Indeed she did—eight years later—but The Seed of Earth wasn't her sort of thing. Eventually, three years later, I sold it to my regular paperback company, Ace Books, and so much for all that high literary ambition.

The year 1958, when most of the science-fiction magazines collapsed and I found myself stranded between my incompatible desires to write first-rate science fiction and yet somehow to earn a first-rate living from my writing, marked the end of a remarkable four-year period for me during which, starting from amateur status, I had sold vast numbers of short stories and novels and established myself as a dependable craftsman upon whom editors could rely for a steady flow of work written to order. Now, though, I would have to find other fields in which to work, since the sort of science-fiction-market that could support full-time writers had disappeared virtually in the twinkling of an eye. 1958 was my last year of prolific science-fiction production for a long time. I hoped to keep my hand in by doing the occasional story for Astounding or Galaxy, but no longer would I think of myself as writing the stuff full time. From dozens of stories a year I scaled back to eight or ten, to three or four, and, by 1961, to none at all. Went elsewhere, wrote other things. And so I entered into the first of the various departures from science fiction that have marked my long career.

———

There aren't many free-lance space-ferry operators who can claim that they carried a log cabin half way from Mars to Ganymede, and then had the log cabin carry them the rest of the way. I can, though you can bet your last tarnished megabuck that I didn't do it willingly. It was quite a trip. I left Mars not only with a log cabin on board, but a genuine muzzle-loading antique cannon, a goodly supply of cannonballs therefrom, and various other miscellaneous antiques—as well as the Curator of Historical Collections from the Ganymede Museum. There was also a stowaway on board, much to his surprise and mine—he wasn't listed in the cargo vouchers.

Let me make one thing clear: I wasn't keen on carrying any such cargo. But my free-lance ferry operator's charter is quite explicit that way, unfortunately. A ferry operator is required to hire his ship to any person of law-abiding character who will meet the (government-fixed) rates, and whose cargo to be transported neither exceeds the ship's weight allowance nor is considered contraband by any System law.

In short, I'm available to just about all comers. By the terms of my charter I've been compelled to ferry five hundred marmosets to Pluto, forced to haul ten tons of Venusian guano to Callisto, constrained to deliver fifty crates of fertilized frogs' eggs from Earth to a research station orbiting Neptune. In the latter case I made the trip twice for the same fee, thanks to the delivery guaranteed clause in the contract; the first time out my radiation shields slipped up for a few seconds, not causing me any particular genetic hardships but playing merry hell with those frog's eggs. When a bunch of four-headed tadpoles began to hatch, they served notice on me that they were not accepting delivery and would pay no fee—and, what's more, would sue if I didn't bring another load of potential frogs up from Earth, and be damned well careful about the shielding this time.

So I hauled another fifty crates of frogs' eggs, this time without mishap, and collected my fee. But I've never been happy about carrying livestock again.

This new offer wasn't livestock. I got the call while I was laying over on Mars after a trip up from Luna with a few colonists and their gear. I had submitted my name to the Transport Registry, informing them that I was on call and waiting for employment—but I was in no hurry. I still had a couple of hundred megabucks left from the last job, and I didn't mind a vacation.

The call came on the third day of my Martian layover. "Collect call for Mr. Sam Diamond, from the Transport Registry. Do you accept?"

"Yes," I muttered, and $30,000 more was chalked to my phone bill. A dollar doesn't last hardly any time at all in these days of system-wide hyperinflation.

"Sam?" a deep voice said. It was Mike Cooper of the Transport people.

"Who else would it be at this end of your collect call?" I growled. "And why can't you people pay for a phone call once in a while?"

"You know the law, Sam," Cooper said cheerfully. "I've got a job for you."

"That's nice. Another load of marmosets?"

"Nothing live this time, Sam, except your passenger. She's Miss Vanderweghe of the Ganymede Museum. Curator of Historical

Collections. She wants someone to ferry her back to Ganymede with some historical relics she's picked up along the way."

"The Washington Monument?" I asked. "The Great Pyramid of Khufu? We could tow it alongside the ship, lashed down with twine—"

"Knock it off," Cooper said, unamused. "What she's got are souvenirs of the Venusian Insurrection. The log cabin that served as Macintyre's headquarters, the cannon used to drive back the Bluecoats, and a few smaller knickknacks along those lines."

"Hold it," I said. "You can't fit a log cabin into my ship. And if it's going to be a tow job, I want the Delivery Guaranteed clause stricken out of the contract. And how much does the damn cannon weigh? I've got a weight ceiling, you know."

"I know. Her entire cargo is less than eight tons, cannon and all. It's well within your tonnage restrictions. And as for the log cabin, it doesn't need to be towed. She's agreed to take it apart for shipping, and reassemble it when it gets to Ganymede."

The layover had been nice while it lasted. I said, "I was looking for some rest, Mike. Isn't there some angle I can use to wiggle out of this cargo?"

"None."

"But—"

"There isn't another free ferry in town tonight. She wants to leave tonight. So you're the boy, Sam. The job is yours."

I opened my mouth. I closed it again. Ferries are considered public services, under the law. The only way I could get a vacation that was sure to last was to apply for one in advance, and I hadn't done that.

"Okay," I said wearily. "When do I sign the contract?"

"Miss Vanderweghe is at my office now," Cooper said. "How soon can you get here?"

I was in a surly mood as I rode downtown to Cooper's place. For the thousandth time I resented the casual way he could pluck me out of some relaxation and make me take a job. I wasn't looking forward to catering to the whims of some dried-up old museum curator all the way out to Ganymede. And I wasn't too pleased with the notion of carrying relics of the Venusian Insurrection.

The Insurrection had caused quite a fuss, a hundred years back. Bunch of Venusian colonists decided they didn't like Earth's rule—the taxation-without-representation bit, though their squawk was unjustified—and set up a wildcat independent government, improvising their equipment out of whatever they could grab. A chap name of Macintyre was in charge; the insurrectionists holed up in the jungle and held off the attacking loyalists for a couple of weeks. Then the Venusian local government appealed to Earth, a regiment of Bluecoats was shipped to Venus, and inside of a week Macintyre was a prisoner and the Insurrection ended. But some diehard Venusians still venerated the insurrectionists, and there had been a few murders and ambushes every year since the overthrow of Macintyre. I could have done without carrying Venusian cargo.

I was going to say as much to Cooper, too, in hopes that some clause of my charter would get me out of the assignment and back on vacation. But I didn't get a chance. I went storming into Cooper's office.

There was a girl sitting in the chair to the left of his desk. She was about twenty-five, well built in most every way possible, with glossy, short-cropped hair and an attractive face.

Cooper stood up and said, "Sam, I'd like you to meet Miss Erna Vanderweghe of Ganymede. Miss Vanderweghe, this is Sam Diamond, one of the best ferry men there is. He'll get you to Ganymede in style."

"I'm sure of that," she said, smiling.

"Hello," I said, gulping.

I didn't bother raising a fuss about the political implications of my cargo. I didn't grouse about weight limits, space problems aboard ship, accommodation difficulties, or anything else. I reached for the contract—it was the standard printed form, with the variables typed in by Cooper—and signed it.

"I'd like to leave tonight," she said.

"Sure. My ship's at the spaceport. Can you have your cargo delivered there by—oh, say, 1700 hours? That way we can blast off by 2100."

"I'll try. Will you be able to help me get my goods out of storage and down to the spaceport?"

I started to say that I'd be delighted to, but Cooper cut in sharply, as I knew he would. "I'm sorry, Miss Vanderweghe, but Sam's contract and charter prohibit him from any landside cargo-handling except within the actual bounds of the spaceport. You'll have to use a local carrier for getting your stuff to the ship, I'm afraid. If you want me to, I'll arrange for transportation—"

My mood was considerably different as I returned to the Deimos to check out. My tub would need five days for the journey between Mars and Ganymede. Now, conditions aboard my ship allow for a certain amount of passenger privacy, but not a devil of a lot. Log cabin or no log cabin, I was going to enjoy the proximity of Miss Erna Vanderweghe. I could think of worse troubles than having to spend five days in the same small ferry with her, and only a log cabin and a cannon for chaperones.

I was grinning as I walked over to the desk to let them know I was pulling out. Nat, the desk clerk, interpreted the grin logically enough, but wrongly.

"You talked them out of giving you the job, eh, Sam? How'd you work it?"

"Huh? Oh—no, I took the job. I'm checking out of here at 1800 hours."

"You *took* it? But you look *happy!*"

"I am," I said with a mysterious expression. I started to saunter away, but Nat called me back.

"You had a visitor a little while ago, Mr. Cooper. He wanted me to let him into your room to wait for you, but naturally I wouldn't do it."

"Visitor? Did he leave his name?"

"He's still here. Sitting right over there, next to the potted palm tree."

Frowning, I walked toward him. He was a thin, hunched-up little man with the sallow look of a Venusian colonist. He was busily reading some cheap dime-novel sort of magazine as I approached.

"Hello," I said affably. "I'm Sam Diamond. You wanted to see me?"

"You're ferrying Erna Vanderweghe to Ganymede tonight, aren't you?" His voice was thinly whining, nasty sounding, mean.

"I make a practice of keeping my business to myself," I told him. "If you're interested in hiring a ferry, you'd better go to the Transport Registry. I'm booked."

"I know you are. And I know who you're carrying. And I know *what* you're carrying."

"Look here, friend, I—"

"You're carrying General Macintyre's cabin, and other priceless relics of the Venusian Republic—and all stolen goods!" His eyes had a fanatic gleam about them. I realized who he was as soon as he used the expression "Venusian Republic." Only an insurrectionist-sympathizer would refer to the rebel group that way.

"I'm not going to discuss business affairs with you," I said. "My cargo has been officially cleared."

"It was stolen by that woman! Purchased with filthy dollars and taken from Venus by stealth!"

I started to walk away. I hate having some loudmouthed fanatic rant at me. But he followed, clutching at my elbows, and said in his best conspiratorial tone, "I warn you, Diamond—cancel that contract or you'll suffer! Those relics must return to Venus!"

Whirling around, I disengaged his hands from my arm and snapped, "I couldn't cancel a contract if I wanted to—and I don't want to. Get out of here or I'll have you jugged, whoever you are."

"Remember the warning—"

"Go on! Shoo! Scat!"

He slinked out of the lobby. Shaking my head, I went upstairs to pack. Damned idiotic cloak-and-dagger morons, I thought. Creeping around hissing warnings and leaving threatening notes, and in general trying to keep alive an underground movement that never had any real reason for existing from the start. It wasn't as if Earth had oppressed the Venusian colonists. The benefits flowed all in one direction, from Earth to Venus, and everyone on Venus knew it except for Macintyre's little bunch of ultranationalistic glory-hounds. Nobody on Venus wanted independence less than the colonists themselves, who had dandy tax exemptions and benefits from the mother world.

I forgot all about the threats by the time I was through packing my meager belongings and had grabbed a meal at the hotel restaurant. Around 1800 hours I went down to the spaceport to see what was happening there. The mechanics had already wheeled my ferry out of the storage hangars; she was out on the field getting checked over for blastoff. Erna Vanderweghe and her cargo had arrived, too. She was standing at the edge of the field, supervising the unloading of her stuff from the van of a local carrier.

The log cabin had been taken apart. It consisted of a stack of stout logs, the longest of them some sixteen feet long and the rest tapering down.

"You think you're going to be able to put that cabin back the way it was?" I asked.

"Oh, certainly. I've got each log numbered to correspond with a diagram I've made. The reassembling shouldn't be any trouble at all," she said, smiling sweetly.

I eyed the other stuff—several crates, a few smaller packages, and a cannon, not very big. "Where'd you get all these things?" I asked.

She shrugged prettily. "I bought them on Venus. Most of them were the property of descendants of the insurrectionists; they were quite happy to sell. There weren't any ferries available on Venus, so I took a commercial liner on the shuttle from Venus to Mars. They said I'd be able to get a ferry here."

"And you did," I said. "In five days we'll be landing on Ganymede."

"I can't wait to get there—to set up my exhibit!"

I frowned. "Tell me something, Miss Vanderweghe. Just how did you manage to—ah—make such an early start in the museum business?"

She grinned. "My father and grandfather were museum curators. I just come by it naturally, I suppose. And I was just about the only colonist on Ganymede who was halfway interested in having the job!"

I chuckled softly and said, "When Cooper told me I was ferrying a museum curator, I pictured a dried-up old spinster who'd nag me all the way to Ganymede. I couldn't have been wronger."

"Disappointed?"

"Not very much," I said.

We had the ship loaded inside of an hour, everything stowed neatly away in the hold and Miss Vanderweghe's personal luggage strapped down in the passenger compartment. Since there wasn't any reason for hanging around longer, I recomputed my takeoff orbit and called the control center for authorization to blast off at 2000 hours, an hour ahead of schedule.

They were agreeable, and at 1955 hours the field sirens started to scream, warning people of an impending blast. Miss Vanderweghe—Erna—was aft, in her acceleration cradle, as I jabbed the keys that would activate the autopilot and take us up.

I started to punch the keys. The computer board started to click. There was nothing left for me to do but strap myself in and wait for brennschluss. A blastoff from Mars is no great problem in astronautics.

As the automatic took over, I flipped my seat back, converting it into an acceleration cradle, and relaxed. It seemed to me that the take-off was a little on the bumpy side, as if I'd figured the ship's mass wrong by one or two hundred pounds. But I didn't worry about the discrepancy. I just shut my eyes and waited while the extra gees bore down on me. The sanest thing for a man to do during blastoff is to go to sleep, and that's what I did.

I woke up half an hour or so later to discover that the engines had cut out, the ship was safely in flight, and that a bloody and battered figure was bent over my controls, energetically ruining them with crowbar and shears.

I blinked. Then the fog in my head cleared and I got out of my cradle. The stowaway turned around. He was quite a mess. The capillaries of his face had popped during the brief moments of top acceleration, and fine purplish lines now wriggled over his cheeks and nose, giving him a grade-A rum blossom, and bloodshot eyes to go with it. He had some choice bruises that he must have acquired while rattling around during blastoff, and his nose had been bleeding all over his shirt. It was the little Venusian fanatic who had threatened me at the hotel.

"How the hell did you get aboard?" I demanded.

"Slipped through the security checkers...but the ship took off ahead of schedule. I did not expect to be on board when blastoff came."

"Sorry to have fouled up your plans," I told him.

"But I regained consciousness in time. Your ship is ruined! You refused to heed my warning, and now you will never reach Ganymede alive. So perish all enemies of the Venusian Republic! So perish those who have desecrated our noble shrines!"

He was practically foaming at the mouth. I started toward him. He swung the crowbar and might have bashed my head in if he had known how to handle himself under nograv conditions, but he didn't, and the only result of his exertion was to send himself drifting toward the roof of the cabin. I yanked on his leg as it went past me and dragged him down. The crowbar dropped from his numb hand. I caught it and poked him across the head with it.

There isn't any hesitation in a spaceman's mind when he finds a stowaway. Fuel is a precious thing, and so is air and food; stowaways simply aren't allowed to live. I didn't feel any qualms about what I did next, but all the same I was glad that Erna Vanderweghe wasn't awake and watching me while I went about it.

I slipped into my breathing-helmet and sealed off the cabin. Opening the airlock, I carried the unconscious Venusian out the hatch and gave him a good push, imparting enough momentum to send him out on an orbit of his own. The compensating reaction pushed me back into the airlock. I closed the hatch. The Venusian must have died instantly, without ever knowing what was happening to him.

Then I had a look-see to determine just how much damage the stowaway had been able to do before I woke up and caught him.

It was plenty.

All our communication equipment was gone, but permanently. The radio was a gutted ruin. The computer was smashed. Two auxiliary fuel tanks had been jettisoned. We were hopelessly off course in asteroid country, and the odds on reaching Ganymede looked mighty slim. By the time I finished making course corrections, we'd be down to our reserve fuel supply. Ganymede was about 350 million miles ahead of us. I didn't see how we were going to travel more than a tenth that distance before air and food troubles set in, and we weren't carrying enough fuel now for a safe landing even if we lived to reach Ganymede.

It was time to wake Miss Vanderweghe and tell her the news, I figured.

She was lying curled up tight in her acceleration cradle, asleep, with a childlike, trusting expression on her face. I watched her for perhaps five minutes before I woke her. She sat up immediately.

"What—oh. Is everything all right? Did we make a good blastoff?"

"Fine blastoff," I said quietly. "But everything isn't all right." I told her about the stowaway and how thoroughly he had wrecked us.

"Oh—that horrible little man from Venus! I knew he had followed me to Mars—that's why I wanted to leave for Ganymede so soon. He made all sorts of absurd threats, as if the things I had bought were holy relics—"

"They are, in a way. If you worship Macintyre and his fellow rebels, then the stuff you carried away is equivalent to the True Cross, I suppose."

"I'm so sorry I got you into this, Sam."

I shrugged. "It's my own fault all the way. Your Venusian friend approached me at the hotel this afternoon and warned me off, but I didn't listen to him. I had my chance to pull out."

"Where's the stowaway now? Unconscious?"

I shook my head, jerking my thumb toward the single port in her cabin. "He's out there. Without a suit. Stowaways aren't entitled to charity under the space laws."

"Oh," she said quietly, turning pale. "I—see. You—ejected him."

I nodded. Then, to get off what promised to be an unpleasant topic, I said, "We're in real trouble. We're off course and we don't have enough fuel for making corrections—not without jettisoning everything on board, ourselves included."

"I don't mind if the cargo goes. I mean, I'd hate to lose it, but if you have to dump it—"

"Uh-uh. The ship itself is the bulk of our mass. The problem isn't the cargo. If there were only some way of jettisoning the *ship*—"

My mouth sagged open. No, I thought. It wouldn't ever work. It's too fantastic to consider.

"I have an idea," I said. "We *will* jettison the ship. And we'll get to Ganymede."

Luckily our saboteur friend hadn't bothered to rip up my charts. I spent half an hour feverishly thumbing through the volume devoted to asteroid orbits, while Erna hovered over my shoulder, not daring to ask questions but probably wondering just what in blazes I was figuring out.

Pretty soon I had a list of a dozen likely asteroids. I narrowed it down to five, then to three, then to one. I missed the convenience of my computer, but regulations require a pilot to be able to get along without one in a pinch, and I got along.

I computed a course toward the asteroid known as (719)-Albert. Luck was riding with us. (719)-Albert was on the outward swing of his orbit. On the basis of some extremely rough computations I worked out an orbit for our crippled ship that would match Albert's in a couple of hours.

Finally, I looked up at Erna and grinned. "This is known as making a virtue out of necessity," I said. "Want to know what's going on?"

"You bet I do."

I leaned back. "We're on our way to a chunk of rock known as (719)-Albert, which is chugging along not far from here on its way through the asteroid belt. (719)-Albert is a rock about three miles in diameter. Figure that it's half the size of Deimos—and Deimos is about as small as a place can get."

"But why are we going there?" she said, puzzled.

"(719)-Albert has an exceedingly eccentric orbit—and I mean eccentric in its astronomical sense: not a peculiar orbit, just one that's very highly elongated. At perihelion (719)-Albert passes around 20 million miles from the orbit of Earth. At aphelion, which is where he's heading now, he comes within 90 million miles of the orbit of Jupiter. Unless my figures are completely cockeyed, Jupiter is going to be about 150 million miles from Albert about a week from now."

I saw I had lost her completely. She said dimly, "But you said a little while ago that we hardly had enough fuel to take us 50 million miles."

"In the ship," I said. "Yes. But I've got other ideas. We'll land on Albert and abandon the ship. Then we ride pickaback on the asteroid until its closest approach to Jupiter—and blast off without the ship."

"Blast off—*how?*"

I smiled triumphantly. "We'll make a raft out of your blessed logs," I said. "Attach one of the ship's rocket engines at the rear, and shove off. Escape velocity from Albert is so low it hardly matters. And since the mass of our raft will only be six or seven hundred pounds—Earthside weight, of course—instead of the thirty tons or so that this ship weighs, we'll be able to coast to Ganymede with plenty of fuel left to burn."

She was looking at me as if I'd just delivered a lecture in the General Theory of Relativity. Apparently the niceties of space travel just weren't in her line at all. But she smiled and tried to look understanding. "It sounds very clever," she said with an uncertain grin.

I felt pretty clever about everything myself, three hours later, when we landed on the surface of an asteroid that could only be (719)-Albert. It had taken only one minor course correction to get us here. Which meant that my rule-of-thumb astrogation had been pretty good.

We donned breathing-suits and clambered out of the ship to inspect our landfall. (719)-Albert wasn't very impressive. The landscape was mostly jagged upthrusts of a dark basalt-like rock. But the view was tremendous—a great backdrop of darkness, speckled with stars, and, much closer, the orbiting fragments of other lumps of rock. Albert's horizon was on the foreshortened side, dipping away almost before it began. Gravitational attraction was so meager it hardly counted. A healthy jump was likely to continue indefinitely upward, as I made clear to Erna right at the start. I didn't want her indulging in the usual hijinks that greenhorns are fond of when on a low-gravity planetoid such as this. I could visualize only too well the scene as she vanished into the void as the result of an overenthusiastic leap.

We surveyed our holdings and found that there was enough food for two people for sixteen days—so we would make it with some to spare. The air supply was less abundant, but there was enough so we didn't need to begin worrying just yet.

We set about building the raft.

Erna dragged the logs out of the cargo hold—their weight didn't amount to anything, here, though I had to caution her about throwing them around carelessly; mass and weight aren't synonymous, and those logs were sturdy enough to knock me for a loop regardless of how little they seemed to weigh. She fetched, and I assembled. We used the thirteen longest logs for the body of the raft, and trussed a couple across the bottom, and a couple more at the top. To make blastoff a little easier, we built the raft propped up against a rock outcropping, at a 45° angle.

I unshipped the smallest rocket engine and fastened it securely to the rear of the raft. I strapped down as many fuel tanks as the raft would hold.

Then—chuckling to myself—I asked Erna to help me haul the cannon out.

"The cannon? Whatever for?"

"To mount at the front of the raft."

"Are you figuring on meeting space pirates?"

"I'm figuring on using the cannon as a brake," I told her. We fastened it at the front of the raft, strapped down the supply of cannonballs and powder nearby it. The cannon would make an ideal brake. All we needed was something that would eject mass in a forwardly direction, pushing us back by courtesy of Newton's Third Law. Why waste fuel when cannonballs would achieve the same purpose?

It took us forty-eight standard Earthtime hours to build the raft. I don't know how many thousands of (719)-Albert days that was, but the little asteroid spun on its axis like a yo-yo, and it seemed that the sun was rising or setting every time we took a breath.

After I had bound the last thong around the rocket engine, Erna grinned and dashed into the ship. She returned, a few moments later, waving a red flag with some sort of blue-and-white design on it.

"What's that?"

"The flag that flew over Macintyre's cabin," she explained. "It's a rebel flag, and we're not strictly insurrectionists, but we ought to have some kind of flag on our ship."

I was agreeable, so she mounted the flag just fore of the rocket engine. Then we returned to the ship to wait.

We waited for three days, Earthtime—maybe several centuries by (719)-Albert reckoning. And in case you're wondering how we passed the time on the barren asteroid for three days, just one reasonably virile ferry pilot and one nubile museum curator, the answer is no. We didn't. I have an inflexible rule about making passes at passengers, even when we're stranded on places like (719)-Albert and when the passengers are as pretty as this one is.

That isn't to say I didn't feel temptation. Erna's breathing-suit was of the plastic kind that looked as though it was force-molded to her body. I didn't have to do much imagining. But I staunchly told Satan to get behind me, and—to my own amazement—he did. I resisted temptation and resisted it manfully.

Meanwhile Jupiter swelled bigger and bigger as (719)-Albert plunged madly along its track toward its rendezvous with Jove. If luck rode with us—translated, if my math had been right—we would find Ganymede midway in her seven-plus day orbit round the big planet.

Time came when the mass detectors in my ship informed me that Jupiter had stopped getting closer and was now getting farther away. That meant that (719)-Albert had passed its point of aphelion and was heading back toward Earth. It was time to get moving.

"All aboard," I told Erna. "Make sure everything we're taking is strapped down tight—food, fuel, air tanks, cannonballs, flags."

She checked off as if we were running down meters and gauges at a spaceport. "Food. Fuel. Air tanks. Cannonballs. Flag. All set to blast, Captain."

"Okay. Get yourself flattened out and hang onto the raft while we blast."

Blastoff was a joke. I had computed the escape velocity of (719)-Albert at approximately .0015 miles/sec. We could have shoved off with a good rearward kick.

But we had fuel to burn. *"Allons!"* I cried, slamming the rocket engine into action. A burst of flame hurled us upward into the night. *"A la belle Ètoile!"* I shouted. "To the stars!"

The raft soared off into space. Erna laughed with delight. As (719)-Albert slowly sank into the sunset, we plunged forward toward giant Jupiter. The only thing missing was soft music in the background.

We rode the raft for three days at constant acceleration. Jupiter grew, and grew, and grew, and gleaming Ganymede became visible peeking around the edge of the great planet. Erna became worried when she saw it.

"Shouldn't we head the raft over toward Ganymede?" she asked. "We're pointed much too far forward."

I sighed. "We aren't going to reach Ganymede for another couple of days," I said. "We want to head for where Ganymede's going to be *then*, not where it happens to be right now. Isn't that obvious?"

"I suppose so," she said, pouting.

We were right on course. Two days later we were heading downward toward the surface of Ganymede. It was like riding a magic carpet. I controlled our landing with the rockets, while Erna gleefully fired ball after ball to provide the needed deceleration. If Ganymede had had an atmosphere, of course, we'd have been whiffed to cinders in a moment—but there was no atmosphere to contend with. We made a perfect no-point landing, flat on the glistening blue-white ice. Lord knows what we must have looked like approaching from space.

We had landed a hundred miles or so from the nearest entrance to the Ganymede Dome. I was dourly considering the prospect of trekking on foot, but Erna was certain we had been seen, and, sure enough, a snowcrawler manned by three incredulous colonists came out to fetch us. I never saw human eyes bulge the way those six eyes bulged at the sight of our raft.

Part of the service I offer is guaranteed delivery, and so, a couple of weeks later, I rented a ship and made a return journey to (7I9)-Albert to pick up the remaining historical relics we had been forced to leave behind—some tattered uniforms and a few boxes of pamphlets. A week after that, a repair ship was despatched to pick up my ferry, and she was hauled to the dockyard on Ganymede and put back in operating condition at a trifling cost of a few thousand megabucks.

These days I run a ferry service between the colonized moons of Jupiter and Saturn, and Erna is head curator of the Ganymede Museum. But I don't take kindly toward getting employment, because it means I have to spend time away from home—and Erna. We were married a while back, you see.

It's a funny thing about General Macintyre's log cabin. Despite Erna's careful diagram, the cabin never got put back together. It seems that the people of Ganymede decided it was of no great value to display the cabin of some Venusian rebel when they could be showing an item of much more immediate associations for Ganymedeans.

So they wouldn't let Erna take the raft apart, and I had to buy myself a new rocket engine. You can see the raft in the museum on Ganymede, any time you happen to be in the neighborhood. If the curator's around, she won't mind answering questions. But don't try to get playful with her. I'm awfully touchy about guys who make passes at my wife.

www.ingramcontent.com/pod-product-compliance
Lightning Source LLC
Chambersburg PA
CBHW020836030726
47496CB00001B/258